I072042O

Welcome to

Hell

Omnibus

Contains:

Welcome to Hell (#1)

See You in Hell (#2)

Mel Goes to Hell (#3)

BONUS Melody Angel's Guide to Heaven and Hell

DEMELZA CARLTON

Welcome

to

Hell

DEMELZA CARLTON

DEDICATION

For all my fellow commuters, corporate and civil workers.

May you never be inspired by a stranger's briefcase.

Job interviews were Mel's personal concept of Hell.

"So, why do you want to work here?"

"I don't," Mel replied.

Raphael sighed. "Come on, Mel. I'm trying to help you. In a real interview, like the one tomorrow, they'll ask you and you'll need a convincing answer."

Mel took a deep breath and tried to think of a reason. After a minute, she shook her head. "Sorry, Raphael. Ask me the next question. I'll have to think about that first one."

"How about telling them it's because you need the money and you've heard they have good pay and conditions? Or because they're the best in the business? Or because you want to make a difference in the world and they're the best place to do it?" Raphael persisted.

"I'll think about it," Mel said. "Try the next question. I still have a whole day before the interview. I might come up with something good by then."

"In your opinion, what's the worst thing about you?"

Mel stared at him. "What kind of question is that? I thought I was supposed to say things that make me sound good and employable, not let them know about my worst habits!"

"Don't tell them your worst habits. Say something that sounds good but that you don't like about yourself," Raphael suggested.

"I can't lie."

"Of course you can't lie — or you shouldn't. You need to say more than that, Mel. I know you've never had a job interview before, but you're not making this easy." Raphael ran a hand through his hair, looking worried. "You're supposed to sell yourself."

Mel laughed. "Technically, this will be my first real job interview and my first paid job. I'd hardly call it selling myself. You make it sound so dirty…"

"Just think of something about you that's really desirable for the job, but that you might not like."

"My boobs are too big?" Mel suggested.

"Oh Hell…Mel!"

"Good afternoon, welcome to Hell–"

Did she really just say that? Mel wondered, staring at the receptionist.

"–lth, Environment, Life and Lands Corporation. How can I help you?"

"Ah, I'm here for a job interview?" Mel left the statement hanging as a question – half hoping she'd be told there was no interview or vacancy, so she wouldn't have to undergo this ordeal.

"Oh, you're from the agency? Take a seat and I'll let

them know you're here," the girl said, waving toward the uncomfortable-looking bucket chairs. She picked up the phone receiver and stared at her until Mel's nervous knees folded, dropping her onto one of the seats.

"Hi, it's Reception. I have an agency girl here who says she has an interview." The receptionist sniffed as if she felt the accuracy of this information was questionable. A pause. "No." The girl's chin pointed at Mel. "What's your name, agency girl?"

"I'm Mel."

The receptionist's shoulders slumped as her eyes implored Heaven for something she evidently lacked. Mel wondered if it was patience, good manners or the ability to smile, as the girl seemed to lack all three. "She says her name is Mel. Just…Mel."

Mel summoned a smile. She could be both patient and polite – evidently it was a rarity in this office, if the receptionist was anything to go by. Perhaps the girl was only a teenager, too young to know better, or maybe she'd had a bad morning…

"She's on her way," the receptionist said as she clicked the phone into its cradle.

Mel considered asking who the girl was referring to, but decided not to bother. She didn't expect any answer from her anyway.

The door beside the reception desk opened and a red-suited woman emerged, scowling. She propped the door open with one shiny, red stiletto. "Melody Angel?" she asked, squinting at the sheet of paper in her hands.

Mel winced. "I'm Mel," she repeated, extending her hand to shake the red woman's.

She ignored it. "Follow me."

The woman turned to her right and entered a small meeting room. No, an interview room, Mel told herself, looking at the office chairs circling the table. The furniture was occupied by two men, a jug of water and some empty glasses.

Oh Hell. I hope all my practice questions with Raphael were worth it — and that I don't forget anything, Mel thought, attempting to keep calm. Please, don't let me stuff this up.

The door clicked shut behind her with a terrible finality as Mel took her indicated seat.

"Why do you want to work for our company?"

Mel paused to choose her words carefully. "The Health, Environment, Life and Lands Corporation is experiencing unprecedented growth in a contracting economy, through turning the government push for cost-cutting, consolidation and privatisation into its primary strength. From securing contracts in health and immigration, to subsequent privatised government departments, the general consensus in the business community is that the Health, Environment, Life and

Lands Corporation will soon control all government services. That's unprecedented power for a private company — and I want to be a part of it, to witness its almost miraculous success."

The three interview panel members sported proud smiles at Mel's praise. The woman ran her fingers through her hair, giving Mel a glimpse of what looked like a small, pointed horn, before it was hidden from sight once more. Mel told herself she was imagining things.

One of the men cleared his throat. "What would you say is your worst quality?" He ran his tongue nervously across his lips and Mel could have sworn it looked forked.

"Three things," Mel replied smoothly. "A trinity, as it were. My eye for detail, my tendency to work too hard to the point of single-mindedness, culminating in my pursuit of perfection. I see things other people gloss over as unimportant and I work hard to ensure that my work doesn't include such errors of judgement. I'm a perfectionist — striving to provide the perfect product, even if I need to work harder to deliver that. That might be why I have a reputation as a miracle worker." She blushed and lowered her head.

Beneath the table, she saw the tip of a pointed tail before it swung out of sight. She coughed to hide her exclamation.

"Would you like a drink of water?" the woman asked, filling a glass from the jug on the table. As she handed Mel the half-filled glass, Mel had the impression that the woman's fingernails bore an eerie resemblance to black claws.

Mel blinked and politely accepted the drink, sipping slowly. She set the glass down.

"How do you deal with working on multiple projects at the same time?" the second man asked. Mel strongly suspected the tail belonged to him.

She smiled broadly. "It's all about priorities. When I have competing deadlines, depending on my personal goals and those of my superiors, I assess my projects very carefully. They get allocated relative priority, based on their importance to both me and the people I work for. I then divide my attention accordingly. My time is valuable and wasting it would be a terrible crime, especially when someone else might need to pay for my oversight. The projects that are the highest priority take precedence." She couldn't keep the edge out of her voice and feared that the second man had noticed it.

His eyes appraised her and she caught a glimpse of red before they faded to brown once more. She resolved to be more cautious for the remainder of her interview. After all, she did want to get out of there alive.

"Do you have any questions for us, or any further information you'd like to add?" the woman in the red suit asked. Her eyes had turned redder as the interview progressed, so Mel couldn't tell herself she was imagining things any more. Lilith – the woman's name was Lilith, Mel reminded herself. She couldn't remember the men's names.

"No, thank you. I believe I've taken enough of your valuable time today," Mel responded with a professional smile. She rose to her feet, smoothing her pale gold jacket and matching skirt.

The three interviewers stood with considerably less grace, making noises that expressed their gratitude for her time, for taking part in the interview, and for not mentioning the pointed tails beneath the table.

Lilith opened the door to release her, waiting for Mel to leave first. Mel stepped out and almost collided with a man in a dark suit.

His coffee splashed high, yet he caught most of it in his cup. Not a spot landed on Mel – just one on the man's shoe. "Damn," he swore, swiping at it with a black handkerchief that appeared almost instantly in his hand. As he rose from his crouch, he took in Mel's attire, from her toes to her raised eyebrows.

He summoned a smile that clashed with the stormy expression in his eyes. "I don't believe I've seen you in the office before, and I make it a point to know all of my staff intimately." He handed the dripping cup to Mel's haughty interviewer. Lilith took it without a murmur, even as some of the coffee slopped onto her shoes.

He held out his hand to shake Mel's. "Luce Iblis, CEO of HELL Corporation."

Mel gave him her fingers, in such a way that he couldn't crush them in his firm handshake. "I'm Mel," she began.

"This is her first time here. She's being interviewed for a position here at Health, Environment, Life and Lands Corporation – as my executive officer," Lilith said.

Luce's eyes stared hungrily at Mel as she lowered her gaze. "Is that so? I suspect I'll be seeing a lot more of you very soon, then. I look forward to welcoming you to the HELL Corporation."

Mel caught the glance that passed between Lilith and Luce before the woman bowed her head in acquiescence. Mel lifted her eyes to meet Luce's, but smiled instead of saying anything in reply.

She felt his scrutiny follow her out to reception, where the red woman thanked her again and said they'd be in touch.

Mel tried to hide her smile as she left. Her stint in Hell was over for the day, and she hoped it would be her last for a long time.

Mel waited on the station platform with all the other be-suited commuters. The train arrived, packed like a sardine tin.

A man behind her muttered, "I survived the London Tube every day – no worries getting on this!"

Mel stood aside for two people to squeeze out of the car before she sidled in, reaching for a metal pole to keep her balance when the train set off. A recorded message warned her that the doors were closing.

"Nope, not getting on this one," the Tube survivor

moaned as the doors shut, leaving him standing foolishly on the platform.

The train picked up speed rapidly and the man behind Mel almost fell on top of her. When he straightened up, she became far more intimately acquainted with the stranger's briefcase than she'd ever thought possible. She thought about accidentally stomping on his foot but decided that would only make the situation worse, because if he jumped, the briefcase would go up, too. With the corner of the briefcase jammed between her cheeks, she idly wondered what would happen if she farted.

Faintly, she heard a phone ring. The generic tone could have been hers, but if it was, she couldn't reach to answer it. Whoever it was would have to wait.

She sighed and closed her eyes. The stranger behind her sighed, too, sending a breath down her shirt to the lucky bra she wore on days when luck needed a little extra push. She struggled to maintain her equilibrium and vowed that if she felt the man's hand move at all, she was going to make sure the whole train knew he was a groper – and not the fish, either.

She didn't know how anyone managed an uncomfortable commute like this, twice a day, every single day of their career. Only an angel or a saint would survive without severely injuring someone in response.

The train stopped at the next station and the man with the penetrative briefcase got out. Seeing a spare seat, Mel took it, straightening her skirt as she sat. She took out her phone and started reading. She'd check her messages when she arrived home — she had no intention of letting the whole train know her business. Especially not after they'd all been unwitting witnesses to her getting a briefcase up the bum.

Mel lost herself in the book she'd picked up. Something about zombies and an Amazonian queen battling on the surface of Mars. Some people came up with the strangest things to turn into stories. She certainly enjoyed their efforts.

She felt almost relaxed again as the train arrived at her station and she trudged up the escalators so she could head home.

"Hello, Helpful Angels Agency. This is Persi. How may I help you?" her sweet voice gushed.

"Good afternoon, Persi. It's Mel, returning Raphael's call. He said it was urgent?" Mel tried to hide her curiosity. What could possibly be so urgent that Raphael had needed to call her before he knew if she'd left the HELL Corporation office?

"Oh! Oh, yes. Um, he's on a call — what do I do?" Persi giggled nervously. "I'm still not used to this switchboard thingy."

"You could put me on hold, or you could tell me a bit more about what Raphael feels is so urgent. I've only been back from Iran for two days. I've spent most of that time either preparing for, or attending, today's job interview as a favour to him, when I was looking forward to taking some time off. I have so much washing to do and there's no food in the house." Mel could almost hear Persi's mind wandering. "How's your mother, Persi?"

"She's good. She's always good. Worried, though. The rumours say the old devil's working on another bid for power and no one's sure when he'll show his hand. They're saying he wants out of Hell and he'll do anything to get it." Another high-pitched giggle. "It's frightening, Mel!"

"People have been saying that for as long as I can remember and Lucifer is still firmly in Hell, Persi. I wouldn't worry about him. If he was marshalling all the forces of Hell for a takeover bid, we'd notice."

"But he's sneaky and this time's different, they say. He might…OH! The blinky light for Raphael's phone is off. That means he's free to talk to you!" Persi squealed. "One sec and I'll –" The beep of buttons cut off her voice before it returned. "Raphael, it's Mel!"

"No, just me," Mel replied. "Did you hit the flash key to transfer after you entered his number?"

"OH! Thank you. Putting you through now, Mel!" Persi said with another giggle.

A single beep, followed by some recorded music –

the unearthly sound of a string quartet, Mel guessed. The music cut off after a few seconds.

"Mel, you're the best and I need you," Raphael said. "You have to take this job."

Mel sighed. "I thought you just wanted me to go in for the interview, to take a look around and report back on my findings. Now you want me to accept a job there?"

"We need an insider at the HELL Corporation. They won the contract for mining this morning. You've seen how they're taking over. First the health and justice systems, then environment, fishing, mining…pretty soon, they'll control all of the privatised government departments. We can't let that happen."

Mel wet her lips. "Why me? Why can't you send an archangel in? I thought Gabrielle was due back from Russia any day. She's experienced and more than qualified. What about Michael? He's good with IT – he fits in anywhere."

"Gabi's still in Russia and Michael…he won't be involved in this one. It's too dangerous." Raphael didn't elaborate. His breathing crackled through the phone line.

"You're not selling me on this, Raphael. Too dangerous for Michael, part of HELL's biggest bid for power in millennia…I'm the last person you should tap for this one. You know I'm better in the background, managing from the shadows. I don't have a taste for danger like some of your guardian angels. I'm…"

"You're perfect," Raphael interrupted eagerly. "They won't suspect you because no one knows you. They'll dismiss you as a brand-new guardian. That's why we'll send you in as a new office temp, so you can…"

"An office temp? The errand girl who answers the phone, takes minutes at meetings and does the photocopying? Are you serious? Was that what I was interviewing for? They'll never buy it. I'm qualified to run their entire company, Raphael. They knew I wasn't an angel-in-training like Persi – from the beginning of the interview. I'm surprised I made it out of there safely." Mel shook her head. "Gabi, Mike…you should be sending in the archangels for something like this. I was planning on heading up to Korea…"

"We can't send Michael in and he knows Gabi, too," Raphael began, but didn't seem to want to continue.

Mel took the bait tiredly. "Who's 'he', Raphael? Michael's not afraid of anyone. After taking on Lucifer himself, Michael's not likely to get nervous around one of his deputy demons."

"We think Lucifer's in charge – directly, this time. If he appears in the office, you know Michael will pull out his flaming sword and all Hell will break loose. He'll set every demon he has against Michael. He won't let Gabi near any sensitive material, either. You're our only hope." Now Raphael sounded scared.

Mel blew out a breath, trying not to laugh. The CEO she'd met looked like he wanted her all over something sensitive – which had nothing to do with the

Corporation. He couldn't possibly have been…
"Lucifer. Out of the Pit and managing a company. Well, I guess I can't say I'm shocked. The whole place was full of demons in suits. The entire interview panel and their CEO, too. Look, I know demons are into the bureaucracy of contracts and such – they've been doing it since Roman times and they've gotten a lot better since Faustus – but surely Lucifer wouldn't be stupid enough to make such an obvious bid for power. It doesn't make sense." She thought of the arrogant CEO, passing his coffee cup to Lilith so he could check Mel out. The way Lilith had bowed her head, as if in respect – but Lilith was one of Lucifer's most trusted lieutenants. If the rumours were true, she was his mistress, too. Could the sleazy man truly have been the Lord of Hell? She couldn't tell Raphael that – what if she was wrong? She'd never had anything to do with Lucifer before and she knew very little about demons. Mel knew she needed to investigate further before she said anything. That meant returning to HELL. "Ah Hell. You think it's a serious attempt, if he's making it known he's involved, don't you?" She didn't want to believe it.

"That's why I need you, Mel," Raphael persisted. "If they think you're insignificant, they'll give you access to more than any other angel we send in. Being you, you'll see to the heart and soul of the matter faster than anyone else can. And…and you'll be well placed to take over the whole Corporation if it becomes necessary. Or get out quickly if he makes an appearance – so you can warn us. No one else can do what you can, Mel."

Mel felt distinctly uneasy. "Take over? You mean dispose of Lucifer? I don't kill demons, Raphael – you know that. Send in one of the Powers – you know this is more their area than mine."

If Mel couldn't hear Raphael breathing on the other end, she'd have assumed his silence meant he'd hung up. "We did," he finally said. "We sent in the twins – Camael and Samael. They were in the office long enough to learn that all the contracts between the Corporation and humans are watertight, before we lost contact with them. It seems they joined the HELL Corporation as part of a more…permanent arrangement. In their legal division."

"They poached our staff? Or is it worse than that? Raphael, if they're corrupting angels, I don't see how you can justify sending anyone in there. The risk is too high."

"Please, Mel," he begged. "You'll be fine. You're not as susceptible to corruption as any of the others. I'll bring in other angels to back you up as quickly as I can. The moment Gabi gets home, I'll send her to you, plus anyone else they'll take. The more power HELL gets, the harder they'll be to take down, and we have to stop them. We can't let Lucifer win."

Mel knew he was right, but that didn't mean she had to give in easily. Especially if it meant trading North Korea for Western Australia. The bulgogi was better in

Korea, for a start, and there was something about the purity of fresh snow in winter. Hell would see snow before Perth did. "All right, Raphael. If they want me to work for them, I'll do it, but you'll owe me a huge favour."

"Oh, thank God!" Raphael cheered. "They already called to say you've got the job. They want you to start on Monday. I can email you the details, or you can write them down now if you like…"

"Send them through via email. I'll have to find something suitable to wear — it's been a long time since I spent any time in an office, and my luggage went missing between Tehran and home. I'm not sure where they sent my suitcase, but it arrived this morning, two days after I did, and it's full of sand. I think some of my underwear's missing, too. I'll need to do a fair bit of washing, in order to have a presentable work wardrobe."

"Thank you, Mel! You're wonderful — I love you."

"Yes, Raphael, I know. You're lucky I know you say that to all the girls. As long as you let me investigate this in my own way, we have a deal."

"Congratulations on your new job. We'll see you in HELL at nine on Monday morning."

See You

in

Hell

DEMELZA CARLTON

DEDICATION

*Sometimes you need to be an angel to get through a
work day.
I've been lucky enough to work beside them instead.
For all those helpful angels who helped inspire this
book and unleash it on the world.
Yes, including briefcase-up-the-bum bloke.
This one's for you.*

"Congratulations on your new job. We'll see you in HELL at nine on Monday morning."

They ended the call and Mel dropped her phone on the bench. Despite Raphael's confidence, she knew this would be her most difficult assignment yet. No angel had ever taken on the Pit and won. Every other angel had failed, corrupted into joining the demons' ranks. She wasn't just the best – she was the only one left. And she didn't have a thing to wear to work.

Maybe if she ironed some of her clean washing,

something would look good. After all, it wasn't like she had to wear pristine whites like she did in Heaven.

"See you in HELL," she murmured, plugging in the iron.

Mel walked into the HELL Corporation building and took the lift up to the sixth floor. To her surprise, today's receptionist was a man. "Welcome to HELL. Can I help you?" he asked with a smile. He raised his eyebrows.

Suddenly nervous, Mel smiled back, keeping her eyebrows firmly down. "I'm here to start work. I'm from the Helpful Angels Agency…"

The receptionist's eyebrows lifted even higher. "I'll get her for you." He paused. "Yes, I have your angel.

Did you want to come get her?"

For a moment, Mel thought he was talking to her, then noticed his almost invisible headset. Embarrassed, she looked out the window at the Christmas decorations in the foyer. It looked like someone had picked up some props leftover from the *Avatar* set and decided to use them for Christmas. In October.

A door opened and Lilith appeared, wearing a red pantsuit, an absent smile on her face. "Hi again, Mel. Call me Lili." She offered her hand and Mel took it. It was so cold and limp, she felt like she was shaking a chicken breast.

"Follow me," Lili said, swiping her card over the reader and opening the nearest door.

Mr Receptionist gave a wave. "Good luck!"

Lili led Mel through a maze in burgundy cubicle land. She stopped at one that looked no different to the others and gestured for Mel to take a red guest chair. Lili seated herself behind the desk, on an ergonomic chair that was just a bit higher than Mel's.

"Right, then. Here's all your pre-orientation training and checklists —" Lili pushed a thick folder of papers across the desk, "— and your login codes — you'll need to change the default password right away —" a single sheet of paper landed on the folder, "— and your desk is next to mine." Lili pointed over the partition to the cubicle next door, between the fire exit and a huge, concrete, structural pole. She smiled at Mel one more time before her eyes slid to her computer monitor in dismissal.

Mel stood and took a step toward her cubicle. "Ah, Lili, you never said what I'm supposed to do here."

Lili lifted her eyes. "First, finish your orientation, then we'll discuss tasks. You're an executive officer, which means you execute orders for anyone in the unit."

Mel looked down at the papers. "So I'll find out next week?"

Lili laughed. "You'll be done with that by the end of tomorrow. Read through the package today and tomorrow you'll be in the group orientation sessions in the training room. Most of the stuff is about safety — what to do if there's a fire. As if we'd ever have fires in HELL!"

Mel had been welcomed to HELL exactly six times since she'd arrived, ninety-two minutes earlier. The presentations had been so enthusiastically delivered that she'd checked her watch thirty-one times and tallied every welcome in her otherwise blank notes.

She felt like making a coffee, just to break the monotony, and it looked like the demons in the room all felt the same way. Two were playing poker, one was watching some sort of video on his phone, one was snoring slightly as she slept on the desk, and the remaining half-dozen demons looked like they weren't far off joining her.

The present speaker gained momentary life as her monotone became uncharacteristically animated. "And now, let me present the CEO of Health, Environment, Life and Lands…Mr Luce Iblis!"

The sleazy, coffee-spilling demon Mel remembered from her interview stepped in front of the projector.

"May I be the first to welcome you to the HELL Corporation," Luce began.

Mel carefully tallied a seventh mark on her page.

"I look forward to working closely with all of you, as we rise from our humble beginnings…"

Hell hardly had a reputation for humility, Mel thought idly. If Luce was a good example of the demon denizens of the place, arrogant beginnings seemed more appropriate. She glanced around at the other demons in the room, for she was definitely the only angel present. They all looked awake and somewhat attentive – or at least their eyes were open and facing front. Cards and phones had vanished.

As Luce droned on, pausing occasionally to deliver one false smile after another, she started to see the patterns. All the demons followed his words, laughing and smiling with him, as if they were afraid to even appear like they weren't listening. It wasn't so much loyalty as blind obedience, or fear. She began to understand precisely what she was facing – a united army who would serve their leader. A man who knew exactly what he controlled. She wondered whether they were quite as sycophantic when he wasn't around.

Her fellow orientees looked more human than the demons who'd interviewed her. There wasn't a tail in sight and they all had very human-looking skin tones. She had seen the occasional vestigial horn, hidden amongst hair, but she'd seen newborn goats with bigger horns. She'd had so little to do with demons in the past that she had no idea if their horn size and human appearance made them extremely junior or senior demons. She turned her attention to their leader, presumably the most senior demon.

"I'm sure it won't be long before the next time someone says, 'See you in Hell!' you'll wonder what department they work in and why you haven't seen them in the lunchroom here at work." Luce's teeth seemed perfect and white as he laughed loudly, joined soon after by his demon chorus.

Luce looked entirely human, Mel decided. Not a horn, hoof or tail out of place. Perfectly manicured nails that didn't make her think of claws. Yet no one could smile that much while their eyes remained soulless, black holes of hate – only a man who'd seen Hell every day for millennia and maintained his sanity. She had no doubts at all. This was clearly the Lord of Hell, she realised, as those dark eyes settled on her.

Mel shivered a little in her seat, in sympathy for how cold the man seemed. Was it the distance from Hell that made him so chilly, like some kind of fiery lizard? How horrible it must be to live such an emotionless existence – no happiness, joy or fellow feeling for anyone. She wondered how a man filled with such cold indifference could seduce so many angels to fall. All she felt for him was sadness. The danger Raphael spoke of seemed distant – she needed to know what this man planned and running off to Raphael right away wasn't going to get anyone anywhere. She needed to stay and observe for as long as she could.

"So, once again, welcome to HELL!" he boomed, with one last practised smile.

Mel regretted that she'd missed his speech while letting her mind wander, but the emotionless tone he'd used had made the words sound like he'd memorised them long before and not varied them much since. She vaguely remembered seeing a letter from the CEO in her notes yesterday – she'd probably already read the content of his presentation. The saccharine message hadn't improved any in his personal delivery.

"And now, we break for fifteen minutes to refresh and have a coffee!" the demon trainer called out. "Fifteen minutes on the dot!"

Mel slipped out to the kitchen so she could finally have a drink. Demons were known for their slavish devotion to Earthly pleasures – surely the rich, dark brew of office coffee would be one of those.

Mel carefully blew on her coffee as she returned to the lunchroom turned training room.

Luce reclined against the tiny bar in the corner, resting his arms on it so his hips were pushed into greater prominence.

Mel recognised his stance as one meant to draw attention to the bulge in his pants. The implied message was clear: the pants could be unzipped for the right girl or boy, if someone played their cards right. Mel had far more experience with such a stance than Luce probably realised – for she remembered a time in Russia when it had merely meant the man was rich enough to own a spare pair of socks to stuff in his pants against the frostbiting cold. Ah, Napoleon had been stubborn and arrogant, too, she recalled, but he'd been good for intelligent conversation. He'd also owned an ample supply of socks.

No one seemed game to speak to the CEO, so Mel took pity on him. Resting her elbow on the end of the bar, she asked, "Do you get bored, delivering the same orientation presentation every month?"

"Of course not," came the easy answer. "Every time I tell new staff about the achievements of the HELL Corporation, I see their pride in being part of my company, knowing the next team of new staff will be hearing about the achievements that they personally helped happen."

Mel laughed heartily. "That sounds like a rehearsed response if ever I heard one. Do you ever answer a question honestly?"

"Of course," Luce replied. Mel barely knew the man, yet she knew he was lying.

She pressed her lips together and gave a little smile in response, before turning her attention to her instant coffee. Attention it didn't deserve, but the muddy brew was an improvement to listening to the demon's rehearsed rhetoric.

Luce seemed to realise that he'd hit a wrong note. "It's Mel, right?"

"Yes," she acquiesced gracefully. "From the Helpful Angels Agency." A careful sip of coffee kept her eyes from meeting his as the cup hid her smile. She waited for the implied warning to sink in: far from being one of his demons, she played most emphatically for the other team.

"Ah. Ah, yes. I remember now. You're the new girl who's working under Lili, right?"

"I'm in the office beside her and I report to her, yes," Mel corrected. "I'm looking forward to seeing precisely which projects she has in mind for me. I understand the company's interests are quite diverse, so I expect the work to be different to anything I've done before, if nothing else."

"So what were you doing before deciding to be my angel?"

Mel gave him her serene smile, knowing Hell would freeze over before she'd ever be his angel. He evidently didn't know that yet, so she replied, "Other temporary assignments, as required. I go where I'm needed, that's all." She took a larger mouthful of her cooling coffee, trying not to grimace at the taste.

"I'm sure I'll need you for something. Lili does a lot of work for me. She may even delegate some of her more delicate tasks to you, if you're lucky. We could be working very closely together on some of my pet projects." Luce grinned. "You'll want to make sure you wear a skirt." He stared at her pants-clad legs hungrily.

Mel wondered what he'd say if she admitted the

closest he'd get to her was precisely where he was now – just out of arm's reach. She chose to say nothing. Instead, she smiled and nodded, then excused herself so she could wash the sludge out of the bottom of her coffee mug. She wanted to wash her whole body – the sleazy CEO made her skin crawl – but she hardly had time before the next orientation session resumed.

She slipped back into the training room, relieved to see that Luce had left. Somehow, she suspected she'd be seeing him again soon, though she hoped the opposite. Slimy snake of a CEO…

Two demons crept into the room behind Mel, smelling strongly of cigarette smoke. Another demon inhaled blissfully. "Oh, that smells so good. I've been on nicotine patches so I don't have to go out for a ciggy, but it's just not the same…"

The trainer pressed some paracetamol out of the packaging and tipped them into her mouth, washing them down with her cup of coffee.

Mel glanced around – all the demons looked like they'd taken the opportunity to grab another foul coffee at the end of the break. Aside from a demon cracking open a can of Red Bull, she was the only one not holding a cup.

"Are we all back? Good. It's time to discuss our substance policy," the trainer began.

A demon sneezed, then blew her nose noisily. She pulled out some hand sanitiser and rubbed her hands with it.

A slide popped up on the projector screen. To Mel's mild irritation, the trainer read it aloud, as if the entire group were blind or illiterate.

"Our policy: No employee is to consume or use drugs or alcohol within eight hours of commencing work to start and/or return to work while under the influence of drugs or alcohol.

"The purpose of this policy is to maintain a work environment free from the effects of the use of drugs and alcohol. Therefore the use or consumption is strictly forbidden. The consequence of breaching this policy is instant dismissal." The trainer paused. "Does anyone have a problem with this?" She picked up her coffee and sipped it.

The demons shook their heads in unison. Mel heard some slurping their drinks, too. Demons. Oh, dear. This job was going to be much harder than she'd thought. If every demon in the place was as sloppy and slipshod as whoever had slapped together the substance policy, she had a lot of work to do. She'd best get started, then.

She sighed and said, "Yes. I do."

"Which part don't you understand? Or is it simply that you don't agree with it?" the woman asked, a superior smile on her face as if she'd be delighted to perform an instant dismissal.

Mel took a deep breath. "Well, the first sentence doesn't make sense. It looks like someone cut and pasted it but forgot to proofread it. Splitting it into two sentences might make it clearer. Ending the first sentence after 'commencing work', then replacing the 'to' with 'No employee is to start...' Admittedly, you'd need to define drugs and alcohol. It isn't clear as it is."

The superior smile widened. "I think our policy makes it very clear. It encompasses use and consumption of all drugs and alcohol. No exceptions."

"In that case, all of us have earned instant dismissal in the last hour," Mel replied. "Including you. We've all had caffeine – coffee, Red Bull and the like – and then there's nicotine, paracetamol and just using alcohol sanitiser."

Laughter erupted behind her as the trainer seemed to choke on a coughing fit. "We didn't mean caffeine or those other things. Those aren't...you can't be dismissed for..." she spluttered.

"Under the wording of your policy, we can. What'll your CEO do when he finds out? Do you think he'll ban coffee or just decide to fire the lot of us?"

The demon's face grew an interesting shade of red and her horns appeared through her hair. "How dare you...He...oh Hell...he'll..." Anger shifted to fear in her face.

She must be terrified of the CEO, Mel mused. Surely only Lucifer could have that effect on demons. Mel smiled angelically. "I'd be delighted to help you reword your policy before he sees it. Perhaps if this orientation programme ends early, I'll have time today to help you before I'm expected back at my desk."

The trainer's face started to fade back to normal as she looked around. "Do you think…you might all go back to work without mentioning this? We can end orientation early, if you like…"

Every demon in the room rose and the orientees left quickly, with surreptitious, grateful nods to Mel. She returned these as politely as she could before she found herself alone with the trainer.

"You'll really help?" the trainer asked incredulously.

Mel beamed. "Of course. I'm an angel. It's what I do. Plus, I'm more than a little worried about what would happen if you banned caffeine from your office. I think Hell would be a happier place than here."

"Ah, Lili? I'm done," Mel announced, relieved that she'd finally finished her orientation and all the getting-to-know-you sessions without giving too much away…and neatened up the substance policy so that everyone got to keep their jobs for another day.

Lili looked up from what appeared to be an engrossing email. "Done all your orientation? Great, let's get you a project." She reached for a stack of folders that threatened to topple over, picking up the yellow one on top. "Something easy to begin with. We need you to research rehabilitation techniques for graffiti criminals."

Mel felt her jaw drop. "You need me to do…what? I've never worked with criminals, rehabilitation or anything to do with justice before. Since when was the justice system privatised?"

Lili gave Mel a perfunctory smile. "After privatisation worked so well for the prison and immigration detention centres, privatising the justice system seemed the logical next step. It's the 'Life' in the name of our Corporation – Health, Environment, Life and Lands. Now, it shouldn't be a problem. Our Research Division has already written a report on this, so all of their references should still be on file."

Mel felt like she'd missed something. "If it's already been done, why do you need me to do it again?"

Lili leaned forward and lowered her voice. "Our Research Division looks at things…rather differently to us. We're not sure they took the research in the right direction. They may have focussed on art therapy because it was the easiest solution, as opposed to the best solution."

Mel laughed. "But surely art therapy would be both the easiest and best solution!"

Lili frowned. "Don't let their research blind you. Our Research Division has their offices next to an art school, which isn't the case with this office, so you shouldn't suffer the same bias as our head researcher."

Mel nodded knowingly. "Ah, an art school. Did your

researcher have to do lots of research in the female life drawing class? I can understand why he'd advocate that solution."

Lili looked shocked. "You can't say things like that. Phil might consider it sexual harassment."

Mel wet her lips, wondering how to correct her mistake. "Well, it does seem like the first thing I'd think of. Drawing naked women would certainly have an effect on the minds of men in prison, particularly those who are already artistically inclined. Things don't change that much."

Lili's face lost all expression. "Sometimes they do, dear. Phil is gay and he's married to the principal of the art school, Lial. I understand the female form does nothing for him. You'll find he can get quite enthusiastic, describing the hard contours of a well-muscled, male body."

Mel felt her face flush. She'd forgotten that some men don't like women. She couldn't blame them – she was particularly partial to a well-muscled, male body, too. Admittedly, it had been a while since she'd been close enough to touch such a body, but she held out hope that she might, sometime soon…

Mel shook herself. This wasn't the time to think about sexy men. She had work to do and any attractive men on her horizon would have to wait until she was finished with her current assignment. Or until she'd at least earned a holiday from it.

"Well, I guess I'll get started then," she said with

false cheer, picking up the yellow file and walking away as quickly as she could.

She sat at her desk and restrained herself from banging her head repeatedly on the laminated surface. She resisted searching the Internet for images of hot men – she knew where that would lead, though the kitten photos that came up were always cute. Instead, Mel took a deep breath and got to work, not lifting her head until the day was done.

When Mel returned from lunch, a small sheaf of papers covered her keyboard. The words, 'NOT complimentary!' were scrawled across the front page in red ink.

She eyed it for a moment and decided that the red pen scrawl over the front of the memo she'd sent was definitely not complimentary, to the point where she considered it quite rude. She took a closer look at the pages.

On the second page, the red ink surfaced again,

carving a ring around the word 'complimentary'. She took a deep breath as she decided that the red-pen wielder didn't like the word. Perhaps they'd prefer something insulting instead?

"…this initiative will be complimentary to our efforts to rehabilitate car thieves and graffiti artists…" she read.

What's wrong with saying nice things about their efforts at rehabilitation? Mel wondered. It wasn't her line – someone up the chain of command had tainted her text with bigger words and, apparently, mistakes, too.

She decided to ask Lili.

Lili laughed when she read the papers. "Ah, the Luce red pen of doom. It's your turn this week."

Mel was confused. "My turn? This isn't even my mistake!"

"Like an impotent man's used condom, our CEO's ego needs reinflating from time to time, usually at least once a week. Last month, before you started, Luce sent out a rant about how many people confused compliments with complements. Something about the first one saying something nice and the second one 'completing me' or some shit like that. You're the first one to make the mistake after his rant, so you get to apologise." Lili didn't look sympathetic.

Mel's confusion deepened. "Apologise? For not getting his email before I started working here and fixing someone else's mistake after this left my desk?

Shouldn't the person who made the mistake be doing this, as they did get the email?"

"You're forgetting that whoever did make that mistake is higher in the company hierarchy than you are, and we'll all delegate the letter to you anyway, whether it was your mistake or not." Lili shrugged. "Hey, it's better than getting his email, ignoring it and having to explain why. At least you have an excuse. Just write up another memo apologising for the mistake and he'll forget about it as soon as he feels his ego is swollen enough again."

"I have to write a formal apology?" Mel was mortified. "Can't I just pull the original memo, fix the mistake and resubmit it?"

Lili smiled. "Sure you can, but that puts your memo at the bottom of the pile, which means it'll be delayed by at least another week or two. Then you'll have to write a memo apologising for the delays to your project instead." She shrugged. "Think of it as one of those, 'Other duties as required,' on your job description. You do what you're told and you get paid for it. At least he's not asking for you to do it on your own time, or when you had leave booked!"

Nor was he asking her to personally deliver her apology to his office, where she'd have to dodge his sleazy advances, Mel consoled herself.

She sighed and returned to her desk. The CEO of HELL threw tantrums that would embarrass a two-year-old because he didn't like someone's choice of words and he had an ego the size of a hot air balloon, which deflated rapidly in the chilly corporate atmosphere. So it was no different working in HELL than anywhere else. She took a deep breath and started wasting her afternoon on stroking the CEO's ego. At least that was all she was expected to stroke.

"Yep, that looks fine," Lili said, pushing the piece of paper across the table to Mel. "Just change it to the font in the style guide and you can take it up to Luce yourself."

"I…what? I thought you said I just had to write it and send it up to him," Mel protested.

Lili's eyes glowed red as if she sensed Mel's discomfort and enjoyed it immensely. "Oh, no. He came down here personally and placed the offending report on your desk. He waited a while, too, determined to make sure you understood his message. He insisted that I send you to report to him as soon as you received it."

Mel felt her jaw drop. "But…that was hours ago!" She felt her stomach and the sandwich inside it start to sink.

Lili grinned fiercely. "Then I suggest you change the font quickly and leg it up those stairs to Luce's office before you're any later."

Struggling not to swear, Mel marched back to her desk to make the letter and offending memo as perfect as she could. Fifteen minutes later, she pulled the pages from the printer and set off for the executive suite upstairs.

She kept a serene smile on her face as she strode through the maze of cubicles, nodding slightly every time she caught the eye of another demon. She'd never recognise them all, but it still seemed a good idea to stay on good terms with them. If her job survived the day and the belated dressing-down from Luce.

She shrugged. If her first job lasted less than a fortnight, so be it. She didn't much like the work, anyway, and there were plenty of demons to do it. It's not as if the HELL Corporation would miss her. She'd tell Raphael that the CEO definitely was Lucifer and let him sort it out while she went to Korea. She could taste the bulgogi already…

The cubicles were bigger now – spacious enough to take several visitors and a large meeting table between them. Mel knew she was nearing executive territory.

"Can I help you?" an imperious voice asked. Mel heard the words, along with the implied message that the owner of the voice would not help her. Mel was perfectly happy helping herself.

Mel's smile lit up her whole face. "Lili sent me to see Luce regarding a report." She proffered the papers.

The older woman's lips pursed as her deep, dark eyes narrowed. She had to be one of Luce's more senior demons. Her demeanour spoke of indescribable age and experience – all of it decidedly dark.

"I'm Mephi, Mr Iblis' personal assistant," the woman said, emphasising the demon's name. "All of his appointments go through me. Do you have an appointment?"

The woman's subtext was amazing, Mel decided. She radiated an aura that said Mel hadn't a hope of getting through her and she'd never be important enough for an appointment. Despite herself, she was impressed. She wondered how many demons balked at this formidable gatekeeper.

"I'm delighted to meet you, Mephi. I wish I'd known to call you first – but Luce left this on my desk and insisted I speak to him about it immediately. Given the urgency, I didn't dare delay." Mel let the slightest look of concern cross her face. "I haven't missed him, have I? I'll wait as long as I have to, if he's with someone. I'd hate to be the one responsible for this getting to him later than he'd like." She slipped on a sympathetic smile that suggested she wouldn't want Mephi to bear the brunt of her boss's wrath.

Mephi held Mel's gaze for a few seconds before she conceded her point and picked up the phone. "Mr Iblis, I have an angel here to see you." She managed to make it sound like something she'd found floating in the staff toilets.

"If you're talking about the girl standing at your desk with the papers in her hand, send her right in, Mephi," came a voice from behind Mel.

Mephi shrugged. "If you say so," she sniffed, clicking the phone handset back into place.

Mel nodded her thanks to Mephi with an unwavering smile, before turning to brave Luce in his lair. His office, she corrected herself, as she entered the airy space. She couldn't imagine a lair containing…

"Are those Pro Hart landscapes?" Mel asked eagerly. "I don't think I've ever seen the originals in oil before – just prints of them. It's the colours. They're always so vibrant, so real…"

"They are," Luce replied, "but you're not here to discuss my art collection. You've kept me waiting and I am far from happy." His eyes seemed to catch the light in odd ways, as if each was a singularity drinking the photons in, with no intention of releasing them.

Mel stepped forward and laid her papers on his desk. "The corrections you requested, along with a letter."

Luce gave the papers a cursory glance before turning

the full pull of those dark eyes on Mel. "Do you know how long you've made me wait?" He lifted his chin. "Close the door."

For the first time, Mel felt a premonition of danger. The demon reclined in his desk chair with his hands in his lap, a picture of relaxed repose. Only his eyes seemed to belie the image — like a crocodile lurking beneath still, muddy waters. Did the crocodile know how much danger he was in?

"No," Mel said.

Luce snorted. "I can have you naked on the desk with the door open or closed. It makes no difference to me. You might be embarrassed later if Mephi hears you moaning, though, which she won't when you close the soundproof door."

Mel struggled not to laugh. She even swallowed her smile before she spoke. "And I can have you up on sexual harassment charges before you can get your hands out of your pants to zip them up. If you'd wanted to see me sooner, you should have left a written note or emailed me, instead of leaving a message with Lili. She only told me a few minutes ago that you wanted to see me." The sounds of furtive zipping confirmed what had only been a guess. "Do you want me to turn my back and wait a minute, while you finish putting your bits away? I wouldn't want anything getting stuck or hurt, with you rushing things and all."

To hide the laughter still threatening to escape, she turned and kicked the door shut. This demon wasn't dangerous – he was ridiculous, she decided.

"Now strip and get your arse on the desk," Luce instructed.

Mel stared at him. He couldn't be serious, could he?

"Every other girl in this building knows how to do as she's told. Do you know how many girls I've had on this desk? You should consider yourself lucky. The last one I had in here was so quick getting undressed that I managed to give her a full fifteen minutes of my time. At this rate, you'll be lucky to have five."

Mel became transfixed by the timber desktop. "Did you wipe it clean afterwards?"

"What?" Luce's face reddened.

"Did you wipe it clean afterwards?" Mel repeated patiently. "I mean, you work on it every day and my report's there now. At the very least, I'd give it a good spritz with the Spray and Wipe and some paper towel before I used the desk again for work. Imagine how many diseases and strange germs each of your, er, accommodating staff members contributed when they placed their bare behinds on your desk."

The shock on Luce's face was priceless. He edged his chair away from the suddenly suspicious surface.

"Did you want me to go ask Mephi if there's a bottle in the kitchen?" Mel offered. "I'm sure I could wipe your desk down for you, just this once, if it makes you feel uncomfortable. We can get the cleaners to include that as part of their regular evening duties, if you like." She coughed. "Ah, you might want to zip up that last inch first..." She glanced away and heard the squeal of a quickly fastened zip. "There. That wasn't so hard, was it?"

A second too late, she realised her poor choice of words and it was her turn to blush.

Luce exploded with laughter. "You have no idea. I'm still trying to work out whether I should remind you that I can fire you if you don't do what I say, but something tells me you know that already."

Mel shrugged. "Sexual harassment and unfair dismissal. You'll be on a roll with the Equal Opportunity Commission with those two. You'll have a trifecta with the occupational health and safety risk of that unhygienic desk."

"It'll be my word against yours," Luce replied. Dark eyes seemed to bore into hers and Mel gave in to curiosity, looking deeper into a darkness that seemed too dense to be true. Did the demon have a soul under that thick layer of shadow, or was that miasma all that was left of his soul? Was his apparent humanity just an illusion?

Mel dropped her voice. "Everyone knows that angels don't lie, but demons do." She held his gaze until he closed his eyes, revealing nothing more.

"You've got balls, angel."

Mel lowered her eyes. "Actually, I don't, but we're not going there. I don't do demons, Luce. I gather there are some girls who like being ordered around like unpaid prostitutes, but I'm more of a dinner, flowers, chocolates and gradual sort of girl. And I really do prefer wings to horns." Her smile was apologetic. "Do you want to discuss my report? I believe the spelling mistakes were inserted by Lili or someone else who altered the document after it left my desk. I agree that my reports shouldn't have spelling mistakes in them, hence the present one is as near-perfect as I can make it."

Luce waved his hand dismissively. "I'm sure the report's fine now. Leave it with me."

"The only thing you wanted to discuss was whether I'd sleep with you?" Mel asked.

Luce seemed surprised. He evidently wasn't used to forthright angels, Mel mused. Perhaps she should have been more careful – or at least less frank.

"Not so much sleep. I definitely want you awake." He paused before adding, "Look, I lied."

Big surprise there, Mel thought.

"When I said I'd only have five minutes for you, that's not true. I don't have any more meetings or appointments today. You can have me for as long as you want. All night, if you like." Another pause. "And it doesn't have to be the desk. There's this chair, or up against the wall, or on the floor...or even on the couch!" Luce sounded really proud of himself. "I'll tell you what. I'll even let you choose."

Mel felt a stab of pity for the man. He had no idea how wrong this whole conversation had been. "Thank you for the truly tempting offer," she began carefully, "but I'm going to have to refuse. I have plans tonight and I'm just about to finish work for the day."

His grin faltered, as he looked shaken. Mel's heart ached in sympathy. "Well, if you're sure...maybe another time, then."

Mel managed to smile politely before making as dignified an exit as she could.

As she reached the stairs down to her floor, she clearly heard him say, "Shit!"

Indeed, she thought, remembering that her plans tonight included stopping at the supermarket to pick up some toilet cleaner on her way home so she could clean the porcelain receptacle. It's not like she'd lied to him about having plans...

There was something oddly satisfying about a freshly-scrubbed toilet. Perhaps it was the way the reflective white porcelain shone. Or maybe it was simply the knowledge that it would be a whole week before she had to inhale bleach fumes again.

"Mel? What's for dinner?" she heard Raphael call.

There was a surprise. He'd wandered in and let himself in with the spare key without telling her he was coming. Had he heard about Luce's ill-conceived attempt at seduction already?

She found Raphael in the kitchen, chugging a beer. "Ooh, I haven't had one of those in a while," she said. "Are there more in the…thank you." She took the open Rogers and smiled as she sipped from the stubby. "So, did you bring me dinner, too?"

Mel registered Raphael's shock and laughed. "If you want me to cook dinner for you, you'll have to call in advance to let me know. I've been running around after demons all day and I'm done for. I was going to make a sandwich or head up to the little Japanese place by Canning Highway. Take your pick and we'll do it."

"How about I go pick up some Japanese and bring it back here? Tempura and tofu?" Raphael offered.

Mel smiled. "If you're offering to buy me dinner with all the extras, you're going to be asking for another favour before the night's out. I shall sit here, drink my beer, and wait for you." She settled on the sofa, bottle in hand. It looked like the neighbours' kitten had sneaked in and curled up on her desk shelf again. The tiny creature would've fitted on a saucer with space to spare. She decided to let it sleep for a bit longer before she carried it home to its owners.

Raphael left and returned with their bento-boxed dinner. Mel used his absence to set the table with chopsticks and condiments, before brewing a pot of traditional Japanese tea.

After slurping artfully at his udon, Raphael paused to wipe his face with a napkin. "How's work?" he asked, fishing for more noodles with his chopsticks.

"I spend all day doing random tasks for demons. If I told you half the pointless things they make me do, you wouldn't believe it. My reports have to be perfect and approved by my superior, Lili. Then she sends the document up to the person she reports to, who makes any changes they want, who then sends it further up the chain for everyone else to do the same…until it ends up on the CEO's desk for him to approve for release. If the CEO likes it, great, but if he decides that one of the commas inserted by someone along the chain isn't where he wants a comma, the report is dumped on my desk with a nasty note or, worse, a demon in person, demanding to know why I'd make such a mistake and insisting I fix it immediately. If I don't, I'm assigned some even less appealing task to do on top of my existing workload…" She wondered if she should tell him exactly what Luce had ordered her to do, but it'd probably shock poor Raphael.

"I would believe it. It sounds like the old government approval process the demons inherited when they took on the contracts. Humans can be even more bureaucratic than demons where government business is involved." Raphael transferred what looked like a piece of chicken into his mouth, followed by more noodles and a big slurp of broth. "Any sign of Lucifer yet?"

Mel hesitated. She was certain the CEO was the Lord of Hell. It felt too far-fetched, though. What could Lucifer possibly want with Western Australia? Weren't there more populated places he should look to conquer first? She wanted more time to find out what he was up to before she left HELL. But she had to say something – Raphael expected a response. "What does he look like? I think I might have seen him once, ages ago. I'm sure his time in Hell has changed him since then."

Raphael shrugged. "We have no idea what he looks like. He changes his form more often than humans today change clothes – he's so good at it, he could pick exactly what would best attract a human. Even as an angel, he was like that. Now…Hell, he could be anyone. Look like anyone. It's his soul you'd recognise. Once you know him, it's hard for him to hide. He has the blackest, most corrupt soul of any demon I've ever met. Charming to a fault, always looking for a way to seduce you to do exactly what he wants. Using any means necessary. Be glad you've never met him, Mel. He's not someone you want to go up against."

"But that's why I'm there, doing whatever menial office tasks his minions come up with, isn't it? To spot him and take over from him?" Mel asked, selecting another piece of tofu.

"NO!" Raphael dropped the clump of noodles back into his bowl so suddenly it splashed soup across the table. "If you spot him, get out and tell me. He's dangerous. Avoid him at all costs, Mel. Do you know what he'd do to you if he knew who you were and what you can do?"

Mel smiled. "I'm Melody Angel, an office temp who

can photocopy a few thousand pages without swearing when the photocopier gets its seventeenth paper jam. Who can answer the phone politely and transfer calls when I get a dozen misplaced calls that should have gone to Reception, some demon or even a building company in Osborne Park with an almost identical number to mine. Raphael, honestly – he'd probably just offer me a permanent job as his office assistant." She laughed. "To be honest, that's not a bad idea – I'd be well-placed to see everything that goes on and…"

"That's not a joke, Mel. He offered Camael and Samael jobs in his legal department and now I can't get them to take my calls or even speak to me. If he offers you a job, promise me you won't take it. Please, Mel!"

Mel had never seen Raphael look quite this scared. "First, tell me what you haven't yet."

"I promised…*I swore*…" Raphael stammered.

"You owe me more than that," Mel said, her voice deceptively soft. "You will tell me why. What danger does Lucifer pose to me alone?"

"He'll take you to Hell with him. Michael saw it. If he ever gets close enough to you to ask for your help, he won't let you go. Your destiny will be to descend into Hell with him."

Mel's voice dropped lower. "When did Michael see this?"

Raphael swallowed. "Before…before the battle when Lucifer fell. Michael swore he'd win, so he could keep you safe. He asked me to help hide you from

Lucifer in any way I could. I've tried – for centuries, I've tried! – but none of us, not even Michael, expected him to take over HELL Corporation personally. And here, of all places, where I know you keep a permanent house to stay in when you're on one of your sabbaticals. I had no one else here to ask – but I don't want you to take any unnecessary risks." He stared at her, as if weighing his guilt. "Please, Mel. None of us wants to see you in Hell. Is there anyone you've seen at the HELL Corporation that you might think is Lucifer?"

Mel sighed. "The CEO might be. I don't know the demon at all. He goes by the name Luce Iblis. Look, it's only a suspicion – the attempts I've seen him make at seduction weren't the sort to be successful. They were just plain sad. The man's definitely a demon of some kind, but Lili seems a far nastier piece of work. Get Gabi here. She'd be able to recognise him, if he is indeed Lucifer. And if not…well, at least I'd have some help around the office. The photocopying is tedious, to say the least."

"Yes! I'll call Gabi in the morning. We can't be too careful. It could just be a ploy to get you to drop your guard after all. She'll help you in any way she can. I swear it." Raphael slurped up the last noodle and grinned as he set his bowl back on the table.

Mel raised her beer in a toast. "To a better day tomorrow, then," she said. After all, it could hardly be worse than today.

"It's Gerry's birthday on the weekend and we're all putting in to get him a present," announced Merih. "What does everyone think about a new tablet and a mankini?"

Mel thought it would be quite expensive, but she didn't say so. She also wondered why Gerry's manager wanted him to have a mankini. She assumed that was a matter between the two of them.

Merih's eyes swept the room. "So we're agreed, then?"

Some heads nodded slowly. Merih's eyes darted to each member of the group before fixing on Mel. "I'll take care of the tablet. Mel, could you arrange a mankini?"

Mel was taken aback. Why would she know where to get a mankini? "I wouldn't know where to start. I've never bought one before." She'd be content to never buy one at all, nor see one on any man she knew.

Merih laughed. "Ah, you'll be fine. I'll leave it to you. We need it for tomorrow, so hurry up!"

Mel saw Lili nod, smiling, so she resigned herself to the task. Executive officers execute orders, she reminded herself.

She sat at her computer and searched for mankinis. She discovered that they used to come as a free gift with Borat DVDs, but not any more. There were plenty on eBay, but there was no way she'd have it by tomorrow. All the other hits were pictures of men who owned a mankinis — one had huge tufts of black hair sticking out of it — or ads for sex shops.

She opened up tabs for a few and steeled herself for unpleasant research. She let out her breath in a relieved hiss as she clicked on the first page. It featured a warning message, telling her the page had been blocked because it might contain pornographic content.

It's a sex shop, Mel thought. Of course it might contain pornographic content.

She clicked on the web address again, but the site was still blocked. She tried the next and the next...but they were all blocked. She jumped up and trotted over to Lili's cubicle.

"Ah, Lili?"

"Mmm?"

"I can't seem to find a mankini online, because the sex shops are blocked." Her voice carried over the cubicles and some heads popped up to glance at Mel before slowly shrinking out of sight.

"You can't look at sex toys at work," Lili whispered.

Mel was both annoyed and confused. "But don't we regulate prostitutes and brothels?"

Lili gave her the smile that made Mel feel stupid. "Yes, but not adult shops." She kept her voice low. "I guess you'll just have to go out to one and see what they have. Ring them first, though."

Mel lowered her voice to match Lili's. "I don't know where they are. I've never been into a sex shop. I wouldn't know what to ask for."

"Oh, the nearest one is on Murray Street," Lili said dismissively. "It's called XXX or something. Their number should be in the phone book – ring them and I'll escort you there so you don't get lost."

Mel rang the number on the phone book's website and explained to the chirpy woman on the phone what she was after.

"Oh, we have them in several colours. Which would you like? They're part of the Bang Him range, sweetie." Mel wondered if the woman was testing out the merchandise under the phone desk, she sounded so cheerful.

"What colours do they come in?"

"Oh, there's fluorescent green and pink, black lycra and black leather with or without studs, sweetie. I highly recommend the studs." The woman gave an excited giggle.

"Green," Mel said firmly. "Is it okay if I pick it up this afternoon?"

"Sure, sweetie," the woman purred. "We have plenty more in the Bang Him range that you might like."

Mel ended the call as quickly and politely as she could.

She and Lili drove to the adult shop and parked right out front, as Lili insisted, though it's not as if the shop had a back entrance or rear car park.

Inside the shop, they were greeted by an excited woman clad in black and silver latex. She couldn't stop expressing how thrilled she'd be to help them. Mel wondered whether this was the suspected product-tester she'd spoken to on the phone.

"We're here for the mankini? I rang earlier?" Mel asked hesitantly.

"Absolutely! Let me show you the whole range," the woman gushed. Her name badge read 'Mitzi'.

She took both girls over to a display that was clearly the province of the Bang Him range. Mel leaned over to look more closely at a strange-shaped item before she read the name and decided she didn't want to know what it did.

"Are you sure you want the green, sweetie?" Mitzi cooed, her hand waving toward a studded black vinyl number.

Mel choked as she spotted a dildo so big she wondered how anyone could use it for anything but decoration.

Lili answered, "Green would be lovely. It's for a work colleague."

"Oh, how delightful," Mitzi said with a wink. "Is there anything else you'd like?"

Mel tried to work out why they had a display of dildos with tentacles and what looked like strange torture implements, at 30% off, no less, in honour of the release of 'Monsters in the Dark', whatever they were, then decided that she didn't want to know that, either. Surely monsters should be kept in the dark, where they belonged...

"No, thank you," Mel managed to say, swallowing hard. She decided she'd rather be in Hell than here.

"Good morning, Gerry brought photos!" Lili told Mel as she arrived on Monday morning of another fresh week in HELL.

"Of what?" Mel asked, her mouth watering at the aroma of Lili's coffee.

Lili took a slow sip, savouring the taste with her eyes closed, before she swallowed and said, "Pictures his wife took of the mankini. He loved it – you're officially his favourite person in the office!"

Mel was ready to jump Lili for the coffee, she was

panting for one. "Great." She forced herself to walk away.

Unlike Lili, Mel's budget didn't stretch to include expensive barista brew from the award-winning coffee shop downstairs, so she took her plain mug to the kitchen for some of the free instant stuff.

She grimaced as she took her first mouthful of watery, brown sludge, but the caffeine began to take effect, however crappy it tasted. She opened her email.

Gerry's big "THANK YOU!" email came with a slideshow. She clicked it open as she took another sip of her cup of almost-coffee – and almost spat it out on the monitor screen. By the time she was done with the slideshow, she knew that Gerry loved his mankini, it fitted him perfectly, he didn't have huge tufts of black hair poking out of it, and his wife really liked Gerry's reverse view, bisected by green lycra. Wait, were those her lips?

Mel decided that she sincerely hoped Gerry won the lottery that night. She wasn't sure she could look at him without thinking of his green mankini and arse-kissing wife.

Fighting to keep her coffee in her mouth, she clicked on the next email at random, certain that it couldn't shock her more than the first. It was from a man she didn't know named Dan. It sounded like a nice, safe name.

She read it. She read it again, before deciding to find Lili. Surely it wasn't possible. This sounded like the story she'd been reading on the train.

Lili was riveted by something on her computer screen. Mel hoped it wasn't a disturbing PowerPoint presentation.

She cleared her throat. "Am I supposed to get conspiracy hoax emails?"

Lili looked up, annoyance clearly written across her face. "What?"

"Is there really an alien invasion?" Mel asked slowly, feeling silly.

"Aliens?" Lili looked blank for a moment. "Oh, yes, probably. You mean Dan's assessment that 'alien invaders don't hold back and if we're serious neither should we,' something about Yanks and 'collateral damage'?"

Mel nodded.

"Well, depending on what they'll affect, we'll probably have to handle it in some capacity. Health, environment, life, lands…justice for whoever let them in…it all comes down to us."

Mel found her voice. "But, seriously…space aliens?"

Lili laughed. "If there are space aliens, we'd be the ones dealing with them. Dan's probably just talking about cane toads again."

"Oh." Mel sighed in relief.

"We'll have the Department of Defence to help with space aliens," Lili said. "For the terrestrial kind, we're on our own. Defence isn't any use against cane toads."

"Don't forget, software training today!" Lili called as Mel headed to the lunchroom in search of a hot drink. Mel nodded and kept walking. She just had time to get the tea and take it to the training room.

Slipping into a seat in the back row, she sipped her tea silently in the darkened room. A PowerPoint presentation lit the screen as well as a nervous Nybbas, who trembled at the front with a wobbling laser pointer in his hand. He looked more scared than she did, standing in front of an audience, Mel mused.

The trainer Mel recognised from her orientation, who she now knew was called Sil, shifted a tiny video camera on a tripod, angling it so it pointed right at Nybbas. "Right. As long as you stay between the tables and the screen, you're in the picture. We can send the training video out to all our regional offices as soon as this session's done."

Nybbas nodded, gnawing on his lip.

"And…you're live!" Sil sang out.

A sickly smile spread across Nybbas' face. "Good morning, er afternoon, er morning, ladies and gentlemen. Today I'm here to tell you how excited I am!" Between his gritted teeth and his stiff-armed pose, Mel's mind suggested several words that would be more appropriate than excited.

"This package will make you gasp in awe. Just one little thing that will change the way you work forever. I'm so excited to be giving it to you, I can barely contain myself. You're going to love it. And we'll be rolling it out across all the offices…"

The room full of bored demons transformed to one full of grinning demons, with enthusiasm far greater than anything Nybbas could show. His strained delivery of the rehearsed copy didn't help matters, either.

Mel pressed her lips together and endured Nybbas' presentation as best she could. He rushed through it so fast that he was done in only half their allotted time. Once the half-hour was up, a smiling Sil reached to turn off the video camera and the other demons congratulated Nybbas on his package, telling him how much the regional offices would enjoy the training session.

"I'll upload the video right away and send it out this afternoon," Sil said happily, cradling the camera.

"Wait."

Both Sil and Nybbas stared at Mel. Everyone else had left, but she still sat quietly in her seat.

"You should review the presentation first. Can we hook it up to the big screen, or only watch it from the recorder?" Mel asked.

"I guess I could upload it here…" Sil said. "I'll just go get the cables and stuff to hook it up. Be right back!"

She hurried out and Nybbas slumped onto a chair. "I was terrible, wasn't I? They were all lying when they said the regional offices would like my presentation…"

Mel took a careful breath. "No, not terrible. Look, if I gave you some suggestions as to how you might improve the presentation, maybe you'd like to record it again. Without an audience this time."

"Like what? I've had Sil coaching me for weeks on how to do a presentation. I have to use all the right words, move my hands, smile…I did all that!" Nybbas buried his face in his palms. "I can't do any better."

"Well, you know how you hold your hands sort of stiff at your sides," Mel began. She waited for Nybbas to nod before continuing, "You might want to consider lifting them a little. Instead of level with your hips, try making the same gesture in front of your chest, and widen your hands to about the width of your shoulders…"

"What do you mean?"

Mel tried to demonstrate. "You know how you hold your arms out like an Aussie Rules football umpire calling a goal? Your elbows bent close to your body, your forearms at right angles to the rest and your fingers pointing forward? Every time you gesture, it's so tight it looks like a pair of synchronised guillotines. If you lift your arms, your gestures are loose and seem more natural." She demonstrated the chopping motion Nybbas had used, then lifted her arms higher to show the difference.

Nybbas nodded slowly. "I could do that." He waved his arms experimentally, looking relieved.

"And keep your hands in front of your chest the whole time," Mel suggested, trying not to smile.

"I can do that, too," he replied. He stared at her. "But…I don't see why I should redo the whole presentation and record it again just to do the hand signals better. It seems such a tiny change. I'm sure the regional office staff won't notice the difference…"

Mel coughed delicately. "I think you'll find the small change in hand gestures will make a significant improvement to your overall delivery. I really do think it's worth it." Please don't make me say it any more plainly, Mel prayed.

Nybbas frowned at her and opened his mouth to protest.

"It's up!" Sil announced, striding into the room. Nybbas closed his mouth. "I uploaded it at my desk and it's on the network. I'll pull it up now…"

Mel closed her eyes and inhaled as she waited for the file to load. Sympathy for a devil was a terrible thing and she couldn't conscionably let Nybbas embarrass himself like this without attempting to intervene.

She bit down on her lip as the picture appeared. Nybbas' arms were held stiffly at his sides, his hands level with his pelvis, perhaps a sock's width apart. Every time his hands made a stiff guillotine chop, they neatly framed his open pants fly. The slight pull on his pants fabric made the unbuttoned gap in the front of his boxers pop open, revealing a tantalising glimpse of flesh.

"…ladies and (chop) gentlemen. Today (chop) I'm here (chop) to tell (chop) you how excited (chop) I am!" It was very clear from the lack of bulging that he was either not the slightest bit excited, or his excitement was contained within a very small space.

Mel forced herself to continue watching, if only for Nybbas' benefit. She didn't dare laugh.

"This (chop) package (chop) will make you gasp (chop chop) in awe…"

The demon on the screen placed his thumb and forefinger a finger's width apart and shook them at pelvis level for emphasis, before returning to chopping.

"Just (shake) one (shake) little (shake) thing (shake) that will change (chop) the way you work forever (chop). I'm (chop) so (chop chop) excited to be giving it to you, I can barely contain (chop) myself. You're going to love (chop) it. And we'll be rolling it out across all the offices…"

Mercifully, Mel reached over and paused the video.

"Holy Hell. I can't believe no one told me. I almost showed my dick to the whole corporation…" Nybbas' eyes looked wider than the distance between his shaking fingers in the presentation.

"And told them it was only an inch long!" Sil burst out, laughing.

Mel kept her voice level. "Sil, could you go get that camera? I'll help Nybbas record a more appropriate training package." She kept her eyes on Sil until the trainer hurried out of the room, mumbling her assent.

"I'll be in your debt forever for this, Mel," Nybbas vowed. "Eternally grateful…anything you need, you just ask. And if you help me do the presentation again without telling everyone about my tiny package, I'll be your personal slave for life."

Smiling uncertainly, Mel waved away the offer. "It's really not necessary. I just like to help."

Nybbas' eyes grew round. "Is it because you think I'm tiny? Honestly, I'm not. I may not be as big as Lord Lucifer, but it's not small and I definitely know how to use it. I helped build the Thai adult film industry, I'll have you know. Here, let me show you…" He unbuttoned his pants and dropped them to his ankles.

Now Mel laughed – albeit gently. "It's okay – I

believe you. I really don't need to see it. Put your pants back on – you'll need them to do your presentation. And make sure that zip's secure..." Mel averted her eyes as he complied. Over her shoulder, she continued, "Would you like to do it right away, or would you prefer to do your presentation some other time?"

"I have to send it out as soon as possible, so I'd better do it now. With HR booking the room every day to work on their group Christmas presentation, I'll never get this meeting room again," Nybbas replied, sighing. "OH! Right after I feed the imps. The last time I was late feeding them, we had horny demons all over the place. Would you like to meet them?"

"Ah…horny demons? No, thank you, I think I've met more than my fair share already and…"

Nybbas laughed. "I mean the imps. Didn't you ever wonder how we manage to hide our existence from humans and blend in so well?"

"Yes," Mel admitted. "Sure. I'd love to meet your imps."

"Come with me. I'll show you where we get their food," Nybbas said, striding out of the training room. He held the door to Reception open for Mel and she thanked him. "Have to go downstairs." He punched the button for the lift, which opened precisely three seconds later. Both he and Mel entered and travelled to the ground floor, before Mel followed him into the shopping arcade beside the HELL Corporation building.

"Their favourite is the peri-peri chips from Nando's in the food court," Nybbas explained. "I get two seriously large serves with extra chili salt once a week. Other days, they get the spiciest Thai I can find. I'll let you give them the chips — they'll love you for it. They don't normally take too well to new people, so their favourite food will help…"

He helped himself to the chips on their lift ride back to the office, before leading the way to IT and the server room. At the door, he passed the chips to Mel and fished through his pockets. Nybbas withdrew a key with his peri-powdered fingers and poked it into the server room door. "They live in here. It has better climate control than the rest of the office." He opened the door and frigid air froze Mel's fingers. "Come on in."

Mel carefully stepped inside the server room, which had a wall occupied by blinking racks of equipment that looked like the office's computer servers. Blue umbilical network cables connected them through the ceiling to the whole corporation, and hanging from the cables were what looked like black bats.

"Chip day, boys," Nybbas called, letting the door close behind them. Wings unfolded and leathery faces peered out, but none relinquished their grip on the cables. "Hold up the bags," he murmured to Mel.

She did, but their response didn't change. Mel set the bags on the small, empty table in the middle of the room and ripped one bag down the front. The spicy smell of the salt wafted up, tempting even her.

Claws ticked on the laminate as a bat landed beside

her hand. The creature regarded Mel with soul-searching eyes that belonged to no bat she'd ever met. She smiled in response. It extended a claw toward her and she took it in her fingers.

"Respect, lady," she heard the creature say, though its mouth never moved.

"Thank you," her spirit replied, equally silently. She glanced at Nybbas. "Can the demon hear us?"

"Demons poor soul-readers. Not like you, lady. For illusion-weaver, soul-talk is simple."

"Illusion-weaver?"

The creature showed her images of his people. "Unweave illusions for you, lady. Sptlk show?"

Mel understood that the string of consonants was the imp's name. "Sure."

Sptlk gazed deeply into Mel's eyes and she could feel the imp's soul touch hers. "Lady now can see illusion or reality. Respect, lady. See demon or batman." Mel followed the imp's glance to where Nybbas had stood only minutes before, but he appeared to have vanished. In his place stood a demon so dark he blended into the racks behind him, only visible because he blocked the blinking lights. With his pointed horns and wings, he did look cartoonish. Batman, indeed.

She turned startled eyes on the imps above Nybbas' head. Instead of bats, they looked more like small, round, winged demons, in varying shades of red and black. Sptlk himself was deep burgundy and he sported a pot belly. He patted it happily. "Many chip days."

Mel laughed and the sound was loud in the enclosed space. She blinked carefully and the imps were bats once more. Another blink and she saw Sptlk's very human fingers reach for a chip. He saluted her with it. "Thanks, lady." Sharp teeth demolished chip and chili salt quickly.

"Just like you like 'em, right, Spike?" Nybbas asked, grinning at the imp.

Sptlk nodded and the other imps seemed to decide this was their cue to celebrate chip day, too.

"So these are imps? And they keep you hidden...how?" Mel asked carefully.

Nybbas shrugged. "No idea how they do it. They weave some sort of illusion that people can't penetrate – it even works on us. Hell, they even do it in Hell. Lord Lucifer said they were living in Hell when he got there and they agreed to help him run the place. No idea what he offered them in return."

Sptlk winked at Mel. "Illusion for illusion. Illusion-weavers build illusions for Hell. Illusion-weavers holiday here with humans. Illusion of intimacy and privacy. Much comedy. Lord of Hell very seductive man. Or woman."

Luce in a skirt. No, Luce in stockings and a corset. Seducing how many while the imps watched and laughed? Mel managed a smile. "I'm sure he is," she replied silently.

"Soul-reader who can see through illusions sees deep truth beneath lies. Respect, lady, and hope."

"Thank you," she said, hoping the imp could sense the depth of her gratitude.

The imp nodded sagely in response.

"Wow — they sure like you. I've never seen Spike acknowledge anyone else who's come into the server room. You're not like anyone I've ever met, Mel." Nybbas blushed.

"Maybe you don't meet many angels," Mel suggested.

He shook his head. "No, I've met a fair few angels. None like you, though. You're definitely different. Hell, I don't know any angel who'd have helped me with my presentation. We should probably leave these boys to it and do that video. I'm so happy it'll be just you watching this time, Mel."

Mel saw Sptlk hide a grin. "Demons fun to watch." She smothered her own laugh as she followed Nybbas back to the training room so he could present his package. Hopefully, with his fly zipped up this time.

"Mel, come to lunch with us," Merih said, glancing at Gerry and Lili. There were a fair few other people grouped behind them, too, all carrying sunglasses.

"Hmm? Oh, no, I brought a sandwich," Mel said.

"You can't sit in the office and just eat a home-made sandwich on Melbourne Cup Day. You have to go out to lunch. If we have to drag you out kicking and screaming, you're coming," Merih insisted. He grabbed her wrist.

Mel felt the jolt of energy that flung Merih back

against the wall. It probably hurt her as much as it had him, but he'd taken the full force of it so she barely moved. "Are you okay?" she asked, concerned.

Merih rubbed his arm as the others backed away, murmuring about how they'd meet him there.

"No wonder angels never see any action. Can't even touch them without getting burned," someone muttered.

"I'm sorry," Mel said. "That's never happened before." She stared at her hand, touching her fingers to the desk to see if there was any further discharge. No, not even the slightest spark of static.

"Well, if there was ever any uncertainty about you being an angel, that's gone now," Merih said with a weak grin. "Damn, I forgot about that. It's been ages since I tried to touch an angel and almost never since I started working in the Pit. Didn't you know angels burn demons on contact? Something about the difference in souls — negative and positive energy annihilating each other. Ah, the engineers in Infrastructure can explain it better than me."

Mel frowned. "But I shook hands with Lili when I first started here and she didn't get hurt. And I'm sure I've bumped into or brushed against people here and not hurt anyone…"

"That's different." Merih shrugged. "Angels can control it — shield themselves, somehow, if they want to. Demons can't. Or maybe it's something about intent — an accidental touch doesn't set it off unless there's intent to harm. It's not body contact so much as souls touching. It also means none of us can jump you in the photocopy room without your consent." He sighed.

Mel laughed. "No one's tried that yet." Except Luce and his attempts at issuing orders, she thought, but that wasn't the same as using force. For all his arrogance, he hadn't attempted to touch her. Perhaps she was safer here than Raphael had thought.

Merih's voice brought her thoughts out of Luce's office and back to her own cramped cubicle. "It's still hard to believe you're an angel, though, even after..." He flexed his hand, wincing.

It had to be the first time anyone had ever doubted she was an angel. "Why?"

"Well, you talk to us," Merih admitted. "Treat us like people, like you're one of us and not one of them."

Mel tried not to laugh, but she couldn't keep the gentle smile off her face. "What do you expect me to do? Wander around pretending you don't exist? I know there are differences between angels and demons, and now that I know I can hurt you if I touch you I'll try to be more careful, but I can't see why I'd want to ignore you. Why would other angels do that?"

"I haven't had much luck getting answers out of them," Merih said. "But from what they say to each other, they're afraid they'll be tainted by contact with us. Even just a word or a glance. Like I'd want to touch some snotty, stuck-up angel who'd probably scream and faint the first time she saw a pair of hairy balls and a stiff prick…" He coughed. "Sorry."

This time Mel did laugh. "I can't recall ever fainting at such a sight. Screaming, perhaps, but that came later…" She glanced up at Merih, registering his shock. "What? Haven't you seen an angel blush before?"

Merih swallowed and licked his lips, looking like there were a few things he wanted to say, but didn't dare. "You've got to be the most unusual angel I've ever met." He eyed her hands warily. "If I can't drag you, I guess I'll have to appeal to your sense of charity."

Mel stared at him. Demons didn't support charity.

"You know how wonderful the coffee here is?" he began. Mel smiled and nodded. "Alright, we actually have better coffee in Hell. The instant stuff here is part of some government contract that doesn't expire for another three years, so we can't get out of it. But the German Beer Café up the road is hosting a huge Melbourne Cup lunch and we've all bought tickets. There are all sorts of giveaways, including a brand-new coffee machine – one that uses those little capsule things. We figure that the more of us who go, the better our chance of winning one and we'll pay whoever wins a share of what the machine is worth to use it, so we aren't drinking shit any more."

"Then good luck. I hope you get it," Mel replied. She turned her eyes back to her computer screen.

"We won't unless you come," he said bluntly. "We only go into the draw if our table has at least ten people and we're nine without you."

Mel sighed. "So I have to come to save you from bad coffee?" Her fingers skipped across the keyboard, locking access to her computer. Swinging her access pass lanyard down from the shelf, Mel said, "There's a story in the making – an angel saving a demon. If it were more interesting, maybe someone might write a book about it one day. Ah, the coffee would have to be pretty foul to be worth sticking in a story."

Grabbing her mug, she downed the dregs of cold coffee, almost choking as the sludge hit her tongue. "Honestly, I think this stuff could have come from the sewers in Hell. Not even the damned deserve to drink this. Let's go."

"Great! You brought her. Now we're ten and we're going to win that coffee machine." Gerry waved the hostess over. "Table for ten from HELL Corporation, please." He turned to Mel and Merih. "We've all ordered. Tell the girl at the counter what you want and don't forget to enter the sweep!"

The others trooped off in the hostess' wake as Merih stepped up to the register. "I'll have a jug of the darkest house beer you have and…how does the food work?"

The harassed-looking woman at the register eyed the

queue behind them. "If you're on a company table, then it's twenty dollars a head for food, and drinks are extra," she said. "How many horses do you want in the sweep? Just one?"

"Sounds good to me," Merih replied, handing over his credit card.

The woman processed his payment and held out a basket full of folded paper slips. "Pick your horse," she said.

Merih dipped his hand into the basket, his nails scraping against the bottom, and pulled out a slip. "Red Cadeaux!" he announced, then frowned. "Never heard of it."

"And you, miss?" the woman asked, looking expectantly at Mel.

"Oh, just a glass of your lightest wheat beer – the Weihenstephaner, please. I'm on the same corporate table and...I need a horse, right?"

"You don't have to," Merih jumped in, looking worried. "It's not like you need to gamble if you don't want to."

"You can't enjoy the Melbourne Cup properly without one," the woman said, giving Merih a dirty look. "It's dull if you're not screaming for your horse for that last lap of the race."

Mel laughed. "I'll take the lunch, the beer and the horse, please. I wouldn't want to miss an opportunity to do a bit of screaming." Out of the corner of her eye, she saw Merih blush as red as the Beck's shield on the wall behind him. She handed over her money.

"I hope you pick a winner, then," the woman said, offering the basket.

Mel shrugged. "Green Moon will win, but it's about enjoying the race, so I'll take..." She selected a slip. "...Lights of Heaven. That's a well-named horse for me."

"You never know. It's the Melbourne Cup. Any horse could win," the woman said.

Mel just smiled and followed Merih to the crowded table where their colleagues sat, already munching on the first round of garlic bread.

The two remaining free places at the table were right beside the window. One of the chairs was bathed in the bright, near-noon sun. Merih sat in the shaded one as Mel reached for the other, only to recoil the moment her fingers touched it: the surface of the metal chair was hot enough to fry her lunch on.

Someone sniggered, but Mel heard Merih say, "We should ask for another chair. Mel shouldn't have to..."

"I'll be fine," Mel cut in. She nudged the chair away from the table with her foot, careful to only touch the scorching metal with her shoe. She reached for the jug of iced water and poured it carefully over the chair, making sure she didn't wet her colleagues. Steam rose and a few chunks of ice clattered to the concrete floor, but she didn't flinch until the jug was empty. She reached for the other jug and did the same. Nine demons watched in silence as the puddle on the floor started to evaporate.

Reaching for the last slice of garlic bread, she whipped the cloth out of the basket beneath and used it to dry her much-cooled chair. Crunching into the crust, she smiled as she sat down. A wide-eyed waiter behind her set her beer on the table with shaking hands and she thanked him. He took the empty jugs from her and promised to refill them.

A platter of tempura prawns arrived at the table, followed by another with a tepee of prosciutto-wrapped asparagus spears, and the distracted demons decided it was safe to start talking again.

Mel ate without speaking, occasionally sipping her beer, as she listened to Lili and the girl beside her discussing some book they'd been reading. It seemed to involve some particularly violent sex and a man called Quincy.

She couldn't help herself. "I'm sorry…a violent, sadistic villain called Quincy? With a name like that, I imagine he has a fair bit to be angry about."

"Have you read the Monsters in the Dark series?" Lili asked, surprised.

"No," Mel admitted. "It sounds a bit dark for me, to be honest."

Lili turned away to talk to the man on her other side.

"So you're the angel," the girl beside Mel said. "I never thought I'd see one of your kind at a Melbourne Cup lunch. I mean – isn't gambling a sin to you? Like drinking…and generally enjoying yourself? Or even talking to the likes of us?"

Mel smiled gently. "The rest of the office were going – it seemed rude not to. And Merih told me you needed the numbers to have a chance at better coffee in the office. I wanted to help. I'm perfectly happy to drink and enjoy myself. I even have a horse in the sweep." She held up the little slip of paper.

"Then you're already halfway to being one of the CEO's little office whores. I swear he has a collection of temps just like you that he's corrupted so quickly you'd think they'd never seen a man before. Has he broken you in over his desk yet?" The girl gave a knowing grin at Mel's shock. "What, did you think you were the first?"

"Ana, leave Mel alone," Merih interjected. "If Luce finds out you've been spreading rumours, it'll be you over that desk and you know it."

Ana gave a disgusted sniff and lurched to her feet, headed for the counter and what Mel suspected would be another drink.

"Don't listen to her, Mel," Merih continued. "Luce does have a reputation for seducing all the new office temps – human and angel – but you're different to them. Just don't accept any meetings alone in his office with him and you should be fine." He became very interested in the plate of spring rolls that appeared in front of him as Lili glared in his direction across Ana's empty seat.

"It's all right," Mel said softly as Ana returned,

bearing a jug of beer and a glass that she thumped down on the table. "He's already made an attempt."

"Ah Hell, Mel, I didn't realise. I'm sorry…"

Mel shrugged. "I turned him down. I also suggested he might want to clean his desk occasionally, given all the action it's seen."

Merih exploded in laughter, spraying beer across the table. It missed Mel but splattered in Lili's face, sending her eyeliner running. Lili jumped to her feet, beer and murder in her eyes.

"I believe I'll get another drink. Would anyone else like one?" Mel asked the table in general.

The others got up to dig through their pockets for cash, neatly boxing Lili in at her seat and out of reach of Merih. Mel heard his muttered thanks before she headed up to the counter, trying to remember everyone's beer preferences. She decided to stick to water. Let the demons get drunk — she had work to do when she returned to the office.

The whole café fell silent. Mel couldn't hear the crunch of a single chip.

"Aaaand…they're off!" the race caller shouted.

Twenty-four horses jumped from their starting stalls on the large-screen TVs, their thundering hooves the only sound inside the café.

The race caller identified the horses and their relative positions as the animals galloped their riders round the first lap of Flemington Racecourse.

That's when the shouting started, rising in a

crescendo as the jockeys whipped their horses down the final straight. It wasn't just the demons, either – every single human in the café seemed to be shrieking their support for their respective horse, though the beasts on the other side of the country certainly couldn't hear them.

Mel watched with satisfaction as Green Moon did, indeed, cross the finish line first, followed by three horses with odd names that were much harder to remember. None of these horses were on her or Merih's slips.

Or any other demon's, oddly enough. The demons flung their slips on the table, with varying combinations of anger, disappointment and disgust. She wondered why they bothered gambling at all – after all, demons' bad luck was legendary.

The sweep winners approached the counter to claim their prizes. One was a man who'd had to reject a promotion because his wife had recently given birth to twins and suffered from crippling postnatal depression. Another was a girl who sent all her spare money home to her family in Indonesia, in the hope that her little sister could come and visit sometime soon. The third winner seemed to live a charmed life, but her boss had excused himself early to finalise the paperwork to make her position redundant – a fate she wasn't yet aware of, but she would be by the end of the day. Mel sighed – such was the way of the world, especially in times like these.

The hostess at the counter picked up a handbell and rang it, sending the café silent again. "We'll be drawing the raffle prizes, too. Last chance to buy a ticket – the proceeds go to the winter blanket appeal for the city's homeless." She gestured at the waitstaff who were waving ticket books.

Mel jumped to her feet. "One for me, please." Nine demons stared at her as a waiter wove through the tables to take her money. It wasn't that she wanted or needed any of the raffle prizes, whatever those might be. She couldn't refuse charity – nor a request for help – and this was both. She ignored the demonic scrutiny as she traded her money for a ticket. Number 888, apparently.

The hostess cleared her throat. "Now, everyone on one of the corporate tables, I'm going to ask you to check beneath you. Taped to the bottom of your chair are your free tickets into the draw."

Mel realised that none of the demons had bought a ticket – all they had were the free ones that were included as part of their meal. No, demons definitely didn't believe in charity.

She reached under her seat for hers and almost laughed when she saw the ticket number. Someone sure had a sense of humour up there.

The first half-dozen prizes were coffee, beer and meal vouchers, which went to various human patrons.

"Next up are two coffee pod machines," the hostess announced, as a grinning waiter carried them forward like he was the proud father of twins. She drew out the first ticket. "Four five seven!"

Mel and the increasingly irritated demons watched as first one, then the other coffee maker were won by humans. It definitely wasn't the demons' day. Not only were they damned, but they were doomed to drink disgusting coffee while they were on Earth.

"And one last prize that only came in yesterday. When our coffee supplier heard what we were giving away, he said he'd provide another prize for one lucky winner who appreciated real coffee. So we'll draw one more ticket for an office coffee maker — the same model we use here — and the first year's supply of coffee beans, all provided by our sales rep." The hostess coughed. "For those of you who don't win, we have some brochures for you to take back to your office, detailing prices and packages for machines and coffee supply..."

The demons perked up considerably at this. One of them muttered in Latin, the words too fast for Mel to make out.

"The winning ticket is...number six six six!"

Someone laughed.

Mel's colleagues looked feverishly through the tickets on the table. Gerry lifted the salt shaker, muttering, "Has to be one of us. It has to be..." — looking for a missing ticket that definitely wasn't there.

"Redraw!" a man seated near the door bellowed. The cry was taken up by several others.

Someone definitely had a strange sense of humour, Mel decided. But not even demons deserved to drink the sewage sludge back at the office and she'd be damned before she'd deny them some hope in their miserable lives. She rose. "It's mine." Holding up the ticket that had been taped to the underside of her Hell-hot chair, the angel calmly made her way to the hostess and handed it over.

"Where do you work?" the hostess asked. "I need the office address for the supplier, as he'll deliver your fresh coffee beans weekly – I only have a week's worth here to go with the machine." She gestured at the huge box that was definitely more than Mel could carry.

"I work for the HELL Corporation," Mel replied, writing down the address.

The hostess snorted. "You'll need all the perks you can get, working in that Hell-hole. I've heard stories…well, at least you'll have decent coffee for when you're forced to work late. I've heard it happens a lot over there."

"Not to me," Mel said cheerfully. "Thank you, though. I think my colleagues will appreciate it when the shock wears off." It was hard to ignore nine demons staring at you, she mused.

"Get a couple of the blokes to help you carry it, then, and another couple to grab the coffee. There's a lot and it's heavy," the woman cautioned.

Mel smiled, nodded and thanked her again, before returning to the table.

Merih clapped hard. "Way to go, Mel!"

Slowly, the others joined in with half-hearted applause.

"I can't carry it back to the office myself," she admitted. "Would some of you be willing to help?"

She was answered by demonic silence.

Mel shrugged. "I guess I could ask if the staff here have a trolley I could borrow. I don't think it'll fit in the kitchen, though. Do you think we might be able to set it up on a table in the lunchroom?"

"You mean you're bringing that thing to our office and not the agency?" Lili blurted out.

Mel laughed. "Of course. I work in your office, not the agency office. I'd say your need is greater, too, and you all did invite me along today…"

Two demons whose names Mel didn't know stood up and marched to the counter. Between them, they lifted the coffee machine. "Are you ready to go?" one asked her.

Mel nodded. "There's the coffee, too…"

Merih swung one big bag of coffee beans into Gerry's arms and hefted the other in his own. "At your service, Mel. We'll have to work out how much we owe you for this."

Mel waved the offer away. "I can't drink all this coffee on my own and it'd be a shame not to share it. You don't need to."

"I'll arrange it with everyone else in the office. We'll call it the coffee club. We'd pay one of our own and just because you're not a demon, doesn't mean you don't deserve..."

One of the machine-toting demons cut in: "Oi, this is heavy, mate. If you're going to stand around and talk, you can carry the coffee machine."

"Right. Right," Merih replied, as he led the procession back to the sixth floor of the HELL Corporation building.

In front of an audience of what seemed like half the office, Mel broke the coffee machine out of the box and attempted to assemble it. It was easier than she'd expected, but the LCD screen wasn't lighting up. It took ten minutes before she realised that no one had plugged it in yet and the dearth of helpful volunteers seemed to be standard procedure in HELL.

"There's a power point under this table. Here, I'll hook it up and we can try that again," Mel said, dropping to her knees to crawl under the furniture. Mel heard the scrape of shoes on carpet and wondered why the demons behind her were moving around. She was wearing pants today, so she knew they weren't jockeying for a better view of her underwear.

"So who do I have to whip to get some work done around here?" Mel heard Luce's voice.

She couldn't reach the socket yet. It was half-hidden under a cabinet beside the table. Scooting along the carpet, her fingers made contact with the dusty power point and she plugged the machine in.

"You won the coffee machine at the Cup lunch? It's about time we had some decent coffee around here. Hell, for that, you can all have the afternoon off."

Nobody moved except Mel, whose fingers scrabbled for the switch to turn the power on. There was so much dust behind the cabinet – or were those cobwebs? It looked like Luce's desk wasn't the only thing in the office that the cleaning staff didn't have time for.

"Who won it, anyway? I'll offer a blowjob to the man, if he makes me the first coffee with that thing."

Stunned silence as Mel covered her mouth with a dusty hand to stop herself from exploding into laughter. She decided to get out from under the table before things got out of hand. No one would believe Luce had offered his employees…much less her…

Mel emerged from under the table, but the demons in the room screened her from Luce's sight, even as she stood up.

"Not from me, personally, of course. You can have

your pick of the office girls. The new one's pretty and has quite a clever mouth on her, too. In fact, I can vouch for her myself."

She couldn't help it any more. Luce was digging a hole so deep, he'd hit Hell soon if she didn't stop him. Her laughter bubbled up and out, breaking the demonic silence. "That would be me."

Demons shuffled aside, letting Mel see Luce's surprised expression. He recovered quickly. "Perfect timing. Now, who's going to turn down this lovely lady's services? All you have to do is make me a coffee…"

Mel cleared her throat. "Actually, I don't know how." She glanced around, wondering who had the manual for the machine.

Luce laughed. "Nothing to it! Just drop to your knees, open your mouth, relax your throat and drink down what comes."

"I think there's a bit more to making a coffee on this machine. Merih, can you please pass me the manual? I'll need a cup, too." Mel accepted the booklet and one of the dozen proffered cups with a smile of thanks. "How do you take your coffee, Luce? Or should I guess? I would say…an espresso. Or a double, given the size of the cup. Just the bitter brew, with no milk, cream or sugar."

Luce's smile was as tight and uncomfortable as a brand-new pair of jeans that was a size too small, but his tone still sounded confident. "That sounds about right."

Mel glanced at the manual, keying in his selection. The coffee machine whirred as it started making his brew. Mel kept her eyes carefully on the filling cup as she heard the shuffle of moving feet behind her once more. She spun on the spot with the hot drink in her hands, holding it out to Luce. "The first cup. Enjoy." Her smile was sincere.

He took it from her and slurped at the contents. The demons who hadn't already made their escape decided as one that this was the best time to do so.

Mel held her ground, not lowering her lips from their smile. She didn't laugh when she saw the scrawled text on the side of the mug serendipity had bestowed on Luce – 'SEXY DEVIL', it said. Sad, frustrated, soon to be embarrassed devil would have been more appropriate, but pity stayed her tongue from saying so. Instead, she said, "How's the coffee? I've never used such a complicated machine before. I'm hoping someone who has more experience can show me how to use it."

Luce carefully set his cup down. He glanced around, checking to make sure they really were alone before he spoke in a very low voice. "You're the one who won the coffee machine, aren't you?" Mel nodded once. "Why did you bring it here, instead of the agency where you work? Angels always look after angels first." He sounded bitter.

Mel kept her voice gentle. "Actually, we don't. We look after those who need it most. Those who have the least. I've never worked for Raphael in that office – just here. This office is a pretty dark place and I thought it could do with a bit of hope. No one deserved to drink the coffee we had here before – damned or not, it was just plain horrible." She managed an apologetic smile. "Besides, angels aren't addicted to caffeine like your staff are. We can easily do without. If your staff weren't so afraid of you, perhaps one of them might have said something before you made an offer you couldn't deliver on."

Luce grinned. "Sure I can. Your pick of the office girls – or anyone else here. The technique might be a little different to a blowjob, but I'm sure they'd do their bit to thank you. After all, I'm always open to a more permanent arrangement with our temporary staff, if you like it here."

Mel shook her head, remembering Raphael's warning. "No, Luce. I'm not getting intimate with any of your staff, nor do I want a permanent job here."

"What about me?" His grin faltered, but it was still there. "I'm quite a sexy devil, you know, and I do have a fair bit of experience." His eyes didn't seem so cold now – the darkness reminded her more of his steaming cup of coffee than the vacuum of space. "I'm only offering this to you, Mel. How about a hot cup of sensuality in payment for this equally hot cup of coffee?"

This took her by surprise. Oral sex from Lucifer

himself — well, there was an offer a girl didn't get every day, much less an angel. He'd even remembered her name. "Luce, all I really wanted was a decent cup of coffee for myself. Giving the same to everyone else in the office is a perk, I guess."

Luce looked thoughtful. "How about I make you one? My coffee machine at home is just a smaller version of this one. I should be able to work it out. How do you take it?"

Mel shrugged. "I usually drink tea. I occasionally have a cup of instant coffee, but not often enough to be able to say I know what I like. I'm sure whatever you make will be fine."

"A macchiato, but I'll make it a double because you have a mug…and top it up. White and fluffy on top, clothed in light brown, just like the suit you wore to your interview, but with a hidden dark heart inside." Luce looked proud of himself.

"It sounds lovely, Luce, but you're wrong about a macchiato — or at least, how it's supposed to be made. The heart of a macchiato is milk-white," Mel said gently. She'd never seen such a clumsy attempt at corrupting her — so much for the seductive devil she'd been warned about. All she felt was sympathy for this devil, not desire at all.

His eyes seemed to darken. "We'll see." He stabbed the buttons on the coffee machine until it whirred in submission. Both he and Mel watched the spout, from the first dark trickle to the last white droplet. "Hmmph.

Maybe you're right," he said grudgingly.

Mel reached for her cup and took a tiny sip. She licked the foam from her lip and smiled. "I usually am, but you made a good call on this coffee. I like it. Thank you."

Luce just stared at her, as if he didn't believe her, or he suspected some ulterior motive behind her taste for his coffee-making skills. Mel sighed and waited. She didn't know how demons managed to live with this sort of distrust.

She took pity on him. "I'm an angel, remember? Angels don't lie, Luce."

It took a moment, but eventually Luce seemed satisfied and he relaxed. "No worries," he said. "You're not like any other angel I've known — and I've known a fair few."

Mel smiled. "So I've been told."

Luce seemed to hesitate, torn between more than one course of action. Mel hoped he didn't do anything else stupid.

He seized her hand and kissed it.

Mel expected another jolt of electricity to throw him across the room, like it had with Merih that morning. Some pain as two opposing souls touched. Or some sort of tingling, core-wrenching reaction that so frequently happened to the heroines in all the human romances she'd read. Yet she felt nothing — just the damp touch of his lips on the back of her hand and a faint impression of stormy clouds. That's all she caught of his soul before he released her.

Where was the darkness she'd seen before? Mel wondered. Storm clouds were nowhere near as dark, nor as thick. Was the absence of darkness an illusion…or the darkness itself? She blinked, twice, but Luce didn't change. Unlike Nybbas, Luce looked the same with or without illusion. No, wait, there was one place he'd want to look more impressive. Staring hard at the front of Luce's pants, Mel tried to work out which bulge was the illusion and which the reality, but they both looked identical.

Luce cleared his throat. Startled, Mel looked up. "If you're feeling the same way, I'd be happy to help."

Mel stared. She felt relieved that she hadn't hurt him. One demon a day was more than enough.

"My offer still stands," Luce continued with a wink.

"Your offer?"

"Of very personal payment for your first coffee," Luce replied, raising the cup in salute. "Any time." Whistling, he wandered off.

Mel almost wiped her damp hand on her pants, but she waited until he was out of sight before crossing to the kitchen, where she washed her hands instead. Who knew where his mouth had been?

"Enjoy your holiday!" Gerry called, grinning, as Mel left for the day. "Don't forget to bring back photos!"

"I'll do my best," she replied, shouldering her way through the door to Reception. If she did bring pictures, she'd make sure there wasn't a single mankini in any of them.

Mel's phone rang before she'd pushed her way through the supposedly automatic doors in the lobby. She glanced at the number before accepting the call. "Hi, Raphael."

"Mel, it's me, Raphael," he said, as if he hadn't heard her. Mel waited patiently for his mind to catch up with his mouth. "I've got Gabi! She's arrived from Russia and she'll be in first thing tomorrow to start her receptionist job at HELL. You won't be alone any more!"

"I leave for Sri Lanka tonight and I won't be back for over a week, Raphael. She'll just have to settle in without me."

"You're going WHERE?"

Mel took a deep breath. "I'm going to Sri Lanka. I've had this planned for months, since well before you asked me to go to the job interview here in HELL. Flights and accommodation booked, the works. I'm not giving up my trip to Colombo for you or this job."

"But why are you going to Sri Lanka? Why now? Can't it wait? How can a holiday be more important than stopping Lucifer from taking over the world?" Raphael wailed.

"Raphael, CHOGM is in Colombo this year. I haven't missed a single meeting and not even Lucifer himself will stop me from attending this one. I have a life outside of the agency and the HELL Corporation, remember? You can keep me from Korea for a bit, but not Sri Lanka. Do you have any idea how much trouble world leaders can cause in a retreat without an angel? You remember the one in New Zealand, back in '95?"

Silence reigned as Raphael remembered, all too well, his failings of that year. "You know I'm sorry about that, Mel. It should have been you in Nigeria, not me, but by the time I realised, it was too late. I…Have a good trip and try to enjoy yourself. Get some rest. Something tells me you'll need it."

Mel once again promised she'd do her best, before ending the call. Slipping her phone back into her bag, she marched off to the train station, mentally listing all the things she needed to pack. She knew it was quite hot in Colombo this time of year. Hell, it was hot in Colombo every day of the year. Thank God her hotel had a pool.

Mel rose from the water, refreshed by her morning swim. With the conference dinner last night, the festivities had ended and she had until the following evening to rest, recuperate and reconcile herself to returning home to her job at the HELL Corporation. Lucifer and his minions be damned. Why couldn't she go back to living the life she was supposed to?

"Don't you just look like the angel of the morning, rising from the foam like Venus," a male voice remarked.

Mel's eyes darted to the reclining man. "Watch your words. Lucifer was the light of the morning, and if that's me, you're in for one Hell of a seduction — that will end with you losing your soul."

"But you're not," he said, sliding his sunglasses from his face. "You're the Melody Angel. An angel far more seductive than that old devil could ever be. I knew there was another angel here, but it wasn't until I saw you in the pool this morning that I knew for sure. I should've known. So much harmony at one of these meetings — so many world leaders singing the same tune…must've been visited by the Melody Angel. And who else would be brave enough to swim in a white bikini?" He lifted his camera. "May I?"

"Sure," Mel replied, flashing a perfunctory smile as the camera clicked. She waited for him to lower the camera before throwing her body into the sun lounge beside his. Mel closed her eyes and heard more clicks. "Patrick, if you don't put the camera down, I'm going to throw it in the pool. Just like the last one, when we were in Perth."

"Good thing it's waterproof, then. I'm learning. What can I get you to drink?"

Mel squinted at him. "This early in the morning? Coffee and juice, which I'm going to drink in reverse order."

"Yes, madam," a hotel waiter murmured. Mel hadn't seen him until he'd spoken. She thanked him quickly.

"Better get me a big coffee, too," Patrick said. The

sunglasses covered his eyes again. "How come you look so fresh after last night's banquet? Didn't you drink at all?"

"Sure I did. A few glasses of wine over the course of the evening. I didn't see you there, though. I bet you finished off all of their best Scotch." Mel shook her head. "You and your whisky…"

"Ah, it's because the weather's too hot here for my kilt," Patrick responded. "If I'd been wearing that, you wouldn't have had eyes for anyone else, I bet."

Mel laughed. "You have me there. You in a kilt and nothing else is a temptation for any girl, angel or not. And I know what you keep under it."

"If I'd known you'd be here, I would have packed it anyway, Mel, and to Hell with the weather," Patrick said. "What do you have planned for the day? Or do you fly out today?"

"Tomorrow night, I fly out," Mel replied. "Today and tomorrow, I'd planned on just exploring a bit of Sri Lanka. Being a tourist for a tiny bit before I go home and…aah, Raphael's got this crazy idea that Lucifer's loose in Western Australia and laying the foundations for a new takeover bid. I'm helping him find out what's really going on."

"Lucifer? Well, that doesn't surprise me. Aren't the caves of Hell in the West Australian desert? He had to move them a while back due to overcrowding and there's plenty of space to expand there, if you don't mind the killer wildlife. Of course he'd start there – it's close to home for him." Patrick sat up. "Spend the day with me, Mel. Tomorrow, too, if you like. I have a boat booked with some friends. Come join me for a bit of wahoo. I know you'll like it." He winked.

Mel looked at Patrick. Even in shorts and an open shirt, he looked sexy as Hell. She didn't do demons, but angels were a different story – especially one she knew as well as Patrick. She waited while the waiter set out their drinks, thanking the man and handing him a tip before he disappeared. Sipping her juice, she replied, "First, explain to me exactly what you plan in terms of wahoo."

"Wahoo! We got one! Ladies first, Mel. Take a seat and I'll strap you in." Patrick pushed her into the chair bolted to the back of the boat as one of the crew placed a rod and reel into her hands.

She could feel the tension in the line – there was certainly something strong at the other end. The two men pulled straps across her chest and shoulders as she tried to protest.

"Don't want him pulling you overboard. There are stories of water dragons in these waters," Patrick said as he tightened the straps. "I wouldn't blame him for not wanting to let you go. I wouldn't want to, either."

"All the water dragons in this ocean are women, Patrick. Surely you know that."

He eyed her. "How do you know that? They're pretty secretive."

Mel smiled. "Their leader is as fond of tea as I am when she's on land. A lovely lady, as long as you keep her secrets."

"So you're friends with the mermaids hereabouts, huh? We'll see by what you catch, then, I imagine." He raised his voice. "Reel him in and we'll have fresh fillets for lunch!"

Mel felt her arms tiring after ten minutes of fighting what she thought had to be a shark, it was so fierce. Patrick seemed to sense her exhaustion and he dropped to his knees behind her, his arms circling her body to help her reel in the monster fish.

"We should let him go. He fought well – for his life, Patrick. I'm tired enough to quit and admit he won. I don't need to torture this fish any more," Mel murmured.

Patrick laughed. "If we don't catch anything, there's nothing for lunch. This one will probably be all we need for the whole boat. Besides, we have to pull him up to release him from the hook. I could just cut the line, but then he'd be hurting with a barbed hook in his mouth. No, he's coming here to give you a big kiss, I'll take a picture of you and your new boyfriend, then you can decide if you want to keep him or let him go." His lips touched the base of her neck. "Have you ever had fresh wahoo, Mel?"

Mel snorted. "It sounds like something done with no clothes in the privacy of a hotel room, not on a boat full of people. I'm not answering that."

"I was going to wait until after dinner to offer my services in the privacy of your hotel room, but now works, too. Or it would if…" Two crewmen rushed forward to the port side, gaffs in hand, as Patrick slowed his reeling. "Here he comes. You caught a real monster, Mel!"

The men hauled the fish aboard and Mel let out a shocked gasp. It looked like it was longer than she was tall – and perhaps weighed more, too.

One of them knelt on the desperately fighting fish while another cut its throat. All the fight left with its spirit and tears sprang to Mel's eyes. "I take it we're not releasing him now," she said.

"No," Patrick replied. "But he'll be lunch and dinner, easy. Right – get in there with him. We need a picture of the lady who slayed the monster!" He gave her a push toward the floppy fish and pulled out his camera.

Despite her protests, the fish was lifted and arranged on the deck, so she could pull his tail up to her chest, displaying the length of him.

"Smile, Mel," Patrick coaxed and she did. The fish's spirit was in a better place now and it would be a shame to waste his sacrifice or the body he'd left behind.

"Now, the boys want photos with your monster fish, too. I think it's a record size for them and they want proof to show the other guys in the pub when they get home. Wash up and grab a drink from the cooler while I do the honours. They'll gut, fillet and cook him fresh for you – all part of the service." Patrick stared at her. "There's really nothing you can't do, is there? Charming the Indian Ocean mermaids, hooking the catch of the year, never missing a conference and…are you seriously hunting down Lucifer? He'd best watch out – he doesn't know what he's in for if you find him. Have you and Raphael…?"

Mel laughed. "Raphael and I will never fly. I think his heart's set on someone else entirely and I hope they're happy together." Patrick's face lit up and Mel impulsively kissed his cheek. "I'll go wash up," she said.

Mel used the head and started washing her hands in the tiny sink. Glancing at the even tinier mirror, she noticed a streak of blood on her shirt from the fish. She scrubbed at it but eventually gave up and returned to the deck, grateful that she'd chosen to wear her bikini under her shirt. At least the transparent cotton didn't show her underwear.

"Raphael's crazy," Patrick choked out. He couldn't seem to pull his eyes from her.

"No, Raphael's gay and in love with my brother," Mel replied gently. Her eyes searched his face. "Will you spend the evening with me? Dinner, drinks and…later, too?"

Patrick beamed. "Your wish is my command. For as long as you like."

Mel sighed inwardly even as she smiled. Patrick might have been the perfect partner if their relationship could ever be equal. As it was, though… "We have until my flight leaves tomorrow."

Mel admired the way the water cascaded over his hard body in the shower. Was it his well-muscled chest, the sculpted way the whole package was put together, or simply how well he put it to use for her pleasure? Patrick had certainly perfected both his skills and his assets over time. She could still remember the first time and how nervous he'd been…

Mel took a mouthful of water, swished it around her mouth and spat into the sink, running the tap to send the toothpaste residue down the drain.

"Say the word, Mel, and I'll transfer to Australia or wherever you're working next. All this is yours for the asking, any time you want." He gestured at his well-built body.

"You're terrified of snakes. Do you know how many reptiles we have in Australia – the really deadly kind, as well as just the cuddly ones? The closest snakeless island would be Tasmania or New Zealand. And what will happen to politics in the UK without you, Patrick? You're not just in Ireland because it's one of the few places in the world without snakes. Any time you're away, I swear violence at least doubles in the north. It seems a bit selfish to let people die just so that I can share a shower with you more than once every year or two." Mel splashed water on her face and dried it with the handtowel.

He sounded wistful. "You could move back to the UK. I'd treat you like a queen – you know that. And we'd love to have you. Politics in Europe isn't the same with this latest global financial crisis, or whatever they're calling this fit of hiccups…"

"And let Lucifer run rampant over Australia in the meantime? I'm where I need to be, as are you. I've been working in the Indo-Pacific region for a long time now and I can't just up and leave." Mel paused to take a deep breath. She hadn't meant to sound so sharp. She exhaled, long and slow, before saying, "We have responsibilities, Patrick – and personal relationships always come second to those. We're angels – this world must come first. No matter how irresistible you are in the shower." Her cheeks heated with a faint blush that she couldn't blame on the steam in the hotel bathroom.

"I think you should come first and let the rest of the world handle itself for just a day." His grin was dirty as he rubbed soap down his thighs. He straightened and threw the bar into the dish, reaching for the shampoo instead. "I've never seen you so worried without a world war or major disaster to deal with. If you spread your spirit too thin, doing too much, you'll need to heal in Heaven until you regain your strength. Does Raphael know how stressed you are? This Lucifer thing is really getting to you, isn't it?"

Mel watched as Patrick leaned back to rinse his hair, his hips thrust forward to maintain his balance. He certainly beat any image search on her office computer and he didn't make her think of socks.

"Mel?"

She shook her head to clear it a little, wondering if it was possible for the steam to leak into her brain through her ears. Her head certainly felt misty enough. "Raphael's worried, too, and he's trying to get more angels into Western Australia, but there are so few of us there. I mean, it's so far from anywhere, which is probably why Luce chose it. That and the resources he'll control. And if it's as close to Hell as you say, that only makes the situation more serious, because he'll have as many demon reinforcements as he needs to take his corporation global. Lucifer's the key to this – I know he is – but if I tell Raphael that he'll panic and pull out. Try to pull me out. I don't know that we'll get another chance at this and it looks like it's going to have to be me." Mel looked up to meet Patrick's sympathetic eyes. "Demons. I've never dealt with demons before. I feel if I understood them, I'd have a better idea of what's going on."

"Hey, I'm not a demon expert, but if I can help…" Patrick held out his hands in an unmistakeable invitation. Mel wished she could take his offer more seriously, but his lack of clothing was decidedly distracting. "Call me – or get Raphael to call me, if you're too busy. I downloaded all yesterday's photos onto your little laptop, so you'll even have those to remind you to call me if you need me. You know I'd do anything for you."

Mel smiled and nodded. She did know – but that didn't help. "I don't want to think about Lucifer or demons again until I'm home. That'll be tonight or the early hours of tomorrow morning and plenty soon enough. Thank you for the offer and if I need you, I will call. Right now…" She sighed deeply.

Patrick's reflection winked at her in the mirror. "You know, we still have a couple of hours before I have to leave for the airport. If you want to do more than just look, there's room in this shower for two of us and there's always the bed…"

She laughed, lifting her dress over her head before dropping it on the side of the bathtub. "We shouldn't use the shower. Wouldn't want to waste all that water..."

"The water's not wasted if I'm with you," Patrick replied, pulling her into the hot water with him. "Every drop and every second is precious with you, *Mel meum*." His hands and kisses helped her forget everything but him.

"Mmm, I miss Latin. So sweet to hear it from you..." Mel closed her eyes as she let her fingers roam.

"*Quid ego faciam tibi, Mel meum?*"

(What will I do for thee, O my honey?)

All too soon Mel found herself back at her HELL Corporation desk. Even as she returned to the task at hand, Patrick remained a warm, if receding, memory. She took one look at her long list of emails and decided to send the few pictures Patrick had taken to those she knew in the office who might care. She plugged in the memory stick with her photos and heaved a big sigh as she started on the boring backlog.

"Jez has just come through with the final pictures. Can you take a look, Mel?" Lili's voice roused Mel from trying to decipher her emails. She wasn't the only one who'd been playing with fish and photos: someone had taken their fetish for 007 a little too far — to the point where they'd stuck a fish in a suit and called the poor thing 'James Pond'.

Lili's head popped over the partition. "Oh, good, you're already reading it. Can you print some colour copies and take it up to Luce to see what he thinks?"

Mel looked at the silly picture. "Of what?"

Lili sounded impatient. "The fish in the suit. That one!" She pointed at the screen.

Surely she couldn't be serious — it looked too silly, Mel thought, but she printed the pages anyway. She brought the papers to Lili. "You want me to take these to Luce?"

"Yes," Lili snapped. "They're the graphics for his presentation on our new Water Unit in the Environment Division. The state government wanted more money to fund the politicians' pay rise so they sold all water, fishing and boating services to us. Luce needs the pictures for our end-of-year staff talk this afternoon. Take them to him right now so we have time to get back to Jez with any changes."

Mel reminded herself for the millionth time that her job was to execute orders. "Sure," she replied, and took the photos upstairs to Luce.

Luce's personal assistant sat perkily at the desk outside his office, guarding it like a lair once again. "Can I help you?" Mephi asked sweetly.

"Hi, Lili sent me with the Water Unit pictures?" Mel let the statement become a question.

"Go on in – he's expecting you." Mephi gave Mel a professional smile before dismissing her with disinterest.

Mel stepped hesitantly into the office, glancing at the bright paintings she itched to get a closer look at.

Luce raised his eyebrows as she entered and watched her without saying a word.

Mel found his scrutiny sleazy as Hell, but she resisted the urge to pull her skirt down so that she showed as little flesh as possible. He made her feel like a million spiders were scuttling across her skin.

There had to be something about the man that was good, she told herself. The pride he took in his appearance, perhaps. His restraint in managing not to proposition her the second she walked in, despite his obvious desire to do so. The fact that he didn't smell of sulphur and brimstone. Mel took a deep breath, appreciating whatever aftershave he used to fend off the whiff of Hell.

"I brought you the pictures for your presentation," Mel began, proffering the pages. "I…hope you like them." And let me leave quickly, she added in her head.

Luce picked up the sheaf of paper and spread them across the desk. "What do you think of these?" he asked.

"I…" Mel started to say, wondering how to tell him she'd thought they were a joke without making Jez and

Lili look bad.

"I think they're shit. I asked for photos that show all the good things about water that we want to preserve. Not fish in clothes pretending to be spies. Bring me something better and next time, don't waste paper. Just email them so I can post them straight into my presentation." Luce glared at her, sweeping the papers into a pile and dumping them in his bin.

Mel backed away, biting her lip hard to hide her smile. For the first time, she agreed with the demon, but she didn't dare tell him. She wondered why he employed graphic designers who couldn't follow simple instructions. Perhaps it was just Jez. Or was it a demon thing – the inability to do a job well?

She sat down heavily in her desk chair, which made her feel penitent when it squeaked in protest. She tried to distract herself by looking at her holiday photos and emailing them out before she had to tell Jez the bad news. She couldn't work out who to send them to, so she just dumped her very small contacts list in the address box and hoped she hadn't missed anyone. "A little tropical sunshine to help brighten your day," she murmured as she typed the words.

Mel hit 'send' just as the phone rang. She spent the next three hours trying to work out who was responsible for dealing with illegal dumping of dead cane toads on the front steps of some monument. She tried the Wildlife Unit, but was told that the toads were pests and they only dealt with native animals. She tried the Pest Unit, but they shooed her away like a blowfly, telling her that she could keep her dead toads or throw them in the rubbish. She went to the Lands Division, searching for someone who dealt with landfills and recycling. She was told not to waste their time. She tried to contact the building cleaner, who told her to clean up her own messes – they only cleaned the inside of the building.

In despair, she turned to Lili, who was pulling on her suit jacket. "Are you ready?" Lili asked.

Mel shook her head. "I don't know what to do."

"Come upstairs. We have the CEO's end-of-year briefing. The one with Jez's brilliant fish campaign." Lili rubbed her hands together in excitement.

Mel's heart felt like it was sliding through her ribs and out the bottom of her skirt. In all the excitement about cane toads, she'd forgotten to call Jez. "Ah, about the fish…"

Lili threaded her way through the cubicle maze to the lifts, apparently not even listening.

Mel gave up and followed her. She wondered if she'd get to see Luce throw a tantrum this time. She resolved to sit up the back and look as small as possible. Let him take his wrath out on a demon who deserved it instead of her. Except that she felt she did deserve it this time. The cane toads had taken over…

Mel chose a seat in the highest row at the back of the seminar room, hidden behind the tallest man she could find. Lili arranged herself in the seat beside her, leaning over to speak with the tall man. He inclined his head toward Lili so Mel had a clear view of the front where Luce stood at the lectern, his presentation on the screen beside him.

He started to speak about drinking water quality and how important it was. Mel lost all interest when the first slide appeared – a picture of her drinking her third large vodka and lemonade at the hotel bar in the garden, laughing. She figured there was some water in there somewhere – perhaps in the ice.

"…stunning natural waters…."

Mel winced at the photo of her emerging from the pool. Patrick had captured the moment perfectly.

"…fun fishing opportunities…"

Mel covered her face as she saw the wahoo against her wet shirt, his tail nestled between her breasts.

"…and beautiful beaches."

At least the sunset had looked nice – it had been a wonderful walk and the weather had been warm enough to do it in just a swimsuit. Mel vowed to throw her white bikini out as soon as she got home. She hadn't realised how revealing it was until it was magnified on the presentation screen to twice life size.

"Thank you," Luce finished, as everyone clapped. He smiled straight at Mel.

She sank down in her seat. Somehow, she'd sent the CEO her holiday snaps and now everyone knew what she looked like near-naked. Heaven help her, she pleaded in her head, hoping no one heard.

25

Mel had just started reading a new book on vampires, not her usual taste, but it was terribly compelling, so she decided to take out her phone so she could read a little more at lunch. She'd just reached the point where the vampire arrived in Hell at the call of a particularly seductive demon who seemed to be wearing nothing but a blanket…Mel was feeling unusually warm when she heard a voice.

"Mel?" Lili's head popped over the partition.

No, Callie. She wanted to know what Callie would

do with…Mel tried to cool her blushing cheeks as she looked up at Lili, reluctantly putting her phone down. "Yes?"

"We've decided to move your desk. You'll be in with the rest of the team. Won't that be fun?"

She wouldn't be reading the rest of this story at work, then, Mel thought but didn't say. Callie and Lucien would have to wait until she took her train home. Unless they were going to test the bedsprings. Lucien sounded like the energetic type. Perhaps she should wait until she got home…

"Sure." Mel summoned a smile. "I'll ask the IT guys to switch my computer over, then I'll start moving my things."

Mel had to shift a surprising number of cabinets to reach the desk – they appeared to be nesting beneath and around it. After translocating the stacks of files that had migrated to the desk during its vacancy and removing the choking layer of dust, Mel looked for the computer. She saw the monitor, mouse and keyboard, but nothing else.

With a sigh, brushing the dust bunnies from her breasts, Mel trudged back to her old desk beside the fire escape. There was no response from IT. She headed across the office to the cubicles where the IT staff holed up, insulated by boxes of computer hardware beside the frozen core of the office computer servers, blinking behind the glass that made up one wall. The imps were nowhere in sight.

All the desks were empty bar one. "Yes?" the man seated at it asked. His eyes were on his screen and not on her.

"They're shifting me to the dusty desk by the big south window and I need your help setting up the computer," Mel said.

He turned slowly to face her, taking her in with an extended glance that ended in surprise when Nybbas met her eyes. "Mel!"

Mel wished she'd worn something with a longer skirt. Why did male demons always seem to stare at her legs?

"You should be fine setting it up all by yourself. I know how good you are," he said with a shy smile. "If you need a little more authority with the printers and the like, I'd be happy to help. I'll stop by and see how you're doing later on today." He gave her a pointed look and returned to his own computer in what was clearly a dismissal.

Mel sighed and returned to her computer conundrum. It had to be here somewhere...

She followed the monitor and keyboard cables to a hole in the desk surface, then tracked them to a tiny, dusty shelf in the deepest, darkest corner beneath the desk. Swearing under her breath, Mel dropped to her knees and crawled under the desk. The dust bunnies under there used growth hormones, she was certain of it.

She brushed them aside, hoping they didn't use

spiders as sentries, and tried to pull the whole unit out into the light where she could see it. She was surprised to find she held a laptop on a cardboard box.

She could hear someone calling her name from behind her and she carefully backed up and out from under the desk. She was still on her hands and knees when he spoke again.

"Oh, no worries, it looks like you're doing just fine. You don't need my help." Nybbas' feet moved away from her. "Give me a shout when you want me." He walked away.

By the time Mel had managed to get to her feet, clutching the dusty laptop, she was alone. She looked down and realised that Nybbas had caught an eyeful of lace that no one should have seen. At least she'd been wearing stockings today. She smoothed her dress down over her hips and hoped he hadn't noticed.

She finished setting up the computer with the promised lack of problems, before she left for the day. As she crossed the road, she realised that the big south window was entirely transparent. The whole street and the admiring guy in the office over the road had seen a clear view of her stockings and more while she'd been under the desk.

Entirely uncomfortable, with a storm brewing in her head to match the clouds above, Mel boarded a train and mentally dared anyone to even approach her with a briefcase today. No one did. When she left the train at her station, she chose to walk home instead of taking the bus. Nothing like exercise to release pent-up frustration.

She lengthened her stride as she saw the dark clouds, hoping to make it home before the rain hit. Thunder boomed above her, adding to her discomfort in the high humidity that reminded her of Singapore and Sri Lanka.

An actinic flash of lightning touched the tarmac, not fifteen metres from her. Mel looked warily at the street and the nearby trees before quickening her pace. Walking home in an electrical storm wasn't the safest thing to do.

Another flash jumped between two clouds above her head. She looked up to see the clouds actually roiling – something she didn't think real clouds did. The only time she'd ever seen clouds do that was when she'd touched Luce – the stormy shroud surrounding his soul. In fact, if she looked closely, this storm appeared to have eyes – two of them, glaring angrily down at her, just like Luce did when he wanted to blame her for something.

She shook herself. Storms only had one eye and that was calm, not angry. She must be imagining such things – two angry eyes in a storm. Preposterous!

A streak of lightning touched the road, now only ten metres from her feet. She took a deep breath, inhaling sharp ozone from the discharge. Her heels tapped frantically on the pavement as she hurried for home.

Idly, she wondered if there was a better way to relieve anger than her misguided walk. Though she wasn't the type to hurl thunderbolts at unsuspecting humans, today she felt she could do with a little target practice, especially if her target was an empty road. It might help her to release a little steam after the stressful day.

On the footpath, she bumped into a man she'd seen before, but had never come close to.

"Hello." He beamed at her.

"Hi," Mel replied, flustered. "I'm sorry…"

"Beautiful weather, don't you think?" he asked. "I'm Jimmy. What's your name?"

"Mel."

"Ah, beautiful like you, Belle," he said, holding out a full-blown, red rose, thorns and all. "For you."

She carefully took the flower from the strange man, thanking him. Both walked on in opposite directions. Mel glanced back, but he'd already disappeared. So had the angry eyes in the sky.

Perhaps hurling thunderbolts might be a better release than going for a walk, but she didn't feel the need to direct any today. Maybe another day, Mel decided.

She turned onto her street as the skies opened, showering her with warm rain. She kept walking, not caring as the precipitation pelted her, for she was already soaked in sweat from the sweltering heat of the day. Any other wetness was an improvement.

She stepped inside, dripping across the carpet, heading for the kitchen to take care of the rose. Mature and red, both the lovely fragrance and defensive spikes marked it as a rose from a garden and not a florist. What was it supposed to mean? Was there some strange symbolism she was supposed to see? Or was it simply a lovely gift to remind her that there was more to life than HELL?

She placed the rose in a pint glass of water. Maybe she could look into learning to throw lightning from on high next week. She was sure some new situation at work would inspire her.

Mel checked the weather forecast before she hopped into the shower. It said cool with the chance of a shower and lengthy fine periods, but outside it looked like a perfect day that was heating up the way it always did in summer. She put out pants and a skirt and resolved to check the sky once more before she dressed. She didn't want a repeat of yesterday's drenching on her way to work today.

The fine sky and dark forecast hadn't changed. She tried to decide between the slim-fitted pants and the light skirt that flared nicely as she moved. In the end, Mel gave in and chose both. The pants first, the skirt over the top. If it was still hot when she got to work, she'd stick with the long skirt, but if it had cooled a bit, she'd take the skirt off and show off her new pants. She vowed not to give the people on the plaza another view they wouldn't forget.

She set off for the train station, the skirt swirling a little in the light north-westerly. The clouds for the promised shower had appeared on the horizon behind her, but she had an umbrella, so she ignored them and kept going.

She was perhaps five minutes from the train station when the skies opened in a brief downpour. She unfolded her umbrella and kept walking, knowing it would end soon, as it always did.

The umbrella kept her hair dry, but the light breeze had grown and the water came at her sideways. The umbrella was no use and the lovely skirt caught the wind and rain with equal greed. By the time Mel reached the train station, her skirt was soaked through and clinging to her legs. Her pants were drinking the water in her skirt like a man determined to find a cure for his hangover.

Bedraggled, Mel thought about heading home for a change of clothes, but that would make her late, so she made her way to the platform and caught the next train into the city. The other passengers avoided her as she fanned her dripping skirt out, trying to dry it.

By the time the train arrived, she was no longer dripping, but Mel was still very soggy. Her shoes squelched with each step from the station to HELL.

On the plaza and the street in front of the office, Mel found hundreds of construction workers in fluorescent shirts, protesting about the lack of local labour employed on a particular mining construction project. She squeezed her way through the angry men, wishing her pale pastels didn't stand out so much in a sea of fluorescent yellow and orange.

Once in the office, she breathed a sigh of relief as she sank into her desk chair, switching on her computer. It was a few seconds before she realised the water in her skirt and pants was quickly wicking into her underwear. She stood and headed for the toilets to do something about it.

Gerry saw her hurry past and commented, "You look wet. Did you get caught in the rain?"

Mel stopped and nodded. "Soaked through."

"Didn't you bring an umbrella or a change of clothes?" he asked sympathetically.

Mel blushed. "I had an umbrella, but it didn't do much, and I didn't plan on needing a change of clothes…"

Lili's head popped up above her partition. "Oh, I keep a spare pair of pants for after-work parties, in case I…" She trailed off and flashed a suggestive smile. "You can borrow them if you like."

Mel smiled at Lili. "Thank you, but I'll be all right."

Inwardly, she shuddered at the thought of wearing Lili's pants without her underwear. That would be terribly awkward, she felt. Not to mention the rumour that Lili was Lucifer's mistress – given Luce evidently slept around a bit, or attempted to, he'd probably been in those pants on numerous occasions.

Gerry looked worried. "Now, you know you'll feel better if you take all that wet gear off." He smiled kindly. "You really should take it all off and take up Lili's offer."

Lili nodded vigorously. "You really should."

Mel managed a sickly smile in response as she shook her head. "Thank you, but…"

Gerry grinned. "I'll just keep telling you to take your skirt off 'til you do."

A shriek split the air. Mephi stood with both hands to her mouth, staring from Gerry to Mel. "That's sexual harassment. Don't you give in to him and take your skirt off, dear. I'll report him directly!" Mephi hurried off into the ladies' loo. Gerry followed her, protesting his innocence.

Mel turned and walked as quickly as she could back to her office, shutting the door behind her. She shared it with three other people, but they weren't in yet. Resigned, she knew the ladies' loo was out, so she was glad she had the office to herself.

With her eyes fixed on the door to make sure no one came in, she shimmied out of her wet pants and underwear, leaving just a skirt clinging damply to her skin. She fanned it out, trying to dry it as much as possible.

A loud cheer floated up from the protesters outside and she turned around to see what had happened. They all looked like they were staring at her building. Maybe someone had unrolled a banner down the side, in support of their cause. She shrugged and spread her skirt out to its fullest as she sat down, turning her computer on and staring at the screen.

Down below, the protesters made unhappy sounds and started to move away from the plaza. She watched them go, for once pleased by the good view offered by her window. When the men had marched out of sight up the Terrace, she looked down at her skirt to see if it had dried at all. Silhouetted between the office lights and the window, she realised the lavender skirt was transparent.

"Oh Hell," said Mel. She really wished she'd worn stockings today.

"...meeting at seven," Lili's voice said.

Mel struggled to remember why she was dreaming about Lili, as she was certain she was at home in bed. It was definitely dark. "Mmmph?"

A sigh of exasperation. "There's been an incident and Luce has called an emergency meeting. You've been tapped to take the meeting minutes, so you'll need to be in at work before the meeting at seven. I had to call your agency to put me through to you, because they wouldn't give me your direct number, so I've wasted enough time already. Get in here."

"Yeah, okay," Mel mumbled. The phone beeped in her ear as Lili hung up. That was enough to wake Mel properly.

Half an hour later, showered, styled and squeezed into a suit, Mel trudged to the train station. She could see the sun just rising behind the building, like the sky was on fire. Pretty, she thought muzzily, stumbling down the stairs to the train at the platform.

Despite the early hour, the train was fairly full, but Mel managed to find one of the last free seats. She sank down onto her seat and pulled out her smartphone. She'd found a romance story set in the aftermath of the American Civil War that looked interesting and indeed it was. She was soon engrossed.

The train pulled up at the next station and another herd of commuters boarded, squeezing in like sardines. The doors closed and the train started to move. One woman, looking as sleepy as Mel felt, didn't hold on to anything and lost her balance. She stumbled into Mel as she tried to regain her footing, but the train lurched and tipped her again. This time she fell face-first into Mel's lap.

Mel opened her mouth to ask if the poor woman was okay, but she was silenced by the sound of Nybbas' voice as he caught sight of her. "Ooh, hello!" he boomed, his eyes widening as he took in the sight of Mel with another woman draped across her lap.

Laughter erupted among the commuters and Mel

felt her face redden, as did the other woman, who quickly picked herself up and squeezed between people to put as much distance between herself and Mel as she could.

She and Nybbas detrained at the same station. He walked beside her all the way to the office.

Nyybas had a broad smile on his face, looking far too alert for Mel's foggy mind. "I didn't know you liked eating out for breakfast."

Mel thought about the raspberry yoghurt she hadn't had time for that morning. "This morning's special," she replied, inhaling the waft of bacon perfume emanating from a plaza café.

"I'd love to have breakfast with you one day then," Nybbas returned.

Mel smiled. "How about after this morning's meeting? I have a craving for bacon."

Nybbas seemed stunned by her invitation. "S-s-sure," he stammered.

"Right, take your coffee. Time to start this meeting," Luce said, waving his hand at the tray of steaming cups that Mephi held. Mel concentrated on powering up her laptop, knowing Mephi would never make a coffee for her.

"Mel," she heard Luce say. She glanced up to see him jerk his head at the remaining cup on the tray. It was hers – no one else here owned a white and gold mug, and the white-hearted macchiato it contained was unmistakeable. Luce must have made Mephi do it –

unless he'd made the coffee himself. She smiled her thanks as she took the mug. So sweet of him to remember.

Mel sipped her fresh-brewed coffee between typing, savouring the flavour.

"When was it found?"

"On the twentieth of October."

"Why haven't we acted on it before now? That was over a month ago!"

"She contacted us to tell us about it, but gave us the wrong phone number and never told us any more. We didn't know how to get in contact with her."

"Why did you bring it up now?"

"She sent us photos and it looks suspicious."

"Where is it? What happened to it?"

"She stored it in the freezer."

Alien invasion commenced on 20/10, Mel typed. **Member of the public found body, reported find but couldn't be contacted. Alien body photographed and stored in freezer for further investigation.**

"Why don't we have the body?"

"We've sent one of our staff to retrieve it. He was due there at seven, when the meeting started, so he'll contact us once he's identified and secured the specimen."

The phone rang. Luce hit the speakerphone button.

"Hello? Report."

"Luce, this is Jez from PR. We have enquiries from

all the main media channels, requesting a press conference with you regarding the alien invasion."

"Ah."

"The online news sites are already running a story about the invasion. We need to comment as soon as possible."

CEO to give immediate press conference to prevent panic, Mel typed.

"Set it up for half an hour? I need to go find a tie." Luce left.

About five minutes after his departure, the phone rang again. Lili hit the speakerphone button, trying to sound as authoritative as Luce. "Hello? Report."

"Hi, it's Phil. We have one specimen, but the other one is gone."

"You've lost an alien?"

"No, not entirely. We know where it is. The alien was mistaken for seafood at a barbeque and met with an unfortunate accident."

Mel's fingers skittered across the keys. **Alien corpse bbqed and served at a party.**

"What happened?"

"Ah, the lady who found it says that it was quite delicious. She gave us the remains of the carcass."

"Can you identify it?"

"It appears to bear some similarity to a local tropical rock lobster species…"

Tropical rock lobster mistaken for alien – report is a false alarm, Mel typed as fast as she could.

"What about the remaining specimen?"

"Definitely a very large tropical rock lobster. We've commandeered the specimen for testing…one of our researchers would like to see what it tastes like with butter."

"Ah, okay. Thanks, Phil."

"Sure, bye."

Relieved murmurs flowed around the table. Everyone else started discussing where they intended to go for breakfast following the meeting.

"Um, Lili?" Mel ventured. "What are we going to tell the press conference?"

Lili smiled, her handbag already on her shoulder as she straightened her shirt in preparation for going out. "It's not the end of the world. Just step upstairs and tell Luce it was a false alarm. He can tell the media that we've averted disaster." She followed the team out toward the lift.

Mel broke into a run up the stairs to the seminar room, where Luce had held the briefing on her in her bikinis. She could hear the sound of voices behind the door, so she silently turned the handle and slipped inside.

At the front, his gaze sweeping a dozen cameras as he spoke into a myriad of microphones, Luce smiled. "The important thing to remember is that, even if aliens are invading and the apocalypse is nigh, this is not the end of the world. We have specialist staff ready to respond to any and all invasion forces…" He caught sight of her. "Yes?"

All eyes and lenses turned to Mel and her insides froze with fear, as they always did when she had to speak in public.

Mel dropped to her knees. It might not be an alien invasion, but it was the end of the world. Her boss had just predicted doomsday from an invasion of lobsters. She didn't dare say that the specialist staff were responding with butter. She couldn't say a word. Oh Hell.

The crowd seemed to surge closer to her with a concerned cacophony of sound, but Luce held up his hands for silence and space as he strode closer. "Are you here to report that the situation has been contained?" Luce asked tersely.

Mutely, Mel nodded. Contained in a steamer, she couldn't seem to say. Tears sprang to her eyes and trickled down her cheeks.

"One of our dedicated staff, ladies and gentlemen, who played a key role in averting disaster." Luce leaped lightly up the steps and held out a hand to Mel. She grasped his arm as she rose, holding on to him for support. All she could feel emanating from him was sympathy – a strange sensation for a demon, she thought, as she permitted him to lead her forward to the lectern. "May I present the heroine who's saved the day, Miss Melody Angel!" he boomed, a supportive arm sliding around her waist when it felt like she'd fall to her knees again. Flashes blinded her, shimmering through her tears.

"No further questions," Luce said, waving them away with his free hand. He stood at Mel's side until the last journalist had left, shutting the door behind him. The unusually solicitous demon helped her sit in one of the front-row chairs.

Mel stared at Luce, trying to work out what motivated this sudden change. First the coffee, now this…what did he want?

He handed her a black cotton handkerchief. "That's the second time this week you've saved me from embarrassment in this room. Thank you, angel."

Mel cleared her throat. "Mel. My name is Mel."

"I know your name. Now, so do all of the media."

Mel smiled wanly, passing his damp handkerchief back. "Great. Please forgive me if I don't thank you for that."

Luce frowned. "But the situation is contained, isn't it? And you are the one who was sent with the good news?"

Mel nodded. "Yes, but…"

"That makes you the heroine who single-handedly saved us all from an alien invasion, as well as me from some hard-to-answer questions. It seems I'm in your debt, Mel. All of us are." He met her eyes. "I hope you intend to stay with the corporation for a while. We could use more staff like you."

"I did nothing but take the minutes in the meeting, and it turned out that the emergency was a false alarm,"

Mel said steadily. "Anyone could have done what I did."

Luce shrugged. It looked like he was trying to hide a smile. "So what would you have done if I'd given you a choice? Announced that I was an idiot, or agreed to be the heroine of the HELL Corporation? You had the chance to tell them yourself."

Tell all those reporters, with their cameras, that Luce was an idiot? Mel felt her will drain from her at even the thought of the audience. No, she couldn't have said it — even if it had been true, which it wasn't. And now Luce knew her weakness — her fear of public speaking. She bet he found it funny as Hell.

"Are you feeling okay?" He looked uncertain. "Do you need a hand getting up, or…"

Mel waved him away and rose. "I'll be fine." She trudged up the steps, putting as much distance as she could between herself and the strange demon.

"Remember, I owe you!" he called after her.

And one day, she'd collect, she resolved, but not today.

Mel sipped her morning macchiato as she checked her emails, wishing she was reading that book she'd found over breakfast, the one about reincarnation. The veiled woman on the cover had looked so mysterious…

"Mel, we're getting lots of calls at Reception on the new legislation. We need you to help field enquiries," Lili said without warning.

Mel looked up, stunned. "What about the alien invasion? Aren't I supposed to stay away from the public after I cried in the press conference?"

Lili shrugged. "Luce took care of that. He put out a media release that the invasion had been contained and we'd remain vigilant. No mention of what species they were. He just called you a 'dedicated member of staff' who had 'worked tirelessly to manage the incursion.' He thinks the photos of you in the paper in tears were brilliant. He specifically requested you to help with enquiries."

Mel sighed. At least on Reception she could take her phone with her and read that story between calls. She slipped the smartphone into her pocket, gulped down the last of her coffee and straightened her shirt. "Sure. What questions will I have to answer?"

Lili handed over a booklet. "The new legislation that came into effect on the first. People have lots of questions and they're all answered in this."

Mel took the booklet and smiled as she headed out to Reception, feeling the heavy bump of the phone in her pants pocket with each step.

She sat next to another girl, who was dressed in a fresh white shirt instead of the HELL Corporation uniform. The girl clunked her phone down before burying her face in her hands.

Mel introduced herself. "Here to help," she added.

"No, I'm here to help," the girl said, a slightly hysterical edge to her voice. "I'm Gabrielle, from Helpful Angels, temporarily here to take phone enquiries. What have I been volunteered for? This is really hard." She turned to face Mel and her eyes widened with recognition. "What are you doing here? Raphael said you were in India or something…"

Mel smiled. "Nope, I'm back and it looks like they've given us the worst job they can think of – ah, it'll be easy for a couple of angels, you'll see. Welcome to HELL. It's not too bad, once you get used to it."

Gabi shrugged. "I probably won't be here that long."

The phone rang and Gabi answered it, turning away. She looked pained.

Mel's phone rang, too, so she took a deep breath and answered it. "Good morning, HELL Corporation. How may I help?"

"This is shit."

Mel fought not to laugh. "What is, sir?"

"The new changes to the laws. We're the Cane Toad Action Group and according to the new animal welfare laws, we can't kill any animal in the State without it being done by an authorised veterinarian. It's BULLSHIT."

Mel agreed with him so she tried to be soothing. "Surely that can't be right. I'm sure the new animal welfare laws were only changed to… 'better protect native species, pets and stock.'" She read the list quickly off the front of the brochure, hoping he wouldn't notice her hesitation.

"Well someone better fix this then, because I'm not going to get a vet to personally kill a thousand cane toads. First, I'm going to ring my mate, who's a reporter with Channel Six. Then, I'm going to put the buggers in a bag and gas them the same as we always do…and you can tell your fucking policy people they're stupid!" The irate man hung up.

Mel made a note of the man's point and picked up the brochure with a sigh. Surely no one could write legislation that protected cane toads from being killed. They were a noxious pest that had to be neutralised on sight…

The phone rang again. This time the enquirer was female. "I have a question about the new laws."

Please don't let it be about cane toads, Mel prayed.

The woman's voice shook. "I have a redback spider in my house and I'm terrified it will bite my dog or me, but my neighbour told me that the new laws mean I can't kill it. I can't afford to get a vet out here to do it. What do I do? I don't want it to kill me…"

Mel privately thought she would have preferred cane toads. "I'm sure the laws don't cover redback spiders. You just spray it, squish it or shift it outside, like you would normally."

The woman sniffled as she agreed to do what Mel said, before ending the call.

Gabi was looking at Mel as she hung up. "So, what's the deal with this legislation?" Mel asked, feeling that she'd been dropped into something she hadn't agreed to.

Gabi's expression darkened. She reached for Mel's brochure, flipping quickly through the pages. "The animal rights activists managed to push through this new legislation, which apparently applies to 'all non-human animals in the state' where they must die a humane death, as administered by an authorised vet. The first query I got was about rats, the next was about fishing…and the list just grows. Apparently you can't kill the fish you've caught without a vet, you can't poison rats, can't spray flies and your pet fish can't die of natural causes…and whoever wrote this isn't living in the real world."

Mel started to laugh. "Well, they'll just have to change it to say some animals are exempt from the law, right?"

Gabi shook her head. "They probably will, but it won't be today. Until they do, we'll be dealing with all the questions."

"Excuse me, ladies," a sleazy voice said.

Don't let it be Luce, Mel prayed. The last thing she needed was for Gabi to positively identify him as Lucifer and throw the office into chaos.

Both Gabi and Mel looked up, eyebrows raised.

"I couldn't help but overhear," the stranger said smoothly, "but is it true that the new legislation is a little, ah, problematic and short-sighted?"

Mel found this smarmy stranger familiar. "Legislation is law. What else it is I'd say is up to the policy makers who have to deal with it." She looked hard at him. "Can I help you?"

"I'm from Channel Six news and I've come to interview your CEO about the new legislation. He's expecting me." He grinned greasily at Mel.

She suppressed a shudder, changing her mind and wishing the man had been Luce instead. This must have been one of the reporters at the press conference where she'd cried. Gabi was already on the phone, nodding as she spoke to Mephi. "You can go on in."

Mel jumped to her feet, hoping to keep Gabi away from Luce for a little longer. "I'll take you up to his office." She led the way to the stairs.

Luce smiled at the sight of her and happily greeted the reporter. The two men shook hands and exchanged greetings as Mel stood in the doorway, wondering what to do next.

"We'll be fine, thank you, Mel. Can you send Mephi in to arrange coffee?" Luce asked. Both his and the reporter's eyes followed Mel as she walked out of the office. She tried to ignore their scrutiny.

Mephi huffed as she stood, having already heard Luce's words, and minced into the meeting to arrange refreshments.

As Mel headed away from the office, she heard the reporter's first question. "So, Mr Iblis, as CEO of HELL Corporation, can you tell us how this new legislation will affect containment of the alien invasion? Are we drafting an army of veterinarians to kill the alien menace?"

Mel almost choked as she headed toward the stairs, hoping to put as much distance between herself and the reporter as possible before she lost it laughing.

Sometimes, working for this corporation was funny as Hell.

"This is getting so dull, I think I need a coffee to keep me awake," Gabi muttered. "Cover for me for fifteen minutes while I go get one?"

Mel nodded as she listened to the very long story some woman seemed compelled to tell her — something about a fish in a shop's aquarium that gave her nightmares. Mel still wasn't entirely sure what the caller expected her to do about it. She evidently needed some form of counselling.

Twenty minutes later, she'd managed to end the call,

hand over six visitor badges to humans who had meetings with HELL Corporation personnel, and handle two over-the-counter enquiries about payments for various licences that they had the authority to issue. She'd smiled politely three times when people recognised and congratulated her for saving them from aliens.

Longing for a coffee herself and a trip to the toilet, she waited patiently for Gabi to return. Her coffee run sure was taking a long time. Mel hoped Gabi hadn't run into Luce in the lunchroom.

She took a telephone enquiry about rain water tanks and transferred it to the demon who dealt with such things.

Luce appeared with the reporter, who winked at Mel as he handed back his visitor badge. She managed to send him on his way without her home telephone number, despite his insistence that she give it to him. She sighed and closed her eyes.

If only Luce hadn't made her out to be some sort of heroine to the press and then allowed this poorly thought-out legislation to pass, her job would be so much easier.

"Would you give me your phone number, if I asked?"

Mel opened her eyes. Luce hadn't left — he leaned against the door to the rest of the office, grinning at her.

"Sure," she replied. "As long as I'm working here in HELL..." She gave him the switchboard number for

Reception – the number it seemed like every crazy human in this city had felt the need to call today.

Luce laughed. "And your personal number? The one for the mobile phone I see you reading so avidly on during your breaks, or the number for the house you take sanctuary in when your work day is done?"

"No," she replied honestly. "I don't want to be worried about work when I'm not here. Especially with this misguided new legislation. It seems everyone has a different question that wasn't considered when whichever cloistered individual wrote it. Was there no public consultation at all?"

Luce shook his head. "Nope. And cloistered individuals sound about right – the pair of angels we got from the agency before you arrived were the ones who wrote it. I don't think those two knew much about humans at all – spent too much time in Heaven, contemplating their own divinity. Holy legislation is what they've given me – in that it's full of holes."

"Angels? You mean Camael and Samael? The ones you poached from the agency? Figures. They're fine debating complicated legal points, but writing the laws in the first place? They're neither experienced nor qualified. I would have thought that your people were better at putting together legally binding agreements. Legislation shouldn't be such a big step; surely you have damned lawyers at your disposal..." Mel paused as she realised Luce was silent. "I'm sorry. It's your corporation. I'm sure you can assign whatever poorly qualified personnel you see fit to the task."

Luce laughed. "I've said it before and I'll say it again. You're not like any other angel I've ever met. Yet I'm incredibly happy we have an angel like you handling all the public enquiries on this mess. No one else could do it. Speaking of which…isn't there meant to be another angel on Reception with you?"

"Yes." Mel sighed. "She said she was getting coffee, but it's been half an hour and she's still not back."

"I'll get you one. The least I can do in exchange for you handling this so well. I know what you like." Luce winked.

Mel couldn't help but laugh. "That would be wonderful."

She waited for one of them to return, hoping it would be soon and not at the same time. If Gabi encountered Luce over the coffee machine, she could do some serious damage with hot water and steamed milk.

Luce was back first, carrying her mug of macchiato alongside his own steaming cup. "Thank you," she said with a smile, raising her cup in salute. "Did you see Gabi in there?"

He cheerfully shook his head. "I should get back to work. I can't be making coffee all day. I have a stack of poorly punctuated reports on my desk to approve." With another wink, he disappeared through the office door.

Mel sighed, sipping her perfect coffee, as she

worried about what had happened to Gabi.

The girl herself breezed through the doors. "What kind of city doesn't have a Starbucks?" she demanded. "No one could tell me where I could get a Frappuccino…so I eventually found a place that did flavoured ice coffees with an espresso base. Look, I got a white chocolate and a French vanilla iced latte. Which one do you want?"

They both looked identical to Mel — creamy-coloured milkshakes. She still had a little of her coffee left, but she didn't want to offend Gabi, so she took the one closer to her and offered her thanks for the confection.

Mel tipped the last of her coffee into her mouth and almost choked when Gabi squealed, "How can you drink that? Is that from the demons' coffee machine? You don't know what they put in there! It could be anything…don't drink it, Mel!" She ripped the mug out of Mel's fingers. Too late — it was empty.

"They put coffee beans and milk in it," Mel protested. "Same as anyone else. It's safe, Gabi, honestly."

"But demons use it. How often would they clean a coffee maker? I'd want to disinfect the whole thing, then wash it again to get rid of the stink of corruption. They're demons — there's nothing good about them and everything they touch is tainted by the contact." She looked grim. "I don't know how you've managed to share the office with them for so long. I can barely put up with the proximity, sitting out here apart from them."

Mel's heart ached for the demons Gabi had denigrated. She knew the coffee machine was impeccably maintained – her colleagues appreciated a quality coffee more than she did. There was nothing tainted or corrupted about her coffee – Luce had made it exactly the way she liked it, as promised. She wondered what Gabi would say if she knew a demon had made the contents of her cup.

"Gabi, they're not that bad. I've met worse humans than some of the demons in this office. They were angels once, too, you know…"

Gabi snorted. "They're demons and everything about them is bad. They can't do anything good. The humans worse than them are destined to be either damned or demons themselves when they die. And they might have been angels once, but they fell for a reason. Don't let them drag you down with them. They'll do it out of sheer mischief – their desire to corrupt anything good. Just focus on what we're here for. We have to find Lucifer, find out what he's up to, and stop him. Then we can get the Hell out of here as fast as possible."

Mel sighed. She knew where he was and what he was doing, but she was happy to let Luce drink his coffee and check reports at his desk. Gabi would surely encounter him in the office soon enough. She was surprised the archangel hadn't met him already. Mel wondered if she'd be as eager to leave as Gabi.

The phone trilled and Mel picked up the receiver. "Hello, HELL Corporation. How may I…"

"They've done it again! There's a pile of dead cane toads at the bottom of the War Memorial this time! I want something done about it! Desecrating our fallen heroes' memories…"

Mel sighed. Maybe there were some things she wouldn't miss.

"Prostitutes have more jargon than I'd realised…do you know what a body slide is? Or how much they charge for one?"

Lili had to repeat her question before Mel realised she was the one being addressed.

"A…a body slide?" Mel swallowed, trying not to imagine it. "Should I know?"

Lili shrugged. "Probably not. You'd go and work in their industry instead, if you knew how much they charged."

Mel found that hard to believe. "Oh, I doubt it. I like it here," she managed to say.

Lili considered this. "Well, I guess you could be a phone sex worker. You have the voice for it. One of my friends did that for a while. She had the funniest stories…"

Mel almost choked, but recovered before Lili noticed. "No, thank you. I'm sure it doesn't pay well, and imagine what they might say!"

"You'd have a script of what to say. I'm sure it would mostly be a matter of what colour underwear to tell them you're wearing today…"

Mel spluttered into silence.

"Anyway, they don't pay us enough here," Lili concluded, to Mel's relief. "I wish some billionaire would marry me and then I wouldn't have to work any more."

Gerry's head popped up from behind a partition. "I think Ginger Rhinestone's available!" He wore a big grin.

"Is she?" Lili asked. "Hmm, I wonder…"

Mel tried to keep her breakfast down. She didn't think that Ginger Rhinestone, a particularly plump, female mining magnate, could ever have enough money to attract her. She found herself wondering how Lili could…she shook herself and hoped she'd dislodged the disturbing image, too.

"Right, they don't pay me enough to keep doing this. Come on, it's time for the Christmas party!" Lili beckoned to Mel, who followed her cautiously to the fancy hotel over the road.

They both accepted glasses of wine from the waiter at the entrance, Mel sipped slowly while Lili knocked hers back quickly so she could seize another.

Lili caught sight of a colleague she wanted to talk to and left Mel standing by the waiter. Mel breathed a sigh of relief and pulled out her phone, thinking about catching up on the story she'd been reading on the train that morning. The girl called Nona sounded nice.

…he knocked her out with what? Mel thought, feeling her face grow red.

"Mel!" Luce's smile looked happy. "Welcome to the HELL Corporation Christmas party! Now, you're not at work, so put your phone away – no working!" He reached for her phone to turn it off.

Mel swiped frantically at the screen, hoping to wipe it of words before Luce saw what had made her blush.

She needn't have worried. He didn't even glance at it.

"I've been meaning to thank you for all your hard work and help – even letting me use your photos for my presentation. They were exactly what I needed!" He beamed at her.

"Ah, no worries," Mel replied uneasily. She slipped her phone back into her pocket.

"Have you checked where you're sitting yet?" he asked, nodding at the noticeboard.

Mel shook her head and leaned closer to look for

her name.

"There you are – on my table!" Luce looked pleased, pointing, as Mel's heart sank. She wouldn't be reading anything else about Nona today.

Mel followed him into the hotel function room to their table. Christmas-coloured balloons rose from a weighted, wrapped gift in the centre. Luce insisted that she sit beside him, next to the dance floor, and she reluctantly complied. Lili slid in on her other side, followed by the other executives.

Mel grew steadily paler. She swore not to drink any more wine, lest she make a mistake. She sipped slowly from her glass and set it down.

Looking around at the room, she wondered who most of them were. Gerry and Merih joined a table which was mostly occupied by men. Other staff wandered in, chatting happily as they sat down. With a sinking heart, Mel realised that she was the only angel present.

The food was served quickly and Mel reached for her wine. Inexplicably, the glass had refilled. Another sip and she returned to her steak, careful to carve it into small pieces so she wouldn't make a fool of herself.

Dessert was a slice made of layers of raspberry and dark chocolate mousse that looked obscenely pink, even in the dim light of the function room.

"Oh, this is amazing," Lili moaned, her spoon in her mouth.

Mel looked at her in alarm, but Lili took her spoon

to the mousse again with a rapt expression, in no apparent danger.

Luce's voice sounded throaty. "You have to try this."

Moans rose from Merih and Gerry's table.

It sounded like the demons around her were all experiencing the same mass orgasm. Mel didn't know where to look, so she touched the pinkness with her fingertip and thrust it into her mouth. She closed her eyes, the better to focus on the taste without the distraction of the others around her. This pleasure was private and Mel decided she wanted more, opening her eyes and her mouth eagerly. A glance told her Luce had seen her sucking on her finger and found it funny as Hell, so she capitulated and picked up a spoon for the next taste.

She finished her dessert with reluctance, wishing there was more to prolong the pleasure. Mel reached for her wine.

It had refilled itself again, though she was sure it'd been almost empty. She shrugged and drank.

The jukebox by the dance floor increased its volume. The medley from *Grease* kicked off this party as it had every other one she'd attended since the movie had been released. Mel waited for the next traditional song – where a man declared he'd walk five hundred miles – and was rewarded by the next track. The dance floor started to fill with her more eager colleagues, but Mel remained firmly in her seat.

A dance track began, the Korean lyrics surprising

her. Something about a warm girl who liked coffee. The dance floor cleared quickly, leaving only eight women, who began to dance with a synchronicity that spoke of practice.

Mel felt her jaw drop. She was sure she'd never seen a version of *Gangnam Style* where the girls rode on female horses who evidently enjoyed the experience. It looked like they were all equipped with items she'd seen in that adult shop up the road, too…

"Aren't they brilliant?" Luce shouted in her ear, over the music. He refilled her glass as he spoke.

"I…" Mel swallowed. "Isn't this one of those things that the company calls inappropriate behaviour? I could lose my job if someone from the Human Resources Department finds out I've been looking at this!"

Luce laughed. "I keep forgetting you're not one of my staff and you still work for the agency – if you'd ever had to put in a leave form or ask about a payslip, you'd know that they are the HR Department – the manager is riding the rather well-endowed horse in the middle. I think she'd prefer you just sit down and watch the show, and applaud loudly afterwards."

Mel regarded the dancing demons. It looked like the horses wore some sort of saddle with odd protuberances strapped on to them. She wondered how anyone was supposed to comfortably ride…

Mel groped blindly for her wine glass with her eyes squeezed tightly shut. Perhaps if she drank enough, she'd manage to forget what she'd just seen her colleagues do.

"Time for the Christmas party!" Lili sang out. "Computers off – you won't be coming back today!"

Mel stared. "I thought we already had the office Christmas party. The one at the hotel, with the dancers and…"

Please, don't make me sit through another dance interpretation of *Gangnam Style*, she prayed silently. She still wished she didn't know what a double delight strap-on was for.

"Of course we did. That was the whole office. This

is just our unit – we're going down to Matilda Bay with the swans for a barbeque."

"We're eating swan?" Mel asked, horrified. After the exotic dancers from HR, nothing would surprise her about office Christmas parties in HELL.

Lili laughed. "No, but they might try and eat us. Gerry got us some steaks and sausages, Ana and Merih have some salads, Gabi is bringing the rolls and I took care of the drinks. Time to make merry, Mel!"

Mel conceded the point and proceeded to shut down her computer. Sausages, swans and steak. It wasn't that heavenly mousse, but it was still a celebration and she wouldn't miss it. Demons celebrating Christmas – who'd have thought? "How are we getting there?" she asked.

"A few of us are driving over to the foreshore. I can give you a lift, if you like. I have one seat spare in my car."

Mel accepted gracefully and followed Lili to the underground car park, inexplicably burdened with more wine than she could drink. She wondered why a lot of it was bubbly and pink – it didn't seem like normal demonic fare, but who was she to judge? Her shoulders were too heavily burdened to shrug, so she kept her thoughts to herself.

Lili took the bags of bottles from her, loading them into the boot of her tiny two-seater convertible. The shiny red paintwork seemed to glow even in the dimly lit basement. Mel's fingers itched to drive Lili's car herself – it certainly looked like fun. Fleetingly, she wondered why no one else would want the passenger seat in Lili's lovely car.

"C'mon, Mel, hurry up or they'll start without us!" Lili insisted. She'd slid behind the steering wheel while Mel had mused.

Mel yanked open the door and buckled her seatbelt. She'd barely slammed the door behind her before Lili revved the engine and reversed.

Mel's question was answered quickly. Lili drove like…well, a demon, she decided. A demon with a death wish. Clinging to her seat, both feet firmly braced in the footwell as if she was braking with all her weight, she couldn't take her horrified eyes off the traffic whizzing past their erratically guided missile of a Mazda. The third time the seatbelt strained against her chest at Lili's sudden stop, Mel tried to shut the whole experience out, praying it would be over soon.

"Oh good! Merih and Gerry have already claimed us some tables!" Lili said, cracking open her door.

Mel opened her eyes and unclenched her hands from the bottom of her seat, hoping she hadn't clawed any of the upholstery off in her panic. There didn't appear to be anything unusual under her nails so she escaped from the car.

She tried to settle her shaky legs as she stepped across the grass to the table where the food was laid out. Both Merih and Gerry stood at the barbeque, each holding a beer in one hand and tongs in the other. "Is there anything I can do?" she asked.

"Nope!" Gerry grinned. "You just sit and guard the table from the hellspawn swans. Grab a drink, Mel!"

Hellspawn swans? They looked like normal black swans, Mel thought, examining the large birds by the water's edge. Surely a demon wouldn't blink at hellspawn, no matter what shape it took…

Lili pushed a plastic goblet of pink bubbly into her hand. Mel thanked her and approached the table. One swan unfolded its legs and stretched its neck in her direction, but didn't move closer.

Mel tucked her skirt beneath her and perched on the picnic bench, glancing at the food spread across the table's surface. Plenty of salad, alcohol, plates, cutlery…and some of the expensive bakery rolls she couldn't usually afford. Her stomach made its presence known as her eyes focussed on the heavily seeded rolls that were her favourite. One wouldn't hurt, she decided, slipping her fingers into the bakery bag. The top of the roll was hard to the touch, yet it yielded beneath her fingers, telling her it hadn't been sitting in the humid office all day or in a freezer for longer – this was baked fresh today and bought not long before.

"Go on," Gabi said softly, seating herself beside Mel. "I made sure to get the ones you like – and a few extra, just in case. They won't miss a couple of rolls."

Both angels looked over to the barbeque, where it appeared Merih had poured a beer over the hotplate, sending up a mushroom cloud of steam. The loud hissing didn't drown out their raucous laughter.

Mel agreed and the paper bag crackled as she extracted her prize.

Merry Christmas to me, she thought as she bit into the crusty roll, crunching through the seeds in bliss.

A high-pitched honk, like the squeak of a clarinet, drove her eyes open. The swan's red and white beak was level with her knees as he cocked his head so his red-ringed eye could make contact with hers.

"You want some of this roll, too? I don't blame you," Mel told him, breaking off a bite-sized piece and holding it before his beak. The swan took the morsel without touching her fingers. As Mel took another large bite, she almost choked with laughter as the swan lifted his head to look for more. Swallowing, she broke off another bit for the bird.

Together, they finished the roll and the swan seemed as eager as Mel for another. Without taking her eyes off the bird, Mel asked, "Gabi, is there any chance I could have another one?"

Paper crackled and something hard, rough and seedy touched her elbow. Mel reached over to take it and her fingers grazed those wrapped around the roll.

Dark clouds roiled, the sort only seen in a seriously strong storm – or surrounding a severely troubled soul. Yet this storm had an eye, a break through which she could see...

"You're not Gabrielle," Mel stated quietly.

"No, I'm far sexier than the stuck-up angel who was

sitting here before," a male voice answered.

"Thank you," Mel continued as if he'd neither spoken nor insulted Gabi. She took a bite and the piece came away bigger than she'd expected — certainly more than she could swallow. The swan stretched up eagerly to help her.

Hellspawn by her side or possible hellspawn at her feet — Mel chose to give her attention to the bright-beaked bird. Acutely aware of the demon watching from the bench beside her, she bowed her head to the swan's level.

"You really shouldn't do that. Those birds will take your fingers off or worse if they get close to your face..."

A careful beak took the bread from her, close enough for her to kiss if Mel felt inclined to do so. Instead, she pulled away and covered her mouth as she laughed. Quickly, she placed another piece between her lips for the swan, which stretched for it. As he took the roll from her, she stroked the soft, dark down at his breast.

"I think this is the first time I've ever been insanely jealous of a bird," Luce said.

Mel laughed again. "There are more rolls, if you're hungry – Gabi said she'd bought plenty, though I'm not sure if she factored you into her numbers. I thought this little party was just for Lili's unit."

"Lili always invites the Executive to any unit meetings or functions – and it turned out that I was available to attend this one. Lucky me!"

Luce stretched an arm back to reach for another roll, splaying his legs out in what Mel hoped was simply an attempt to maintain his balance on the bench. His thigh pressed against hers as his shiny, shod foot nudged the swan.

The swan angrily lifted his wings a little, as if unsure whether to fly or fold them again. Luce leaned forward, a piece of bread extended toward the bird, and his feet landed heavily as his centre of gravity shifted. One shoe hit the grass, while the other found a webbed foot.

Wings unfolded fully, the swan hissed menacingly at Luce, before taking the food and a chunk of flesh from his hand. The ungainly bird waddled back to his little harem by the water's edge.

"Damned devil birds," Luce growled, swiping at his bleeding hand with a handkerchief as black as the blood seeping through his fingers. She'd never seen black blood before, but she tried not to stare. "I've seen drunk demons cause less trouble."

"He was well-behaved for me," Mel said. "If you hadn't stepped on his foot…Here, let me help." She reached for his injured hand, shifting the handkerchief away so she could see the damage. The small nick in the webbing between Luce's index finger and thumb looked too tiny to have bled so much. In fact, the skin didn't even look as if it had broken…She wiped away a little of the blood with the burgundy cotton in her hand to get a closer look.

The black handkerchief had turned dark red. Oh Hell, she thought.

Mel quickly released Luce, hoping he wouldn't realise what she'd done. She resolved to control herself better in future – changing the colours of demons' clothing while she healed them would only lead to trouble. She had to subdue her normal angelic instincts or risk exposing herself.

Too late – Luce fingered the red fabric thoughtfully before returning it to his pocket. "That doesn't mean the infernal bird isn't a demon – just that he's smart."

Luce lowered his voice. "I'd lie down and be as docile as you desire for a piece of you, angel. Provided I get what I want from you in return…"

A chorus of honks was all the excuse Mel needed to turn her back on the dirty-minded demon, for she now had three hungry swans to contend with – the male and his two female friends. She filled three beaks with bread before she spoke. "I prefer to be called Mel, Luce. And just because a bird has black wings, doesn't make it a demon." She nodded at the male. "He's only a juvenile. His mother, though, has all her feathers." She offered another piece of bread to the female closest to him. Mel slid her hands down the bird's sides, causing her to open her wings and give them a few flaps before folding them again. The white feathers edging both wings stood out like the frill on the hem of Mel's skirt. "No demon or fallen angel has white feathers in their wings. All three are simply beautiful, magnificent birds. Let me show you."

Mel cupped Luce's limp left hand in hers. She could feel the darkness surrounding his soul far more strongly now, but she paid little heed to it. It didn't seem so dark…as if the thick layer of blackness was merely an illusion and the reality was more like the storm clouds she kept sensing. Clouds that parted at her delicate touch. Beneath, shrouded in shadow, there was so much she hadn't seen before.

Reaching for Luce's right hand, Mel placed the last piece of roll between his fingers. She extended his unresisting arm to tempt the swans with the bread. She could feel his fear. How could this demon be so terrified of a bird? "It's all right," Mel murmured, wrapping her own fingers around his so that she'd take the brunt of the swan's beak if it was startled. She felt Luce relax a little.

The larger female stepped forward to accept the offering and Mel brought Luce's empty hand to the bird's breast. She helped him stroke the dark feathers as she probed his soul.

It wasn't the bird that frightened him. He feared...pain. She dug deeper. Despair, darkness and disguised light, hiding behind...

The bird honked softly and ambled away.

"You're brave," Luce said, pulling his hands back as his voice darkened to an ominous depth. "You shouldn't have done that."

Mel heard the hollow echo in the empty threat and ignored it. Instead, she tried to hold on to the impression she'd felt, which slipped away faster than the swans waddling back to the water. She'd thought a demon's soul held nothing but darkness, yet she'd seen so much more. There was tenderness, too, and...something so slippery she couldn't grasp it, though she doubted Luce could yet, either.

"Brave? How?" she asked. "For showing you that the beauty of a bird is part and parcel of his black wings?"

"I don't think any other angel's tried to touch me

without my permission before – and definitely no demon has. Afraid that with one touch, I could taint them. With a word, seduce them to surrender their souls to me. It wouldn't be the first time. You…you should know the risks you take. Believe the warnings and stories the older, more experienced angels tell you about me – chances are they'll all be true. You have the makings of a good angel, if you last long enough in the job. Isn't there an archangel in your unit? She knows who and what I am. She knows how best to protect herself, too. That one would probably walk away instead of having a conversation with me." He jerked his head at Gabi, who was grumpily crossing the grass a hundred metres away. "Don't you fear for your soul, Mel?"

She lifted her eyes to meet his, wondering if he knew how much she'd already read of his soul – and how much more he revealed to her in his dark eyes now. She smiled as she said, "Perhaps I have less to lose than the others. I rarely regret my actions and I don't now. It seemed sad that you would curse a creature for the colour of his wings – calling him a demon for defending himself. I've always loved the black swans here – for their contrast of darkness and light. Pure white wings can get very boring when that's all you see."

"I rarely see white wings at all." Luce didn't break her stare, letting her even deeper inside. "You really like swans, don't you?" If he was trying to read her soul, he'd soon learn that she had nothing to hide. Unlike him.

"Yes," she said simply. As she delved into his innermost soul, she found the need to continue. "Perhaps because I see more than most and it's hard to fear what you know so intimately. Darkness concealing light, at a depth where most won't look. A destiny that can't be stopped, only delayed. A desire for…vindication. A broken heart that wishes to be healed. A penchant for proof, but not destruction. A soul hidden deep within ice. Yearning, yet a strong fear of pain. Loneliness and longing for…"

His mouth hung open and his eyes held something that looked like fear. Mel wondered what else the demon could possibly be afraid of – his soul was damned and his place in Hell was permanent. What had the power to frighten Lucifer so much that it could take his power of speech and leave him struggling to say something?

He swallowed a couple of times before he could croak out, "Mel…"

"We have salt and pepper!" announced Ana, holding up two china shakers. "Thanks to the café up the way."

"Thanks to her theft from the café," Gabi grumbled, slumping to the bench across from Mel.

Mel felt bereft as Luce yanked his hands from hers. She couldn't remember taking them – or had he given them freely? Regardless, by holding his hands and staring into his eyes she'd seen so much of his soul that she was stunned. Luce was no soulless demon – he was as complex as any angel, though the illusive shroud of darkness had seemed so thick. He was hiding so much sadness and pain, too…

"Mel. Mel!"

Mel lifted her eyes to Gabi's face, wiping her tears away. "Yes?"

"You should go help those boys bring the cooked meat back. We'll set things up here at the table," Gabi said. Her eyes flicked suspiciously to Luce before returning to Mel.

"Sure," Mel replied, getting up. She felt Luce's eyes following her to the barbeque, but she didn't acknowledge the attention. She had a job to do and it didn't involve comforting despairing demons – no matter how deep his soul.

"She said we were just going to the café to get drinks!" Gabi hissed in Mel's ear. "I grabbed a couple of bottles to take up to the register, paid for them, and the demon had vanished! I didn't see her until I got outside, when she told me she'd stolen the salt and pepper shakers while I had them distracted. She even congratulated me on being a decoy. I'm an accessory to theft. They won't let me back into Heaven and all because of that damn demon…"

Mel nodded and made sympathetic noises as she

tried to fork her lettuce into her mouth without getting salad dressing on her nose. Perhaps there was some trick to it that she simply didn't know? She glanced around the table – no, it seemed everyone struggled with the lettuce, too. Even Luce, whose eyes shifted quickly from her to his plate when her gaze settled on him.

Smothering a smile with another lettuce leaf, Mel eyed her steak, wondering if it was well-done enough not to bleed all over her plate.

"Cooked to perfection," Merih said, sticking a large piece of pink-hearted meat into his mouth.

"I wanted rare," Lili complained, lifting her well-browned beef to her lips with distaste.

"It is rare," Gerry chortled. "How often do you get a meal cooked by Merih and me? Merih even burned his hand making it. Now that's dedication!"

Merih held up his hand, which looked a little redder than usual.

"Oh, let me help you with that," Mel said, reaching for the demon's injured hand.

Gabi's loud laughter made Mel turn to the angel in surprise. "Don't waste your time. Angels can't heal demons, Mel. You'd only burn him worse."

"Oh!" Mel remembered Melbourne Cup Day. "I'm sorry," she said to Merih. Yet she wondered how she'd managed to heal Luce, less than an hour before…

Mel decided her steak was worth the risk and cut herself a slice. It seemed demons weren't too bad at barbequing flesh. Perhaps it was all the practice they had in Hell.

"...and what will I do? We're angels. We're supposed to be perfect, not engage in petty theft on some lowly demon's demand!" Gabi hissed, her eyes filling with tears.

Mel carefully swallowed her morsel of meat. "Angels aren't perfect, Gabi. We're just good." She attempted to fold another piece of lettuce onto her fork, which flipped off just before she managed to insert it into her mouth, slapping her wetly on the nose.

"Not just good," Gabi insisted. "We're better than everyone else. At everything."

Mel laughed. "Better at stealing salt shakers, too?" she asked gently.

Gabi reddened.

"What's the joke, Mel?" Gerry asked, drawing her eyes away from Gabi. "It must be pretty good if it can make an angel blush."

Demonic laughter sounded on all sides.

Mel lowered her eyes. "It's...well, it's sort of a private angel joke. You probably wouldn't find it very funny. Even Gabi didn't like it – so I shouldn't really have said it in the first place."

"Tell us another one, then!" Merih insisted.

Mel smiled and shook her head. "I don't know many and the few I do know aren't very good. How about you tell one? I'm sure you know better ones than I do."

Merih grinned back. "Well, I do know a good one

about the day Anna Nicole Smith and Princess Diana arrived at the gates of Heaven for judgement. Heaven was full and St Peter said they only had space for one more..."

"Why is he staring at you? He shouldn't be staring at you like that. It's so rude..." Gabi hissed in Mel's ear.

Mel turned to see who Gabi was glaring at. Luce averted his eyes again, so she looked back at Gabi.

"Um, you have mayonnaise on your nose, Mel," Gabi whispered, handing her a serviette.

Mel wiped her nose carefully, wondering how long she'd been wearing her lunch on her face. She hoped it had just been the last, floppy lettuce leaf that did it.

"...and St Peter said, 'Well, a royal flush beats a pair any day!'" Merih finished.

Mel laughed right along with the demons as Gabi grumbled about how judgement didn't work that way and Heaven was never full.

"I have one," Luce said. The whole table fell silent. He pulled out his red handkerchief and laid it on the table. He glanced up at Mel. "It's about a magic carpet."

"A man walks into a Persian rug shop and asks the salesman for the best rug he has. The salesman grins and tells him that his best rug is in fact a magic carpet. All he has to do is sit on the carpet and say, 'Magic carpet, rise,' and the carpet will rise and fly him wherever he wants to go. They bargain for a while, but when both feel they have a good price, they agree and the man goes home with his Persian rug/magic carpet."

Luce looked up at Mel expectantly before he continued, "So, the man lays the carpet on the floor of his living room, sits down on it and says, 'Magic carpet, please rise.' Nothing happens. He tries sitting in different positions, standing on it, shouting at it, cajoling it – all to no avail. The rug just sits there, looking pretty on the floor.

"The next day, he's having a beer with friends, and one's an engineer for an international airline. They get to talking and he asks the engineer for help with his magic carpet. The friend agrees and comes over to see what he can do for the carpet.

"The engineer takes one look at it and says, 'No wonder it won't fly. It doesn't have any wings!' and he gives it wings."

Mel leaned forward to see Luce fold the handkerchief, as if he was starting to construct a paper plane. She wondered how handkerchief planes flew.

"After his friend left, the man sat on his carpet again, saying, 'Magic carpet, please rise.' Still nothing. Annoyed, upset, but not ready to give up yet, the next day he decides to go ask a mechanic for help. So, he loads the carpet into the car, takes it to his mechanic and shows him the carpet.

"The mechanic looks at the carpet, the same way he looks at the man's car when it's going to cost a lot of money to fix, and finally says, 'Of course it can't fly. It doesn't have an engine!" So, the mechanic puts an engine on the carpet."

Luce folded the handkerchief again, tucking part of it underneath the rest, so it didn't look like a paper plane at all. He caught Mel's eye and winked. Intrigued, she crossed her arms and gave a slight nod, inviting him to continue.

"He pays the mechanic and takes his carpet home again. He lays it out on the floor, hops on, and says, 'Magic carpet, please rise.'" Luce paused for effect. "And…nothing. The carpet just sits there, looking like an ordinary Persian rug, with wings and an engine. Angry, he loads the carpet into his car, determined to take it back to the shop to get his money back.

"On his way back to the rug shop, he drives through the red light district, and the girls are out on the street, looking for customers. He has to stop at an intersection and a girl wearing not much at all leans into his open window, offering to cheer him up for a price.

"Feeling like it's the best thing that's happened to him all week, he agrees and he takes her back to his place. She notices the carpet and asks about it.

"He replies, 'It's supposed to be a magic carpet, but it doesn't matter what I do. It just won't rise!'

"The prostitute laughs and says, 'Baby, trust me, I can make anything rise.' So she gets her hands on the carpet and…"

Mel looked at the red origami penis rising in front of Luce and burst out laughing. The demons were strangely silent.

Luce gave Mel a cheeky grin. "Glad you like it."

The other demons took this as their cue that the joke was over and it was time to laugh, but Luce's eyes locked on Mel's and he seemed not to notice the others at all.

"I need a coffee," Gabi announced, shoving away from the table. The force of her push toppled Mel's wineglass over – right into her lap.

Gabi hunted around the table for a spare napkin to mop up the mess, but the napkins seemed to be gone. Mel rose and attempted to wring some of the wine out of her soaked skirt, hoping it wouldn't hurt the grass.

Luce stood, too, giving his ruddy penis a flick so it hung limp, an ordinary handkerchief once more, before holding it out to Mel. "Please," he offered.

Mel took the handkerchief, to the combined gasps of Gabi and the other demons, and used it to mop the moisture from her skirt.

Mel felt Gabi's hand close on her arm. Gabi was so agitated, her soul felt like a violently shaken snow globe: a blizzard of white with glimpses of colour. "Give it back," Gabi hissed, digging her nails in. "We'll go get napkins from the café."

Mel held out the well-used hanky, inclining her head to Luce. "Thank you."

He winked again. "Any time."

Gabi's grip tightened further as she almost dragged Mel away from Luce and the other demons, marching as fast as her legs could carry her. She looked close to tears. "That was Lucifer. The infernal Lord of Hell. In perhaps the sexiest body I've ever seen him in. And you…you took his dick and wiped your wet patches with it. Are you trying to tempt him to taint you? He's the most dangerous demon there is!"

"Relax. It was just a joke, Gabi, and it was a handkerchief, not the man's genitals. I'm hardly in danger from him," Mel tried to tell her, but Gabi seemed to be muttering under her breath, so she probably didn't hear.

Privately, Mel wondered what Gabi would say if she told her she'd touched more than Luce's suggestive handkerchief today. She didn't want the demon's body — she wanted his stormy soul.

"We should go back to the agency office. Raphael requisitioned a team of surveillance angels — Grigori — and those guys look like the best in the business. Living Greek statues, the lot of them, and they obey orders like you wouldn't believe. Tell Raphael you need one for the weekend. You take your pick of the Grigori boys and…well, once you're done, that demon's hot body won't work on you. You should never go up against demons without making sure there's no desire for temptation…"

Mel burst out laughing. "Gabi, I'm not using any of the agency staff as sex toys."

Gabi looked hurt. "Not sex toys. A willing partner who'd do anything for you…"

"Gabi, have I ever told you about my friend, Patrick?" Mel asked carefully. She waited for Gabi's head-shake before she continued, "A few weeks ago, when I was in Colombo, I ran into him. I think I have a couple of photos we took on our wahoo cruise…"

Mel heard a clink and noticed the stolen salt and pepper shakers in Gabi's pocket. Gabi was certainly a conscientious angel today. Mel wondered how the barbeque would have ended had Gabi not been there.

She'd enjoyed the break over Christmas and New Year, but it looked like the peace was over. Protesters were camped out in front of Mel's office building again. Sighing, she slipped past them and wondered what the problem was this time. They looked like environmentalists – she could see very few shoes among any of them. There were plenty of placards and even one poor person in what looked like a black bird suit. Mel hoped he didn't get heatstroke in the hot weather that was forecast for the day – perhaps he'd head home before that happened.

She wished the security guard a good morning before she stepped into the lift. She could see him shaking his head at the strangely dressed protesters as the steel doors slid shut.

Reaching her desk, Mel flicked on the power to her PC and debated whether to take one of her tisane tea bags or if she'd need the buzz of a coffee.

Lili appeared. "Ah, Mel — you're needed over in Regulation. Zaq has some protesters causing trouble, so his report suddenly became a lot more urgent to the Minister. Something about cockies or corellas or kookaburras — ah, birds, anyway. Go find out what he needs done."

Mel nodded. "Sure." She set off in the vague direction Lili had waved toward. Her drink decision could wait until she worked out what her workload would be.

Thanks to the nameplate by his desk, Mel found Zaq, a stressed-looking demon who didn't even look up as she stood beside him.

She waited, watching him grit his teeth and tap the keyboard for almost a full minute before he grunted, "I'm busy. Go away."

Mel smiled. "I'm Mel and I'm here to help. I believe you have a protester problem?" She pulled out the visitor chair and perched on the edge of it.

"No, they're not a problem. They just don't like the airport expansion project we approved last week." He shoved a report at Mel.

Mel took the booklet and glanced at the cover. It wasn't the international airport – it was the one for small planes, not far south of her house. "I thought they were already so busy that the state government's trying to move them somewhere else," she said. "Why do they want more traffic?"

Zaq shook his head irritably. "They don't. They want to stop the traffic jams on the tarmac, waiting to take off. And then there are the flight schools…"

"There are flight schools there? I had no idea…" Mel marvelled.

"Sure. A couple of really big international airlines have their flight schools at Cockburn. Or they did. One of the accommodation blocks was lost in a bushfire last week."

"Oh, how awful! I hope no one was hurt."

"Only the guy cleaning the barbeque. He was looking for a hose and the only one in the courtyard belonged to the wastewater treatment system – the gardener occasionally used the water on the lawns. Anyway, it was curry night in the cafeteria two days before and the tank was pretty full, so he opened the tap. The septic tank was under a fair bit of pressure, so some of the air escaped and the hotplate was still on. The methane hit the flame and…well, the explosion took out half the accommodation block and the adjacent shower block. Left a big crater, too. The student was lucky – we think the sewage sludge saved him from the worst of the burns. They had to pump his stomach, though, because they think he swallowed some of it..." Zaq chortled. "That's when the shit really hit the fan. Turns out there were disused aviation fuel tanks under the dorms and maybe a plane or two, as well. The whole lot went up, just under the air conditioning units for the other accommodation block. Until they get the mess remediated – and best estimate is two or three years for that – they need new accommodation built quickly. The airline's insisting it can only go on land that the airport can guarantee isn't contaminated, which pretty much only leaves them the virgin bushland buffer. So those old trees have to go." He shrugged.

"Ah, so the protesters are upset about the loss of the trees?" Mel asked.

Zaq snorted. "Only because they think some endangered cockatoos need them. Someone should tell the protesters that any cockatoo in an airport is endangered until it's dead. Should've called it Cocky-burn Airport. It's the busiest airport in Australia – a quarter of a million takeoffs and landings every year. The cockies don't need the trees. The airport had experts come in to do surveys. They said it was too far north for the cockies, but they agreed to plant some trees to replace these, just in case someone got upset. So, no worries!"

Mel wet her lips. "So, what exactly is the Minister worried about, that he's putting you under so much pressure?"

"He needs a presentation that he can deliver to the press conference tomorrow, with briefing notes on the cockies. You know how to use PowerPoint?" Zaq eyed her critically.

"Sure," Mel replied, hoping he wasn't thinking about Luce's end-of-year presentation. "So all the info I need is in this report?"

"Yep," he said. "The expert reports are in the file on the network. I'll email you the link now. What's your login?"

Mel grimaced. "Melody Angel."

"That's a weird name for a…" He stopped. "Are you an agency girl?"

Mel nodded swiftly. "Yes, I'm from the Helpful Angels Agency."

Zaq's eyes narrowed. "Are you sure? You're not like the others. Even the boys in Legal…they have that 'I'm-better-than-you-and-I-know-it' air to them. You seem almost normal – like a human or something. I guess you haven't been an angel for long enough to get a trumpet up your arse or whatever makes them so stiff."

Mel laughed. "No, nothing musical in me at all. Just the name."

"And your voice," he said immediately, then blushed. He stared into his lap as he continued, "So, can you get that presentation to me by the end of the day?"

"Sure," Mel said. She brandished the booklet. "Cockies, here I come!"

"I see why Lord…I mean, Luce recommended you," Zaq said.

Mel stopped dead, then proceeded cautiously with, "Lord Lucifer recommended me for this project? Why?"

"He said you were the best assistant he'd ever had for a presentation and to beg Lili to let me have you," Zaq mumbled to his lap.

Mel tried hard not to laugh. "You had to beg Lili for me? I bet she liked that."

Zaq laughed, lifting his head so he could look at Mel again. "Better you than her. Will you help me with the presentation? I'm terrible at them."

"Of course. Helping people is what angels do," she responded with one final smile, before turning to go.

Lord Lucifer, she mused. So it was true and Gabi was right. Luce was the Lord of Hell. She'd expected him to be darker inside, to be honest, but she only knew what she'd heard of the demon – Mel had never spoken to him before she'd set foot in the HELL Corporation offices. He just didn't seem as dangerous as Raphael and everyone else had warned her.

Ah, he was known as an expert in deception – perhaps he was capable of using that demonic deception on her, Mel decided.

She carried the report to her desk and swapped it for her mug. A tisane today – preparing a presentation on birds sounded like fun.

Mel was almost done with the presentation, which was full of pretty pictures of planes and the wildlife that did live at the airport, including some unusual orchids they seemed to be going to great lengths to protect. She couldn't work out how one of them could be called a praying virgin orchid – it looked more like a bird bending over to drink.

After checking the brief summary on the cockatoos in the report, Mel decided she needed more detail. She dug the expert's report out of her email and took a sip from her second cup of tea. It looked like he'd done a complete biological survey, counting birds, snakes, lizards and even moths.

Mel headed downstairs to pick up some lunch so she could eat while she read the lengthy report. She glanced at her phone and noticed the missed calls from earlier that morning. Raphael had some urgent issue again, she saw – three calls and a misspelled text message told her so. Alone in the lift, she dialled and held her phone to her ear.

Mel only waited for Persi's greeting before interrupting the girl to ask for Raphael. Persi's switchboard skills had improved – she managed to put the call through to Raphael on her first attempt.

"Why the barrage of messages?" Mel asked.

"Where are you? It sounds noisy. Can you come to the office this afternoon? I'd prefer not to be overheard," Raphael said.

"That's all? You want to see me? If you want privacy, come to my place. I'm cooking tonight – I'll make sure there's enough for you. I'll pick up fresh mushrooms on my way home for the risotto, if you bring some wine. I'll probably use all of mine in the cooking."

She stood in front of the Yummi sandwich shop and counted. As she expected, she didn't get past three before he said, "All right. What time?"

"Make it seven, just in case I get caught up at work," Mel replied. A Turkish bread caught her eye. Chicken, pumpkin, feta, baby spinach…her stomach rumbled its agreement.

Raphael agreed and they ended the call. Mel slipped her phone back into her pocket, caught the shop assistant's eye and claimed her sandwich. She waited while it toasted and carried the hot, papered bundle upstairs, her mouth watering all the way.

With every delicious bite, she learned more about the birds the biologist called forest red-tailed black cockatoos. He stated three times that the birds were native to the southern part of the state and rarely appeared on the Swan Coastal Plain, which Mel knew was where she stood. She paused in her reading to pop a few cockatoo facts into the presentation, including the expert's adamant statement that the birds didn't live, eat, sleep or breed at the airport.

She skimmed the rest of the report, hoping she'd see more pictures of the wildlife the eminent doctor and his team had encountered during their survey. She admired the pretty pictures of the tawny frogmouth and the legless lizard that looked like a snake, before opening to a large spread on cockatoos.

She was arrested by the detailed pictures of a small flock of the black birds. They seemed to hang effortlessly in the air, not a single one flapping its wings when the shot was taken. She counted them – nine, no, ten of the birds. Another shot showed the same birds soaring in front of a building that looked suspiciously like an airport control tower. She looked more closely –

it definitely did look like the blocky tower at Cockburn. The caption beneath confirmed it.

So much for the cockatoos never coming to the airport. Perhaps they were holidaying – without eating, sleeping or breeding, she mused. The biologist dismissed them as an unusual occurrence – ten birds was hardly a viable population – and they'd never been seen before the 2009 survey. He considered it unlikely that they'd return, especially with the trees removed. They'd most likely move on to better places to feed, breed and whatever else they did in between.

Mel finished her lunch and her presentation before emailing the link to Zaq. She headed for his desk to ask if he needed any more assistance before she left for the day, and found him avidly reviewing her work.

He glanced up as she approached, but his eyes drifted back to the screen. "I love it! This is perfect," he gushed. "I know why Lord Lucifer's so in love with you. I'm more than halfway there myself. You're an absolute angel!"

Mel carefully kept her face blank as she considered his strange choice of words. Demons didn't – couldn't – love. It was against their very nature to do such a thing. Even the thought of a demon fancying himself in love with an angel was a crazy concept. Zaq must be more overworked than he appeared. "Well, that's what I am," she said.

"I owe you dinner. What are you doing tonight?" Zaq asked. His eyes shone with a fervour that Mel might have called lust, then amended it to excitement. He was staring at her face, after all, and not the rest of her body.

"I already have plans," Mel said gently. "I'm having dinner with a friend of mine tonight."

"Oh." The light in his eyes died, but then a tiny spark kindled again. "I still owe you one. If you ever need a favour, anything at all, just let me know. I'm your man." He grabbed her hand and kissed it.

Just like Luce – no sparks, no electricity.

The momentary contact was all Mel needed to see the man's soul – or the darkness surrounding it. His was a deep, velvety black – so dense she couldn't pierce the shroud at all. He may as well have had no soul, for all she could perceive. Yet the darkness seemed to be stretching, as if some tidal force dragged it toward her. Shaken, she pulled her hand out of his grasp.

Mel heard Zaq's mumbled apologies and thanks as he blushed profusely, but she was too lost in her own thoughts to do more than acknowledge him with a nod as she headed back to her desk.

She dropped into her chair and tried to sort through her findings in her head. The CEO was a demon, the Lord Lucifer she'd been warned about more times than she could count. But his soul and its demonic shroud were lighter and less dense than those of the demons he commanded. Was he a demon at all? How could the ruler of Hell be anything but a demon? And this talk of demons and love. That she knew to be impossible.

Zaq's demonic soul-shroud had brooded with menace as she'd approached it for a closer look. Even the love in her soul had irritated it — love in a demon's soul would have the shroud attacking the soul it was supposed to protect. A cold soul, untouched by any outward emotion, locked in with itself. So lonely...was that why Luce had allowed her in?

HOW had Luce allowed her in?

The calendar on her computer trilled, telling her it was time to go home, so Mel shook the strange thoughts from her head and packed her bag to go. She powered down her computer, shouldered her bag and strode out. She needed to get this new information straight in her head before she shared it with Raphael. It wouldn't do to be uncertain — Raphael shied from risks, and letting her get this close to Luce looked like the biggest one he'd taken in a long time.

Time to catch the train, she reminded herself. Then get the best mushrooms and start dinner. Mushroom risotto was enough to make her night — and tonight she'd get to share the pleasure. What more could an angel ask for?

It never ceased to amaze Mel how the crowd on the train could disperse so quickly once they'd left the station. It was less than a hundred metres from the station platform to the other side of the road, yet a hundred people were reduced to two – and then, just one, as Mel's fellow passenger disappeared down a side street.

She crossed the tiny park, where a dozen residents seemed to be exercising their diminutive, yappy dogs and casting dirty looks at the family who were playing with their golden retriever. Perhaps it was because the retriever's size and bark dwarfed their precious pets into insignificance. Actually, the fat tabby cat regarding the animals warily from a nearby fence was bigger than most of them.

Mel stumbled over a pile of gumnuts in the grass, only just catching herself before she fell. It looked like someone had stripped the little marri tree of its nuts and just left them lying there. All the nuts looked strange, though, as if someone had shredded the flared end of them with a sharp pair of pliers.

A nut landed beside her foot, so mangled that only a shallow bowl was left of it. Mel looked up in time to see a large, black bird spread its wings and soar, kaa-raaking as it fanned out the bright red feathers in his tail. He settled in another tree a few metres away and selected a nut, delicately holding it in one claw as he attacked it with the sharp tool that was its beak.

Another raucous call sounded from the other side of the tree, but Mel couldn't see the second bird. She kept walking.

She paused to wait for traffic before crossing the road to the tiny strip of local shops. A chorus of kaaa-raaks was all the warning she had before the birds skimmed over her, all ten...no, eleven of them, Mel counted. Solid red fans and striped red-and-yellow tail fans, marking them as both males and females. Six females. They rode the sea breeze erratically – some sideways, some so close to the road that a car almost hit one before it lazily flapped and rose above the ute's roof and roll bar.

Perhaps the biologist had miscounted the cockies or his photos hadn't captured the whole flock, Mel reasoned. She threaded through the parked cars to the grocer's, loaded a bag with their award-winning mushrooms – as proclaimed by the row of Royal Show ribbons pinned to the wall above the mushie fridge – and added a small box of shaved parmesan. With her arms full of food, Mel headed for the counter to pay for her purchases. After an exchange of money and pleasant words, Mel tucked her purchases into her canvas shopping bag and headed for the small supermarket next door.

She stopped at their display of garden and pet supplies, spread across two shelving units on either side of the doors. 'Your garden can never have enough sun,' proclaimed one sign, illustrated with a line drawing of the harsh summer sun beating down on a line of daisy-like flowers. Beneath it was a shelf stacked with bags of sunflower seeds.

Mel considered the sign for a moment, then gave in. It would be lovely to have the gold flowers adorning her garden bed along the fence – and she'd probably be in the house long enough to enjoy them. At least working in HELL had some compensations. She slung a bag of seeds over her arm and headed into the shop in search of rice and pine nuts.

Her arms weighed down by two well-matched

shopping bags, Mel left the shopping centre for the trek up the hill to her house. The cockies looked like they'd preceded her – they were making a racket and dropping gumnuts from the tree on her neighbour's lawn when she unlocked her front door.

Dropping her food purchases on the kitchen bench, Mel hefted the bag of sunflower seeds and took it out to the backyard, placing it carefully on her little outdoor setting table. She'd scatter the seeds in the morning – tonight, she had dinner to prepare for herself and Raphael. She hoped he wouldn't forget the wine, for it looked like she barely had enough for the risotto and it didn't taste the same without it.

Placing her largest pan on the stove, she crossed to the stereo for a little cooking music. Beethoven today, she decided. The CD that started with his Ninth…Mel waited for the cellos to start before she headed back to the kitchen.

Humming along, she washed and sliced the mushrooms, then heated a little oil in the pan. She tipped what had to be a whole kilo of mushrooms onto the hot metal, stirring it distractedly with a spatula. It seemed like only yesterday that she'd first heard this played in Vienna. Ah, the quality from the CD simply wasn't the same, but that wasn't a reflection on the musicians – merely her old speakers. Perhaps she should get some new speakers and transfer the music to her phone or her laptop…

Mel switched the stove off and heard a strange

sound that definitely wasn't Beethoven. She glanced out the kitchen window and saw far more black than should be in her backyard. Oh, no…

Sunflower seeds were everywhere, the plastic packaging ripped open by a combination of beak and talon. The birds were perched on her back fence, as well as on the backs of her garden chairs. One was waddling through the mess of seeds spread across her outdoor table. It keeked at her before picking up a seed and cracking it with its beak.

Mel stood on the back step, not entirely sure what to do. All eleven cockatoos had decided to come to her place and they evidently liked sunflower seeds. The female one on the table – the one who looked smaller and lighter-coloured than the rest – keeked at her again and the female perched on her garden chair kaa-raaked in response. Mum and her baby, most likely, which would make the male eyeing her from the other garden chair Dad…

Of course they didn't breed or feed at the airport. They seemed to be doing it in her backyard and probably the bushland nearby.

Well, it's not as if she needed sunflowers, Mel decided. The red-tailed birds were a noisy and colourful addition to her garden – plus, they didn't need watering, what with the lake at the bottom of the hill. She resolved to sweep up the mess in the morning, when they were done, before she bought them some more seeds to entice them back.

Mel headed back inside and started on the rice. More oil, some spring onions, rice, wine and stock…Beethoven's Ninth gave way to his Fifth.

"That smells like Heaven," said a male voice. Mel smiled. Light fingers landed on her shoulder, followed by whisper-soft lips on her cheek. "Or maybe it's you."

"Good to see you, Raphael. Could you pass me that other carton of stock? I figure this'll be done in about fifteen minutes…" She pointed and he complied.

"I'll get some glasses and open the wine, then?" Raphael suggested, reaching for the cupboard above the bench and surveying the small selection of glassware. He didn't wait for an answer and Mel trusted his judgement.

Over the sizzle of the pan in her hands, Mel heard the sounds of bottle opening and liquid glugging into glass. Raphael passed her a glass of chilled white. "In honour of a job well done," he murmured, clinking his drink against hers before he took a mouthful.

Mel sipped cautiously, rolling the creamy blend around her mouth before swallowing. "I didn't think you had any of this left. Age has only improved it, too…" She took a larger sip. "The job's not over yet."

Raphael gulped down more wine, as if steeling himself for a painful task. "Your part in it's almost over."

"Oh?" Mel smiled as she tipped the mushrooms into the pan with her cooked rice. The liquid hissed into steam as it hit the hot metal. She sprinkled pine nuts on top.

"Gabi told me about the picnic."

"There were sausages and salad, some lovely rolls that she bought and I shared with the swans, plus a few bottles of wine. The demons told dirty jokes and one of them scared her by stealing something. It was a HELL Corporation event. I could hardly invite you, Raphael." She kept her eyes on dinner as she stirred.

"She said there's no doubt. Their CEO is Lucifer. And she told me he wouldn't leave you alone – spent the whole time trying to charm you, while you encouraged him!" He sucked in a breath, trying to bring his voice down. "Please, Mel…we have to get you out of there quickly. If he's starting to take a personal interest in you, best you leave before he finds out anything about you."

Mel switched the stove off. "He's lonely, Raphael. Luce likes office girls and he's looking for someone willing to listen to him for more than five minutes. Yes, he evidently likes me. I listen because I want to hear what he has to say. Once you get past his brand of sleazy, he says a whole lot more than he should. What better way to find out what his plans are than to ask him and let him tell me in detail? You're making this out to be much harder and more dangerous than it really is." She pulled a serving spoon from the drawer and started dishing up.

"So you're saying someone less qualified than you could do this? If all he's after is a bit of friendly companionship, someone to smile and nod as he spills all his secrets...your job really is done." Raphael watched Mel sprinkle shredded parmesan on top of their dinner. He looked like he wanted to rip the bowl from under her hands, he seemed so eager.

Mel handed him his plate to hide her hesitation. "Maybe," she said finally. "They'd need a good memory and they'd need to be willing to get closer to him than most angels would. Up to and including sex, perhaps, if you want this wrapped up quickly. I don't know many angels who'd be willing to let Lucifer touch them, let alone make him think they like it..." She stopped at the sight of Raphael's fierce grin. "Who do you have in mind?"

"Persi," he said. "She's not an angel yet, but she's looking for a way to prove herself so that she can be. She's not averse to using her body to get what she wants…remember that motorcycle gang she took on, whose leader was possessed by a demon?"

"I remember," Mel replied, hiding her smile. Persi had come out of that with a penchant for ink and some very creative tattoos. The girl had shown her, too – an ornate halo that only her suitors or a midwife would ever see, surrounded by a montage of kneeling men that spread across her thighs and seemed to be creeping up her back. The artwork reminded Mel of Luca Signorelli and she wouldn't have been surprised if Persi had given the tattoo artist pictures from Orvieto Cathedral to copy. The faces of the damned were decidedly modern, though – and Mel was certain she'd recognised a couple of the bikies amid the crush of flesh. From the little she knew of Luce, he'd probably appreciate the artwork more than most. Perhaps it would even remind him of home. "You're right, she wouldn't shrink away from touching Lucifer. Quite the opposite…"

Raphael smiled happily. "So you agree – Persi's perfect for this. All we have to do is find a place for her in the office, where she can get close to the CEO, and you can bow out safely. No worries!"

Mel almost choked on her first mouthful. Anything involving Persi was hardly without worry. She swallowed, recovered, and replied, "She's still very inexperienced and that puts her in far more danger than I am in her place. Luce might spot that and exploit it. I'd feel terrible, having to tell her mother that we'd thrown Persi into Hell as cannon fodder to protect me. Give me a few more weeks, Raphael, while you try to find somewhere to slip her into the corporation. And don't place her anywhere that needs switchboard skills. She can't transfer calls to save her life!"

Raphael nodded, his mouth full of food. Mel had never seen him eat anything so fast. "Okay. It'll take me that long to find a vacant place to put her forward for. Tell me if anyone's secretary or PA is going on holiday. That'd be the easiest way to get her in..." He shovelled another large forkful of risotto into his face.

Mel was barely a quarter of her way through her food when Raphael jumped up to take his empty bowl to the sink. "I'll get changed in your spare bedroom, if that's okay. Do you want me to help you wash up, or do you mind if I eat and run?" he asked.

"I can take care of the dishes this time," Mel replied. "Why, do you have a date?" She smiled, recognising his eager excitement.

Raphael turned red. "I have a meeting in Heaven and I thought I'd dress up for the occasion..." He gestured at the shirt he'd hung over Mel's lampshade — one of his sexier ones, she was sure of it.

"Sure. Pop your business clothes in the laundry basket — I'll take care of them when I do my next load of washing. I think I still have a couple of your shirts in the guest room, from the other times you've popped in on your way through to Heaven." She leaned forward and kissed his cheek. "Tell my brother I said hello and give him a kiss for me."

Raphael's cheeks flushed redder still as he beat a hasty retreat to Mel's guest room. Mel wondered how much longer it would take before Raphael and her brother admitted the truth — and who would be the one to tell her.

I love Valentine's Day, thought Mel. It makes you think…

"I hate Valentine's Day," an annoyed voice began behind her. "Having to buy flowers and a present, this big commercial thing…and you know she expects it…"

"I'd like to make something for her for Valentine's Day, you know, kind of personal," another male voice replied.

"But would she like that?" the annoyed voice countered.

"Well, she'd have to say that, because she'd sound really shallow if she didn't, but she really wants something bought..."

He laughed. "I like that I can just buy flowers and chocolates and things, it's so much easier. Have you tried to get a restaurant booking?"

Now both of them were laughing. "Valentine's Day and Chinese New Year in the same week? I'd never get a table! We'll be having dinner at home tonight. I hate going out for dinner on Valentine's Day, it's always so crowded, expensive and romantic. " He made romantic sound like the worst adjective of the three. Mel ducked her head to hide her smile.

"Yeah, mate, me too. Who wants to go out to dinner on Valentine's Day?"

Mel thought that she'd enjoy it, to be among so many happy couples, celebrating their love together. The atmosphere could be absolutely blissful. Still, she'd never be able to enjoy her meal, knowing that her table could have been occupied by another couple instead of her self-indulgent self, so tonight she planned to stay home, too. But first, they all had a full day's work to do before that could happen.

The train stopped and Mel turned, recognising the shirts the men wore, marking the men as employees of a consulting firm in the building across the road from the HELL Corporation. She couldn't recall what the company did – its logo featured the same mysterious combination of three letters that most such companies had. The crowd of commuters leaving the train soon separated her from the two anti-valentines and she exhaled her relief.

It was hot already, so she kept to the shaded walkways for her stroll to the office. Beneath the glass ceiling on the plaza, someone had hung red lanterns to celebrate the start of the Year of the Snake. Below the lanterns, a florist had placed a huge display of red roses. "Only $99, a dozen roses delivered to YOUR Valentine!" said the sign painted on the window.

Mel walked past the florist. Something smelled beautiful and it sure wasn't the phalanx of red flowers. She entered the shop and the scent mystery was solved. She waited patiently for service from the angry florist and her stressed assistant.

"Why did you order so many Asiatics? No one wants Asiatics for Valentine's Day — everyone wants red roses! Now we won't have space in the fridge for what we really need!" The florist's face was growing as red as the flowers she was shoving into the refrigerator. "And chocolates — how could you order gold hearts when everyone wants red? We'll never sell these and they'll melt out of the fridge in this heat!"

The assistant looked about fifteen and ready to cry. "I didn't...you told me..." She proffered an order pad, pointing at handwriting that looked too old to be hers. "What do I do with the liliums?"

"Put them out on sale! If we can't sell them at four o'clock to the desperate men who forgot to order roses, you can throw them in the bin!"

Mel stepped up to the counter. "How much for the liliums?" The smell of them was tantalising. It had been so long since she'd had any.

The assistant looked at the florist, who didn't deign to reply. "O-on sssale today. Twenty dollars a bunch."

Mel smiled. "How about those chocolates?"

"Cost price plus GST," the florist said, her eyes showing her eagerness. "Thirty-three dollars."

Mel held out her Visa card. "Can you make up a large bunch of three of these, along with the chocolates, please?"

"Yes, ma'am," the assistant replied, trying to hide her smile from the florist as she made Mel's flowers as pretty as possible with pink paper and ribbon.

Five minutes later, her nose buried in the unearthly scent of her enormous bunch of liliums, Mel carried her flowers and chocolates into the office.

"Wow," said Lili as Mel passed her. "Who are they from?"

"An admirer," Mel replied. An admirer of Asiatic liliums who couldn't walk past them, she thought but didn't say.

Mel placed her flowers in a vase on her desk by the window, where she could smell and admire them all day. She took a pair of scissors to the large box of chocolates, so they were easy to reach in their display tub.

This was her favourite part.

"Good morning, happy Valentine's Day!" she sang out, handing chocolates to all of her colleagues, or placing them on the keyboards and mouse mats of those staff who weren't in yet. "Happy Valentine's

Day…"

"Thank you," said Lili, looking stunned. "This is the only Valentine's present I've had in years."

"Thank you," said Merih.

"Happy Valentine's Day!" replied Gerry.

"OH!" gasped Nybbas, turning red as he lost his ability for coherent speech.

Mephi smiled at Mel – the first such smile Mel had seen. "That's really lovely of you, dear. My husband doesn't even know what day it is."

Mel's smile wobbled with sympathy. What kind of life would it be, to live as a demon without love? She could barely imagine it. Wavering, she debated whether to give chocolate to the CEO, too. No one could be as lonely as Luce, the head demon himself, lusty looks and all. Perhaps she could just leave it with Mephi or on his desk. "Can you tell me if Luce is in?" Mel asked, peeking into the demon's office.

"He's at a meeting, but he'll be back shortly. Why? Did you want to see him about something, dear?" Mephi asked. "If you do, I'll be happy to slip you into his schedule. Just let me know and I'll arrange it." She winked.

"Ah, no, but thank you," Mel said quickly. "I just thought I should leave him a chocolate, too. In the interest of fairness…" She hurried to his desk, placed the gold heart on his mouse mat, then escaped before he returned.

With a considerably lighter tub of chocolates, Mel

returned to her desk. She unwrapped one of the gold foil hearts for herself. It wasn't like the foil colour made a difference to the taste, she thought, as the high-quality chocolate hit her tongue. She decided to have another one.

Gabi bounced into Mel's office. Mortified at missing her fellow angel from Reception, Mel offered the girl her pick of the chocolates. Gabi took several with a smile of thanks as she announced, "You have a delivery!"

Behind her, a courier struggled under an awkward armload of boxes. "Melody Angel?"

Mel cringed inwardly at her full name, but smiled and nodded. "That's me."

He carefully laid the boxes on the meeting table in the middle of the office. Heads rose above partitions, meerkat-style, turning toward her. "Sign here?"

Mel signed his electronic pad with one hand, reaching for a chocolate with the other. She handed them both to him. "Thank you."

He looked surprised.

Mel smiled. "Happy Valentine's Day. Call it a small thank you."

The courier left, looking somewhat bemused.

"Go on, open them!" Gabi urged, her eyes shining.

Mel cut the ribbon on the first long box. A dozen long-stemmed roses lay nestled in tissue paper, topped by red ribbon and a card. "From a secret admirer," the card read.

The other two boxes contained identical displays, only differing in the handwriting on the cards. Mel leaned over the boxes in hope, but she was disappointed. The long-stemmed roses didn't smell. What was the point of giving roses anymore? Florists' roses didn't smell. It was the scent in the oil that was an aphrodisiac. Mel sighed as she remembered receiving scented roses. It seemed so long ago…wait, no it wasn't. There was that rose from the mysterious, disappearing stranger. The mature, red, thorny one that had made her think about…

"So are you my Valentine?" Luce asked with a grin, appearing out of nowhere with a gold heart between his fingers.

Mel's heart sank. She'd so hoped not to see him, watching his eyes wander as he said his insincere thanks. Too late now.

"Mel's wonderful," Gabi gushed. "She brought chocolates for the whole office to share and she's been delivering them to everyone. So sweet of her!" Mel held her breath as Gabi held out her handful of hearts, making Luce's single one seem insignificant.

Lili stuck her head in the office. "Thanks again, Mel!" She shoved her chocolate between her teeth as she withdrew.

For the first time, Luce looked stunned. Mel wasn't sure if she wanted to laugh or cry at the demon's expression. He'd come in with such self-confidence and now he was crushed.

"I wasn't sure if I'd have enough for everyone, so I only gave people one each," Mel said quietly. "I'd be happy to give you more, if you'd like." She started to smile again. "But only if you don't tell everyone else. I'm not sure if I have enough for everyone to grab a whole handful like Gabi did."

Gabi stuck her tongue out, then unwrapped a chocolate and popped it into her mouth.

Luce's dark eyes stared at Mel as he held up his heart. "This is the first gift I've ever received for Valentine's Day. Thank you." His expression was all seriousness – but he appeared sincere for once, Mel thought.

"You're welcome," she said with equal sincerity. She let her lips lift in a slight smile as Luce's scrutiny continued. A lesser angel might have looked away, but Mel was more than a match for poor, lonely Luce. She felt her sense of pity awaken.

He glanced away.

"Whose are those?" Luce asked, nodding at the boxed flowers.

Gabi swallowed her chocolate with a gulp. "Mel's!" she said, appearing more excited than Mel.

"Really?" Luce asked, looking Mel up and down. "You're a popular lady!" He hurried away without another word.

"More for you, Mel!" Gabi sang out an hour later, interrupting Mel's lunchtime reading. She was quite growing to like the book about nephilim – the heroine reminded her strongly of Persi, with her penchant for shoes. She wondered if it was a distinctly nephilim quality or simply one Persi didn't share with the angelic half of her family heritage.

This time, Gabi held a large display box of orchids, in shades of fuchsia, gold and white. Mel picked up the card. "For my office angel, with compliments from a secret admirer," she read. She recognised Luce's handwriting, for his not-complimentary written rant was still clear in her mind.

Gabi didn't seem to want to leave. "Ohhhh, I love orchids," she cooed over the flowers. "Who sent you such beautiful ones?"

Mel caught sight of Luce, watching her avidly from a nearby cubicle. She turned her eyes to the flowers. "They're really lovely," she admitted. She leaned over to sniff these, too, but she could feel the chill in the petals as soon as she got close. Fresh from a florist's fridge, these wouldn't smell until they warmed a little. Disappointed, she just smiled at Gabi before going back to her project. She lost herself in looking for graphics for the unit's new phone app.

By the end of the day, Mel had moved both the orchids and the roses in their vases to the middle of the meeting table, where the whole office could admire the display. Only the liliums remained in the vase on her desk, still wrapped in paper, waiting for her to carry them home.

Her computer clock ticked over to knock-off time, so she shut it down and rose. She stared at the orchids for a moment, wondering whether to take them. Gabi liked them so much – she didn't want to deprive the girl of her favourite flowers. She bent and inhaled deeply, hoping to catch the scent of them to help her decide.

Nothing. The strongest smell came from the greenery surrounding the flowers.

With a sigh, she straightened again. They were so pretty, which almost made up for the lack of smell. Still, it would be near impossible to manage the box of orchids and the bunch of liliums on the train – and there was no way she was leaving her liliums behind.

She gathered her things and turned to go, her arms full of marbled pink and white blooms.

"Don't forget your flowers," Luce said, striding into the office. "You might drive one of your Valentines to despair by leaving his gift behind."

Mel smiled. "They're all from secret admirers. I thought we could all admire them here. Maybe having them on display will give some of the admirers the courage to admit who they are." Her eyes met Luce's and she knew the others would never say, for fear of his reaction. Poor Nybbas, Merih and Zaq. "I'll have my hands full on the train, anyway." She lifted her liliums up, so the divine scent wafted through the office again.

"I could give you a lift home, if you like, and help you carry all of these down to my car," Luce offered eagerly. "We could go out for dinner afterwards. I know this wonderful seafood restaurant, right on the water, which does the best oysters…"

"No, thank you," she said, edging past him. The last thing she needed was a demon – especially this demon – knowing her home address.

"Come on, Mel, you won't get a better offer than The Old Brewery. Fresh oysters, wagyu beef cooked to perfection, marron…the beautiful view over Melville

Water as the sun sets…and you'll be with me." His grin widened with each new temptation, as if he felt he was saving the best for last. Mel was sure that, in his opinion, this was the case.

"Actually, I have plans for dinner already," she admitted.

"Who with?" he asked. He may as well have asked for the details of a serial killer who needed to be put away for life, Mel thought, not liking his tone.

"With the person who bought my liliums," she said gently.

"The cheapest flowers the florist had," Luce scoffed. "You can do better than him. Stand him up – come out with me instead. I promise you'll enjoy it."

"The flowers with the most alluring scent that the florist had, making them more than just beautiful," Mel corrected. "From someone who knows they're my favourite because of their perfume. Someone who didn't need to hide behind the anonymous name of Valentine or admirer." She looked Luce firmly in the eye. "Good night, Luce. I hope you enjoy your evening and your oysters. See you at work tomorrow."

She strode out, not slowing her step until it had carried her into the train carriage and the doors slid shut behind her.

A kind man offered Mel his seat and she took it gratefully, balancing the flowers between her knees. She held her phone out and looked for a short story to help her pass the time on the train, having finished the nephilim book at lunch.

While she searched, she heard a familiar voice.

"So, did you get her present?" the annoyed anti-Valentine of the morning enquired.

"Yep, flowers, chocolates and some earrings," replied the other. "We're going out to dinner tonight, at that new teppanyaki grill at Nishi. You?"

"My missus booked us into Beethoven's, for their special Valentine's banquet," the now-more-stunned-than-annoyed voice replied. "Have you ever been there?"

"No, but I've heard it's good. Have fun, mate!"

Mel hid her smile behind her flowers. The two men who wouldn't go to restaurants had booked dinner at two of the more expensive establishments in the area, but she knew from experience that the prices at both were certainly worth it.

She found a short story competition with a Valentine's Day theme and settled in to read some of the entries. Romance, unusual gifts and her favourite day of the year, with flowers and chocolate to scintillate her senses as she forgot all about Luce and his devious demands.

She happily headed home, ordered a pizza and opened a bottle of wine to share with herself. Amid the scent of her favourite flowers, she thought of Luce, dining alone amid a multitude of couples, lonely with his oysters by the river. Once again, she pitied the demon and anyone else who couldn't enjoy a day that was about love – whoever you spent it with. Perhaps she should have joined him. He would have spent the whole time ogling her and missing out on the lovely atmosphere places only had on Valentine's Day.

Poor Luce. It must be so sad to be a demon on days like this.

Mel felt self-conscious as she stepped into the office. On the train, she'd been talking to a particularly talented artist who'd admitted to painting pictures inspired by the books she'd read and the discussion had turned to mermaids. What Mel hadn't said was that she knew for a fact that mermaids existed – and she'd met some. She and the demons could pass as humans among humans, but with mermaids it was a completely different story.

She dropped her bag on her desk, glancing at the big south window. Her computer was already on, which seemed strange.

"Good morning!" boomed a voice behind her. "What are you looking for?"

Spinning on the spot, Mel came face to face with a man she'd never met before. "I'm looking for my coffee cup, so I can have some caffeine before I check my emails," she replied uncertainly.

"Oh, were you the girl who borrowed my desk while I was away? I had your clutter moved to the desk by the fire escape, where it belongs." He dismissed her with a wave of his hand. "Try looking over there." He enthroned himself on what had been Mel's desk chair and ignored her as he placed his hand possessively over her former mouse.

Mel summoned a smile. "Thank you," she said as she left the bright shared office to return to the cramped, dark desk by the fire escape.

Gabi was waiting for her with a box full of Mel's belongings, the box of orchids balanced precariously on top. As soon as she saw Mel, her expression turned from bewildered to sad. "Mel, some new man told me I had to pack up all your things and move them. I didn't know what else to do – you weren't here and neither was Lili…"

Mel was calm and collected. As temporary staff, even her desk was only a temporary arrangement. Today, she wouldn't have to worry about showing off her stockings to everyone on the plaza. She could wear skirts as short as she pleased. "No worries, Gabi. It was too bright by the big south window and the air conditioning couldn't cope with the sun coming in on hot days. Thanks for taking such good care of my things. Now, if the rumours I heard downstairs on my way in are correct, we're very well placed for…"

The fire alarm began to sound over the office PA system. Gabi's eyes widened. The beeping lengthened to whooping as Mel smiled. They were the first to evacuate via the fire escape stairs.

Standing in Central Park as all the other staff meandered in, Gabi said, "You'll have to take your angel orchids home. They won't survive without some sun."

Mel shrugged. "Cut flowers never last long, anyway. They were lovely while they lasted – much longer than the roses, at least."

Gabi's eyes grew round. "Your angel orchids aren't cut flowers. They're in a beautiful pot, with soil and everything. I've been watering them for you every week – it was the least I could do, in exchange for you sharing them with me. It was heavy, but I couldn't just leave them there!"

Live orchids. Luce had bought her a large pot of live…had she said angel orchids? "I've never taken care of orchids before," Mel admitted. "Aren't they meant to be really delicate? What kind are they? I'll have to look up detailed instructions on keeping them alive. I'd hate to kill them."

"They're moth orchids – but yours are a really rare angel colour-morph. I've only seen angel ones in fuchsia and pink, but yours are white with tinted lips and a delicate blush…it must be someone who knows you really well. And he must really like you – those are insanely expensive. Do you think it might have been one of the Grigori boys from the agency? I went down to watch them play football one lunchtime and they were the no-shirts side…" She blushed. "Well, if it weren't for Uri, I'd seriously consider a bit of fun with one of them. Those boys are built!"

Mel laughed. "No, I don't think they're from one of the agency angels, however well-built they might be. Wishful thinking, I'm sure – I don't blush anywhere near as much as you do."

"You should keep them in your bathroom, so you can admire them when you're all steamy in the shower," Gabi continued dreamily.

"What? The shirtless Grigori football team?" Mel tried to control her laughter. "They wouldn't fit in my tiny bathroom."

"No, your orchids. They like it warm and humid. I bet the guy who gave them to you would love to know his flowers share your shower every morning…"

Mel shook her head. "How long since you've seen Uri? Did you leave him in Russia?"

Gabi nodded sadly. "I haven't seen him in months. What with the next winter Olympics in Russia, he's worried and trying to keep an eye on everything. But I know I'll see him again eventually. It's you I'm worried about. How long since you've seen a man in all his naked glory?"

Mel opened her mouth to reply.

"Good to see you ladies made it out unscathed," Luce's voice came from behind her. He nodded to Mel and Gabi as he breezed past, grinning. "Don't forget the Minister's visit later on this morning!"

Neither of them were likely to have any contact with the Minister – temporary staff were hardly going to be high on his list of people in the corporation to meet on his much-touted tour of the facility. Mel and Gabi didn't respond, letting Luce continue walking until he was out of earshot.

Hoping he hadn't heard their conversation, Mel's thoughts drifted to Luce's flowers and his Valentine dinner invitation. Perhaps she should have accepted, after all. The orchids had been a very kind gesture – more thoughtful than she'd given him credit for.

"See? I knew you couldn't remember," Gabi said. "Next time you're up at the agency, wink at one of the Grigori boys and take him home for the weekend. Share a shower with a man instead of just his flowers. I guarantee you'll be glowing come Monday morning."

She might do dinner with Luce, Mel decided, but sharing a shower with the demon? Hell, no! When this assignment was over, she'd socialise a little with the other agency angels and see what came of it, that's all. Or perhaps even pay Patrick a visit...

The red-hatted fire warden demons were signalling the all-clear, so Mel and Gabi started to move back to the office. The foyer was full of demons and humans, for there were still a few humans in the offices on the other floors. The lifts were leaving, packed with people.

"Mel," a voice hissed.

She saw a beckoning hand and followed it around the corner to the service lift, where an elderly security guard stood, smiling. "Care for a lift, Mel?"

She laughed and accepted, thanking him. Reaching her floor, she steeled herself for another day at work. Sitting next to the fire escape did have its benefits, even without a window, Mel mused.

Thanks to the quick-thinking security guard, Mel was one of the first people to return to the office after the fire and evacuation drill. That meant no queue for the coffee machine. Mel dug her mug out in readiness for the luxury of a real coffee while her computer started.

The milk stood in crates by the fridge, cascades of condensation dripping down the sides of the bottles, while a new box of coffee beans sat unopened by the machine. The delivery must have arrived just as the fire alarm sounded, so Mel decided to take advantage of the surplus to serve herself precisely what she wanted. She selected a double with a little extra froth to fill her mug, and watched the drink make itself.

Mel carried the steaming concoction back to her desk and set it down so she could start unpacking her belongings.

The orchids were first. She looked around for a suitable spot where they might get a little sun and still be out of her way. Mel temporarily settled for the top of her filing cabinet, swearing she'd take them home on the train that night – they didn't deserve to die on her dingy desk, displaced by the demon from their accustomed window.

Pens and papers were much easier to place – two minutes saw everything in order once more. Mel sat to start work. She took her first sip of coffee as she checked her emails.

The girl she'd been talking to earlier that morning had sent a link to some of her recent character artwork, the first email told Mel. Mel clicked on the link and waited patiently for the gallery to load.

"Here's my little angel! Minister, I'd like you to meet Mel, our miracle worker in averting alien invasions!" Luce's beaming face was the first thing Mel saw, with another be-suited man behind him.

Trying not to grit her teeth as she smiled, Mel stood and offered her hand to the newcomer, recognising the Minister for Productivity. He was the man who'd decided to start selling off government services, so the government of the day could fill what seemed to be a whole galaxy of budget black holes. Mel had always wondered whether giving government services to the Pit had been such a wise decision, but she'd never had the opportunity to ask the Minister his thoughts on the matter. Now was her chance.

She opened her mouth, trying to arrange the question carefully so she'd receive an answer.

"Wow! Isn't she a beauty?" the Minister exclaimed with a smile.

She closed her mouth quickly, wondering if the man was Luce's brother. Or his son. Or some close, salacious relation who Luce had trained in…

"You are a talented lady, aren't you, Mel? When did you paint that?" Luce asked, his eyes intent on Mel's monitor.

"I'd like a copy on the wall in my office!" the Minister declared.

"Oh, no, my friend did it. She just sent me a photo so I could see…" Mel trailed off, unsure how to introduce the subject of mermaid fact and fiction with a minister.

Both Luce and the Minister started walking away.

Mel sank gratefully into her chair, watching to make sure neither man was looking to return. Her computer had blacked out to her screensaver, so she nudged the mouse to wake it up. She almost spat out her coffee.

A beautiful blonde mermaid, her breasts on full display in glorious colours, beamed from Mel's screen.

She was, indeed, a beauty.

Never. She'd never agree to go to dinner with Luce, and she hoped never to lock eyes with the demon again. He'd seen naked mermaid pictures on her PC.

Mel felt her cheeks go well past pink, approaching the colour of those clearly visible nipples. "Oh Hell," she whimpered.

"Another report for Luce?" Mephi asked, glancing up from her magazine.

Mel nodded. "Yes. This one's on cemetery sustainability. Who'd have thought cremation was more environmentally friendly than burial? Not to mention cheaper in the long term. It's all there – along with the economic assessment. I have a lot of pictures from my facility tour, but I didn't put them all in. The crematorium waste looked like something you'd scrape out of a baking pan after making a pork roast with plenty of crackling…" She saw Mephi's face turn white and then pale green as she set what looked like barbeque pork and fried rice down on the desk. "Sorry. It surprised me, is all."

Mephi coughed and wiped her mouth with a tissue. "It sounds…fascinating. You can take it straight in to Luce's office – pop it on top of the pile in his in-tray. Do you want me to schedule an appointment with him so you can discuss it? I can squeeze you in any time this week, as long as you don't tell anyone else I did it. He'll be back from his meeting with the Minister in an hour or two."

"No, the whole thing's pretty self-explanatory. If he wants to know any more, we can always arrange a meeting later," Mel said, moving to deposit her report on Luce's desk. As she returned, she caught sight of what Mephi was reading. It wasn't a magazine at all – it was a travel brochure for Thailand. "Are you headed off on holiday?"

Mephi looked uncertain as she set the brochure down. "Part of the arrangements for working here include paid holiday leave for all staff. I've never taken a holiday before and I wanted to spend the time at a spa resort somewhere, where it's warm and I can just relax."

"You've never…" Mel's sympathy for demons flared up. "Thailand is lovely. So's Malaysia, and Singapore, and Indonesia…or there's Mauritius…and Sri Lanka."

"But my husband wants to go skiing – he wants to see snow and spend his time somewhere cold before he heads back to…where he normally works," Mephi wailed.

"Snow can be wonderful, too," Mel said. "Very pretty – and the ski resorts usually have lots of warm food, well-heated rooms and plenty to drink."

Mephi looked stricken. "He said that he'll go without me if I won't go to a ski resort, and he refuses to go anywhere near the tropics. Too hot for him, he said. We've never been on a holiday together and I was so hoping…" The demon looked close to tears.

"You could do both," Mel suggested.

"He can't stand the heat," Mephi replied sorrowfully.

Mel hesitated for a moment, then took pity on the demon. "How about a ski resort with hot spring spas? That way, he could ski while you relax, and in the evenings, perhaps you could share the spa…" She winked. "The hot water certainly gets the blood flowing, I've heard."

Mephi stared at her. "What would an angel know about…about…" She blushed.

Mel laughed easily. "My friend, Koyane, lives in Japan. When I visited him in '97, we spent some time in the hot springs around Kyoto and Nara and they proved quite steamy. I had some spare time, so he took me up to the Nagano region and showed me some of the natural hot springs, outside in the snow. There was this one little town…Nozawa Onsen, it's called. It's a ski resort, but it's named for the sulphur spring onsens. Between the apple ice wine, the hot springs, the snow and Koyane…well, I wasn't in a hurry to come home."

"Bob would like that, if there's skiing, and if there's some sort of spa for me…" Mephi looked wistful. "Is there anywhere you can recommend for us to stay?"

"Sure. There was this lovely traditional guesthouse, owned by a Japanese lady I met in an onsen. I was feeling ill because I'd had far too many shiitake with my soba…ah, you don't need to hear about that. Anyway, I can email the details of the place, if you like, and you and Bob can make your trip something of a second honeymoon. In the traditional guesthouses, the beds are all futons on tatami — wall-to-wall mattresses. More space than the average couple know what to do with. The honeymoon suites with their king-sized beds here don't know what they're missing…"

"It sounds wonderful," Mephi admitted. "Four weeks there sounds almost as good as going back to Heaven…"

"Oh — have you and…ah, Bob been together for that long?" Mel asked, trying to hide her surprise.

Mephi nodded. "We met before the battle and we sort of got together before the fighting started…" She blushed again. "When Lucifer fell, we refused to be parted and we weren't allowed back in." She sighed. "It was a long time ago and the fires then have sort of burned down to a dull glow, but I still remember what that first night was like. I'd give almost anything to have that again with Bob."

Mel couldn't hide the tears that sprang to her eyes.

Demons who still had the memory of a love that preceded their fall. Admittedly, it could hardly be more than lust now, but even that was something, after all this time. Who'd have thought that Mephistopheles and Beelzebub were even capable of love in the first place? Maybe there was hope for them, after all. "I'll go get their contact details and send them to you straight away," Mel promised and hurried away. First, she'd find the details of that ryokan for Mephi. Then, she'd call Raphael and tell him she had the perfect job for Persi — as Luce's PA. Serendipity, indeed.

"It's time for you to finish up in the office. Book your flights to Korea whenever you're ready. Persi got the job and she can clean up the last details," Raphael announced, rummaging through her cupboards. "Where do you keep your coffee?"

"I don't have any," Mel replied absently. "I drink more than enough at the office. What makes you think it's over?"

Raphael stared out the window, which Mel thought was definitely suspicious. "You've said Lucifer is looking for some female company. Persi's more than willing – she'll start as soon as his PA leaves the office. You can mentor her for a week or so, but it's time to pull you out of there before it gets too dangerous."

Mel snorted with laughter. "The office is dangerous? Raphael, they're just demons. I can handle myself just fine."

He whirled and met her eyes. "They're not just demons. It's an office full of demons led by Lucifer. Do you know how dangerous he can be? And he's paying a lot of attention to you – you've said it yourself." His fingers plucked nervously at his tie. Mel had never seen the man look so unsettled.

"I've managed to keep him at arm's length for this long, Raphael. I'd prefer to see this through personally, or I'll be worrying the whole time I'm in Korea. Persi isn't all that experienced and you don't seem to be so worried about Luce getting his hands on her."

"Please, Mel. None of us wants to see you in Hell – get out while you can. Let Persi finish this up, so you can stay safe."

Mel shook her head. "I still don't see how sacrificing Persi for my safety is acceptable. She's unpredictable and inexperienced, but she might make a good angel if she gets the chance. Sending her in as cannon fodder for Luce is a waste."

Raphael managed a weak grin. "She said the same thing – about wanting a chance. And this is it. I'm giving her a chance to prove she deserves to be an angel. It's what she wants, she said."

"I don't think…" Mel hesitated, then began again. "I realise she's eager to prove herself, but this is a Hell of a responsibility for someone like her. Even if I'm not in the office, I'm not leaving for Korea before her task is complete. I want you to make it clear that she's to call me if she has any news – good or bad – and if she needs even the slightest bit of help. Day or night. And I will be watching her, because I don't trust Lucifer."

Inwardly, she sighed. She still wanted his soul, but she'd have to wait and give Persephone her chance first. Luckily, she had eternity.

Mel took a bite of her sandwich. Time for lunch, she thought, wondering if she'd have time to start reading that story about a grumpy unicorn and a gunslinger. Mermaids might exist, but unicorns were definitely the stuff of fiction. Romancing a rhinoceros, really. Or like passing Persi off as an angel. Add a rider and… She pulled out her phone and started looking through her library.

"Ah, Mel?" Lili's head popped up over the partition. "You're not busy tonight, are you? There's a big executive meeting last thing this afternoon, to fit with the CEO's schedule, and Mephi's gone on leave. Could you stay to take the meeting minutes and write them up afterwards?"

Mel looked up from her phone. "Shouldn't it be one of the usual admin people in Executive, who know more about confidential, high-level stuff?"

Lili looked abashed. "Well, yes, but Mephi recommended you to Luce and he requested your services, so…"

Mel felt her lips curl in a customary smile. "Of course. I don't have plans tonight after work." Except eating dinner, she thought but kept to herself. "I'd be happy to help out. Does that mean I'll get time off in lieu of the extra hours, or do you just want me to put the hours on my timesheet as overtime?"

Lili shrugged. "Your call. I don't mind. Can you ring Mephi to tell her you'll do it?"

"Isn't Mephi away?" Mel asked, mystified.

"Yes, but there's some temp doing her job until she comes back. She'll be at Mephi's desk." Lili dismissed her and disappeared.

Mel picked up the phone and dialled Mephi's extension.

"Hello, HELL Corporation Executive. This is Persephone. How may I direct your call?" The breathless voice sounded like a child's. Mel envisaged pink, bubble gum and knee socks, carefully camouflaging what she knew to be a very naughty tattoo, framed in black lace. If Persi remembered to wear underwear at all, Mel mused, recalling one incident in the US where Persi had refused to wear something Americans called panties, to the delight of the media crew. She hoped Persi could do a better job this time. This was too delicate a task to leave details hanging in the wind.

Mel took a deep breath. "Persi? It's Mel. Just calling to say I'll be taking the minutes at the executive meeting this afternoon."

"Oh!" Persi squeaked, giggling. "I'm so nervous! I've never had so much responsibility – personal assistant to a CEO and all. He's so attractive, too…"

Mel smothered a smile. "Sounds like you're doing fine, Persi. Can you tell Luce for me, please?"

"Oh…oh, sure!" Persi bubbled. "One second…sir! Miss Angel has confirmed that she will be available to attend the executive meeting!" She sounded like she was going to burst with excitement.

"Can you transfer her through to me?" Mel heard Luce ask.

Mel prayed the girl would remember how to do it. All she had to remember was how to transfer to one number…

Persi pressed some buttons, which made noise but did nothing else. "I don't know!" she squeaked. Mel's heart sank.

"Then I'll just borrow your phone," Luce purred. His voice swelled in volume as he approached Persi's desk. "You don't mind if I lean over your desk, do you?" His tone didn't change after crackling noises told Mel the phone had changed hands. "Hello, Mel."

Mel shook her head, already worrying about the younger girl. Luce was laying it on a bit thick for poor Persi, especially with her so young and inexperienced. Bikies were fluffy bunnies compared to demons. "Hi. Lili's told me you need me for tonight's meeting. It starts at four in the boardroom, right?"

Luce laughed throatily. "That's right. Did she tell you that I'd require your services afterwards, finalising the minutes from the meeting and the like?"

Mel smiled in response, even though she knew he couldn't see her. "Of course. See you at four." She carefully placed the receiver back in the cradle.

Four came around. Mel claimed the keyboard in the boardroom and time ticked away as she took the minutes for a thoroughly boring executive meeting. She kept her eyes on the screen and didn't look up, except to identify the presenter of a particular point.

"And for the very last time for a while, meeting adjourned!" she heard Luce say with some satisfaction, followed by a chorus of chairs pushing away from the table in unison. Heels and polished shoes tramped out the door to her cymbal-sigh of relief.

A pants-clad leg appeared on the table beside Mel. She sighed again and looked up as Luce beamed down at her.

"I had the girl order us dinner," he said with a wink. "I'll call the restaurant and tell them to deliver it."

Mel nodded wordlessly and returned her eyes to the screen. After one last check, she'd be done writing up the minutes, and free for the evening. She figured she might as well stay for dinner. At least until he'd reviewed the minutes so she could complete them.

She hit save as the leg returned. "Dinner's ready, dear," Luce said with a chuckle.

Mel glanced up. "I'm Mel, not Mephi or your wife. Can you check this over while I go find some cutlery?" She stood and walked out of the boardroom to the adjacent kitchen. She took her time selecting the cheapest plastic cutlery and giving it a wash first before returning to the boardroom.

Luce reclined in her still-warm seat, his eyes following her appreciatively as she entered the room. "It looks perfect to me."

"Good," Mel replied with a perfunctory smile. She held up the white plastic knives and forks. "Where's the food?"

Luce rose. "In my office, of course." He led the way out.

Mel noticed he'd removed his jacket, so she had a clear view of his well-cut shirt and pants as she followed him. She wondered if she could get pants that showed off her behind so well. Shrugging, she dismissed the idea. Hell, she probably couldn't afford them, anyway.

"Your dinner," Luce said with a smile, gesturing at the meeting table in his office.

Room service, Mel thought. Of course.

The normally naked meeting table now wore a white tablecloth and dinner service for two, and Mel recognised the plates from the Christmas party at the Hilton. Her mouth watered at the sight of the chocolate raspberry mousse. She clutched at the plastic cutlery as she took in its stainless steel cousins on the white cloth.

"You won't be needing those." Luce nodded at her clenched fist of forks and friends. Mel released them onto the table, where they blended in with the cloth. He pulled back a chair for her and gestured for her to sit, before rounding the table to seat himself across from her.

Luce offered a bottle, tilting it over Mel's glass. "Wine?"

Mel's curiosity was piqued. "What kind?"

Luce shrugged. "Some white the hotel thinks goes well with the entrée."

So much for the suave, wine connoisseur of a CEO. Mel laughed outright as she tilted her head to read the label. She recognised it as one she liked but couldn't often afford, from the winery with the beautiful gardens down in Margaret River. "Yes."

The entrée was oysters. Mel didn't touch them.

Luce slurped through his before he noticed hers

were untouched. "What's wrong with your oysters?" he asked through a mouthful.

Mel's stare was as cold as the bed of ice beneath their shells. "They're still alive."

"Not for long!" Luce grinned as he swallowed the last of his. He waited, but her expression didn't defrost. "Aren't you going to eat them?"

Mel lifted her wine glass and sipped, savouring the light wine. "No."

He reached for her plate. Slurp, slurp, slurp and Luce gulped his own wine with a grin, surveying the empty shells. "Do you know why I asked you to stay back tonight?" he asked.

Mel placed her glass carefully on the table. "Of course. It's your last day, as you're flying to take up some new position in the company that involves a lot of travel, and you wanted to check over the minutes before you left for good. I'm sorry I missed your farewell morning tea — I heard your speech was quite touching."

"Oh. Yes." Luce looked miffed, as if Mel had stolen his thunder. "Do you know why I'm leaving?"

Mel gave a small smile. "I had heard it was to do with your health..." She thought there might be some truth in that particular rumour, as the dark circles beneath his eyes betrayed him. She wondered what sort of malaise a demon could possibly suffer from.

Luce coughed. "Yes. The climate here is not what I'm used to. I need somewhere warmer, drier..."

"And with more smoke and sulphur?" Mel finished for him with a smile before she could stop herself.

"Where smoking is far less frowned upon than here, certainly," Luce replied uncertainly. It appeared Mel had stolen not just his thunder but his entire storm. "Shall we have the main course?"

"Sure. I'm starving," Mel said as she uncovered her plate. She thought longingly of the steak she had at home, but the one before her was seared and saucy, reclining on a bed of vegetables and crowned with a baby carrot. She tried not to laugh — he'd evidently asked the chef to make the meal as suggestive as possible, and so it was.

"More wine?" Luce said suddenly, grabbing a bottle of red and sloshing it into his own empty glass.

Mel drank the dregs of her white before tilting her glass toward him. "Please." The red ran smoothly into her glass, almost as dark as the steak. More Margaret River wine, but this time it was from Devil's Lair, Mel thought as she glanced at the label, tasting the unmistakeable shiraz.

Luce emptied his glass before Mel had set hers down, so he refilled it before tackling his meal. Mel smothered a smile and started slicing her steak into small pieces.

Mel kept her eyes down and Luce seemed to need to slurp his shiraz courage with increasing frequency. When she was sated, Mel carefully placed her cutlery side by side on the plate. She carefully wiped her parted lips with her cloth napkin before delicately taking another sip of wine.

"I want you to come with me. I need you," Luce blurted out. His knuckles were white as he clutched the empty wine bottle.

Mel touched her wineglass to her lips once more, holding the rich red in her mouth for a few moments before swallowing. "I'm needed here."

Luce swallowed and tried again with some difficulty. Mel wondered if he'd had too much wine. "I need a personal assistant in my new job and I want you. I'll be travelling a lot, incorporating new acquisitions into the HELL Corporation. I'll need an absolute angel who can do anything to be my assistant – an angel like you."

Mel smiled. "Like me? Would another angel do?" Her heart went out to the demon, but she knew this was the perfect opportunity to replace herself in his affections or whatever his feelings for her were.

Luce looked uncertain. "What do you mean?"

Mel tried to keep the wickedness from her smile. "Well, only half-angel, really. Your new PA, Persephone, is perfect for what you need. She's far more helpful than I could ever be. She'll keep everything in order to the last detail – she'll be able to tell if you're missing a pomegranate seed from your breakfast."

"You mean the girl with the glasses? A half-angel, really? What's the other half?" Luce looked stunned. Perhaps it was the wine.

Mel permitted herself to laugh. "My cousin – her mother – insisted that he was some sort of Greek god, but he was about as much use as a marble statue. I didn't enquire further." Her smile turned prim. "You might want to ask Persephone about her halo."

"But you said your cousin isn't a full angel. How can she have a real halo on her head?" Luce asked, laughing.

"Ah, no, not on her head," Mel replied, biting her lip so she didn't say any more. He evidently hadn't persuaded Persi onto his desk yet, or he'd know exactly what she was referring to. "She's even a fan of unusual art, like the pictures on your wall. You'll like Persephone." And she might like him, if his tongue was smoother than it was tonight. Mel reached for her dish of mousse and dipped her spoon. Heavenly, as before. She resolved to learn to make this, for she could hardly afford dessert from the Hilton every day.

"Are you sure you want to refuse my offer?" Luce watched Mel.

She felt sorry for him, but she'd promised Raphael and Persephone that she'd leave him to them. Her sympathy for the demon was clouding her judgement. Time to make good on her word.

Mel dropped her spoon in her dish. "Yes. My place is here." She wiped her lips with the soft cloth once more before dropping that, too. Mel stood and Luce mirrored her movement. He looked so forlorn; she pitied the demon more than she thought possible. Perhaps it was best that Persi would be his downfall and not her. She didn't have the heart to rip out his.

Mel rounded the table to his side. On impulse, she kissed his ruddy cheek. "Farewell, Luce. Thank you for the lovely dinner and the orchids you sent me secretly for Valentine's Day. I wish you the best, both in your new job and your health. If your travels bring you back to my city, I'd love to catch up again for dinner and drinks. Persi will know how to get into contact with me." She stepped away from him. "Now, I must go home to get some sleep."

"I have a couch here. We could share!" Luce shouted after her, more than an edge of desperation in his tone.

No, Persi would not share. Even a prince of darkness would be putty in her pretty hands in this state. And her halo…oh Hell!

"Goodnight, Luce."

Mel fought her laughter as she left the building, laughing so loud and hard on the train that the other passengers gave her a wide berth, which was just as well. If she stopped laughing, she'd cry. The lost, lonely look on his face as she left had smote her heart. She hadn't even been able to say her final goodbye.

She hated to admit it, but the office was dull without Luce. The work was the same, but it seemed to lack a vibrancy that she now thought had stemmed from his presence. It wasn't that she missed him – all the demons seemed to be more somnolent. Of course, that could be partly because there'd been some incident with the delivery truck so that there weren't any coffee beans left – and there wouldn't be any more until the following Tuesday.

Lili seemed to ask less of her, while she spent longer

and longer at lunch or generally away from the office. More than once, there were new shopping bags on Lili's filing cabinet in the afternoons. Perhaps there was some truth in the rumour that Lili was Luce's mistress, for she definitely seemed to be pining away for something.

Mel shut down her PC and headed home. Today Persi was due to call in her first weekly report and Mel was curious about the girl's progress.

The call lasted fifteen minutes. Persi used the word "fine" at least thirty times by Mel's tally and asked more questions than she answered. She wanted to know how Luce liked his coffee, what his favourite foods were, and whether he preferred her to initiate sex or would she have to wait for orders. Mel almost choked on her tea at this last one, before she managed to suggest that Persi try taking the initiative. Evidently Luce hadn't liked the desk in his hotel room, or Mel was sure Persi would have spread herself across it at even the slightest suggestion that he wanted sex. Persi was certainly no angel in that respect.

The only question she did answer, fortunately, was the most important. "What sort of deal did he sign at the meeting yesterday?"

"Some sort of agreement to provide government services in the United States," Persi said slowly. "Health services, I think. I didn't think the US government provided health services…but he has a meeting tomorrow with some fancy real estate agent about office space. Not just here, but all over the world.

Donald Dump or something, I think he said his name was..." She giggled.

Glancing at the itinerary Persi had given her, Mel decided to pay the two a visit and see precisely how fine their business was in...New York, she read, and they were staying at what appeared to be called the Trump hotel – not a dump at all. Ah, she'd soon find out.

Mel stretched out to sleep, feeling her spirit shake free of her tired body. As a pure angel, with no human limitations aside from the universe's laws of physics, she could swim through the atmosphere as sentient light. She couldn't leave her body for long, as the constructed form would start to disintegrate if untended, but an hour or two would be more than enough time to travel to New York and back – far faster than flying in any aircraft. She'd check on the couple and return home, with no one the wiser. Better yet, she'd be invisible to human eyes in her angel form.

She revelled in the refreshing sensation of fast flight and it felt like mere seconds before the trees of a very different Central Park appeared below her, in chilly morning sunlight. The snow surprised her, until she realised the reversed seasons and higher latitude placed the park in very early spring. She'd been working for the HELL Corporation so long, she'd missed winter in Korea, too.

She reached out, for she knew Persi's soul well. The agitated girl was in a hotel room overlooking the park and Mel could hear Luce's voice, complaining that she'd picked the wrong hotel. He never accepted favours from Trump, though he offered his hotel every time. Something about the rich Carlton...no, the Ritz-Carlton.

"But they had no suites left with park views, sir, and you said you needed both..." Persi whined. "Let me help you with that, sir."

Mel would have laughed at the repeated "sirs" but she was trying to stay as subdued as possible. Luce might be able to sense another spirit in the room – and she didn't want to be seen.

She couldn't see Persi at first – just Luce, sitting at a desk, frowning at his laptop, a cup of coffee on the glass surface beside him. The dark circles beneath his eyes seemed to have worsened in the week he'd been away – jet lag, she presumed.

Persi was...under the desk, plugging in the laptop power cable. "I see something else I can do for you, sir," she said. Mel heard unzipping, then slurping, as she realised precisely what Persi was doing for Luce. Luce shifted uncomfortably in his seat, nudging her away with his foot and Mel heard Persi's voice say thickly, "Oh, please, sir..."

Mel felt a desire to gag – quite a feat without a throat or digestive tract. Where in Hell had Persi learned to be so sickeningly submissive?

"Fine. Make it quick," Luce grunted, closing the document he was working on. Instead, he opened a presentation and Mel's attention was drawn to the screen. He'd pulled up the picture of her in her wet swimsuit in Sri Lanka and his eyes were fixed on the picture with an intensity that made Mel blush – or it would have, had she brought a body.

To Mel's relief, Persi did indeed make it quick, crawling out from under the table less than five minutes later, wiping her mouth. "If you like, sir, I'd be happy to provide a more complete service any time you please. Whenever and wherever." She winked, but Luce wasn't looking at her. He'd quickly opened up his email and was scrolling through one message so slowly that Mel wondered if he was trying to memorise it. She looked closer – it was the email she'd sent him with her Sri Lanka photos.

"Get out," Luce said shortly. "We leave for our first meeting in an hour and I need to work without interruptions until then. Close the door behind you. I'll grab you when it's time."

Persi pouted and glided to the door to her adjoining room. "If you're sure…" she purred, lifting her skirt a little to give Luce a lovely glimpse of her tattooed skin.

Luce didn't even look.

The door closed quietly as Persi slumped onto the bucket chair in her room. After a minute, she headed to the bathroom to brush her teeth – twice, Mel guessed, as it took so long and required a significant amount of spitting. Mel slipped back into Luce's room, wondering what work was so secret that it couldn't proceed in front of Persi.

Luce's fingers stroked the sunset shot on the LCD screen as he murmured, "My God, what I'd do for a single ray of your sunshine, Mel."

Stunned, Mel tried to shrink back into Persi's room. He was more perceptive than she'd realised – and she'd tried to be so careful...

He buried his head in his hands. "It should be you here instead of that...that...little lamprey. I'd take five minutes in the same room as you over a whole night naked with her. Hell, I'd give Trump back his millions and tear up the contracts if it meant you could be here. I'd give anything. Anything. Ah Hell..." He crossed to the bar fridge and extracted a small bottle of amber liquid. He wrenched it open and poured the contents into his coffee, then drank it down in three gulps that sounded surprisingly like sobs. "Melody..."

Luce's soul writhed like a nest of snakes having a violent orgy. In her spirit form, Mel could see the turmoil more clearly than ever before. He gritted his teeth against the pain. "I'll take this corporation global and then I'll come back for you, Mel. You won't have to be a temp, doing Lili's dirty work in a boring little city far from everywhere. You can have any job you want in any city you please. I'll give you the world...even if you don't want me."

Wishing she could help or even say something to comfort him and knowing she couldn't, Mel swept out, winging her way home to where she knew Luce wanted to be. She resolved not to look in on him again – it broke her heart to see the demon so lonely. And the way he'd said her name…Much more of this and she couldn't help stepping in – she couldn't bear to see such suffering.

Of course, it could all be a front to win her sympathy and enslave her soul, Mel mused as she passed the Equator. If he'd suspected she was in his hotel room, he could have lied through his perfect teeth. Luce had a reputation for being the most seductive demon there was and he was certainly arrogant enough to make the attempt. She kept thinking of the storm in his soul, though, for that had been real. Luce was at war with himself – that she knew for certain.

She'd promised she'd stay out of it until Persi needed her help. And the girl couldn't help but fail, with Luce like this.

In the meantime, Persi was her responsibility – and she would watch over the girl as carefully as she could, while avoiding the depressed demon next door.

Mel settled back into her body, rousing from slumber so she could shift it from the bed to the phone.

Flexing her fingers, she dialled Raphael's number and heard his sleepy voice. "Mm? Mel? What is it?"

"Persi called. This isn't just a fact-finding mission like you thought – the meetings are contract negotiations. Luce is taking the HELL Corporation global. He's sourced offices in several countries and he already has a signed contract with the US government –

for their health services, the largest portfolio in their budget."

"Oh Hell."

"We need to gain control of HELL Corporation and remove Lucifer. Do you want to tell Persi? She'll have to get him to sign the documents somehow."

Mel could almost hear Raphael thinking, before he finally said, "You tell Persi what she needs to do. I'll have some of our legal boys draft the contracts. Tell her to sell herself into slavery if she has to — but she needs to get him to sign those documents, whatever the cost."

"I draw the line at her soul, Raphael. Her body is hers to do what she wants with, but I won't support her selling her soul."

"Hers or yours, Mel — I'd hand hers over any day. It's a fair price to pay to thwart Lucifer in his bid for this much power."

Mel sighed. She'd have preferred to proceed differently — with Luce's soul as the bargaining chip — but it was out of her hands now. At least, it was for the moment. "When she calls next, I'll tell her. You have a week to produce watertight contracts. Ones even American lawyers can't find loopholes in."

"Are you a first aid officer?" a harried-looking man asked Mel.

She put down her phone reluctantly, her mind still on the book about a writer's romance. "Yes. What's happened?" She rose from her seat.

The man led the way through the cubicle maze. "We've had another incident in the store room. One bloke's unconscious and bleeding on the floor, while one of the girls from HR has injured her wrist, apparently with one of her heels. She says that the injury was sustained in self-defence…"

Mel hurried after him, her own heels padding on the carpeted floor. Something seemed very strange today.

The HR manager walked past, clutching a file to her chest and shaking her head. "This is bad, very bad. It's the third one today – the tenth this week – and it's only Tuesday…" she muttered to no one in particular.

She reached the doorway of the store room and stopped, stunned.

A man was indeed unconscious on the carpet; his head and shoulders had landed on the bottom of one of the shelving units. Through his forearm was a red stiletto heel, the gel cushion insert hanging out like the man's tongue. Black blood seeped from his arm onto the pile of telephone message pads beneath him.

An hysterical Ana clutched a ream of paper to her chest, the fingers of one hand wrapped around the wrist of her other hand. "He deserved it! Thieving policy officer…"

Mel noticed blood and some of the man's equally dark hair sticking to the wrapper around the ream of paper.

She summoned a soothing smile and reached past Ana for one of the first aid kits. Without taking her eyes off the hysterical woman or the limp man, Mel said over her shoulder, "Could you call me an ambulance, please?" She looked at Ana, who had kicked off her other red heel, looking ready to use it. "Make that two ambulances, for two casualties?"

"Sure," the other man replied as he hurried away.

"May I?" Mel asked, extending her hand to Ana.

"You can't have it! We're completely out!" Ana shouted.

Mel smiled her most angelic smile. "Not the paper. I'd like to examine your wrist."

Mel prodded for a moment until the woman yanked her hand back with an cry of pain. "It looks like a bad sprain. Best get you to hospital. Did you want to go wait in Reception?"

Ana gave a curt nod. "Right after I get this paper in the printer." She marched off to HR, still hugging her bloody ream of paper.

Mel turned her attention to the man on the floor. She didn't know him, but she didn't expect to – there were plenty of HELL Corporation policy officers she hadn't met. She hoped he'd recover enough from his head injury to be able to tell her his name. Sighing, she lightly patted his face and hands. "Wake up, please, and tell me if you can hear me. Are you okay?"

The man groaned and moved, but he didn't say anything she understood, so Mel repeated the exercise.

"Ffff…ucking bitch," the man mumbled after a while.

Mel pressed her lips together. "Can you tell me your name?"

"Mo," he mumbled.

"Mo? Your name is Mo?"

"Yyy…sss," Mo replied with difficulty.

"Right, well, I'm Mel and I've called you an ambulance, which will take you to hospital so you can get checked out."

"Good. Call….p...lice…too," he mumbled.

"We're sorting that out right now," Mel said carefully.

Luckily, the ambulance officers didn't take long to arrive and they took Mo away, relieving Mel of her responsibilities. She headed back to her desk, detouring to wash Mo's blood off her hands first.

Lili appeared, looking flustered. "Oh, Mel! Could you sort and staple these documents in time for my meeting in five minutes?" She dumped the ream of printed paper on Mel's desk and wandered off without waiting for Mel's answer.

With a sigh, Mel pulled out her stapler and started dealing with the sheets.

She made it to a third of the way through before her stapler protested and died. Patiently, Mel tapped it on the desk and checked the staples. She added some more, just in case. The stapler didn't do anything.

She peered into it and thought perhaps a staple had gotten jammed. She tried to pry it out with a pair of scissors, but they were too big. She needed something smaller, like…

Mel picked up a pen and inserted the point into her stapler, trying to get the wayward staple out. The pen point snapped, shattering the plastic with it. Mel dropped the pen into the bin by the desk. She searched her desk for a letter opener or something else she could use, but came up with nothing.

She headed over to Merih's desk. "How do I order a new stapler and a pen to replace the ones I just broke?" she asked.

He shrugged. "You can't. You have to fix them or do without."

She stared at him. "What? I can't have a new pen?"

He pulled up the internal network screen and tapped his monitor. "That's why."

"...the Minister has issued a media statement announcing immediate saving measures across government. These measures include: a temporary freeze on all expenditure on the procurement of non-essential goods and services (consumables such as stationery, use of consultants, non-essential travel)," she read. Mel looked at Merih. "But stationery is essential! This is an office!"

Merih shrugged. "Apparently not, according to the Minister. Haven't you noticed the fights breaking out in the store room where the stationery used to be kept?"

Oh.

Two hours later, Mel had taken her stapler apart, sustaining several bleeding cuts in the process, and reassembled it so it worked once more. Leaving bloody fingerprints on the documents, she finished dealing with the papers and delivered them to Lili's meeting. Then she went in search of a first aid kit to clean and cover her cuts.

By that time, the work day was over. She slipped her phone into her bag and lifted it onto her shoulder.

She'd wasted a whole work day over ten dollars' worth of stationery – a stapler and a ream of paper. That was…almost three hundred dollars of wasted time and money. How was that saving?

Hell will freeze over before she found out, Mel decided. Her laughter bubbled up as she realised the reality. No, Hell had already frozen over. On the Minister's orders.

"No, there's no more paper," Lili said before Mel could even ask why her documents hadn't printed. "We used our last ream yesterday and I swear I saw one of the Environment boys stealing from our printer this morning. No one wastes as much paper as the Environment Division…" She hungrily eyed the pen in Mel's hand. "You're lucky you still have a pen. Everyone else's went missing overnight."

"Actually, I have two. If you need one…" Mel offered her pen and Lili snatched it from her. Mel sighed. "Is the Minister's freeze still in effect? I don't see how it affects us. It's not like the government's paying for our stationery – I thought the HELL Corporation costs were factored into your initial bid to provide services…"

Lili shrugged. "It's the look of the thing. All government departments are making funding cuts to allow for renovations to the premier's new palace to include a brothel in the basement. They say it'll save millions, but not before it's open for business. We can't look like we're spending lots of money when all the other government services are skimping…"

Mel smothered a laugh. "I still think there are better ways to save money than not allowing us to have stationery. I can't get anything done."

"Go get a coffee," Lili suggested. "Maybe by the time you're back, Merih and Gerry will have scrounged enough paper to print."

Mel nodded, but bypassed the kitchen for the stairs up to the executive suite. Luce wouldn't have agreed to such stupid austerity measures and she'd be damned before she'd sit around and do nothing, wasting their money by doing no work.

Mel was surprised to see Mephi back, not to mention smiling blissfully and humming. Had it really been a month since she'd left? Luce had been gone for just as long. The office was definitely a different place without him. Mel found she actually missed the man. His conversation, more than anything, as well as the occasional coffee he'd made for her. Coffee and conversation. Mel tried not to laugh. She was certain Luce would have preferred that she miss parts of his personality and anatomy that started with C, though Persi was probably doing her best to ensure he forgot all about Mel. And so she should.

"Mel! Oh, you won't believe how wonderful it was! Bob and I…we…were arrested by the Japanese police." Mephi blushed, looking absurdly proud.

Mel wasn't sure whether to laugh, smile or look concerned. "I'm happy to hear you enjoyed your holiday. I hope it was all a misunderstanding," she said carefully.

Mephi giggled, sounding eerily like Persi instead of her usual efficient self. "Public nudity, disturbing the peace, property damage, inciting public violence, rioting, misuse of public property…oh, it was incredible. Bob and I spent half the night naked on the futons, but we got too hot and decided to try a romp in the snow. My knees went numb, so I insisted we visit the hot springs, but the indoor ones wouldn't let us in together, because they keep men and women separate — can you imagine? So we found some up the hill that were outdoors and not segregated…"

Mel coughed. "Up the hill…you mean the cooking hot springs? The ones that are too hot for humans, with all the warning signs?"

"Humans, maybe, but they were just a warm bath to us demons, dear. And we steamed them up a fair bit more before we were done. So we had another roll in the snow...and fell through someone's basement window. We climbed out, had another wash in the hot springs – just to disinfect, of course, the cuts from the broken glass, but one thing led to another and...by that time some of the townspeople were up and they were very rude, so Bob broke off a length of the chain fence and used it to protect me..." Mephi's eyes misted over at the memory.

"Wow. Sounds like an exciting holiday," Mel managed to say. She didn't think she'd ever understand demons.

"It was." Mephi sighed. "What can I do for you, dear? Just name it. Bob and I will be in your debt for eternity."

Mel took a deep breath. "I'd like to see whoever's doing Luce's job. I want to discuss the austerity measures."

"Let me just check..." Mephi frowned at her monitor. "He's free now and for the next half hour. Go right in."

He sat at Luce's desk. The office looked no different, but the man who occupied it was a shadow compared to the charismatic Lord of Hell. "What is it?" he asked, rubbing his face with both hands as he looked up. "And who are you?"

"I'm Mel," she began. "I want to hear it from you – why the entire corporation is under these austerity measures. I'd like to assist, but I can't unless I know why."

He shuffled through the papers piled up over his desk. Luce had never had that much paper in his entire office, let alone his desk. "There was a memo from the Minister. I had Mephi send it around..."

Mel wet her lips. "Oh yes, I saw that. It doesn't explain why. The HELL Corporation's profits are rising steadily and it's picking up more government services every week. The only reason I can think of is the need for capital elsewhere – if Luce is thinking of expanding his corporation on a global scale. If this is the case, then reducing its productivity here by not ordering paper is pointless."

Cold, dark eyes regarded her, but he didn't say a word.

"You've got an office full of staff, fighting over stationery and doing nothing else. Half of them are spending their entire work day stealing paper from the other half, who are out on coffee and smoke breaks because they can't do anything else. Zero productivity will only make the company look bad when Luce wants it to appear at its best, in the media and otherwise. All it'll take is one person to talk to the media and the press will be all over it – and office humour like this will go viral, reaching the furthest corners of the globe wherever Luce is. Luce wouldn't have authorised this and he'd stop it if he knew."

The man folded his arms. "Are you threatening to talk to the press or Lucifer? He left me in charge and said that anyone who doesn't follow orders will go right back to the Pit for insubordination or inciting trouble. That's a Level Eight offence – and you'll be on the receiving end for as long as I see fit." His demonic grin was the picture of fierce anticipation.

"I'm agency staff," Mel replied coolly. "If you want me to work outside of the CBD, you'll have to renegotiate my contract with the agency and I have to agree to it. Keep your threats for the staff you can control. Admittedly, if you don't have any stationery in the office, there's really no point in me or any of the agency staff being here, as our productivity is worse than that of your regular, demonic staff. You see, we fill out paper timesheets that have to be signed by hand. At the end of this week, if there's no paper to print our timesheets, we won't be working because, unlike demons, we don't do anything based on empty threats and no reward."

"Fine. You're fired, then," he said, waving his hand as if ridding himself of a bad smell.

Mel kept her face expressionless, despite her initial desire to smile. If she wasn't required to spend all day in the office at the demons' beck and call, she could keep better track of Luce and Persi – and be available to fly out the moment Persi called for help.

After a moment, she nodded. "I suggest you terminate the contracts of all agency staff at the end of this week and use the money for stationery. Luce will thank you for it – instead of sending you to whatever level of Hell is reserved for idiots who waste resources." She turned on her heel and left.

She heard the man scramble to his feet and follow her. "Mephi!" he called. "Send a note to…whoever. Tell them to fire all the agency staff."

"But, Bob…that's Mel. She's the angel who suggested our holiday destination. You can't…" Mephi protested.

Mel stopped. "It's all right," she said. "We're all temporary staff and we're only here for as long as we're needed. The agency will have another assignment before I reach home tonight, I'm sure of it."

Mephi drew herself up, shedding all semblance of humanity. Mel watched in fascination as the immaculate skirt split to reveal a well-muscled red leg that matched the demon's furious face. A ruddy finger stabbed the air to emphasise each word. "Beelzebub! How DARE you. I won't let you send Mel out of here in disgrace after what she did for us…for our marriage! If you EVER want me to touch you again, you will see to it that she has a job for life or a proper send off – WHATEVER she asks for. And if she asks for your gift-wrapped genitals as a going-away gift…I will tie the blood-spattered bow myself!"

The man in the suit seemed to shrink. "Yes, dear."

Mel smiled politely. "A morning tea would be plenty. As for a fitting farewell gift…a pen is fine. Something small to remember you all by."

Mephi's skin faded to normal. "I'll see to it that

catering is ordered for ten on Friday. We'll miss you, Mel."

Mel couldn't say the same, so she said what she could: "Thank you."

Merih cleared his throat noisily. "We all want to thank you for everything you've done. The quality of the coffee. The wording of our laws and policies. The paper-purchasing freeze. The protesters. The training sessions. The CEO's end-of-year presentation. Saving us all from aliens. Saving the CEO from a swan. Mephi and Bob's second honeymoon. And who can forget the chocolates on Valentine's Day? Everything you've touched here is better because you've been with us. We want to thank you in the best way we know how. Now, every man among us wants to give you a good six inches…"

"And the ladies," Ana said under her breath, lifting her six inch stiletto heel.

"Or more!" shouted Nybbas, turning red.

"Or more," agreed Merih, "but we figured we'd give you something just as long and hard that lasts longer than five minutes. Something to remember us by."

He handed her a small, gift-wrapped box, dwarfed by the huge card accompanying it. Mel smiled, thanked him, and opened the card first. It was full of tiny writing – from what looked like all the staff she'd ever met, or given chocolate to on Valentine's Day. Tears sprang to her eyes. "Thank you," she said again.

"Open it!" Gerry hollered. "Ana said what you needed most was a vibrator because you'd never see any action any other way. We all want to see what sort of sex toy fits in a box that small!"

Mel laughed and blushed. "If you insist." She unwrapped the paper with care and pulled out the box. "Ohhh…that's so kind of you. What a lovely surprise. I want to use it right away…"

"Is it a gift voucher for the sex shop on Murray Street?" Ana asked loudly.

"No. Much better than that. It's a beautiful pen," Mel said, holding up the gold writing implement so the light caught it.

"We had your name engraved on it, too," Merih murmured, pointing at the three letters that spelled out her name, to her relief.

Her tears escaped. "Thank you so much."

"SPEECH!" Nybbas bellowed.

"I...I can't," Mel whispered as every demonic eye settled on her. Forcing herself not to run and hide, she tried to clear her throat to find her voice. If she closed her eyes, perhaps she could.

"Thank you. Thank you so much. I hope...I only hope I helped."

There was silence as the demons waited for more words – perhaps they wanted something like Luce's long speeches, but Mel had no more.

Clapping started behind her and someone whistled. The room erupted in applause and Mel dared to open her eyes. It was over. Her time in HELL was over.

It hadn't been so bad after all. Who'd have thought?

"Morning, Mel. I need your help. How do I…"

"I swallowed a whole German sausage in front of him and he barely blinked! Every other man in the place offered me a job or a bed, but Luce locked me out of his room! What else do I have to do to…"

"What do I do if…"

"He said I have to wear a scarf over my head for the meeting. He said I can't go unless I cover up. How am I supposed to seduce him if the only skin I can show is my face without any makeup? Help me, Mel, I don't know how to..."

"We had to drink this foul-tasting brown spirit that burned all the way down. I coughed so hard I lost my voice. What should I do tonight so I don't..."

"We're meeting with the Treasury Minister in London tomorrow. I have all the documents prepared, just like you said. Do you really think I should open the meeting with..."

Mel kept her voice calm and kept talking until she knew Persi had understood. "What you need to do is..."

Every day. Sometimes two or three times a day. Constant phone calls, text messages and emails. Persi would panic and Mel was her panacea. Mel longed for the day that she was only a placebo, so she could wean the girl off her blind obedience. She needed so many instructions just to get through the day...

Yet the girl was improving – and she was trying to look after Luce, too. Mel couldn't bring herself to turn a completely blind eye to Luce, even if she only saw him through Persi's panicked perception. Persi made sure he was always on time and immaculately dressed, that he ate and drank, and that his coffee was perfect. She vetted the restaurant menus and presented them to Mel until she learned what Luce liked to eat.

Mel didn't how she'd have managed to do this on top of her daily drudgery at the office, and was doubly glad she didn't work for the HELL Corporation anymore.

Day by day, she wondered when she'd receive Persi's resignation – when would the girl admit defeat? So many of her questions were about how to attract Luce – despite her repeated offers, Luce wouldn't sleep with the girl and he'd threatened to find a new PA if she crawled under the desk or into his bed again.

Luce without lust – Mel couldn't help laughing at the very thought of it, for it was so hard to believe. The demon she knew would have happily taken any willing girl on his desk here in Perth – what had left him so impotent now?

With every phone call, her understanding deepened and Mel wished again that she'd disregarded Raphael's advice and accepted Luce's offer. She'd be holding his soul in her hands by now, instead of having to talk Persi through even the simplest of negotiations. Or offering the girl advice on seducing a man she'd never slept with, and didn't intend to.

The front windows rattled ominously thanks to yet another strong gust of wind. Mel paid little attention to it – her windows had withstood sixty years of such storms and the glass was only a little loose in the frames. She was more worried that she'd lose power before the kettle boiled for her cup of tea. She'd developed quite a taste for her floral tisanes and she wanted her drink in hand when Persi called again.

The rain pelting on the tin roof drowned out all other sound for a few minutes – she only knew the kettle was ready because the light had switched off. Dropping one of the tiny pyramid teabags into her cup, she tipped the kettle to pour her tea. The smell of jasmine steam made her smile as she closed her eyes, simply enjoying the scent. Even angels were allowed guilty pleasures such as this. She lifted the cup and took a small sip.

The downpour desisted and Mel heard the rattling again – this time, both her windows and the front door. That was unusual – for a wind gust to swirl through her carport and reach the door, it would have to move around corners.

"Mel!" she heard a voice sob. "You have to let me in. I don't know who else to turn to. Please help me!"

The door shuddered in its frame as Mel realised it wasn't just the wind knocking at her door in the storm.

"Please, Mel!"

She sighed and set down her tea. No one should be out in such a storm – especially not someone who knew her name and address.

She turned both locks and swung the front door open.

"Oh, thank God. Please let me in, Mel. I'll do anything."

She couldn't see his face in the carport shadows, but pity drove her not to care. She unlatched the screen door and swung it out into the darkness. "Come in. You must be soaked."

He stumbled on the steps and she held out her hand

to help him. His wet fingers closed gratefully over hers as he stepped over the threshold.

Mel stood back to stare. It had been weeks since she'd last seen Luce and those weeks had not been kind to him. His suit sagged from his shoulders under the weight of water it held, the smell of wet wool overpowering the delicate scent of jasmine tea. His hair, plastered to his head, dripped down his face, highlighting the dark circles beneath his eyes. He folded his arms across his body, trying to stop the shivering. "Thank you," he said.

"What happened?" she asked carefully. She suspected she knew, but that didn't explain how he was here, in her house.

"She…that devil woman…took everything. Slowly at first and then…I had no control any more. Do you know she has a halo on her…on her…and she wanted me to…" His eyes widened in horror, yet the horrors could only be in his head.

Mel noticed the puddle forming on her carpet at his feet. She touched a cautious hand to his back. "You should get out of those drenched clothes and into something warm and dry. How about you take a shower while I see if I have anything that might fit you." She guided him to the sunny yellow bathroom and closed the door.

Pressing her lips together, she headed for the guest room, where she kept the clothes Raphael had left at her house – he could certainly spare them. Particularly if it was his fault there was a man in her house who needed them. With the weight Luce appeared to have lost, he'd have no trouble fitting into Raphael's clothes.

She took a shirt, pants and a sweater to the bathroom, rapping on the timber door with her knuckles. "I have some clothes for you," she called. She couldn't hear the water running, so she cracked the door open a little and passed the pile of folded garments through the gap.

Luce's hands covered Mel's briefly before he took her offering. "Thank you."

Once her hands were empty, she quickly pulled the door closed. "Let me know if you need anything else. Use as much hot water as you like. The towels are clean – I brought them in from the line just before the storm hit." She waited for the hiss of the shower starting before she strode to her bedroom with grim purpose.

Picking up her phone from the charger, she noticed a missed call from the one person she needed to speak to, timed to match the beginning of the downpour.

The line rang twice before it was answered. "Hell—"

Mel cut her off. "How goes your assignment?"

Persi giggled. "Mission accomplished. I now have control of all his interests in the HELL Corporation."

"At what cost?" Mel ground her teeth.

"Almost nothing. It felt too easy, Mel. I barely had to do anything – I didn't even have to sleep with him in the end. It was like he just gave up."

"What was his price?" Mel asked urgently.

"Just your phone number and home address. Nothing!" Persi insisted. "He's powerless now, Mel. It's not like you have to answer, talk to him or even let him in. He doesn't matter any more."

Mel thought of how the demons in the office had responded to Luce – like marionettes to a puppeteer. He could sign over everything in the world to Persi, but he was still the unchallenged master of Hell and all it contained. It was both his strength and his curse. "You're wrong. He does matter." Mel heard the water in the shower stop flowing. "Report to Raphael. Tell him your assignment is complete – earlier than expected, too. Convey my congratulations to you both on a job well done. I'll finish up here." She terminated the call, taking a deep breath to strengthen herself. She had a damp demon to deal with.

Mel settled onto the sofa, sipping her still-warm tea. She set a second, steaming cup on the coffee table for Luce.

The floorboards outside the bathroom door creaked under his weight, drawing her eyes from the cup to her guest. Raphael's shirt was too big and the pants would have fallen off him if he didn't have a belt. He looked slightly less lost now.

"You kept them," he said in wonder.

"I did?" Mel asked, unsure.

He nodded slowly. "The flowers. The orchids

I…secretly bought you for Valentine's Day, but you knew, all the same. I thought you didn't like them. Yet…you took them home and cared for them. They look as perfect as they were in February. Surely those can't be the same flowers!"

Mel smiled. "They are. They seem to like my bathroom. Perhaps it's the humidity." She took another sip of her tea so she could avoid his eyes. The intensity of his gaze was more than a little disconcerting.

"It's you. You breathe the tiniest whisper of your vitality into everything around you and it's as if the whole world comes to life. Even I feel better and I'm…I'm…"

Mel waited for Luce to finish his sentence, but he didn't seem able to. "Please, sit down. Have some tea."

Luce nodded and accepted, inhaling deeply as he sank into an armchair. He slurped the hot liquid. "This is good," he said in surprise.

Mel nodded, taking a deep draught of her own. After swallowing, she said, "I'd like you to tell me again what happened. Take as much time as you need and, please, don't hold back on details. You mentioned a devil woman with a halo?"

Luce nodded, lowering his cup from his lips. "Your…cousin. The half-angel. Persephone. Oh God, she was my PA. The perfect assistant, just like you said she'd be. She kept my schedule so well I only had to ask her to know exactly where I should be. She knew it all. New York, Berlin, Singapore, Johannesburg,

Dubai...she had my coffee in hand before I knew I needed it. Took the minutes, prepared all the documents...read them so she could brief me on the plane, or assist me in the meetings. Then London...she effortlessly took control of the negotiation. And when we got back to the hotel, we had adjoining hotel rooms and she left the door open. When I got out of the shower, she was naked on my bed. She spread her legs and...she has a...a..." Luce swallowed and looked horrified.

"Halo tattoo?" she suggested, not needing a graphic description.

"Y...yeah," he managed to say. "I took one look at her and I couldn't. You marked me, so I felt nothing for her. Nothing!"

This was news to her. Mel tilted her head. "I marked you? When, and how?"

The disconcerted demon blushed. "When you kissed me goodbye. An angel's kiss is redemption for us. You gave it willingly, without...and you wished me well! It took me a fortnight to figure it out – what you'd done to me with that one touch. While I was distracted, she just took more and more until, one day, she asked me to sign over everything to her. The company and everything I owned. So I did – if she'd tell me how to find you again."

A redeemed demon? Could there be such a thing? Mel could think of only one thing that could cause such a transformation and it wasn't her farewell kiss. It might help explain his obvious ill-health, too. Not to mention why he'd been stroking pictures of her on his laptop in New York. Mel regarded him over the rim of her cup as she drank the remainder of her tea. Did the man know the source of the sickness in his soul? She'd never seen a soul at war with itself before.

She kept her voice light as she said, "It was hardly a kiss. A peck on the cheek, perhaps. An angel's kiss usually annihilates your kind, or sends you back into the Pit. You were Persi's charge, not mine, and you seemed so happy to have her. Yet you left her and came here in the middle of a storm. Why?" Even as she tilted her head, she kept her eyes on him.

Luce flashed a rueful smile. "I left so quickly, I barely noticed the storm start. I didn't want to turn back and return to her. I just wanted to find you." He held out his hand. "Here, let me get you another cup of tea."

Mel surrendered her empty mug and watched him carry both his and hers to the kitchen. She'd left the box of tea on the counter, so he didn't have to hunt for it. Ten minutes later, he returned, carrying two steaming cups.

She inclined her head in thanks as she accepted her drink, setting it on the table to cool. "Give me your hand. I want to see this for myself."

Luce swallowed, almost choking on his tea. "You want to see my soul? Why?"

"I want to understand better. I have seen it all before, Luce," Mel replied, trying not to laugh. "Yes, even yours. Remember? In front of the swans on the foreshore, before you told dirty jokes to try and make me blush."

"You didn't blush. The other angel did. You laughed." Luce looked at her, as if conducting some form of assessment. He came to a decision and held out both shaking hands, palms up. Mel took them. She drew a deep breath and looked into his eyes for a long time. "Your eyes are still just as beautiful," he murmured, but Mel shushed him.

The war was over – but which side had won? Mel wondered. Oh, my…

She released his hands first; shaking her head when she was done reading his soul. "I don't understand. How can the shadow on your soul be simply…gone? Changed, somehow. It looks almost as clean as an angel's. How can you be the demon who tried to seduce me in the boardroom, your office, the work Christmas party…how can you change this much?"

He grinned. "I told you, you marked me. And you're partly right. I'm not redeemed yet – not completely, anyway. I'm toying with the idea of pinning you to the couch, ripping your clothes off and having my wicked way with you. I still might."

Decisively un-demon-like, Mel mused. A normal demon, like the Luce she knew, would have seduced her out of her clothes and waited for her to ask (or beg) for him. Demons didn't do rape – their aim was to damn the soul they seduced. Luce sounded more like a lusty human than a demon – and he didn't seem to realise it. Her suspicions swirled, coalescing into very curious thought-clouds.

Mel took up her cup again. "You could try, but you're no match for me, if you ever were. They entrusted you to Persi, but still you pursue me. Only me. Not Persephone." She watched as his grin faded in fear at her cousin's name. Inspiration struck. "You signed over everything to her, didn't you? Your kind are big on written contracts. You gave her the shadows from your soul as part of the contract. You sealing such a bargain…summoned the storm."

He shrugged. "She can't wield my power without a bit of demon in her. I wasn't going to give her any other part of me. I gave it all up for you."

Renouncing everything for her. Redemption. Mel gasped, setting her cup down before she dropped it as realisation exploded in her mind. Redemption might be possible for him, and she knew how. "But it's not enough. You may have given up everything, but if you're truly after redemption, you'll need something a little more powerful than a peck on the cheek to complete the transformation. Is that really what you want, Luce?"

Luce clunked his cup on the table beside hers, sliding off the couch. He dropped to his knees on the rug, his hands out in supplication. "Please, Mel. Help me. I'm begging you. Finish what you started. I can't enter your world, yet I'm no longer a part of mine. Send me back or take me with you. Make me whole again and I'll do anything you ask."

56

She stared down at the demon kneeling at her feet. She ached to help him, but to grant him the angel's kiss he asked for could hurt him more than she cared to. "I can't refuse to help you, but I don't know what will happen if I try. I might just banish you back to the Pit, where you'll stay for centuries until you can return."

Luce winked. "I'm willing to take the risk for one kiss from you. I promise I'll be good. Do my best not to corrupt you. Believe me when I say I don't want you to fall, Mel. Your kindness in letting me enter your house, when I could harm you so easily…you're too trusting, but I owe you for that today. You'll make the best kind of angel, I know it. One day, I want to see how beautiful your wings will be."

"One day – will be?" Mel laughed so hard it took her almost a minute before she could continue, "You think I'm a fresh-faced Grigori, or an angel-in-training like Persi, waiting to earn my wings, and one kiss can corrupt me. Oh Hell – I really thought you'd have realised by now. Your soul is in far more danger than mine could ever be. Luce, look at me. Love isn't my weakness, but my strength." She rose to her feet, feeling all pretence of humanity slip away as her wings unfurled. Feathers brushed both the floor and the ceiling as her soul's normally concealed glow lit up the room. "If you wish to be like me, you must rise with me." She saw her radiance reflected in his eyes and ruthlessly reined it in before she overwhelmed him, but she also saw his eyes shine with hope. He wanted this. Truly, he did.

Luce stood up stiffly. "Mel…who are you? Your real name and rank, I mean. Like I'm Lucifer, Light of the Morning. I was one of the Seraphim, until…" He swallowed. "You should know who I am before we go any further. I've never met an angel who could withstand me – and then, not for long."

She touched his arm, her sympathy overflowing. "I know your history, Luce. I witnessed it all from Earth, for my responsibilities keep me here," she said gently.

"Just because you haven't met an angel stronger than you, doesn't mean we don't exist. In my true form, I am Muriel of the Hashmallim."

Luce stared at her, his mouth wide. He swallowed a few times before he laughed shakily. "A Domination? You're a Domination. The only female Domination, who I've never met. No wonder you managed to turn me down flat. I should have known."

Mel persisted. "I've known Earth and all its pleasures for longer than you have. You cannot corrupt me, but one kiss from me might destroy you, Luce. Are you willing to take that risk?"

"Hell's hot, but so are you. I'll take my chances," Luce insisted. He licked his lips – Mel suspected out of nervousness more than lust. "You almost sound like you'd be sad if you destroyed me. Why did you enter my company and challenge me, if not to put an end to me?"

"I've always spent most of my time on Earth, dealing with leadership matters here. I guide and teach, not kill, Luce. You and your corporation were not aligned with my objectives." Mel bowed her head. Centuries of watching and guiding the leaders of her world gave her the strength she needed to try to redeem a demon. How much harder could it be?

"Close your eyes," she said softly. It wasn't necessary, but she was nervous and didn't want him watching her. It was, after all, her first time. No one she knew had ever redeemed a demon – it wasn't meant to be possible. She expected him to vanish in a burst of light as she banished him back to where his kind belonged. She didn't want to see the betrayal in his eyes if she failed, as she surely would.

But there was something different about him…something that made her willing to take the chance. If this was what he truly wanted, then perhaps it was possible…

She drew closer, brushing her lips against his until she could feel his breath through his parted lips. He was correct – she would be saddened to send him home. Mel knew she was too kind-hearted for killing demons.

Drawing in a breath that tingled with jasmine, from his tea and hers, she tasted his lips. Sweeter and softer than she expected. Sharing air, skin and warmth, she gave him her tongue, too, trading it for his. A deep sound rumbled in his throat, but he didn't break their connection. Mel touched her fingers to his temples, wishing she could see his thoughts to know why. Was redemption worth so much to him, or was there more? She didn't want to hurt him.

Her lips sealed in his breath and she closed her eyes, too, as she opened her heart. Breathing her own spirit into him as part of a passionate kiss should have destroyed the salacious demon. Yet his arms closed carefully around her, a reverent embrace as he responded to her kiss.

So much sensation, touching far more than two bodies. In a kiss this deep, she felt the communion of two souls twining together – with no taint of corruption to darken the moment. She waited for him to fade from her arms as she sent him back to Hell, for the moment to end – but still their kiss continued. A true angel's kiss, so what did that make Luce?

She felt the spark of contact between her soul and his, igniting something in him that opened his heart to her. The flood of feeling from him swept away all illusions – she knew the depths of his soul and the intensity overwhelmed her.

A deafening explosion outside, accompanied by a bright burst of light, couldn't break the contact between them. The afterimage burned through Mel's eyelids even after her house was plunged into darkness.

Dimly, she became aware of the power in the house draining away. The refrigerator's hum silenced and the sole sounds were their shared breathing beneath the rain hissing down on the roof. The room was lit only by her golden glow. No – not anymore.

She'd turned a demon – and, possibly, blown the power transformer for the whole suburb in the process. She hoped the damage could be repaired – but it was a small price to pay for the redemption of a soul.

Mel pulled away, feeling the change as Luce began to give off light, too. Not as bright as Mel, but enough. "Luce, look," she said softly. "See what you've become."

He opened his eyes and looked down. "Thank you," Luce breathed. He flexed his fingers, the faint light from them shimmering in his eyes.

"How do you feel?" Mel asked, wondering what a

redeemed demon was supposed to experience. She had no comparison. She allowed her radiance to dim into darkness, as she tried to focus on the faint connection she still seemed to have with his heart. When she faded, Luce was the only light in the room. A light she'd helped rekindle, which made him her responsibility.

"Some things are different, but some stay the same. I still want you as much as ever. I almost wish you'd rejected me. The thought of taking you on the couch has turned from enticing to all-consuming. I want...more." He stared at her hungrily.

Mel took his arm, looking up to meet his eyes so he could read her soul if he wished. "Careful, or you'll wind up back in the Pit, right back where you started. Congress between angels and demons is forbidden, but two angels...Love is a very important part of life as an angel." She waited for her words to sink in.

"No, I'm sure I just want to seduce you out of your clothes so I can make love to you 'til morning." It took him a moment for his mind to catch up with his tongue. Luce looked shocked as he said, "I love you?" He shook his head hard. "No. Demons aren't capable of love. I can't love you. Unless..." Mel could see his eyes widening as he sensed it. "How did you do it? I do love you." The former demon's confusion was complete.

Mel laughed gently. "So it would seem." She leaned in close. "For future reference, I prefer the bed to the couch – more space. Come." She beckoned. "I don't want you to be alone tonight. So, tell me, Luce. How good are you in bed?"

Luce chuckled as he followed her. "I can make an angel think she's in Heaven."

Sunlight kissed her eyelids and Mel slipped out of bed.

Luce still slept soundly and she didn't want to wake him, so she left only a light kiss on the former demon's cheek. She padded quietly to the kitchen with her phone, lifted it and dialled. Two rings later, he answered.

"Hello?"

"Raphael, you know how you owe me a favour?"

Mel Goes to Hell

DEMELZA CARLTON

DEDICATION

For Opa, who made an angel swear in Heaven while I was writing this book. She must have spent all day preparing his place up there – only for him to decide he was staying on Earth for a bit longer.

Soft lips brushed his cheek. Luce turned his head to claim a kiss for his mouth, too, but met only air. He opened his eyes, searching for the source of the soft kisses, just in time to see her back depart through the doorway.

He glanced at the room, taking a moment to remember the events of the previous night. Persephone, signing the contracts, before he left in the downpour...

He scrambled out of bed, trying not to make a sound before he made sure his memories were accurate.

"You know how you owe me a favour?" Mel's lovely voice said.

Luce's breath caught in his throat as he walked faster. He needed to see her to be sure.

She was talking on the telephone, resting her forearm on the bench so she could lean across it. One ankle was crossed behind the other, her toes tapping lightly on the carpet. Luce stood transfixed at this vision.

Mel had invited him in, given him a spectacular kiss, before demonstrating that she was heavenly in more ways than he'd imagined.

"Don't worry. Persi is aware of her mistake and she won't make it again. If he finds you, don't let him in – call us and we'll take care of him. It's hardly a favour – just us protecting a valuable member of our staff," a muffled male voice sounded through the phone line.

Mel's caller was talking about him, Luce realised. Not to let him in, because he was the mistake. But Mel had, and she'd taken better care of him than anyone else would or could. She was the best kind of angel.

"No, it's not that," Mel replied. "Look, can I meet with you in person, some time this morning? I'd prefer to discuss this face to face."

"I have a meeting at nine, but I'm free from ten. How about then?" the voice said.

She turned to look at the clock above Luce's head. He didn't have time to hide himself or conceal how he'd been staring at her, so he brazened it out, meeting her eyes when her glance lowered to his face, before her gaze dropped lower still.

"Ten sounds fine. See you then," she said, turning away from Luce.

Sprung, Luce didn't waste time. He strode across the carpet to Mel, reaching out to touch her. "You should've told him it's too late – I've already found you," he whispered, feeling her tense up. She dropped the phone on the counter, letting Luce see that she'd ended the call.

"I'd like to keep you to myself for a little longer, first. I'm not sure what I've done to you and it wouldn't be fair to desert you so soon," Mel admitted.

Luce's heart sank. "So I'm under observation, like some sort of medical case, Mel? Not because you feel something for me, except maybe morbid curiosity?" he asked bitterly. He glanced up at the clock. "And you'll discharge me at ten, when you have a meeting with a secretive somebody who thinks I'm a mistake."

Steel-strong hands grasped his as her eyes bored into his soul. "You're coming with me to that meeting. Afterwards, I'll be all yours. After all, we're both unemployed. Perhaps you should start thinking about what we'll do together."

Luce's mind whirled. Together. All his. Mel.

"So what would you like for breakfast?" she asked.

Luce chuckled. "You – or, failing that, anything else you're willing to offer." He pressed his lips lightly to her neck, praying that she wouldn't pull away as he drew a deep draught of her scent. Heaven. She smelled of Heaven – or did Heaven smell of her?

"You are a sexy devil, aren't you?" Mel laughed, shaking her head.

Luce shrugged. "I have no idea what I am now, but still sexy, I'm sure."

Mel filled the kettle and clicked it on, but nothing happened. She flicked the switch a couple of times, with no result. Next, she tried to switch on the kitchen light — unnecessary with the bright morning sunlight streaming in — but that didn't work, either. "The power must still be out from last night," Mel murmured, frowning.

"The power's out? When did that happen?" Luce asked. "Must have slept through that."

"No," Mel said softly. "We did it. We...blew the

transformer when we kissed. I hope it isn't too much trouble to repair. I'll have to remember not to redeem demons in the house again if it is." She smiled, but Luce thought she looked a little sad, too. "How are you feeling this morning?"

"Better than I have in years," Luce admitted, grinning. "A couple more nights like last night and I'll feel like the king of the world again." The look of horror on Mel's face made him realise what he'd said. He held up both hands in surrender. "I mean that in a purely metaphorical sense. I gave that up – I swear."

Mel nodded gravely, but she still didn't seem convinced.

"Look, let me make you breakfast. A small thank you for everything you've done for me. Power-hungry demons don't make you breakfast, right?"

"What are you going to make, given that the power's out? I can't even make tea," she said.

Luce eyed the gas stove. "Where do you keep your pots and pans?"

Mel pointed at the cupboard beside the stove. Luce rummaged through it until he found a saucepan and a frypan. He filled the pot with water before setting both on the stove. He turned the control knobs for the burners, hearing the hiss of gas but not the click of the igniter.

"The ignition is electric," Mel said. "It won't work."

"Maybe not for an angel like you, but I've been playing with fire for a very long time," Luce said grimly, touching his index fingers to the gas jets. Both burst into brilliant blue flame. He scooped a tiny flickering tongue of flame onto his fingertip, lifting it to show Mel. She stared at it as if mesmerised.

"Angels can't do that," she said softly, looking worried. "Luce..."

He laughed and blew out the flame. "Maybe I'm not entirely redeemed after all." He peered into his pants. "Yep, I'm still up for a bit of action on the couch – and I am seriously hot." A wisp of smoke curled up from his extinguished finger.

Mel laughed, but her heart didn't seem in it. She was hiding something, Luce decided, but there was no point in trying to push it out of her. It must be something to do with her early morning phone call.

"So what are you making me for breakfast?" she asked.

"Got eggs and milk? Mushrooms, bacon, ham, cheese...anything I can fold into an omelette?"

"I have all but the bacon," Mel said warmly, opening the dark fridge.

Together, they laid out the ingredients for a decadent omelette, before Luce insisted that Mel sit down and let him do the work. She laughed a little but acquiesced, settling into one of the dining chairs in the alcove just beyond the kitchen.

Luce opened the tiny tin of mushrooms and drained it. He started slicing them, pausing occasionally to smile at the watching angel.

The longer he looked, the more he saw. Mel wasn't beautiful in a classic or a modern sense, so she didn't stand out. She wasn't ugly, either – he'd call her pretty. Her form fitted the soul it contained, sure, for her radiant smile shone through that face like the sun itself. He wondered why she hadn't chosen a more striking body – it was almost as if she were trying to blend in or hide among humans. An angel with power like hers faced little danger from anyone. What or who could she possibly be hiding from?

He became aware of a stinging pain in his finger. "Ow...oh shit!" Instead of cutting a mushroom, he'd hacked off half his own fingertip. Red blood was leaking across the cutting board, creeping closer to the mushrooms.

Luce stared in fascination. He hadn't seen red blood flow from his veins since...since the night he fell. The blows from Michael's sword had burned as they cut, and he could remember seeing his own blood on his hands. The last thing he saw before he fell...and his blood had been black ever since. Until now.

"Luce. It's all right," Mel soothed, her hands prying the knife from his. His blood tainted her fingers, yet she didn't shrink from it.

He tried to pull his hand away, his mind whirling at what to do. Hospital. He should get to a hospital, where they'd be able to stitch his finger back together. Before he lost too much blood.

Mel's fingers felt like steel – stronger than any set of

handcuffs he owned – yet her hands were smaller and slimmer than his. He couldn't break her grip, even as she brought her other hand toward his severed finger. Sickened, he saw the bone between the blood and tissue, before her hand hid his from sight. Some of the salt had seeped into the wound and the stinging became unbearable.

"Stop," he gasped. "Please. Take me to hospital. Need some painkillers and they can fix this."

"Kiss me," Mel murmured. "It will help."

Luce snorted. "How?" Half the word was swallowed by her lips connecting with his. His whole hand was on fire and her kiss was just a pleasant distraction, but not enough. Tears of pain coursed down his cheeks – he could taste the salt and he was sure Mel could, too, but she continued to kiss him as she kept his hand captive.

He broke away from her. "Mel. Please..." He was embarrassed to hear it come out sounding like a sob. It felt like his hand was going numb from the blood loss – or was it Mel's strong grip?

"Here, let me wash the blood away so I can get a better look," she said, pulling him toward the sink. Cool water trickled across his skin and he didn't dare look at the damage, though it wasn't hurting as much. Perhaps the water had numbed it further.

She forced his injured hand up between them, level with her lips. She started to kiss his fingers. First his thumb, then his index finger. He felt the touch of her tongue on the tip of his middle finger, dreading the pain when she touched his next, injured finger.

"Mel, please, stop," he begged. This was worse than the humiliation Persephone put him through. But Mel was an angel, the kindest he'd ever met. She wouldn't hurt him like this...

He felt another tear slip out of the corner of his eye as he squeezed them tightly shut, the tiniest defence against the pain he knew was coming.

Her lips grazed his pinkie, then pulled away. He could feel her breath on his hand as she said, "Open your eyes, Luce."

He knew what was next, but he heard the command in her tone and he had to obey. He couldn't not do it. Her fingers shielded his, so he couldn't see the last joint of his finger just hanging, blood trickling... He felt his knuckle graze her lips and wondered what in Hell she was doing.

"But you're an angel. An angel, Mel. Please..."

She set his finger alight as she gently sucked on the length of it, from base to tip. He fancied he could feel her tongue tickling his injured fingertip, but that wasn't possible – he'd seen the severed nerve. He'd seen...

He saw her pull his finger from her mouth, whole and healed as if it had never happened. He'd been able to heal when he was an angel, but never as fast or as perfectly as this. "How?" he gasped.

Her eyes held him. "Love, Luce. When you love someone, you'd do anything for them. Take away their pain. Heal their hurts. Lift them when they fall. Help them when they need you most. Love is my greatest strength, Luce, and I love you." There was power in her voice – he was under no illusions that it was anyone less than Muriel of the Hashmallim who had him mesmerised.

Giddy from the blood loss, misty-eyed at the heavy attraction for both Mel and the power she held over him, Luce couldn't think straight. He didn't have to. He seized her in an embrace that would have crushed a weaker woman. Not Mel. Her body was firm against him – not resisting, but not compliant, either. His kiss was clumsy and rough, but she responded as if he'd been skilful and seductive, for she was both.

He wanted her...oh Hell, how he wanted her. Blearily, he peered over her shoulder at the couch. He wouldn't make it that far. Maybe if he lifted her onto the bench...His back slammed into the fridge and he forgot about the bench. Mel's body pinned his to the metal and it didn't matter where as long as it was now. Oh God, MEL...

She released him and he almost fell. He stared at her, hurt. What had he done wrong?

"The water's boiling and we should probably turn both burners off if we're not going to use them," Mel said, wiping her mouth with her hand. She looked as flushed as he felt, but her grin showed no guilt.

Luce glanced at the stove. The water was boiling over – hissing into steam as it threatened to extinguish the burner flame beneath it. How had he missed the sound?

"I'll make us some tea and you make breakfast. We need to get into the city for that meeting at ten," Mel said, regret in her tone.

"And maybe later we can finish what we started?" Luce asked eagerly.

"Yes. Later, Luce." The look she gave him held unmistakeable love. No one had ever looked at him like that before.

His heart swelled in his chest. Miracles did happen. He was an angel again and Mel loved HIM.

Dressed in his still slightly damp suit, Luce slid into his car. He'd parked it halfway up Mel's street, in the only available spot, but the walk seemed a lot shorter now in dry daylight with Mel by his side. He couldn't keep the smile off his face as she climbed into the passenger seat beside him.

Her eyes were serious. "If you drive like a maniac, I will get out and walk. You only get one warning."

He winked. "Yes, ma'am. I'll be the smoothest chauffeur you ever had, I swear. I'll have you naked in the back seat before you can –"

"Luce. That really is enough."

He waited for her to click her seatbelt into place over her pale grey suit skirt before he pulled his black Jaguar smoothly out of the tight space, letting his blissful mood infuse his driving. He was in no hurry.

Mel watched the traffic as he drove, occasionally glancing at him but shifting her gaze before he could meet her eyes. He wondered what he'd missed of her telephone conversation before he'd interrupted and what sort of favour she'd be asking for – and from whom.

He turned into the HELL Corporation garage entrance, swiping his passcard to open the gate as he nodded to the guard. He drove automatically to his personal car bay on the second level down, only to stop in shock as he saw it occupied by a bright yellow smart car.

"Persi's car," Mel said.

Luce yanked the steering wheel around and parked his car in the general HELL Corporation space beside the tiny irritant in his parking spot. He sat glowering at it and all it symbolised, before realising that Mel stood outside his door, waiting. He hurried to get out so she wouldn't leave without him, but she didn't seem to be in a hurry. He locked the car and turned on the alarm at a touch. Mel extended her hand toward him.

He held out the keys, unsure. "What do you want?" An unfamiliar desire to give her anything she asked for swept over him, confusing him even more.

She smiled gently. "Your hand, Luce. I'd like to walk down the street, holding your hand, if you don't mind. I don't keep secrets easily – I prefer an open declaration, where possible."

He shoved the keys in his pocket and grabbed her hand. "Let's go."

Mel's laughter echoed through the underground car park, but Luce liked the sound. There was no cruelty in it – she laughed for joy, he knew.

As they stepped out onto the street, joining the crowds of commuters hurrying to or from coffee shops for their mid-morning caffeine hit, Luce gave in and asked, "Where are we headed?"

"The agency that employs me," Mel responded, glancing at the traffic before stepping out onto the road. "Raphael owes me a favour or three and I think today is an ideal occasion to cash in."

"You mean the Helpful Angels Agency? I'm not going to be very welcome there," Luce admitted. "I could just camp out in a coffee shop somewhere and wait for you to come rejoin me so I can buy you one. It might be easier."

Mel's fingers tightened around his. "Oh, no. You're coming in with me – whatever they think and say. You have a right to be there, as the favour I'll ask for involves you – intimately, I think. They need to know how serious I am about this and your very presence will help to emphasise that."

She sounded like she was planning for battle – a battle she'd surely win. "If you'd accepted my offer to be my PA instead of Persephone, nothing could have stopped us. With you at my side, I bet I'd never have been thrown out of Heaven," Luce blurted out.

Mel glanced at Luce, pressing her lips together. "Perhaps," she said, picking up the pace so he had to hurry to keep up.

He almost missed the doorway, which was set between two shops, with the winged HAA logo stencilled on the glass. Luckily, Mel didn't let go of him as she seized the doorknob with her free hand, leading Luce up the stairs behind her.

At least he got a nice view of her arse to bolster him up the stairs – a small, unexpected slice of Heaven, Luce decided, slowing his ascent to make the most of it.

4

"Good morning, Mel! It's wonderful to see you," a warm voice greeted her. "We've been so worried..."

Luce couldn't see the girl's face yet, but he doubted he'd get such an enthusiastic greeting. Hell, he'd never heard one like it at HELL Corporation, either. As his head rose above the banister, he got a clear view of the receptionist. He recognised Gabrielle instantly.

Mel's grip tightened around his fingers, so he plastered a grin on his face as he pounded up the last few stairs to the landing. "This is my friend, Luce. He'll be coming in to see Raphael with me at ten," Mel said with a beaming smile.

Gabrielle's smile turned to a look of horror. "Mel, that's...that's..."

Flashing a smile and a wink to the archangel receptionist, Luce held out his hand to shake Gabrielle's. "Luce Iblis, recently retired CEO of the HELL Corporation. I'm sure you've worked under me in our office." Gabrielle hid her hands beneath the desk, so he reached for Mel's hand instead, pulling her fingers to his lips. "Mel has kindly arranged a meeting for me with Raphael." From the corner of his eye, he could see Mel's professional smile, giving nothing away. Mel could hide more secrets with her open, angelic smile than he held in all of Hell, Luce mused.

Gabrielle jumped up from her desk. "I'll go see if he's through with his nine o'clock," she said breathlessly, hurrying in her heels to one of the enclosed offices along the back wall.

"Shall we sit?" he asked Mel, waving at the sofa against the wall. Mel nodded and followed him to the seat. She carefully placed herself on the cushions so her skirt sat perfectly, then waited for Luce to take the other half of the couch. He wasn't as worried about appearances as she seemed to be – he stretched out his arms as he relaxed into the white leather, one along the armrest and the other around Mel. She straightened her back the tiniest bit, but didn't move to push him away.

Both were silent as they heard panicked voices from

the office with the partially closed door — it appeared that Gabrielle had forgotten to close it.

A male voice said, "She's here. By some miracle, she made it through the night without him finding her. He's probably hunting her now — I'll keep her safe, I swear. If I have the whole agency guarding her, I'll find somewhere to hide her that he'll never think to look. Find me some crisis on the other side of the world we can use to coerce her to leave. North Korea, Canada, UK, Siberia, Ukraine...there has to be something. Find out and call back within the hour, while she's still here." The phone rattled into its cradle, as if the man's hands were shaking. Gabrielle's voice murmured quietly — too low for him to discern the words. Luce figured they were probably about him, anyway.

"Wherever you go, I want to come with you," Luce whispered and Mel nodded. He wondered what she was agreeing to — his company or just his desire? His thoughts were interrupted by movement across the office.

Raphael emerged behind Gabrielle, his face whiter than his shirt. His eyes flicked briefly to Luce, but his attention was on Mel. "Please, God, no," he whispered, just loud enough to carry to Luce's ears.

Luce wondered what he was so worried about. Did the angel think he'd managed to corrupt Mel? The world would end before he'd succeed at that — which sounded good to him.

"Mel, I'm so sorry about the imposition on you,

particularly when you're on leave. I'd like to discuss it with you privately, if possible," Raphael said, not acknowledging Luce at all.

Before Mel could respond, Luce chimed in, "Fine by me. If you have company secrets to discuss, I'll just sit out here and keep Gabrielle company. Keep her from getting lonely and all." He grinned at the receptionist, who blanched as she sank onto her desk chair.

"Gabi won't be alone for long, Luce. I'm sure she's just holding the fort until everyone else returns with coffee. It might be best for everyone if you're not sitting at the top of the stairs when a whole pack of coffee-carrying Grigori come up." She lifted her eyes to Raphael. "It's fine. What I'm here to discuss can be said in front of Luce."

Raphael evidently didn't agree, but he also didn't seem to want to argue with Mel, so he gestured toward his office, leading the way. He offered them both a seat before hurrying around the desk to put its laminated width between them.

Luce wanted to laugh at how nervously these angels seemed to treat him, as if he might explode at any moment, but he didn't want to embarrass Mel. He was as eager as Raphael seemed to be to hear what she had to say.

"How are you, Mel? Are you well?" Raphael began, staring at her with worried eyes. "You didn't experience any damage last night in the storm?" He seemed to be searching for a reply without saying what he really sought.

"I'm fine," Mel said, her serene smile speaking volumes to Luce that Raphael didn't seem to understand.

"Are you sure? Nothing different at all?" Raphael persisted.

Luce lost patience. "By all that's holy, I haven't corrupted the girl. I showed up at her house last night in the storm, with nothing but my car and the soaked clothes I stood up in. Mel was kind enough to take me in and let me stay until the storm was over. Your precious angel is as pristine and perfect as I found her." He reached for the letter opener on Raphael's desk, which turned out to be surprisingly sharp – perfect for his needs. "The problem is THIS." He dragged the blade across his palm, and a line of ruby blood erupted.

Raphael's eyes widened. "How...? Demon blood is black. How can you have blood like ours?"

Mel touched her fingers to Luce's palm, causing the cut to close.

"Thank you," Luce said in surprise.

"Demons can't be healed by angels! What in Hell?" Raphael exclaimed, jumping up and backing into the wall, away from the sight before him.

"I'd say your precious angel has corrupted me into something like you."

"That's not possible!" Raphael replied. "Demons are damned, never to be redeemed!"

"If you have a better explanation, I'd love to hear it.

Because I've got nothing," Luce snapped.

"What have you done?" Raphael stared at Mel, looking scared. "That's not just any demon you've changed. You've redeemed the Lord of Hell!"

"He came to me and begged for my help. I'd do no less for any other human and he seemed little more than that, with the power Persi stripped from him. He was shivering, standing on my front steps in a soaked suit." Mel shrugged. "What can I say? He makes a good cup of tea."

"You owe me a favour, Raphael," Mel stated. "I'd like to use it to clear up some of the mess resulting from this assignment."

"If you want him changed back into a demon, I'm sure Michael would be happy to help," Raphael replied eagerly.

"No!" Mel and Luce said together. Luce looked at her in surprise, but she had more to say.

"I want you to arrange an invitation for Luce to re-enter Heaven, Raphael. He's been kept out for long enough. I'm happy to explain his case up there in person, if required."

Both men stared at her.

"Michael won't be happy about this," Raphael said, shaking his head. "I should never have brought you in on this assignment. Now..."

"Michael's never happy," Mel replied abruptly, but she didn't elaborate.

Luce looked from one to the other, wondering what was going unsaid in this exchange. He hoped it was more about Michael's insecurities than anything to do with him. He'd never liked Michael, not after what he'd done to him. If Michael was miserable, that was fine by him. Served the righteous bastard right.

"It'll take some time and a lot of work, Mel. I'll find him somewhere to stay in the meantime," Raphael muttered, as if Luce wasn't sitting right in front of him. "It won't be up to his normal opulent standard, but if he's serious about joining our ranks, he'll just have to make do..."

"Luce, you're welcome to stay with me for as long as you need to," Mel said.

That sounded pretty good to him. Luce cleared his throat. "Thank you."

"Michael really won't like that at all," Raphael said, looking even more worried.

Mel rose to her feet. "Michael isn't my keeper. Perhaps he needs to realise that there are some things he can't control." She bowed her head slightly to

Raphael. "Thank you. Let me know when you have more to tell me."

Luce stood, too, opening the office door so they could leave the stuffy space.

"Mel, you know Michael's only trying to protect you," Raphael said urgently. "Don't let his charm win you over. Remember who and what he is."

Mel's voice was cold. "I know what Michael's trying to do and it wouldn't be necessary if he'd taken my advice, instead of picking and choosing the bits he liked best. I'm under no illusions about Luce. I wish I could say the same about Michael's perception of me."

Luce couldn't hide his smile. It sounded like Mel and Michael had a history that hadn't ended well. He swore he'd be better to her than that idiot of an overprotective archangel. Whatever it took.

Luce tried not to show how relieved he felt to hear the HAA door close behind them as they reached the street. "Would you like to grab a coffee or maybe an early lunch?" he asked Mel.

"Sure," she said.

They headed to a nearby café, where they both ordered coffee before sitting at a table at the very back. Partway between the coffee rush and the lunch rush, Luce knew the café's emptiness wouldn't last, but they could take advantage of it while it did.

Luce opened his mouth to ask Mel about her relationship with Michael.

"Gah! That was a bloody waste of time," a loud, male voice complained. Timber creaked as the man sat down at the table beside Luce and Mel.

"No, it wasn't. Those suits were perfect. You'll match the bridesmaids and the flowers, so it'll be a real wedding to remember. Just think of the photos..." the girl said dreamily as she sat in the chair across from him.

Mel covered her smile, clearly trying not to laugh. She evidently knew more about this couple and their wedding than Luce did.

"I AM thinking of the photos – we'll have them for the rest of our lives. I'm not getting married in a hot pink suit!" the man protested.

Luce burst out laughing.

The girl glared at Luce, then pursed her mouth as she turned her eyes back to her fiancé. "I thought you'd do anything for me. Now you won't even wear the suit I want you to at our wedding. Maybe you don't want to marry me at all." She rose to her full height, which would barely have reached Luce's chest. She gave a little snort and a nod, before turning her back on her fiancé to stride angrily out of the café.

Mel reached over and touched the man's arm. "Tell her you would do anything for her. Swim through sharks, give your life to save hers," she whispered.

The man pulled his arm irritably away from Mel as

he stood up. Luce felt bad for her – she'd only tried to help, after all. He hoped she wouldn't be hurt. After all, humans weren't known for taking advice from strangers and maybe the bloke was better off without his bridezilla.

"Jess, I would do almost anything for you!" the man shouted. "I'd swim through a school of sharks at Trigg Beach to get to you. I'd fend off an entire gang of bikies if they threatened to hurt you."

The girl stopped and turned around.

Luce recovered from his shock quickly. "Say you'd walk through Hell for her," he suggested. "Naked."

The bloke stared at him. "That's a fucking crazy idea. Who'd walk through Hell naked?" He turned back to Jess. "And I'd marry you in my birthday suit on Swanbourne Beach if that's what you want, but if I make my brothers and my best mate wear pink suits, they'll kill me before the wedding!"

Some of the other café patrons started cheering and Jess sported a hot pink blush. "I couldn't get married on Swanbourne Beach. I've already ordered my dress and my underwear..."

The bloke shoved his way through tables to get to her and the cheering grew louder as the couple kissed. They left without ordering.

Luce turned back to Mel to find her staring at him. "What?"

"Who would walk through Hell naked?" she asked.

Luce shrugged. "I do it all the time. Well, usually

with the horns, the tail, the red skin...you know, the whole works. People seem to expect it on occasion. Keeps the other demons in order, but clothes would just spoil the effect..." He broke off as he heard the rattle of crockery.

"Your coffee?" a frightened-looking waitress stammered, the tray shaking in her hands.

Luce's espresso contrasted nicely with Mel's macchiato, he thought. She hadn't seen his wings yet, though she'd certainly seen the rest of him last night. He'd been proud to be able to please an angel with his physique, when she was so accustomed to angelic perfection. She'd certainly appreciated his technique, too...

"Luce," Mel called. It sounded like it wasn't the first time, either.

Luce focussed on her face, trying not to remember what it looked like in her more passionate moments —

like this morning. He could inspire her to remind him later. "Yes?"

"I asked what you wanted to do this afternoon. Given both of us are unemployed and relatively free, for the moment – your call." Mel smiled.

Luce thought he'd like to get her out of her conservative clothes and show her the devil of a good time. He'd happily do that all afternoon and into the evening, too.

"Clothes?" Mel asked.

Luce stared at her. Had she read his mind? He'd heard there were angels who could read thoughts and his had been fairly graphic. He felt a blush colour his cheeks. "What about clothes?" he ventured.

"Don't you need more clothes? All you have are your current suit and shirt. You're going to need fresh ones for tomorrow."

Luce shrugged. "I can buy some more before we leave, I guess." He tried not to show how relieved he felt.

Mel shook her head, still smiling. Luce didn't want her to stop smiling – ever. "I assume Persephone made you sign over your house, along with everything else, but she'd have no use for your clothes. Wouldn't it be easier just to ask her if you can have them?"

When Mel put it so reasonably, it sounded like the easiest thing in the world – but she couldn't know Persephone as well as he did. The half-angel, which he suspected was also half-demon, would probably insist he do something incredibly degrading for every single sock. He still had horrible flashbacks about her tattoo. Hundreds of damned, writhing, naked...all scrambling and fighting to get closer to her unholy halo...

"Do you want me to call her and ask for you?" Mel asked kindly – once again, as if she could read his mind.

Luce shivered and said, "I'd really appreciate it if you would. Buying new might be easier, though."

Mel pulled out her phone and made the call. After less than a minute of speaking to Persephone, she ended the conversation. She turned her eyes to Luce again. "She said you can have all of your clothes, shoes, accessories and toiletries. I'd like to smell your aftershave on you again." She slipped her phone into her bag. "We can go over there this afternoon while no one's home, if you still have your house keys. Otherwise, we can go pick up the keys from her in the office."

"I still have my keys, so we can do it without having to see her. Thank you – for everything," Luce said, dazed. "What did she ask for in return?" He dreaded knowing, but he knew he needed to.

Mel laughed. "Persi is deeply in my debt for giving out my phone number and address to a demon without my permission. She wouldn't dare ask me for anything until long after she's made reparation for that."

She'd been giving Mel's details out to random demons? Luce's hands clenched, ready for combat. "If any demon comes near your house..."

Mel laid her fingers gently over his fists. "There was only one demon – you, Luce. I'm sure we can come to some sort of arrangement for me calling in a favour on your behalf."

"In other words, I'll be in your debt?" he suggested. "Even deeper than I am already, of course."

"That sounds tempting. In the meantime – it's time for you to show me where you lived, Luce."

He thought of his Crawley penthouse. "With pleasure."

"There's the restaurant I wanted to take you to on Valentine's Day," Luce said, pointing. "Really fresh oysters..." He stopped. "Sorry, I know you don't like oysters." He didn't think she'd heard him as she didn't respond.

Mel's curiosity was clear in her wide eyes as she followed him into the old brewery by the river. "How long have you lived here?"

"I bought this apartment off the plans. Why?"

"Well, this bit of land has a reputation for being

cursed. Apparently, there's a huge snake that lies in wait for the unwary here. I'm just wondering how much you had to do with the origin of that particular legend..." Mel wore her wicked smile, the one Luce found hard to believe he was seeing on an angel's face.

"Big snake? Sounds like my style," Luce replied, wondering just how much Mel knew about him. She had said she knew his history, but realisation dawned on him that she could have meant far more than his initial fall from Heaven. In contrast, he knew almost nothing about her.

How was that possible? There weren't that many angels as old as she was — and he knew a fair bit about all of the others. He'd fought with or against all of them in the past. Given she was still an angel and hadn't fallen with him, she must have been one of those against him, but he knew he'd never seen her before she'd walked into the HELL Corporation offices. It was almost as if she'd been deliberately avoiding him — or hidden from him by someone else.

Worried, he shoved the key into the lock and almost broke it off as he wrenched it around. The key twisted and unlocked the door, but he hesitated before opening it for Mel. The view from the arched windows was absolutely stunning, and he wanted her to enjoy it.

"Are you ready?" he asked.

"For what?" she replied.

He grinned. "Entering the devil's lair. I could have a den with whips, chains and all sorts of torture implements in here. Aren't you worried about what you might find? Or that you might not make it out?"

Her smile didn't waver as she looked deep into his eyes – no, into his soul, he realised. "You don't torture people for pleasure. You tease and torment, yes, but pain is reserved for those who you feel deserve it – those who have caused similar pain. I don't think you enjoy it, either – or you would never have left Hell. You could be hiding poor taste in decorating, though – the walls of your place might be plastered with naked pictures of all the women you've slept with." She laughed. "If that's the case, the worst you'll do to me is make me blush."

Now he was more worried than ever. She knew him almost as well as he knew himself – details he'd never really thought about, and she saw so much! What if she thought he had bad taste?

Mel's smile softened and she stopped laughing. "It's all right. If you really do have naked pictures on the wall, I'll do my best not to look, so I don't embarrass you. Oh...unless the naked pictures are of you?"

Luce laughed aloud. Why in Hell would he want to see naked pictures of himself? "Okay, just as long as you feel you're ready." He threw the door wide open and strode in, beckoning her to follow him. He stood beside the windows, his eyes fixed on her and not the view of Melville Water. "What do you think?" he asked anxiously.

"The view is really beautiful. You can almost see

clear to my place from here." She turned sympathetic eyes from the panorama to him. "It must have been hard to give this place up."

He'd never really thought about it until now – this place wasn't his any more. Instead, he had Mel. Or he'd had her for a night. Cautiously, he laid an arm around her shoulders, wondering if she'd pull away, even as he pulled her to him. His relief hissed out with his breath as she rested her head against his chest.

"It was worth it," he responded. "I mean, you or a big snake. The choice was easy."

She laughed. "I know what I'd prefer." She didn't enlighten him. Instead, she said, "We should really start packing up your clothes, or we'll still be here when Persi gets home. I don't think I've ever seen you wear the same black shirt twice, until today. It'll take us a while to get them all packed."

She'd noticed. He felt absurdly gratified to hear it. He wondered what else she'd noticed but feigned indifference to.

"C'mon, Luce. You won't shock me with your extensive wardrobe. I've seen you wear a lot of it at work." Mel stepped away from him, headed for his bedroom. He hurried to follow, hoping he hadn't left any of his sex toys out where Mel could find them. Or worse – if Persephone had found them after he'd left. How could he explain his handcuff collection to an angel like Mel?

Countless trips later, he'd filled the car with his clothes, shoes and other personal items. He'd managed to hide at least three sets of cuffs without Mel seeing, or at least, he hoped so. The pair weighing heavily in his coat pocket had featured prominently in a particularly elaborate fantasy about Mel. He didn't even want to contemplate Persephone touching them.

As he headed back up in the lift to the apartment one last time, Luce wondered whether his whiskeys counted as personal items. Persephone hated whiskey and some of the more mature ones would definitely be wasted on her. He'd ask Mel what she thought about taking the bottles. After all, she'd made the bargain with Persephone – she'd know whether the alcohol was included with his stuff.

He found her standing at his bedroom window, staring out across the water.

"Did you know you could see the dolphins from here?" Mel turned her eager eyes on him and held out her hand. "Come watch them play."

He took her hand, letting her reel him in, before dropping it to wrap his arms around her. Mel pointed at the fins cutting through the water, near Matilda Bay. They'd stroked the swans together on that shore and he'd wanted to bring her here ever since. "There," she said.

Luce peered out at them over her shoulder, then shrugged. "Are you sure those are dolphins? I always thought they were baby bull sharks. There are a fair few of them in the river."

Mel laughed. "No, the sharks are smaller, with different tails. They're far shyer, too. Look at their tails. Sharks swim with their tails flicking from side to side, like this" – she moved her hand to demonstrate – "and dolphins are mammals, so they undulate up and down, like this," she said, rippling her arm like the dolphins in the bay below.

"I should've had you up here a long time ago, just so you could tell me what I was seeing." Luce glanced at the bed. "I'd still be happy to have you here now. It's just us, my king-sized bed and the amazing view..."

Mel turned cold. "It's not your house or your bed any more, Luce. It all belongs to Persi. Even with the wonderful view, someone else's bed simply doesn't appeal to me. Have you packed up all your things? The car must be pretty full by now. I think you own more shoes than I do."

Luce felt his face redden. The way she said it, it sounded so sordid. Like offering her his dirty desk. Again, she was right. Persephone had cuffed herself to this bed and it was soiled by sheer association. It didn't even look like she'd changed the sheets. Hell, the whole penthouse was polluted by her presence, the venomous little viper. Now he wanted to leave more than Mel did. There were the whiskeys, though...

"I have all my clothes and shoes in the car. I was wondering about my whiskey. Do you think they count as personal items? Most of the bottles are opened," he said.

Mel tilted her head, considering. "Does Persi like whiskey?"

Luce laughed. "No. When we were in Japan last week, I was given some particularly fine bottles of Hibiki. She almost caused an incident when she choked on her first mouthful. I think the bottles are here somewhere..."

"I've never tasted Japanese whiskey, though I admit I'm quite fond of the Scottish ones. Something about the peat they use there. It's certainly improved a lot since the early batches in the 1500s, too. They called it the water of life back then, though." Mel nodded slowly. "If they fit into your car, you can take them. I'll arrange it with Persi when I speak to her next."

Mel liked whiskey? Luce brightened. He'd pack every single bottle he owned – and throw out all his shoes to make room in the car if he had to. Surely she'd appreciate the twenty-one-year-old Hibiki. He headed for the walk-in pantry behind the bar, where he kept his spirits.

"Mel? Are you still here?"

Luce almost dropped his best bottle of Laphroaig at the sound of Persephone's voice. He tried to pull the door shut, so she wouldn't see him. But, because he couldn't close it completely without making noise, he still heard her clearly.

"I'm in the main bedroom, admiring the view," Mel called back.

"Oh, Mel, I'm so sorry! Raphael shouted at me so much last night that I cried! I should never have told him how to find you. It all seemed so easy, so simple, that I thought you wouldn't mind and Raphael was so angry. I didn't know..."

Was Raphael the one who'd tried to hide her from him? Luce wondered. Or was he just doing it now, for someone else? Whoever he'd been on the phone with this morning...

"It's all right," Mel's calm voice interrupted. "Have you spoken to Raphael yet today?"

Luce tried not to make a sound as he packed the remaining bottles into the box. He definitely didn't want her to know he was here.

Persephone's inane giggle set Luce's teeth on edge. "No! He'll only shout at me again and I didn't want to cry in front of all those demons at the office. Your call was a godsend. I couldn't leave you to pack up all the demon's things by yourself, so I got off work as early as I could and raced over here to help you. Do you want me to get started on the shoes? I've never known a man who had so many. I don't think I've met a man like him, ever. I still can't believe he wasn't the slightest bit interested in me – I even offered him his choice of handcuffs! Do you think it might be because he doesn't like women?"

Mel coughed to cover what Luce thought sounded more like laughter. He hoped she wasn't laughing about the handcuffs. "Maybe he just likes good shoes. Actually, most of Luce's things are already packed and downstairs. There's not really much more for you to do."

"Are you sure? You shouldn't have to deal with the demon's things like this. I definitely don't need any of them. Raphael should have sent some of the boys from the agency over to do it, or I would have when I got home. I'd have had a courier deliver them to...wherever Raphael wanted them. Are you sure there's nothing else I can do to help?"

"It's fine. Like I said, all taken care of. Oh, there was one thing I was wondering about. His whiskey. Would it be all right if I took that, too? It'd be a shame to waste it."

Luce held his breath, hoping. The little minx would probably pour them all down the drain if she knew they were for him and not just Mel.

"Take anything you want," Persephone said warmly. "He keeps the best alcohol in the cupboard behind the bar..."

Luce had only a moment's warning of her approach, but he had nowhere to go with the box of bottles in his arms. The door flew open – and Persephone's mouth did, too.

She pursed her lips almost immediately. "Mel, did you know the demon was hiding in the cupboard?" She glared at Luce, who backed up involuntarily. "You were going to jump her when she came to collect the whiskey, weren't you? If you hurt Mel, you'll have every angel in the agency, and Heaven as well, after your hide. If you so much as touch her, I will personally chop your willy off!"

Was he imagining it, or did her eyes look more red than brown for a moment there? Luce wondered, trying unobtrusively to cross his legs where he stood. Just in case.

"That won't be necessary, Persi," Luce heard Mel say. He tried not to show how relieved he felt. "I brought Luce over to pack his own things. He can carry the whiskey down to the car for me, too." She pulled Persephone out of the way, so Luce had space to edge out of the cupboard, using the box as a shield between his body and the angry half-angel.

He hurried out of the apartment with the bottles, then took his time carrying it to the car park and loading it into the car. He debated whether to wait for Mel in the car or return upstairs to his former home and PA, wishing he didn't have to see Persephone again. Still, he knew he'd have to face her at some point.

Gah, when did she change from being simply a nuisance to something that scared him? As if her touch tainted him, when all he wanted was Mel. Who was waiting for him upstairs.

He sighed and trudged back up to the apartment, hoping Persephone would leave before he made it there.

"Mel, you really should let some of the Grigori boys take care of him. I should never have let him leave. Should have asked Michael to send him back to Hell where he belongs so he can't..." Persephone broke off abruptly as Luce shouldered past her to wrap an arm around Mel. He needed her like a lifeline.

"Are you ready to go?" he asked her, doing his damnedest to ignore the half-angel. "If we leave now, we can beat the peak-hour traffic and I can have everything put away at your place before dinner. I know this wonderful little seafood restaurant down by the water that serves the best oysters..." He grinned.

"I'm not eating oysters," Mel objected.

Luce let his grin widen. "You won't have to. I'll happily eat enough for both of us. You can order whatever you like and I'll drive you home after."

Mel's face lit with a genuine smile. "That sounds lovely." Her fingers closed around his. "See you later, Persi, and thank you for the whiskey."

Together, they walked out of the apartment, leaving a shocked Persephone behind them.

"These old wardrobes must've been built when people only owned a few clothes. It won't shut!" Luce grumbled.

Mel appeared in the doorway, the empty whiskey box in her arms. "Here. You take the box out to the recycling bin and I'll see if I can help. You can always put some of them in my wardrobe if you have to. I'm sure I have space for more."

Luce agreed and left her to it. He'd never had to deal with furniture that fought back before.

He returned to the guest room to find Mel squeezing through the doorway with an armload of his clothes. "Let me help," he said instantly, taking them from her.

"They'll have to go in my room. This one's full." Mel nodded at the now-closed wardrobe that housed his clothes and shoes.

He dumped his load on her bed and opened Mel's wardrobe door. It was pitifully bare – she had perhaps a dozen items hanging from the rail. Hell, he had more clothes on the bed. He recognised all of them, too – that one she'd worn to work on Melbourne Cup day; there was the suit she'd worn to her job interview, beside the skirt she'd worn on Valentine's Day. And the suit she'd worn on the day of the alien press conference, when she'd ended up as the HELL Corporation heroine. No, wait...there was one dress he'd never seen her wear. The shimmer of silk as it caught the light made him certain of it. He'd have dropped to his knees and begged if she had. An angel in deep gold silk...the gift!

"I got you a present while I was away. I forgot to give it to you last night," Luce said, leaving his clothes where they lay to look for his suitcase. He knew he'd left it...ah, there it was. The box was slightly squashed at the corners, but the contents looked like they were intact. No leaking liquid or anything. Luce returned to Mel's room and held out the misshapen box. "For you."

Mel's eyes lit up as she looked at the package and

carefully took it from his hands. "Thank you." She kissed him, but it was over so quickly that Luce barely had time to respond. He watched her peel off the crumpled plastic wrap and open the box. "How did you know?" she exclaimed, staring at him in wonder. She pulled out the bottle of perfume, holding it over her wrist in anticipation.

"You wore it every day at work. I came to see if you were free for lunch a few times, but you weren't at your desk. Once, there was this scent...like I'd just missed you and you'd sprayed your perfume on before you went out. I went through your desk drawers and then your filing cabinet, looking for it. I found it, but the bottle was almost empty. When I saw the same perfume in an airport duty-free shop, I had to get it. I wanted to give it to you...but I also wanted to keep it to remember you by." He closed his eyes, determined not to look at her. He sounded like some sappy romance hero, instead of the stern Lord of Hell. "Every day I was away, I thought of you. Wished it was you with me instead of that...that..."

"Lamprey?" Mel suggested.

"Yes!" Luce exclaimed. "You don't know what it was like. I mean, first it was just the short skirts and skimpy tops so I could look at the goods, as if she wanted me to ask how much she wanted for them. Then she left buttons and zips undone, like she wanted to take it all off. Then the constant offers. Sex, sex and more sex. She started offering with her clothes on, but they came off quickly. First, she wore those skimpy little French knickers, then switched to stringier and skimpier things until she left off underwear completely. Any excuse and she'd bend over to pick something up, flash that horrible tattoo and give a coy smile or a wink, like she thought I wanted to see what she had between her legs. I couldn't eat or drink anything when she was around, because I knew I wouldn't be able to keep it down when she dropped her fork again...Oh, Mel, you have no idea. I shuddered at the sight or sound of her – my own secretary! Not being able to get any work done around her, because of the constant offers of sex..."

Mel's gentle smile looked sympathetic. "Actually, I do. Some demons are more subtle than others, but your office had plenty of men who deemed themselves my prospective partners. One was particularly persistent."

"The demons at work hounded you like that half-angel pursued me? I'll send them all back to Hell in disgrace. I had no idea. You'll never have to see any of them again, I swear..."

"I don't work there any more and neither do you, so it's not really an issue now. And it wasn't as difficult for me as it was for you. I knew I could never accept any of the offers. I didn't want to hurt anyone, is all. As long as you were a demon, the most I was ever willing to offer you was dinner." Mel's smile turned sad and she turned away, busying herself with his clothes on the bed.

"You agreed to dinner tonight," Luce reminded her, starting to feel uneasy.

"I did," she said. She started hanging his shirts beside her dresses, pushing her meagre wardrobe aside to make more room for his. She stopped to finger the last one. "I've never seen you wear this to work."

Luce looked at the silk shirt that had caught her interest. "That's because I bought it in New York and I didn't trust my PA to get it dry-cleaned properly, so I haven't worn it yet. But for you, if you like...I'll wear it to dinner." He made swift work of his buttons, stripping off his shirt so he could change. "Or I could just go topless, for your viewing pleasure." He grinned, spreading his arms in an open invitation.

Mel laughed heartily as she stepped closer. "Are they real?" she asked, caressing his rippled muscles with her fingertips. It felt...indescribably good.

"All real. All...yours." He pulled her closer, wishing his pants didn't feel so tight. Maybe he should take them off, too. "And there's more, Mel." He kicked his pants away from the puddle they'd formed around his ankles. For a moment, he wondered if her silence was because he was being too pushy, like he'd been in the office. Could he ever do the right thing around her? "But only if you want me," he said, hoping.

"Before or after dinner?" She gave his lips a light kiss.

"Both, if you like. An aperitif, then dinner, followed by a decadent dessert. I want to treat you like you deserve, Mel. You've done so much for me and I want to repay you in any way I can." Luce waved at himself before gesturing more broadly. "Me. The world. I'd give you anything, Mel. All you have to do is ask."

"I don't need you to give me the world. For now, you're enough," she said, giving him a deeper, more heavenly kiss.

"And after?" Luce's voice growled, to his surprise. He'd never heard himself sound so feral. Like some lust-crazed human about to jump her without her permission. But he wouldn't. Not Mel. After so many weeks without her, he needed to know she wouldn't leave him. She'd laugh if she knew, he was sure of it. The Lord of Hell, lost without Mel.

"You promised me dinner and dessert, my love. I'll hold you to that," Mel said, smiling. "Now show me what you have in mind for an aperitif."

She wore white – an angel in the kitchen, contrasting with the honey-coloured timber cabinets. Her hair was pinned up as it usually was in the office, baring her neck so that it fairly begged him for a kiss. He couldn't refuse her, so he moved as quietly as he could until she was close enough to touch. Maybe he hadn't used up all his oyster influence last night...

"What is it about white that makes you look so angelic?" he murmured as he kissed her neck.

Mel jumped and gave a yelp. Liquid splattered on

the bench.

Luce lifted his head and realised she'd been handling hot tea. She moved quickly to the sink, running her red hands under the cold tap.

"I'm sorry, Mel. I didn't realise..." he began, wishing he'd thought to announce himself more safely. She was hurting because of him and he couldn't stand it. He'd give anything to be able to heal her as she had him.

"It's all right," she said breathlessly. She nodded at the half-full cups. "You drink yours. I'll get to mine in a minute, if I get time."

"What's the hurry?" Luce asked, slurping the steaming liquid. He hadn't had a cup of tea in centuries until arriving at Mel's place and now it seemed perfectly natural to drink several a day. He wondered if there was anything she couldn't persuade him to do.

"Raphael called. He said he can get permission for you to enter Heaven again, but you'll have to go through judgement, like any mortal. I said it was ridiculous and I fully intend to argue your case in person. Raphael evidently didn't make it clear..." For the first time, Mel looked annoyed. No, like an angel filled with righteous anger, or at least indignation. He pitied whoever she'd be arguing with; they hadn't a hope in Hell against her.

"Are you sure it's worth the trouble?" he asked. "I mean, it's been so long, I barely remember what it's like up there. It's not like I need to go in – the place is full of righteous angels, being sickeningly kind to each other with no idea of the reality down here. You know I have no patience for them, with their snowy-white reputations and ideals. I don't belong there."

"I'm one of them and so are you. You have every right to be there, just like they do. I have the same ideals, Luce, and you seem to like me just fine," Mel said through gritted teeth as she shut off the tap, shaking her fingers dry in the sink.

Now he felt bad. She seemed so different to all the other angels he knew. None of them knew the conditions down here as well as she did. Delusional, living in their cloudy paradise...they'd never believe her, unless they saw him bleed for themselves. He'd spill his lifeblood for Mel, but not a drop for any of them, he swore. And they'd turn on her like they'd turned on him all those centuries ago. For doing what was necessary – stating the truth.

"I'm coming with you," he announced.

She shook her head. "No, Luce. They'd...react differently to you. I'll go on my own and smooth the way for you. It's better this way."

He snorted. "You expect me to sit here, like some damsel in distress, while you fight my battles for me? Why don't I just wear one of your dresses and you can call me Lucia, too? Even then you'd have to chain me up here to keep me from coming with you. Oh Hell, that brings back memories..." He couldn't help laughing.

"What memories? Do you have a torture room with chains somewhere that you haven't showed me yet?"

Mel asked. "Or did you just forget about it until now?"

Luce did his best to regain control of himself. "No, not any more. I did have a fun couple of decades as Madam Lucia, though, and we had a couple in the Lair. The things those girls could do..."

Mel's face turned blank, almost deliberately, Luce decided. "You worked as a brothel madam? Why doesn't that surprise me? I bet you could've filled up Hell with the people in your whorehouse..."

Luce sobered. "The customers, yes, but most of the girls were absolute saints. The things they put up with from the clients, the pay, the conditions...actually, I never saw their souls again, once they left my employ. Of course, there were a few...the ones who thought it was a fun idea to rob the customers and leave them in an alley somewhere, sometimes still breathing...well, Hell always needs a few more demons."

"You...I'm sorry, Luce, I'm just trying to imagine you in a dress, let alone running a brothel..." Mel shook her head, as if trying to shake the image out of her ears.

Luce tried to smother his grin. "You know, I could show you," he offered eagerly. "There was a lot of leather involved, but I believe some of my favourite designs are still in vogue in modern adult shops. I think they'd suit you better than they ever did me, though."

"Luce." Mel's piercing gaze brought him out of his fantasy. "We weren't discussing your fetish for leather. We were discussing how you should stay here while I'm in Heaven, at least for the moment."

He met her eyes without flinching. "The only way you'll get me to stay here while you're fighting on my behalf is with a strong set of restraints – which brings us nicely back to leather." He let his grin break free. "I fight my own battles in person, Mel. Later, we can celebrate with leather, if you like."

Her expression was priceless and he couldn't help laughing.

"Please stay here and wait for me," Mel said as she slipped her shoes on. "You won't help your case any by pleading it personally, I swear."

"What are you so worried about? That I'll upset someone? Those angels should learn to take themselves less seriously if just the sight of me offends them," Luce grumbled.

"Angels have long memories, Luce, and you...many of them still blame you for the fall of their loved ones — the angels who followed you and fell with you," Mel said gently.

Luce stopped dead, ignoring his half-laced shoe. "No one fell with me. I fell alone, Mel, and I was left where I landed, shattered. It was dark and cold and hurt like Hell and there was no one to help me. The other angels were banished for what they chose to do, but by the time any of them found me, I'd recovered sufficiently that I didn't need their help. Every one of them made their own decision and I won't be held responsible for their choices and actions!" For a dark moment, he was lost in his past pain in the very depths of a private part of Hell.

Mel's soft kiss to his cheek pulled him out of the Pit, her arms holding him firmly in the present. "Show me," she whispered.

It was as if the ground had dropped away beneath him. Falling through stone and darkness until agony engulfed him and the shadows closed in, but the sensation was dulled, somehow. Maybe it was Mel's embrace, still secure and strong. Blindly, he groped for her in the dark and his lips found hers. He couldn't kiss her hard enough to banish the memories, but they began to fade all the same as she returned his kisses. He tasted salt – oh God, was he crying again? What in Hell would Mel think of him? His eyes jerked open to find out.

Tears cascaded down her face from eyes brimming with sympathy. Not his tears – hers. For him. More precious than any he'd seen before, let alone tasted.

"I'm sorry, Luce. I didn't know – and I can barely imagine what it was like to go through it alone." Her sweet, salty kiss was a balm to his slowly healing soul.

"I don't trust your heavenly hosts one little bit. You shouldn't go alone, not to speak on my behalf. I won't let them hurt you like they did me. Let them judge me – they're no better than I am." He regretted the bitterness in his tone, but it was there all the same.

"Luce...please. You're right – any form of judgement is unnecessary and that's exactly what I need to explain. If you come with me, if they judge you today..." She swallowed, as if she wanted to choke down her own words before she spoke them aloud. "I see only darkness. The future is not clear."

Luce grasped her shoulders and looked deep into her eyes, but she turned away to hide her soul. "What aren't you telling me? Mel..."

Closing her eyes, she breathed deeply. "What I swore I wouldn't say. Don't ask me to lie, Luce, for I won't. Please, take my word and trust my advice – that it is a bad idea for you to accompany me to Heaven today. For once, swallow your pride and accept help when it's offered." When her eyes opened, they shimmered with tears. Clouds threatening rain.

If she cried at the mere memories of his fall, there was no way he'd stand by and let them throw her out on his behalf. Luce cemented his resolve. "I'm not sitting here on my arse while you plead for my soul. I intend to be where I belong – by your side. They can judge me to my face."

"I still think it's a bad idea, Luce," she conceded reluctantly. "You should wait."

He shrugged. "If they won't let me in, then I'll sit on the kerb outside the gates, drinking out of a bottle in a brown paper bag, until you reappear." His fingers twitched and the bag appeared in his hand, crumpled around the bottle's metal cap. "And I won't share my single malt with anyone but you."

She laughed and shook her head. Luce wished she'd look less sad, as if she was more worried than she was willing to say. So much for a triumphant entry into Heaven after all these centuries. "To the gates?" he suggested, taking her hand.

She squeezed his fingers strongly. "Yes. With you tagging along, I'll have to do things the old-fashioned way and use the gate."

Together, they translocated to where they could just see the gates. Bathed in misty cloud, the bars shone like pearl in the bright sunlight. Luce felt his dread build as he approached the portal that had kept him out for millennia. Before his eyes, they changed from the happy vision to one that better fitted his mood. Cold iron, brick and desolation, rising from ashen snow.

"The gates of Auschwitz? Luce, that's really not funny," Mel murmured.

Luce left them looking dark. They matched the foreboding he felt as he tightened his grip on Mel's hand. They were going to separate him from Mel, he was sure of it. Let them try. He'd fight with every speck of his spirit, like nothing they'd ever seen.

He focussed on the crunch of snow underfoot. If he stared at his feet, he wouldn't see the looming gates he knew would always keep him out.

"Halt!" a male voice commanded.

Luce looked at the angel on gate duty. A bloke in a white dress, no less. No wonder he looked nervous. He had his wings out, poised for flight, as if he thought it made him look more angelic, instead of like a giant seagull.

Mel gave a little sigh and he felt the softness of her wings making their presence known. She gave him a radiant smile and he was reminded of their first kiss, the night she'd changed him.

"Should I?" he whispered.

Mel nodded encouragingly. Luce breathed deeply. He'd never shown her his dark wings – in fact, few people had seen them. He'd lost count of the number of times he'd lost feathers to the rough rocks in the narrow tunnels. The smell of singed feathers had plagued him so much in Hell that he'd given up showing them altogether centuries ago. Feeling more nervous than ever, he envisioned the vulture he always thought he looked like. The weight on his shoulders told him they were visible. He stretched, feeling the power in his wings for the first time in too long.

"Impressive wingspan," Mel whispered with a wicked smile. Her fingers caressed the leading edge of ebony feathers, making him wish he'd broken his wings out earlier.

Every bit of his being was telling him to enfold her in his arms and fly away with her. He dismissed the silly sensation and folded his wings instead, turning his steady gaze on the now-even-more-nervous angel.

"You need to get in line like everyone else. You'll be called when it's your turn for judgement." The angel pointed a shaky finger toward the long line of white benches, which were occupied by a diverse array of people.

"Sure," Mel replied, tugging at Luce's arm as she led the way to the first empty patch of white wood. As they passed, he noticed people staring and whispering, but none would meet his eyes.

She settled her wings behind her with a shrug of her shoulders and Luce did the same. Looking up at all the people before them, he realised that the only black in the sea of people was what he was wearing – his suit and his wings. The one place in the universe where black didn't let him blend into the background.

He sighed and wished for the first time that he was invisible. This was going to be a long wait.

"So you're the one who redeemed a demon! Everyone's talking about it," the angel sitting beside Mel gushed. "I didn't think it was possible!" She stared avidly at Luce. "I'm Therese, by the way."

Mel introduced herself, offering the girl her hand. "How long have you been an escort?"

Luce choked with laughter and tried to hide it with a coughing fit. An angel escort?

Therese's eyes shone. "Only a few weeks, I think — it's difficult to tell, with no concept of time up here.

This one will be the tenth soul I've escorted to Heaven," she said proudly, gesturing at the girl on her other side.

The teenager stared into space, much like the corpse she probably hadn't left behind very long ago, judging by the modern cut of her clothes.

"You've been around a lot longer, I'm sure. I've heard it takes at least a century before we get wings and yours look so majestic..." Therese added.

Mel smiled modestly at her feet. "Thank you, I have. I've rarely seen the gates this busy, though. What's happened?"

"I heard there was a typhoon in the Pacific, but weekends are always busy lately," Therese said, her expression turning sad.

"Why weekends?"

"Teenagers killed in car accidents, like this one," Therese said softly, nodding at the girl beside her. "The driver, and the passenger who gave him the tequila, were sent elsewhere, but this one was in the back seat when the car hit a tree. None of them were wearing seatbelts. It's like teenage kids think they're indestructible."

Mel smiled sadly. "That hasn't changed. They've been doing that since the first humans – though baiting a rhino or a mammoth with nothing but a pointy stick is perhaps safer than racing in a Ford V8."

Therese's eyes widened. "You've been around that long? Since...since cave people? Is that why you were sent to escort the demon here?"

Mel's smile widened. "No, I volunteered for this one." Luce felt her fingers weave between his, still hot from her scalding this morning. Once again, Luce wished he could heal the damage he'd caused.

Therese lowered her voice, as if she thought her whisper wouldn't carry to Luce's ears. "Where did you find him? I mean, I've never heard of a redeemed demon before..."

"Lucifer's office in HELL."

Therese gasped. "The depths of Hell? But he looks too attractive to be a demon. I heard they had horns, tails, hooves, red skin and things. That one...well, I think I'd volunteer to escort him places, too." She blushed.

"Would you like me to strip and show you the whole package?" Luce offered, turning to face the angel. "I mean, if you want to admire me as a fine piece of meat, I'd hate for you to miss anything."

She turned redder still. "Are you sure he's redeemed? He doesn't sound it. Shouldn't someone lock him up or something, until they're sure?"

Luce crossed his wrists and lifted them. "Mel can handcuff me to the bed any time she likes and test me until she's satisfied." He realised he still had a pair of cuffs in his jacket pocket, which spurred him to turn on the full force of his wicked grin. "Any beds in Heaven?"

"Shh. Later, perhaps," Mel whispered.

"I didn't think there were submissive demons. I

thought they were all arrogant and into whips and chains and things..." Therese's eyes widened. "If you found him in Lucifer's lair, he must be the devil's lover. What will you do when Lucifer comes looking for you?" The little angel looked terrified.

Let him in and give him a cup of tea after letting him use her shower, Luce thought.

"I'm sure I'll manage," Mel replied, looking like she was trying not to laugh.

Luce was struggling, too. The fresh-faced angel without wings had no idea who he was, despite his dark wings. "Mel's definitely a match for Lucifer, any day of the week," he managed to say. A perfect, sublime match, he thought as he glanced at Mel's shapely legs below her skirt.

"Oh, no – they say no angel is, which is why they banished him to Hell. I'm sure I'd be terrified if I so much as saw him," Therese squeaked in fright. "Imagine all the terrible things he could do to you! They say he can corrupt you with just a word or even a look!"

Luce gave her his friendliest smile. "Then it's a good thing I'm on my best behaviour today."

Therese stared at Luce in terror as she realised who he was. "God help me," she murmured.

"Next!" called the gate angel.

Therese looked to be deep in prayer and the line before her had vanished.

"You're up, Therese," Mel said, nudging the girl. "It was lovely meeting you."

"And...and you," the young angel stammered, pulling the teenage girl's saved soul after her as she hurried to the gate angel's podium.

"You didn't need to scare the poor girl, Luce," Mel said.

"I was just trying to be friendly," he protested. Under her knowing gaze, he relented. "Oh, okay. I've been tempting innocent morsels like her for millennia. Old habits die hard. It's not like I was going to..." He drifted off, not actually sure what he'd have done to the little angel if he'd had her. He stuck his hands in his pockets and scuffed at the snow with his shoes. His fingers closed around the white leather cuffs in his pocket and he brightened. "You know, I meant it about the handcuffs. Any time you think I might be reverting to my old ways, feel free to chain me to the bed. I always keep a spare pair in my pocket, just in case." He started to pull them out so he could show her.

"Shh, put them away, Luce. You'll give everyone the wrong impression. C'mon, it's our turn." She stood and strode toward the gates.

Luce followed her along the row of now-empty benches to what he hoped was his final judgement.

The dude in the dress swallowed and loosened his collar a little. "N-n-name?" he managed to say.

Mel's mellifluous voice rang out before Luce could open his mouth. "Allow me to present the redeemed angel, Lucifer, Light of the Morning, for re-entry into Heaven."

"L-L-Lucifer?" the saint squeaked. "Does he...does he submit to judgement?"

Luce wanted to ask for an angel who could enunciate properly, but he held his tongue. He didn't want to embarrass Mel. "He does," he said instead.

The man riffled through the pages of his book. Luce stood patiently, waiting.

"You hereby express your contrition for the following sins. Pride, the war against Heaven, the subversive activities of the HELL Corporation, seduction and corruption of one hundred and fifty three thousand, five hundred and sixteen angels..."

Luce tuned out a little at this point, feeling his face flush as he looked everywhere but at Mel. He'd lost count after the first dozen or so. That was millennia ago and they did add up, but he hadn't realised that there were quite that many. A thousand or two, maybe, but surely not a hundred thousand...

"Is that how much practice it took to get as good as you are? No wonder you're the best I've ever had," Mel murmured.

Luce stared at her in surprise and found himself lost in her smile. She was an angel in every sense of the word. "I didn't sleep with all of them," he confessed, then added virtuously, "Some of the men said I wasn't their type."

The angel cleared his throat before continuing, "Impersonation of the Virgin Mary in a strip club on five occasions, salacious thoughts about Melody Angel..."

The strip clubs had been funny. The first time, he'd seen grown men crying and some even praying. A bunch had hurried home to their wives. It was like watching a hilarious movie for the second time – he'd just had to do it again. As for the thoughts about Mel...ah, those were nothing compared to the reality. Maybe he should mention some of his early fantasies to her, just in case she was interested.

"...and the violent rape of Persephone."

The WHAT?

"I never touched Persephone, the little devil!" Luce protested.

The gate guard seemed to grow in stature, as if he enjoyed being argued with. "Says here the last sin you committed was the violent rape of Persephone, the half-angel who worked as your personal assistant. You left her tied to your bed, bleeding."

"She's lying! I swear I never touched her!" Luce replied hotly. He hadn't. She'd cuffed herself to the bed. If she'd managed to cut herself or rub her wrists raw while trying to get out of the cuffs herself, it wasn't his fault.

"So you don't repent of your final sin?" the guard prompted, the pen shaking in his hand with apparent eagerness.

"I can't repent for something I didn't do. Aren't you supposed to be omniscient? Or the book is, anyway? Check again," Luce insisted. He felt his dread build. He'd given Persephone everything – the powers, the authority, all that came with the darkness in his soul. Did that also mean she had his capacity for deception – that she could accuse him of rape he'd never committed and manage to get it written into the Book of Judgement? He wished he'd killed her instead. Maybe he should have done what they said he had.

"It says here..."

"I vouch for him," Mel interrupted, her voice ringing out across the snow as she strode toward him. She tapped the book with her finger. "He was with me that evening, not Persephone. I spoke to her while he was in my house and she was both uninjured and not restrained in any way. After that phone call, I kept him occupied until I left him in no state to do anything to Persephone that night...or the next morning."

It was the guard's turn to blush. He evidently wasn't used to forthright angels – or perhaps not female ones. Luce grinned. He wondered how much hotter that blush would get if he knew precisely how Mel had kept him occupied.

A woman stormed through the gate toward Luce. "I swear by all I and my daughter hold holy: that demon seduced my daughter, tied her to a bed and raped her when she wouldn't submit to him!" she screeched. "He's not redeemed – he's the demon who's seduced more angels than any other. I'll swear to his guilt. You can't let him in unless he does proper penance for what he did to my daughter!" The gates clanged shut behind her, vibrating a little with the force of the closure.

Luce had never seen her before in his life, though she did bear a passing resemblance to Persephone. Idly, he wondered if the girl's mother knew about her tattoo – or whether the mother had one, too. She looked far too youthful to be Persephone's mother, but appearances were deceiving in Heaven. He'd spent too long in Hell – he wasn't used to souls choosing their age. In Hell, they looked their worst, on principle.

"Why doesn't your daughter speak for herself, Cousin Demeter?" Mel asked reasonably.

Demeter pointed a shaking finger at Luce. "She doesn't trust him not to do it again. Even the thought of him scares her!" Her mouth set in a grim line. "He left my poor girl to take care of his company, doing his job, while he cavorts with another angel, no doubt trying to corrupt her, too! He has no remorse!"

Luce swallowed. "I have no remorse for Persephone. She said if I gave her everything – my company, my power, all of it – she'd tell me how I could find Mel. She took it willingly. All she gave me in return was an address, a phone number and her word they were Mel's. I'd do it again – with less hesitation." Mel's fingers tightened around his. He couldn't look at her. She'd let him into her house and her life. He couldn't remember joy like she'd brought him. She didn't deserve a demoted demon – she deserved an angel of equal rank. He'd do whatever it took to achieve that again – even if it meant surviving this inquisition. He took a deep breath. "I'm sorry if anything I've done caused Persephone pain or grief. That was never my intention." He gritted his teeth.

"So...so you do repent all of your crimes?" the gate guard cried in relief, sweat trickling down his cheek. Luce realised he wasn't the only one under pressure in this interrogation. The gates slowly started to swing open. "In that case, I can permit you entry into..."

"NO!" boomed a new voice. "I haven't stood guard for countless centuries against him and his kind, only to let a demon in now. I banished him to Hell as he deserved. Demons cannot be redeemed. I won't stand by and permit the most damned demon of them all to sneak into Heaven on an angel's skirts." An armoured angel stepped in front of the gates, lifting a sword that burst into flame. "You shall not pass!"

Oh Hell. He had to pop up, just when everything seemed to be going so well. If he had a nemesis, it was Michael. Mel was no match for that flaming sword.

Mel burst out laughing. "You've been watching too many movies, Michael. Even I've seen that one. As for my skirt..." She shimmied out of the garment, letting it puddle in the snow at her feet for a moment, before reaching down to retrieve it. Flashing her white cotton undies in the process, she ignored Luce's wide grin, the gate guard's blush and Michael's attempt to turn his head away. "If I remember correctly, Michael, you were just as eager as Luce to get into my skirts. Here!" She balled up the white skirt and lobbed it at the armoured angel.

Awkwardly, he batted it away with the sword, setting the skirt alight as it tumbled to his feet. He did a clumsy, clanking jig on the spot to put out the flames. The resulting black scorch marks up his legs spoiled the shiny armour. Luce smothered a laugh as Michael ripped the metal helmet off his head. Red-faced, he demanded, "What are you laughing at, demon?"

"Well, I can certainly see why the lady prefers me," Luce drawled.

"All the more reason to keep you and your kind out!" declared Michael. "You deserve an eternity in Hell for corrupting just one angel, let alone a hundred thousand, five hundred and..."

"A hundred and fifty three thousand, five hundred and sixteen," the gate guard corrected.

Michael stared at him in panic. "A hundred and fifty three thousand..."

"Five hundred and sixteen," the guard repeated, with some satisfaction.

"Look, I've said I'm sorry for any wrong I've done.

But there's more to it. Every one of those angels was a willing participant," Luce said. "And after seeing you two, I'm not surprised. Skirts and dresses and metal — haven't you seen what men wear on Earth these days?"

"I'll send you right back to the Pit before you can make it five hundred and seventeen with Mel!" Michael shouted, waving the sword so the flames streaked through the air. Demeter stood with her arms crossed, nodding. She still kept her distance from Michael, her eyes firmly fixed on the erratic sword. "You're only using her to get back into Heaven so you can try to take over again!"

Luce turned to Mel. "I swear that's not true. If this weren't your home, I wouldn't want to set foot in there ever again. Mel, please believe me. I might've fantasised about corrupting you before, but now that I know you, I couldn't. You can see into my heart" — he thumped his chest — "and into my soul. You know I wouldn't do that to you, don't you?"

Mel nodded serenely, her eyes intent on Luce's. "I know exactly what you would and wouldn't do," she said.

Luce felt a chill sweep across his heart. Did she know him better than he knew himself? Had she brought him here, only to betray him so Michael could banish him more permanently to the Pit?

No, she wouldn't do that. She was too kind for that — and she'd tried to dissuade him from coming with her. Surely she wouldn't...she was the only one who believed in him, that he could be redeemed. His hope was all hers.

"You may have her convinced, but never me. I will not let you pass into Heaven!" Michael shouted, lowering the sword like a parking barrier across the gate.

"What about my daughter? What reparation will he make for what he did to her?" Demeter growled, looking from the gate guard to Michael.

Both men shrugged. "He said he was sorry..." the guard ventured.

"The Hell he's sorry!" she shouted. Her eyes glowed with fury. "I'll send him back to the Pit myself."

She pulled Michael's sword from his steel grip. The blade flared up, giving her eyes a ruddy glow, as she held it like a cricketer about to hit a ball for six. She charged forward, her eyes fixed on Luce.

No one seemed able to move.

Luce recovered first, summoning his traditional bident to block the blow he could see angling toward him. He wouldn't let that blade blast him to Hell against his will again. That was one blow to the balls he wouldn't take.

Mel recovered second, moving between Demeter and Luce. Her resonant "NO!" was enough to freeze Luce.

Faced with a righteous angel, Demeter faltered and the flame fizzled. She dropped the sword, but it was too late.

Luce tried to lower his weapon, too, but both barbs had already pierced Mel. The bident had passed right through her chest, the red-glazed prongs protruding from her white shirt.

"No," Luce moaned. "Mel..." He dismissed his weapon back to the depths of Hell, so it wouldn't do any further damage to Mel's body. His eyes fixed on the fading bronze fork until it had disappeared altogether.

He pulled her against him, trying to let her down gently onto the snow, which now felt incredibly cold and hard. Beneath his knees, the snow turned to cloud – much softer and warmer for Mel, he realised distantly.

Blood blossomed over Mel's breasts, like obscene flowers on a corpse. There were tears in her eyes.

Luce didn't care who was watching him. He kissed Mel's lips and tasted the salt of her blood. A nagging thought crossed his mind that angels couldn't be killed, but Michael's sword and his own fork weren't normal weapons – they were imbued with more power than anything else he'd encountered. He'd been banished from Heaven by one of them...and she'd been touched by both.

Mel didn't deserve his fate.

"Hold on, my love. Everything will be as it should be. You'll see." She smiled and a bubble of blood appeared at the corner of her lips.

"You'll be all right," he said, praying for it to be true. "Just lie still, Mel, and someone will heal you.'"

If he were the angel he once was, he could have

healed her at a touch. Instead, he was forced to beg for help from the angels who'd condemned him. "What are you staring at?" he shouted. "Someone help her. Help her!"

No one moved.

The light in Mel's eyes started to fade. With what looked like great effort, she swallowed. "I love you," she whispered. She looked at him one last time and her eyes closed.

Luce couldn't take his eyes off her. He thought it was his sight blurring, as sunlight tinted his tears of grief to gold. The body in his arms became lighter, though, so that he couldn't help but notice. Her skin was turning to gold, dissolving into a fine mist. The mist curled upward, forming a cloud above his head. The bloodstained shirt in his hands fell limp with no body to fill it.

The cloud roiled, streaming like cirrus in a high wind, then faded into nothing. She was gone.

He crumpled the shirt in his arms, still warm from Mel's body and smelling of her perfume. Actually, it was lumpy with her underwire bra, so he folded it carefully so as not to show her underwear to anyone. He looked around for her knickers and scooped them up, too, hiding them inside her shirt. He didn't trust Michael with them — not that he trusted Michael at all, self-righteous bastard.

Luce felt his fury build. Mel was his everything and they'd taken her away from him by standing there doing nothing. "You killed her," he accused Demeter, before shifting his glare to Michael. If Michael hadn't brought his infernal sword and barred their way...if Demeter hadn't snatched it from him to attack Luce...if Mel hadn't felt he needed to be protected... "She didn't deserve to die!"

"No," the gate guard piped up, looking scared, "you did. It's right here in the Book of Judgement. You brought your Hellish weapon here and thrust it through her body."

Luce gasped for breath. He did it. He did it. He'd killed her – the one person he'd ever loved.

"She didn't deserve you, either," Michael said. "You'd only drag her down to Hell and hide her from all those who love and need her."

I love her, Luce thought. No, I loved her. For she's forever gone to me, whether she lives or not. If she ever sees me again, her eyes will accuse and condemn. For I killed her. I killed her.

"Some things can't be redeemed," he muttered. "Now I know what it is to be damned."

Shadows swirled, summoned back to his dark soul. There was no light for him, not any more. Perhaps there never was. He belonged in Hell.

"You will never know the domination of Earth or Heaven. Your realm will be Hell and the boundaries of your rule. For your advisors, take the angels who fought for you, for they, too, will fall from Heaven, never to return. GO!" Michael waved his sword and the flames seemed to blaze higher than the angel behind them.

Luce could feel fear in the archangel, but the sword Michael wielded was more powerful than any other weapon the worlds had known. Nevertheless, Luce knew he was right. "Those beings aren't perfect and they never will be. They will destroy all we've created here. They are few now, but they will outnumber us in time and, when that happens, they will stop listening. What will you do with them when they are not fit for Heaven or Earth any more?"

"Why, we'll send them to you, to Hell. You and yours can punish them as you wish, as a deterrent to the rest. They can join you in permanent exile," Michael announced. The angels who followed him laughed.

"What will you do when Hell is full?" Luce asked.

"It won't be full until this world is ended. Then, we will speak again," Michael said, drawing back his sword.

"Take your best shot," Luce growled, opening his arms wide. He wouldn't show fear or weakness, though he knew the other angel had won. Even exiled to Hell, he wouldn't acknowledge defeat. "And do not miss, for if I see you again, be assured that I will kill you."

The burning blade drove deep into his chest before he could close his mouth.

The pain was blinding, sending him to his knees. Luce struggled to speak, but Michael gave him no opportunity. He ripped the sword, now dripping with blood, from Luce's body. If Luce thought the pain from the entry wound was bad, he wasn't prepared for the agony of the exit. His vision went dark.

"Fall, demon. You have no dominion here or on Earth. No one will help you now."

Luce felt his body plummeting through darkness. The cold cling of cloud, the furious rush of wind, weightlessness in his limbs, yet still he fell. His body burned as if cloven in two by the sword before it was torn free, but this became his only feeling as the icy plunge took his sense of touch along with his sight. He heard the air scream past, though he couldn't summon the breath to scream. He could taste his own blood like tar in his throat and wished the torment would end.

His prayer was answered. He hit unyielding rock, pain exploding as his bones shattered from the impact. When the icy air stole his pain, it was a relief.

Only darkness, silence and the cold kiss of stone, sending him into oblivion.

Wonderful. Now he was having flashbacks about his first fall from Heaven. Luce waited impatiently for the memory to fade enough for reality to return.

In the absence of sound, the first thing he became aware of was scent. Coconut and lemon. No, mandarin and neroli. Jasmine, sandalwood, lavender and...myrrh. His lips lifted in a smile. Only Mel smelled like that.

He opened his eyes dreamily, so he could see her as well as smell her, but he lay in darkness. The scent was so clear, though, as if she was right there with him. He lifted his nose, trying to work out where she was, and felt the touch of cotton on his face.

Mel's ripped shirt.

Luce jerked up, shivering on the cold, stone floor.

Mel. Gone forever – by his hand.

Pain exploded anew, worse than his first crash into Hell.

He'd never see her again.

"I love you," she'd whispered, even as she'd died at his hands. What kind of tragedy ended with words of love for her murderer from his victim? Who would write such a fate for anyone?

William Shakespeare. *Othello.*

Luce wondered if there was a circle in Hell reserved for authors who killed their characters in stupid circumstances, as he'd killed Mel. Or maybe just the bitches who tortured their heroes, subjecting them to the sort of pain gnawing at his heart now. If there wasn't, he was going to create one, with boiling pools of ink...or pages that delivered countless paper cuts...or computers that only had dodgy touchscreens with terrible autocorrect...

Mel was no Desdemona. She wouldn't have let him wallow in his misery or any other feeling. She'd have insisted on a shower, a change of clothes and some tea. Yes, he was damned, but he was the Lord of Hell. He'd damn well make sure the other damned souls regretted their crimes as much as he did his. Killing his beloved angel...

He climbed laboriously to his feet. Balled up in his hand were the remains of her clothes. He buried his nose in the bloodstained shirt, wanting to catch a whiff of her perfume. Neroli, jasmine and myrrh. Oh God, Mel...

He spread her clothes out on his desk. The pierced shirt. The white, lace-edged bra... that had holes in it, too. Only her knickers were intact. They were all he had of her — the last clothes she'd worn, stained with her lifeblood and marked with her scent. He'd treasure them until the world ended. He folded the underwear carefully inside the shirt and placed the whole bundle in his desk drawer. It wouldn't do to show his weakness to the lesser demons of his realm. What would she have wanted him to do if he lost her?

She'd want him wearing a clean shirt. The one he wore to dinner with her in the office, the night she'd first kissed his cheek. He summoned the item with a thought, stripping out of his soiled clothes.

Fresh shirt, then fresh pants, underwear and socks. Tie. Hair brushed, face washed and shaved. Teeth sparkling. He was dealing with demons and damned souls. None of them deserved to know about the hole in his heart, the place reserved for her.

He turned the climate control thermostat down, hoping it would help him maintain his icy calm. Just the way Mel had in negotiations with anyone, angel or demon.

I love you, too, Mel, he thought. Like no one else before or since. If the remainder of his existence was to be a living Hell, at least he'd be in the right place for it. No one else would notice the difference.

Mel felt her body slowly coalesce. No one had told her just how much it would hurt to be stabbed and then disintegrate. Raphael owed her big time for this; as did Michael. She couldn't recall ever being this furious, but she'd never heard of an angel offering false judgement before. They'd have Hell to pay on this one – and that was after she was done with them. Heaven wasn't happy with them, either.

When she could feel her fingers moving, she dared to open her eyes. She took stock of her surroundings before moving from her crouch. "Where's Luce?" she asked. "More importantly, where are my clothes? Little brother, if you think hiding my clothes is funny..."

Michael's metal-clad foot nudged the small pile of ash. "Well, this was your skirt. Why'd you tell him I used to dress up in your clothes when I was a kid? He'll think I'm..."

"He doesn't know you're my little brother. I'm sure Luce didn't...where is he? I thought you said you'd wait for me to return before you opened the gates for him." She stretched as she stood up, feeling the flex of her muscles in her rebuilt body. "And where did he get that fork from?"

"We think he summoned it from Hell. He can't have given up everything – he must still be the Lord of Hell. That makes him very dangerous," Peter piped up.

Mel dismissed the danger. "He gave up everything he owned – all the power he had – to Persephone. His dominion over Hell is a sacred trust – he can't give that up. It's part of who he is. I saw him use that power in my house and again when he brought that weapon here from Hell. Angel or demon, Luce is still the Lord of Hell – and, ultimately, the leader of every demon there is. I need to know where he is."

Michael cleared his throat, turning his back on Mel. "He vanished, just after you did. We think he banished himself back to Hell permanently."

Peter took the cloth from beneath his book and tossed it to Mel, who began wrapping it around herself like a sarong. As he set the book down again, a loose sheet of paper slipped out into the cloud at his feet.

"Why?" she asked. "He passed your damn test, with your trumped-up charges on that little memo. I'm sure you're not allowed to add extra pages to the Book of Judgement. Your little unauthorised tribunal. I agreed not to reveal my identity until after you were done, but if I'd known what you were going to do with NO authority whatsoever, I'd never have permitted it. Oh, and if I ever see that sword again, it'll be too soon. I swear I'll have it welded into a city sewer main. Do you know how much that hurt? When I see Raphael, he's going to be in my debt for the next millennium, at least. And someone owes me new clothes and matching underwear. Tell me you at least let Luce know he was free to enter Heaven."

"He disappeared before we could tell him," Michael whispered hoarsely.

"Why didn't you follow him?" Mel demanded.

"He's gone to Hell. We can't follow him there — can't even see him. He's masking himself from us, somehow," Michael replied, a little louder.

"But not from me," Mel said softly. "He carries a part of me with him."

Michael seemed to gain stature. "He has WHAT?" he exploded. "You sold your soul to Lucifer? What happens when he finds out who you are? What possessed you to do something so...so...STUPID?"

Mel turned cold eyes on her brother, feeling all

restraint slip away. Standing in her full glory, she saw reflected gold glitter in Michael's fearful eyes. Too little, too late for Luce. Her voice held more power than she intended as she said, "I sold nothing. I gave it freely, for it was my only hope of helping him. He already knows who I am. I thought I could send him home to Hell when his soul repulsed the spirit I breathed into him, but he welcomed me...with love. Our souls bonded and some small spark remains with him – I can sense it still." She reached out to the soul that was so closely connected to her own. "Screened by a thick cloud of darkness, and in the middle is despair. What did you tell him?" She couldn't hide the horror in her voice. She'd never sensed a soul in so much pain before. And a soul who didn't deserve it.

Fear seemed to have stolen Michael's ability to speak. He knew she knew.

"He really thought he'd killed you," Peter said.

"So he condemned himself to Hell? You realise I'm going to have to go in there after him," Mel stated. She struggled with the thick fabric, which wouldn't quite meet. There simply wasn't enough of it.

"You don't have to," Michael ventured. "You could just leave him to his fate. He is the ruler of Hell, after all. He does sort of belong there."

Mel shook her head slowly. "You don't get it, do you? We can't bond with demons or the fallen without falling ourselves, and I am as I ever was. Instead, he changed – for me. He's an angel – the same as us. He doesn't belong there any more than we do. Makes me wonder how many others are there who don't need to be. He's there because of me and I won't let him suffer any more. Enough is enough."

"But, Mel, no angel who's ever made it out of there has remained, well, an angel," Michael hedged. "Most never leave. Don't go – it's too great a risk, to lose you for a demon you think might have changed." Far from a command, he sounded like he was begging. "Please, Mel..."

"Are you volunteering to go in my place?" Mel asked. "Someone has to set this right."

Michael shook his head violently. "Please. I only did it to protect you. I couldn't...I wouldn't...and he'd never listen to me. Let alone forgive..."

"Nothing can justify what you did to him. If my fate is to enter Hell, then I will follow it. And let you live with the knowledge that it's your fault. You won't stop me, Michael."

He dropped to his knees and grabbed her hand, his eyes entreating. "Mel, don't. No angel can survive Hell without being tainted. Just look at him..."

"Show me." Mel looked at Michael's face and deeper, too – to the very depths of his soul. She saw an angel forcing another to fall into Hell...for her. Somehow, that angel had emerged as the demon she'd met on the day of her interview. She snapped, "You're suggesting I should leave a redeemed man in Hell because it's too hard and you're too scared to do it yourself? After what you did to him? There's a reason you're standing guard on the gate, little brother, while I've been guiding the governments of the world for centuries. No one else has ever redeemed a demon – until me. You three just sent an innocent man to Hell without a word of protest. And I know this isn't the first time." Mel stared at Demeter and the two men until they found the cloud beneath their feet fascinating. "Michael and Peter, you agree that he passed your test – and you won't cause any further trouble to prevent him from entering Heaven?"

Both men nodded.

"Yes, Lady Muriel," Peter managed to say, backed up by Michael's scared silence.

"Demeter, he never touched Persi, though she offered herself to him. I watched over her myself – I was worried about the outcome, too, yet events spun out as he said." Mel kept her gaze on Persephone's mother.

Demeter bowed her head. "I believe you, Lady Muriel. Persi never said what he'd done – simply that he left her naked and hurt in his home. I didn't realise all he hurt was her pride. You do understand why I had to see for myself, if he really could be redeemed, as you say." She swallowed. "I'm sorry I burned your shirt. I wish you luck. A redeemed demon...gives us hope of redemption for the others."

Mel took a deep breath and released it, feeling the strength in her newly formed body. She'd need it in

Hell. "I'll see you all on my return and Heaven won't help you if you stand in my way again. From HELL Corporation to the Pit itself. Now, more than ever, it's time for me to go to Hell."

With barely a gold shimmer in the air, she was gone. The tiny tablecloth fluttered in the firmament, buoyed by the breeze of her passage.

"What do we do now?" Peter asked Michael.

"Pray," Michael replied. "I'd prefer to let a hundred demons into Heaven with my blessing than agree to let Mel go to Hell."

"Why did you let her go, then?" Peter persisted.

Michael's laughter was hollow. "Nothing can stop Lady Muriel from fulfilling her destiny. Not you, not me, not Raphael. Not even all the forces of Heaven combined."

"What about the forces of Hell?"

Michael closed his eyes in defeat. "We're about to find out, aren't we?"

Much like Luce's inability to enter Heaven without passing through the gates, Mel knew she couldn't translocate herself directly into Hell. There were protocols to be observed. Instead, she placed herself in the desert sand a short distance from the entrance, in full view of the cave mouth. She'd expected a fiery portal, like the stories said, but she'd take this cold, rocky alternative if it meant she wouldn't singe her wing feathers on the way in. She did have to keep up appearances, after all.

She reached out once more for Luce, sensing his despairing soul amid a collective moan of so many others. So much pain, concentrated in one place. That was Hell. She couldn't understand how any angel could want to stay here. She could feel tears forming in her eyes already and she wasn't even inside.

She passed between jagged rocks, wondering how many souls it would take to wear them smooth. She knew it was a matter of perspective – she saw Hell this way, while others saw the inferno, their worst nightmares, or, in Luce's case, perhaps a friendly welcome mat. No, surely not even he saw that.

The imps had told her that Hell was as much a place of perception as Heaven – perhaps this place had inspired post-modernist thinkers to formulate their theories on perspectives and reality. She smothered laughter as she stepped into the darkness, letting her body glow just a little so she could see clearly. If she'd known the fires of Hell would be extinguished for her visit, she'd have brought a torch.

Now it was only a matter of time before her natural radiance brought her to the attention of some of Hell's darker denizens; demons and souls who had inhabited the place for so long that they were unrecognisable for the angels and humans they once were. She shrugged. The one she searched for was the oldest, darkest and most powerful of them all – and he loved her. Nothing else mattered but finding Luce.

Mel shivered as a cold breeze caught her. She looked

down and realised she'd lost the tiny tablecloth somewhere along the way.

A naked angel, taking on all the forces of Hell to claim their leader. Oh, someone up there sure had a sense of humour. So be it. No one could say she'd chosen the easy way, she mused, chuckling quietly. Her laughter seemed an odd sound in this dark place, but no less unusual than her own, glowing self.

"I'm coming for you, Luce," she said, her words ringing out in the darkness. "I've redeemed you once and nothing will stop me from doing the same again. I know your soul."

Only silence greeted her statement, until she swore as she smacked her foot on a rock.

Limping slightly, she strode on. Luce's soul was worth more than a simple stubbed toe.

The words were carved deep into the stone:

All hope abandon ye who enter here.

Mel half expected despair to settle on her like a heavy blanket, but her hopes were higher than ever. Luce was near – she could feel his presence. She had to hope, for not doing so would be to lose Luce to despair and a fate he didn't deserve – something she couldn't do. He'd asked for her help, even if it had taken him millennia to do so.

She'd come so far – she'd drag hope kicking and screaming to the very depths of Hell. She paused to look at the dark letters. She didn't want to deface something that had evidently taken a lot of time and effort to carve, but she wouldn't leave without leaving her own mark on the place. Eternity in the absence of hope had never been her intention.

She concentrated and summoned a short, pine plank. The wood developed a shiny white sheen as Mel's idea took form. Letters appeared in tacky red gloss, cursive suiting it better than the plain Latin letters her sign would cover. She paused and thought for a moment, before adding a spray of red glitter, spread across the sign's surface. Not hiding her smile, she hung the sign above the doorway, so that it concealed the stark letters beneath.

She looked up at her handiwork. "A sexy devil lives here," she read aloud, before starting to laugh. She raised her voice to shout, "Luce, the longer you leave me to my own devices, the more I'll decorate your domain! I hope you like red glitter."

She was answered by silence, but her own amusement was enough. She wanted to see Luce's face when he noticed the sign – and she hoped it would be soon.

The cavern was dim and Mel waited for her eyes to adjust. Her own luminance brightened to compensate — she stood out so much anyway, a little light wouldn't make much difference. She could hear the trickle of water as a stream ran deep into the cave system.

She stumbled over some unevenness on the ground and reached for the nearest rock to steady herself. The rock moaned under her hand and she realised her mistake. The soul that had once been a man was grey and huddled, shaped much like a rock, and his stillness only added to the impression of stone. She let her fingers linger on the man, closing her eyes to see what he did, if only for a moment.

Loud buzzing drew her attention to the cloud of wasps surrounding them. The insects flew in to sting the man, who had his hands over his face instead of trying to brush them away. Mel tried to shoo the cloud from him, but it paid no attention to her. She waved her hands more widely, hoping to give the man some small relief, but the wasps disappeared as she broke contact with the damned soul.

The man endured eternal torment – in his own head, she realised. Tears sprang to her eyes. How could anyone sustain hope when they were tortured by their own imagination? Imps and illusions.

She touched another crouched soul – this one appeared vaguely female. She heard the woman's hoarse screams as maggots crawled through the gaping wounds all over her body. Mel reeled back, letting the woman go, as the wiggling, white larvae vanished from her sight – though not from her memory.

She looked around. These two souls were not alone – there were thousands of huddled figures in the cavern, stretching out into the darkness. She stifled a sob. This was Hell – this sea of hopelessness. She wasn't surprised that Luce had been so eager to leave. She'd leave now if it weren't for him.

Out of the darkness, she heard an old man's cackling laughter.

"This is no place for you, angel. Go back to where you belong."

Mel proceeded carefully toward the voice, only to stop in surprise. The trickling stream caressed her toes as she stared. Spanning the tiny rivulet was a flat riverboat, sitting like a bridge from one side of the water to the other. A man stood in the bow, his head hooded, a pole suspended from his hand into the shallow water. "Go home to Heaven. Hell is not for your kind, unless you wish to fall."

Mel drew herself up. "I am here for Lucifer and I won't leave until I've spoken with him."

"Then you'll never leave, angel. How will you withstand Hell when even the damned souls in the vestibule can drive you to tears?"

She felt more tears trickle down her cheeks, adding salt to the stream. "This is horrible enough — and it's not even Hell?" She couldn't leave him here. How could she leave any of them?

"No, little angel. Go back to whoever sent you. If the Lord of Hell wishes to see you, he'll find you, and you'll wish he hadn't," he said, sounding kind.

She thought she recognised the voice, though it had been a long time since she'd heard it. "Charon?" she asked.

"Everyone knows I'm the ferryman here, angel. If you're a new escort, so fresh you'd never heard of me before today, you should leave quickly. No angel lasts long here."

"You'll see more clearly if you take your hood off, Charon," Mel said with a smile. "Don't you recognise me?"

Down came the hood. The old man beneath squinted at her, looking puzzled. Some spark of recognition kindled in his eye and his shock showed. "Lady Muriel? What are you doing here?"

"I told you – I'm here for Lucifer," she said sadly.

"No. The risk is too great. You're needed on Earth – among men, where you can make a difference. Here, there is only despair."

"Charon, you know better than to tell a Domination what to do. I will enter Hell and descend to whatever depths your Lord has hidden himself in. He can't hide from me."

"I won't take you across the river, Lady Muriel," the old man said firmly, his hand shaking as his fingers grasped the pole.

Mel laughed as she took another step into the stream. Even in the middle, the water was barely above her ankles, a cleansing coolness between her toes. "I don't need your boat. I can walk across just fine."

His eyes widened in shock once more. "You can see through the illusions? Even the Lord of Hell traverses the River Acheron by boat. Lady Muriel...don't lose yourself in the darkness here. Some of the shadows here are darker than anything on the surface."

She bowed her head in thanks. "I will do my best. If you see Lucifer, tell him I'm looking for him. Remind him that he is in my debt and I will collect."

He bowed in response. "I will, Lady Muriel, and I wish you well. My hopes go with you."

"I never should've bought that round. Buying rounds only ever ends badly. Someone else always orders the most expensive cocktail and you're left to pick up the bill..." a voice slurred. "Should've stuck to drinking mead."

Mel laughed. "Buying rounds is always trouble. I miss mead like we used to get."

She followed the sound of more slurred imprecations and found a man sitting submerged in shallow water. She splashed across to him. "Where was the best mead made?"

"Larissa, in Aeolus. Did you ever taste it?" the man asked dreamily. "I owned the first tavern in Larissa and none could compare to it. They tried to copy my recipes, but making good mead is an art..." The man looked blearily at her. "Do I know you? No one's talked to me in so long. It's like I'm invisible..."

"If you make the best mead in Larissa, then you must be Acheron, Demeter's son. I believe I did taste it once, but that was a long time ago. What happened to you?"

"Bunch of men were all that was left of a huge army. Defeated, they came into my tavern for a drink. Wanted to drown their sorrows before heading home. I poured a round of mead, took their coin, then headed to the cellar for another jug when I heard their story. My shout and all. When I came back up, the crazy general of the winning army was wrecking my tavern. Some idiot named Zeus. Him and his men broke everything. I tried to stop them, but some of them picked me up and dragged me to the river. I woke up in the water and I'm waiting for the dawn, so I can see to walk home. My wife'll be waiting."

Mel understood Demeter's desire for redemption of those here now, seeing her son sitting like a drunkard in the gutter. She hadn't the heart to tell him that his wife and family were long dead, as was he.

"I saw your mother recently. She sends her love," Mel said instead.

"Mother's the one who taught me to make mead," Acheron said happily, stretching out in the water, his hands behind his head. He started to snore.

Mel sighed sadly for Acheron's fate. To everyone else, he was simply a part of the river that bore his name now. She resolved to find some mead when she reached the surface once more, to drink to Acheron's memory.

Mel thought she could see a flicker of light in front of her, wavering as if reflected on water. She strode forward more confidently. Perhaps she'd finally found some of the hellfire she'd heard about. This place seemed far more dank, dark and depressing than the fiery place of torment she'd been led to believe it was. All she felt for the denizens of this place was pity. And Luce – lost among them, somewhere. She could feel his presence still, but she knew he was much deeper than she'd reached thus far. Her heart ached for him – he seemed so lonely. "I'm here, Luce. You'll see me sooner if you come to me. I'm dependent on your demons for directions." She sensed no change in him, so she doubted he'd heard her words. She ploughed on.

Mel squeezed through a narrow crevice and found the cavern widened considerably after it. It had to, to accommodate the columns stretching as far as she could see. This cave was lit from above, faint moonlight or sunlight shimmering through the dripping water and slick stalactites to reach the pool below. The whole room looked like some sort of castle, with towers and walls made by limestone accretions over many millennia. Even the columns were natural formations, where stalactites and stalagmites, or stalactites and the floor, had met and married.

She hadn't expected to stumble across something so beautiful inside Hell. She wanted to ask Luce about it — what dark secrets did this place hold? Or was this place somewhere he came to for respite from the darkness throughout the rest of Hell? She stepped carefully into the pool to take a closer look at a glimmering column, noticing glow worms for the first time. This cave must have been close to the surface, to capture and keep Earth insects.

Something bumped her foot and she looked down. A blissful-faced man floated on the surface, his eyes wide open and glazed, as if in a drugged stupor. Mel carefully backed away from him, apologising, but he didn't reply. Only now did she notice that the pool was full of such floating figures – all of them drifting upon the surface, staring up.

She left the water completely at this point, not wanting to make contact with any of the other strange souls. Perhaps this was where Hell's denizens were rewarded for good behaviour – or it could be some form of torture she couldn't fathom.

She left them to their pretty play of light on water and limestone. When she found Luce, she could ask him about the place. Hell was stranger than she'd thought – but still sad. Drifting in a dream was not much of an improvement on living in fear of an illusion, as the souls in the vestibule had been.

A soft sound made her look down. A pink bundle of feathers lay at her feet – it looked like it had flown into the cave but had been unable to find the way out. She lifted the bird, feeling the faint vibration of its fast-beating heart. "This is no place for you, little one," she whispered, kissing the cockatoo's back. The bird turned its head to regard her and let out a shriek as it lifted its crest, flashing a sunset spectrum of feathers.

Mel closed her eyes and traced the light to its source in the desert sky above. She breathed on the bird, sharing her knowledge of the way out. "Fly," she said, releasing the Major Mitchell cockatoo. White wings spread, flapped and sent the creature flying upward and away. A final shriek of farewell filtered through the caves in its wake.

She shook her own wings, wishing she could follow

the cockatoo from darkness into daylight.

"I'll see you fly out of here, too, Luce! You're going to spread those wings for me, because I love you and I won't leave you here," she shouted.

A pink feather landed by her foot and Mel leaned over to pick it up. Pink fluffiness was as out of place in Hell as she was. Luce should have come to confront her by now. Perhaps she hadn't made her presence clear enough to him yet.

Mel's eyes darted around the cavern, looking for a flat stretch of wall for her canvas. This time, she'd try her hand at cave painting instead of sign writing. Metaphorically speaking.

She heard the cockatoo shriek faintly again, joined by the sound of several more birds. A flock in flight, she decided, in garish pink and red, holding the image of the birds in her head as she summoned the coloured pigments she'd need to bring the image to life. White and pink, red and yellow...Mel opened her eyes to survey her handiwork. Larger than life, the pink cockatoos soared on the limestone, headed up and out. As she would be, as soon as she found Luce.

She'd carry him out in her arms if she had to, like a reclaimed soul for Heaven. For that's what he was. And if there was hope for him, then there was hope for all the others here, too.

The two junior demons shuffled their feet and stared at the stone. Luce knew he'd remember their names if he thought about it long enough, but he didn't want to waste any more time or thought on them. Luce found he grew more impatient the longer they took to get to the point.

"Why haven't there been regular reports on the number of new souls entering the gate?" he demanded.

"We've been working in the office and..." one mumbled.

"But you've been back a week, without a word between the two of you." Luce looked from one to the other and still couldn't see their eyes. "What's wrong with the gate?"

One of them jerked his head up, his wide, frightened eyes meeting Luce's. "We don't know who did it! Everything was fine – a bit quiet, maybe, after the dangerous drivers came in for the weekend, so we stopped for a smoke..."

"You were smoking on the premises while on duty?" Luce boomed. "You know there are human laws about that sort of thing..."

"We weren't in the office – we went back inside to light up, like we always do. It was raining out," the second demon whined. "There isn't a procedure about smoking in Hell. Just outside and in the office."

Luce took a deep breath. He'd forgotten. It'd been that long since he'd smoked anything, after spending so long in the human world, that it'd completely slipped his mind that it was normal to smoke here. "Go on. The gate?" he prompted.

"Yeah, the gate," the first one continued, glancing at his companion. "Look, it was fine. No one around and no trouble. So we stopped for a break and when we came back, it was there. We didn't see who it was. But there was this stink of angel around..."

"Just the stink – no sign of the angel, though," the second piped up. "We looked around outside – got wet and everything – but couldn't find him anywhere."

Luce grunted impatiently. "Did you think to check inside?"

"What angel would be crazy enough to come into Hell?" The two guard demons looked at each other and laughed.

"Angels do nothing without a reason," Luce said softly. "So if the angel left – what did he do before he left?" He kept his eyes on the squirming guards.

"He defaced the sign, sir! Left a note," Demon Two said helpfully.

"A note." Luce couldn't have made his voice more expressionless if he tried. "And what did this note say?"

The guards exchanged nervous glances. Demon One coughed. "Best if you see for yourself, Lord Lucifer. You'll probably understand it better than we could."

Luce nodded and stood. On his signal, all three of them transported directly to the cave entrance. The rain had stopped temporarily, but the damp on the ground and in the air, compounded by the heavy cloud above, promised that their reprieve was brief. God, the desert rain smelled good.

One of the demons lit a cigarette with shaking hands, dropping his match in the damp sand. A wisp of smoke writhed up as it extinguished.

A flash of light caught Luce's eye. For a moment, he thought the match had flared up again, but it looked redder than the tiny sulphur flame. He scanned the wet ground. It looked like flecks of metal or glittering stone on the red desert sand. He glanced up at the gate arch.

Red glitter. He scuffed at the flecks in the mud, seeing the colour bleed out, leaving only the silver behind.

Michael. Who else could it be, but the cross-dressing angel who hated him so passionately? Only Michael would be cruel enough to taunt him about the loss that was still raw in his heart – and in such a childish way, like a teenager with a spray can in an alley on Earth.

"If you see any more angels, I want you to subdue them on sight and then bring them to me. We won't tolerate this kind of disrespect. Hell is not a place for jokes," Luce said shortly, trying to hide his pain. He'd give anything to hear Mel call him sexy again. Hell, he'd give anything to hear her laughter at one of his jokes.

"What do you want us to do with the sign, sir?" Demon One asked timorously.

Luce shrugged. "Leave it where it is. It's true." He turned and said, "Remember – any more angels – bring them straight to me, in my office. I don't have time to be traipsing all over Hell because of some silly angel's idea of a prank."

As he shifted from the gate to his desk in the depths, he caught one guard whispering to the other, "So which demon is the sign talking about?"

He wanted to turn and shout at his subordinates, if only to release some of his anger and frustration, but his grief floated too close to the surface. He sank onto his desk chair as the tears started to fall. He summoned the precious red handkerchief – the one that Mel had transformed from black to its current colour – to catch the droplets before they could hit the desk. Demons didn't cry – definitely not the Lord of Hell. God, what would the others think of him if they saw?

But the Lord of Hell had never lost his beloved angel before. He'd never had one to lose until now and he'd barely had her for a moment before they took her away.

To Hell with everyone and everything. Luce sealed his office to everyone else and lost himself in grief.

Mel rounded a corner to find her wings caught on the rough rocks enclosing a narrow passage. Folding them out of sight, she surveyed the line of shadowy, sad souls blocking her progress. Some of them were shaking where they stood, while others shifted their feet constantly, as if looking for firm ground to stand on from which to plead their case.

The scene reminded her a little of those awaiting judgement at Heaven's gates, but there were no angels or demons to be seen. Perhaps the damned didn't qualify for escorts, Mel thought. Or the escort demons didn't care enough about their charges to wait with them. Neither would have surprised her.

The passage looked too tightly packed with people to squeeze through, so she resolved to wait patiently. The line did appear to be moving, and more swiftly than the line of souls awaiting entrance to Heaven.

She touched the shoulder of the man before her. "Excuse me," she began, "can you please tell me what we're waiting for?"

"Accommodation assignments," the man replied over his shoulder. "There's a boss up ahead who says where you get to stay. Someone said I'll probably be down on Level Three."

"Level Three?" Mel enquired politely.

"Yeah, Level Three. That's where drug addicts go. I mean, I wouldn't have killed all those people if it weren't for the drugs, see? Some I was too high to remember and the others should've known better'n to get between me and the money for another hit. The girls who wouldn't put out for the punters had it coming, too..."

Mel carefully tucked her hands behind her so she wouldn't touch the man again. The hazy impression she'd received from his mind had initially reminded her of a Jimi Hendrix song, but now that she knew why, she didn't want to know any more of it. How many deaths had resulted from this man's habit? How many lives ruined, how many hurt or... She felt tears streak her cheeks.

"Hey, it's all right, sweetheart. If I had any on me right now, I'd give it to you. It'd send you straight to Heaven, instead of Level Two, where they put the little lusty ones. Pretty girl like you, they'll go easy on you."

She met the eyes of the addict in surprise. He was Hellbound, no mistake, but the man still had a heart, somewhere deep beneath the dark haze. "I'm worried for a friend of mine who's in the deepest level here, I think. I need to see and speak to him. I'm not staying."

His eyes widened. "You're not here for judgement? Fuck me, I heard it was only angels who could leave once they were in. You a real angel?"

Mel lowered her eyes and nodded. "He's here by mistake. I won't leave until I've seen him. The others are waiting in Heaven for me to return with him."

The man snorted and it turned into a phlegmy cough that made him spit on the stone floor. "Fuck. First I ever heard of angels judging someone and making a mistake. Wish I had an angel looking after me. Here, I'm in no hurry. How 'bout we switch places and you go first?"

He sashayed to the side of the passage, ushering her past. Mel thanked him and moved forward.

"OI!" the man's voice rang out. "We got an angel here, says there's been a mistake. Let 'er through!"

Bowed heads lifted and turned to stare curiously at Mel. Embarrassed, she kept her head down.

"I SAID MOVE!" he hollered. "Who's in a hurry to

get into Hell five minutes faster? Fuck'n MOVE for the angel!"

Shuffling footsteps scraped on stone as people moved aside. Thankful that she'd already hidden her wings, she sidled past as many as she could, trying not to meet anyone's eyes. She didn't want to see inside any of their souls – just the first man in the queue had saddened her enough. She'd sink under the knowledge of all their sins. So much harm...

"I'm coming for you, Luce," she murmured. "I won't leave you mired in this despair. Hold on, my love." Determination drove her steps, more sure with every word. Luce needed her and if she faltered through fear, he would pay the price – a debt she would need to repay.

With all her will bent on the soul at her destination, Mel didn't see the body before her until she bumped into him.

"I'm sorry," she said, stopping.

"Yeah, everyone's sorry, but not sorry enough, which is why you ended up here," he said roughly. "What did you do that everyone's so eager to see you judged for?"

Mel glanced back and saw the crowded passage, full of people craning to get a good view. Her courage failed. "I'm here for Luce," she whispered.

Something snaked around her waist and tightened, threatening to crush her. "It's Lord Lucifer here, and you'd best remember it. The Lord of Hell doesn't forgive or forget. And neither do I." The tail gave her a squeeze. "Now, tell me the truth. I'll know if you lie. Who are you and what was the worst sin you committed?"

"I ate the last dozen Valentine's chocolates by myself and didn't give them to my colleagues." A searing pain deep in her soul made her want to double over, but the man's tail held her upright. "Luce," she wailed weakly. The pain wasn't hers but his. A sudden stab made her scream, yet her skin was unharmed. What could hurt Luce so badly? "Hold on, Luce," she mumbled as the pain overwhelmed her.

The grip on her body lessened, but the pain didn't change. If anything, it grew stronger. Mel felt stone under her knees and she forced her eyes open. She couldn't fall. She needed to find Luce. A heavily built man glared down at her. "Who are you?" he demanded. "Judgement is worse for those who don't confess completely!"

His name surfaced in her thoughts. "Minos," she managed to say.

"Yeah, that's me," he replied. "Who in Hell are you?"

"I'm Mel." Her voice died to a whisper.

"Nope, don't know a Mel. Try again," the man said.

Her soul ached again. "Luce. I need to find Luce. He's hurting..."

"The Lord of Hell hurts a lot of people, girl — it's his job. Tell me your name or you can go wait at the back of the line until you remember it. I'm in no hurry and there's plenty more where you came from."

Mel swallowed, trying to block the pain. It felt as if, somehow, Luce was doing the same. Welcoming the reprieve, she forced the words out quickly before it returned. "Lady Muriel of the Hashmallim. I'm here to see Lucifer."

Minos doubled over with laughter. "That's a good one, girl. The day I see an angel like her down here...hahahaha...pull the other one!"

Looking deep into his eyes, Mel gritted her teeth and said, "Angels don't lie, Minos."

A fresh wave of pain punched her in the gut and she fell into blackness, haunted by the sound of her own scream.

Luce had been there – drifting in the dark – but he'd disappeared. So much pain...

The light was dim and the pain was gone. The pallet beneath her rustled as Mel shifted. Straw covered by coarse cloth, with the solidity of stone supporting the lot. No pillows. This wasn't the bed of a modern man.

Feeling a little bruised, she sat up, wincing. Her body was intact – that, at least, she could tell. She squinted at her arms and her chest, remembering the agony that had taken her consciousness. Mel couldn't remember the last time she'd fainted. She reached out for Luce, but she only felt him faintly – as if he was asleep, or heavily shielded from her, though not far away. Somewhere below...

"I ask your forgiveness, Lady Muriel." Silhouetted in the cave entrance, Minos knelt with his head bowed. "I hope I didn't harm you. The stories some of those damned souls come up with...I thought I'd heard them all. And a girl claiming to be you...I'm sorry I didn't recognise you immediately."

Mel clambered to her unsteady feet. "It's been more than three thousand years, Minos. You were human then."

His eyes stayed firmly fixed on the floor as he shook his head. "It's no excuse. You remembered me."

"If you'd told me last week that today I'd be talking to you in Hell, I wouldn't have believed it. Yet here I am and I won't leave until I've seen Luce." She regarded the large man with thoughtful eyes. "Can you help me find him, Minos? It would certainly make my task easier."

Another heavy head-shake. "Lord Lucifer is in his lair, in the deepest part of Hell, where I can't go. Word is that he doesn't want to be disturbed." Minos lowered his voice. "The rumour I've heard is that he suffered some sort of setback on the surface. Something to do with a girl."

Mel smiled and waited.

Minos stared at Mel. "He didn't try to seduce you,

did he? I mean, you calling him...that...and coming here to see him might make people think...Michael would be ready to declare war on him again, if he knew!"

Mel's suspicions rose. "What do you know about Michael and Luce? And where did you hear it?"

She watched in fascination as Minos clasped his hands as if in prayer – though his people never prayed in this way. "Please, don't be angry with me. I have a beer or two with Peter every other week – he's fond of barley beer and I know where to get the best, just like we used to have at home – and occasionally Michael comes, too. Judgement is a thankless job and sometimes you just need to talk to someone who understands, or you'd go mad." He paused, as if waiting for Mel to say something, but she simply smiled. "Okay. From what Michael's said when he's had a horn too many, he's terrified that his premonitions will come true."

Mel was confused by the reference to horns, so it took her a moment to realise that drinking vessels were the least of her worries. "What premonitions? Michael's been getting premonitions about me? Since when?"

"Always the same one. Since just before the Fall," Minos whispered. He glanced around, as if looking for eavesdroppers. When he seemed satisfied, he stood and crept into the room. He gestured at the pallet. "May I?"

Mel nodded.

He sank into the straw, shifting his crown so he could scratch his thinning hair beneath it.

Mel seated herself beside him, curling her knees to

her chest as she rested her back against the limestone wall.

"You know in the Heavenly War, that Michael and Lucifer each led an army?" he began, before looking sheepish. "Of course you know. I've just seen so many new demons that weren't around then. Michael met with you and he agreed with your idea of offering Hell to Lucifer so he'd surrender without a fight, what with the offer of his own realm to run and all. Well, on the eve before battle, Michael dreamed of you. He saw you meet with Lucifer and Lucifer fell to his knees before you. The dream ended with you walking into Hell. And when Michael donned his armour the next morning, he swore he'd keep you from Lucifer, so he could never lead you into Hell." He swallowed. "Your brother's army won and he banished Lucifer here, never to enter Heaven again, but he couldn't keep him from Earth. Every time he heard rumours that Lucifer had returned to Earth to make another bid for power, he sent someone to investigate..."

Raphael, Mel thought. Michael was in a lot more trouble than she'd realised. "Why haven't you told Luce this? He's the Lord of Hell and your boss."

Minos reddened and stared at his lap. "Lord Lucifer never asks for my advice on matters of strategy or policy. All he wants from me are numbers — who went where and how many — and I send them to one of his senior demons every month. I believe he finds my knowledge of politics...outdated. He doesn't know I had the best advisor any king could ever have, in the past, present or future, and I learned more from her in one human lifetime than he has in all his time to date!" He'd risen to his feet and Mel saw the king she'd known so many centuries ago. "Leave while you can, Lady Muriel. I'll tell him nothing. Michael will be relieved to see you home safe and the world will be in the right hands again."

"Not all leaders see mine as the right hands, Minos. Your own grandson..." Mel broke off.

"You mean my namesake – the murderer of Athenian children? I think he's down on Level Eight and I hope he rots there," Minos spat. He turned worried eyes to Mel. "You mean he did worse things than that?"

"He betrayed me," she admitted. "He listened to my counsel on countless occasions and sometimes even asked me to administer justice to his people. There was a woman...ah, she was accused of some terrible crimes that she didn't commit. It was so long ago – I don't even remember her name. She was the last in a long line of people he asked me to judge that day. I pronounced judgement in front of a large crowd that had gathered in the court at Knossos – I told them that she was innocent. I wasn't aware that the king had promised them her death in order to save the guilty party – a woman he'd taken a fancy to. I stated one judgement, their king another...and when he heard, he screamed at the already angry crowd that I must have helped the woman. The crowd...it was a riot. I tried to shield her with my own body, for I knew that the body I wore didn't matter and I could construct another. I couldn't protect her. They tore our bodies apart. And I've never been able to speak in public since, for I remember the feeling of all those eyes on me, then all those hands tearing, tugging, gouging...and the sound of her screaming as they did the same to her." Mel shuddered delicately. "Even that small crowd today was enough to freeze my voice in my throat as it dropped me to my knees. Lady Muriel, advisor to chieftains, secretary-generals, emperors, presidents and kings, but unable to voice a single word when a dozen might hear me." She gave a snort of laughter.

"I'll see him moved to Level Nine with the other hypocrites and traitors," Minos swore, clenching his fists. "You should leave, Lady Muriel, before Lord Lucifer hears you're here and tries to keep you. The world needs you whispering in their leaders' ears — as I know, all too well."

"I can't leave, Minos. I must see Luce and I won't stop until I have. Michael's premonition — it has come to pass, for I have entered Hell, as you see. I won't leave until my task is complete." She patted his shoulder. She sensed only concern — not the despair so prevalent among the others in Hell, or the darkness surrounding the demons' souls. Minos was neither damned nor demon — but not quite an angel, either.

"What do I tell Peter and Michael? Michael's going

to be furious." Minos wrung his hands.

"Tell them...tell Michael that we will have words when I return. Sending an innocent man to Hell in order to save his sister from a fate he had no right to prevent...tell him I will speak to him again only when I have healed the damage he has done, as I see fit. He will wait for my summons." Mel heard her voice resonate in the little cave, as if she were pronouncing judgement on her brother. In a way, perhaps she was.

Minos licked his lips nervously. "Are you sure? He's got that sword and it can do a fair bit of damage when he's angry. I can handle him, but a lady like yourself..."

Mel rose to her feet. Her voice was soft as she said, "Are you a gambling man, Minos? Michael tells you I will not leave Hell, based on an incomplete premonition, and I tell you I will – with its Lord, no less. Not a premonition – a promise. On whom would you bet your harvest?"

Minos grinned, his eyes lighting up with her reflected radiance. "Lady Muriel, I'd bet my kingdom on you. I bet Michael spits his beer out when I tell him so, too. I wish you well." He bowed deeply. "If you are ever in need of my assistance, only call and I will be there. If you change your mind and wish to leave Hell, summon me and I will escort you home." He winked. "Lord Lucifer owes me a favour or two, and I'd happily collect on them to repay my debt to you."

Mel's laughter sounded loud in the small space. "You did learn a lot, didn't you? Thank you, Minos. If you could point the way to Luce's lair, that would be plenty for the moment."

She followed Minos through a labyrinth of narrow caverns and passages until he stopped. "This is Level Two, Lady Muriel. Once again, I wish you well – and I hope to see you soon in Heaven, for a horn of good barley beer." The man bowed and disappeared into the dark.

Mel took a deep breath and set off once more, wishing she knew what had caused Luce such unbearable pain – and why his soul seemed so silent now.

Damned and down here, where no angel would ever find him, to taunt him about the joy he'd almost had. Mel would never follow him here – wouldn't or couldn't. He didn't want her here, either – this was no place for an angel like her. Her realm was Heaven; his was Hell. Surely she'd seen that in the last moments before her body sublimated.

Angels and demons didn't get to live happily ever after. Destiny wouldn't allow it – and Destiny was a bitch to him on a good day. Mel deserved better –

better than he could ever be. She'd soon see that, if her soul had been able to escape to Heaven. The other angels would help her. Heaven was full of those who hated him. It wouldn't be long before she did, too – unless she was dead.

Dead or indifferent – did it matter which? With his Hellish weapon, he'd driven away all hope of a future with her. He'd never wanted to drag her down here to be with him – nothing could be allowed to taint someone as pure as Mel. Luce fingered the prongs on his bident. A thin patina of Mel's blood still stained the weapon, though it had dried and wasn't likely to drip on the desk.

Idly, he wondered when this desk had last been cleaned – his desk in the office on Earth was sprayed and wiped daily, after Mel had turned him down and pointed out its poor hygiene. She'd even made him laugh, though he'd been furious at the time. Mel had made each day worth living, not just something to be endured until his next goal was achieved. What were his goals, anyway? Just a way of keeping score until the world ended.

But that world with Mel had been one he never wanted to see end.

The work Christmas parties, in the hotel and with the carnivorous swans. He'd planned on avoiding or sleeping through them both, as he did every year. Yet he'd seen her heading off, her arms full of alcohol, and his heart had leaped at the thought of a party – any party – with her, alcohol-uninhibited and...aaah... She'd laughed and enjoyed herself, inspiring him to do the same. With her help, he'd stroked a swan – one that would have devoured his fingers.

It was Mel. Always, it was Mel. What creature wouldn't lie down and let her have her way with him? Heavenly, for she'd never hurt him. Hell, he'd even reacted like the swans when she'd stroked his dark wings – what he'd give for her to do it again. Any part of him. Or a kiss...

She wouldn't. Mel would never touch him again. He was too far beneath her. In the dark. Damned. For letting her die. He deserved it. All this and more.

He touched the blood on the bident again. Her blood.

Could the Lord of Hell's weapon kill an angel, like Michael's flaming sword could force one to fall against his will? He could think of no better test subject than himself – for no angel deserved to die as much as he did. If the bident could kill an angel, then his surely had stolen her life. Maybe Mel would be waiting for him...

Oh God, what would he give for it to be true? Everything. Even his life. For her.

He pulled up his sleeves, then took his shirt off altogether. He wouldn't need it any more. He wanted to plunge the damn thing through his heart, if he still had one, skewering it like some sort of spiritual satay stick with his heart beside hers.

Practicality won out – he wasn't sure he had the

strength to push the long-handled weapon through his own breast.

Was it darker in the room, or was it just his eyes dimming?

The bloodied bident prongs, like obscene nipples piercing her shirt through her breasts. Oh God.

He should have known they'd never let him have her.

"Hold on, my love," she'd said, believing everything would be all right. He could almost hear her voice saying it now.

He buried his face in his hands. Nothing could stop the tears. Look how the Lord of Hell cried for the loss of one woman. One, after more than a hundred and fifty thousand – his downfall had been the woman who'd made him rise. A woman so kind she'd seemed incredibly innocent, instead of so worldly-wise that even he couldn't fault her. He'd held out hope of love and life with her in Heaven, for she'd said it was possible. For the first time, she'd been wrong.

Luce reached for her shirt and breathed deep, savouring her perfume. Heaven smelled of her. Myrrh... He hoped the weapon was capable of killing him, for he didn't want to wake without her.

"Luce," she'd called him, her voice caressing the name he used among humans on the surface. In his heart, she was calling him again. He couldn't refuse her.

He dragged the fork from the desk, holding it between his thighs so it came to his chest. No, he couldn't impale himself as he had her. With a dagger or a sword, perhaps. This had to be the instrument of his death, as it had been hers. If only he could work out how.

Lifting his arms above his head, he prayed for guidance – for what he feared would never come. Oh God...he was crying again.

He dropped his hands and felt the sting of a sharp point pierce his palm. He watched the blood well up, a red rivulet that trickled down his wrist. His prayer was answered. It would be slower this way, but Heaven knew he deserved the pain.

Luce lined his arms up, so each barb centred on the vein bisecting his wrists. He lifted his arms once more, clenching his hands together as he concentrated on keeping them steady. Please, let him strike true on the first time. The tears were flowing too fast for him to see clearly any more.

Mel. Oh God, Mel...

Luce drove his arms down, grunting as bronze met bone. Blood spurted, but the pain was nothing compared to the hole where his heart had been. Empty without her.

The blood would flow faster if he pulled his wrists off the barbs. He'd see her sooner.

Gritting his teeth so hard he thought they'd crack, Luce wrenched his arms up. He saw chunks of his own flesh impaled on the weapon that had been his, before he toppled over onto the floor and forgot all about it.

Nothing hurt like the loneliness inside. He crawled away to feel the cold stone beneath his body one last time, bringing his arms before his face so he could watch his lifeblood draining out through the gaping holes; marking the flow of time until he could hold her in his arms again, or oblivion would claim him and he'd never know this pain again.

Please, let this old demon die. He has nothing left to live for.

"Luce," she called again, fainter this time.

"I'm coming, sweet Melody," he said, before he sank deep into a darkness from which he hoped never to wake up.

29

Mel didn't want to enter the next cavern. It looked like it was full of people lying on the floor, having fits. They were spread out on the stone floor, much like the others had been in the cave pool, but these ones were moving jerkily as if they had no control over their own bodies.

She knelt to touch the shoulder of the nearest body — a young woman, she guessed. Immediately, the cavern roof vanished in thick cloud and a spattering of hail headed for her face. She felt the force of the wind on her body, blowing them both away from the skinny young man the girl reached for. The girl's wail of despair as she was torn away from the boy before she could even touch him rasped on Mel's heart. Mel let go of the girl and both the storm and the boy vanished.

Her hands trembling, Mel reached for an older woman crouching on all fours and crying. The storm resumed – just as fiercely as before – only this time the woman was being swept away from what appeared to be her whole family, as a man banged her relentlessly from behind. Mel released this woman, too, and the rutting man vanished along with the children shrieking for their mother.

Mel's heart ached for all of them. They knew despair she never could. Even if Luce was just a faint presence somewhere deep and distant, she wasn't being forced away from him. Quite the contrary – she knew she was getting closer. What could they possibly have done to deserve such despair for eternity? She could feel the grief etched into these souls. Why couldn't this be enough?

She stumbled through the bucking bodies, not wanting to touch another. Yet a familiar face caught her eye – a ruler who had ignored her advice in order to pursue his lust, much like Minos' grandson and namesake. Without thinking, she reached for his shoulder.

The storm seemed to centre on this man, who saw others outside the whirlwind and reached for them as they appeared and vanished. What also seemed to vanish were bits of the man's body – swept up in the twister encircling him and whirled away until they, too, vanished from sight as he screamed. Mel watched the man's hand slowly disintegrate, a piece at a time, before it was followed by his genitals. Repulsed, she yanked her hand back.

In life, the man had ordered all lepers to be executed, for his own infirmity had been his greatest fear. Now, by some irony, he was forced to feel his own body fall apart as those he'd loved or lusted after in life looked on without helping him.

But that had been centuries ago. Centuries. No...at least a millennium. Maybe close to two. How long was enough? Eternity was too much.

"LUCE!" Mel shouted. "Why don't you stop this? Suffering must have an end some time!"

As always, there was no answer. Incensed, she reached for him. Faint, but there; despair and then...gone.

"No!" she gasped, falling to her knees. "Don't you disappear. Luce!"

Illusions, Mel told herself. All the despair was an illusion and somehow she'd let it wash over her. She knew where Hell's illusions originated and they would answer to her. "Spklt! Lift the illusions in this cavern," she shouted with her voice and then deeper, with her spirit.

"Lady, Spklt has Lord's orders..." The imp appeared amid the bodies, accompanied by many more, as his words touched her soul.

"MY order is to lift the illusion. It is too strong and I say it is enough."

"Agreement with Lord..." The imp's thoughts drifted off.

"Tell him I ordered it and let him pursue me," Mel insisted, hoping this more open challenge to his authority might bring him out of hiding. A whole level of Hell disrupted.

"As you will, Lady. Lord will be angry. Very amusing." The imp bowed, as did his colleagues. They straightened and stilled, and Mel caught a glimpse of the imps' shared excitement at seeing Luce aroused in anger and lust. They hoped for an epic battle, but they would settle for explosive sex.

Mel couldn't help laughing. Nothing stirred up trouble as much as an imp – and their mischievous imaginations would put a human author to shame. She'd never heard of most of the things they hoped she and Luce would do.

Luce. She reached for him again, but still she couldn't find him. She refused to give up. "I'm coming to save you from yourself, for I won't lose you, my love," she murmured. "And if you take love advice from any of the imps today, you'll have to find yourself a human contortionist, because I will not..." She heard the imps' amusement and shut the thought down.

She glanced at the prone and supine souls, seeing some start to move toward their peers, murmuring names. Mel heard a wet kiss and whispered endearments, along with some pet names she'd have preferred not to know.

Wondering what a pookie was, and why it seemed so essential to so many of these damned souls, she stepped through them to the tunnel that led to the lower levels.

Let Luce see her handiwork. If he wanted to maintain control over Hell, then he'd have to come to her. If he made her walk all the way to his lair...she'd ensure all Hell broke loose above him.

Mel felt the imps' agreement. They would be her allies in this, for there was no amusement for them while Luce locked himself in his lair.

Behind her, she heard a moan of pleasure and not pain. She quickened her steps.

30

A bark broke the silence, followed by what sounded like a pack of dogs. Mel headed in the direction the sound had come from – she had heard tales of Cerberus, but the dog never left his guard post. She knew her path lay beyond the creature, so she summoned her courage and sought him out.

The once-pitiful, poorly mutated puppy did indeed have three heads and all were barking, creating a cacophony of echoes in the cave. The huge creature wasn't chained or restrained in any way, but only its heads moved toward Mel, alternately sniffing and baying like three separate dogs. She saw the food bowls at its feet, but they were all empty. The poor creature was hungry.

Concentrating, she summoned a snack for the beast – some pork sausages she'd planned to cook with Luce on the weekend. Perhaps the meat would see better use here. She held them out. Two heads extended toward her, while the third hung back, afraid. The two stretched, sniffed...then snarled and fell on one another, fighting over the meat neither of them could reach. All the while, the beast's four feet didn't move. Three heads controlling one body – poor, confused creature, Mel thought. She split the sausages into three portions, tossing them into the dishes. No wonder it was so huge, with three heads to eat but only one body to sustain. It didn't look like anyone had fed him recently, though, as she watched him devour the fresh meat.

All around them, water plinked and flowed to the floor, muffling the sounds of mastication.

One of the beast's heads abandoned his meal to deliver a menacing growl at her.

"That's not a good idea," she said, fixing her eyes on the growling head. With all her attention on Cerberus, Mel jumped when she felt something damp clamp around her ankle. The firm grip anchored her to the ground as she tried to twist around to see what had seized her. Something even slimier enveloped her toes.

It was a mud-covered man, his mouth sucking

blissfully at her foot. Horrified, Mel pulled out of his grasp and shifted closer to Cerberus. Two heads were now growling at the man, straining to snap at him.

The man subsided into the mud from whence he'd come, a foetid swamp that stretched as far as Mel could see in the dim cavern. Wondering where the clay had come from to create a swamp so deep in a cave, Mel saw a human figure rise from the muck and relieve itself, before sinking down into the filth once more. The surface writhed with bodies, Mel realised, horrified. She wondered what sort of sins those on this level had committed. Did toe-sucking count? She couldn't quite recall if that was a sin or not. Surely it wasn't worse than the lust that had condemned those on Level Two. Mel didn't want to touch one of the damned to find out — their crimes might be far worse than she'd thought. Perhaps there were some things she didn't need to know.

Mel looked at the expanse of mud, thinking she'd found the sludge layer of the world's largest septic tank. After curry night in the demons' barracks, she decided, remembering the septic flight school explosion she'd heard about when she worked in the HELL Corporation office. No wonder the demons had found the incident funny — when they were accustomed to this sort of sewage every day.

She wondered if there was a way around, not wanting to soil herself with any more of the nightsoil than necessary. The suspicious mud on her foot and ankle smelled awful already. Only one way to find out...

Mel shook out her wings and rose to hover over the mire. No, it looked like Level Three was wall-to-wall mud. Sighing, she figured her wings could do with the exercise. After all, she rarely had an excuse to fly on Earth. Dodging the stalactites would be a fun test of her rusty flight skills.

Stranded beside the cesspool, Cerberus started barking again, the sound echoing through the cavern as she left him behind.

"Come out and feed your dog, Luce — and get someone to see to your septic tank. If anything needs pumping out, it's that," Mel said softly, wishing he'd hear her and dreading that he wouldn't, even if she shouted.

Mel heard the sounds of shouting from up ahead and landed lightly on her feet, folding her wings out of sight so that she might better navigate the narrow passage between one level and the next. She emerged from the tunnel into a cavern filled with yelling people. Thousands of them, all seemingly engaged in heated arguments and shoving matches with each other over...nothing. Mel touched the woman nearest her and was transported into an ancient, bustling marketplace. The woman seemed to alternate between shouting at the merchant for the items she ardently desired and those crowding around her for getting in her way. Mel released the woman as a man bumped into her and began shouting at her. Mel glimpsed a modern department store, emblazoned with signs that read, 'Black Friday SALE,' before the man took umbrage at a woman who appeared to be lifting a foot spa from a display table, leaving Mel alone to vent his spleen on her instead.

Mad. They're all mad, Mel decided, trying to squeeze through the milling crowd.

A tinkling sound grew louder as she crossed the cavern, the only high note among the deeper voices of the crowd. Like small bells, Mel thought, wondering why they were present. Their purpose could hardly be anything good.

Wishing she was tall enough to see over more of the crowd, Mel moved through them as best she could, following the chiming toward its source. She tripped over a box and nearly fell, but regained her balance in time. Reaching down, Mel lifted the foot spa box she'd seen earlier, wondering what such a strange item was doing here. Figuring she'd best get it out of harm's way, she carried it with her through the crowd.

The throng thinned as she approached the far wall and Mel saw that the cavern had a raised dais, with rough steps cut up one side. She ascended, knowing she was close. Laying the box by the wall, she approached what looked like a waist-high frame with objects suspended from it with string. Closer, she saw what made the sound. Each object was a chiming cat toy being vigorously pawed and batted by a belled calico cat. Their poses reminded her of the waving good luck cats she'd seen in Japan – Maneki Neko, the statues were called. But these were the real thing – live cats, willingly waving for infinitely greater luck than any statue could provide.

Why cats? she wondered, unable to resist a closer look and a chance to play with them. The moment she dropped to her knees, the nearest cat left its toy to saunter over for some investigation. The beast sniffed and then licked Mel's soiled ankle until no mud remained – just the faint fishy scent of the cat's saliva.

Laughing, Mel summoned some fish to repay her cleaning companion – some of her lunch pouches of tuna, tipping the contents onto the stone ledge. All chiming ceased as the other cats scented the treat and padded to join the impromptu feast.

Wishing she could spend more time with the cats, but knowing she'd have to continue, Mel thought of the box of ping pong balls in her shed. Perhaps they'd like to play with those, too – especially with such a large space. Bringing the box to her hands, she waited for the cats to finish cleaning themselves before she upended the box. Balls spun erratically in all directions, ably assisted by enthused cats.

Mere seconds passed before both cats and balls had vanished from the dais and they were careening between the crazed shoppers on the floor below. Mel watched, enchanted.

"My luck!" shrieked a voice. It belonged to a dark-haired, diminutive man clutching a wad of what looked like betting slips. "Where is my luck? My kitties. My kitties!" The man's hands fluttered like frightened birds, showering the stone with paper.

"It's all right. They're still here. I'm sure they'll return when they get hungry," Mel said.

"But the battle! The epic battle! Bets have just closed and the next ten minutes will decide the winner. And they're not even interested!" the little man insisted shrilly.

A half-dozen cats couldn't distract thousands of people, surely, Mel thought, scanning the crowd. The quiet, still crowd. By all that was holy...how could a playing cat capture the fascination of so many? Even Mel thought it a miracle of sorts. Who'd have thought?

"They're not fighting for the foot spa! The bets are on who wins the foot spa today!" he wailed.

Mel glanced at the box that he hadn't seemed to have noticed. "That would be me. It was just sitting on the ground, so I lifted it out of harm's way. I must admit I've never used one before and my feet are a little sore from walking bare on the stone today. Are they hard to use?"

"You? Who are you?" the man spat.

Something about the way he moved and pouted reminded Mel of Persi. "You're my cousin Demeter's other son, Ploutos," she said slowly. "I'm Mel."

"Mel? Mel?" Ploutos squawked. "I don't know any Mel – OH!" Dark eyes grew round. "Lady Muriel! What the Hell are you doing here?"

Mel managed a smile. "Looking for Lucifer. I need to speak to him."

"What will Lord Lucifer say when he sees this?" Ploutos wailed, waving at the happy, cat-watching denizens of Level Four.

"Tell him an interfering angel came in and disrupted your perfectly run part of Hell," Mel replied. "The sooner I find him, the less disruption I'll cause to his realm."

Ploutos swallowed noisily. "Yes, Lady Muriel. I must warn you, though. Don't use the foot spa. Just leave it here. It's faulty. This is Hell, after all. The nearest relaxing foot massage is probably in a day spa thousands of kilometres away. I hope you get it, Lady Muriel. Lord Lucifer is...surlier than usual, lately. He sees no one and none have entered his lair in some time. I wish you every success, but an angry Lord Lucifer is not something you should see. My half-sister, Persi, seems to have some sort of crazy crush on him, but even she's scared of his temper. Yet she keeps coming here, wanting to see him..."

Mel raised her eyebrows. "Persi? Here? That's...disturbing news. She should be running the HELL Corporation back on Earth, where I left her."

"She has it bad for Lord Lucifer and she's

determined to have him at any cost. Can you speak to her? Tell her what she's risking?"

"When I see her next, I will certainly speak to her. The last place she should be is here in Hell. Not if she wants to be an angel..." Mel said.

"This is why we need you so much. Who would do what you do if Lord Lucifer...if he...I'm sorry, Lady Muriel, but his fury is frightening. If he summoned all the powers of Hell and unleashed them on you...he could do untold damage. I wouldn't want him to hurt you."

Mel laughed. "Thank you, Ploutos, but I think I've seen his temper already. Honestly, Luce is about as dangerous as those cats."

Ploutos managed a sickly smile. "I hope you're right, Lady Muriel. I wouldn't want to be in your place."

Mel nodded and decided she'd dallied long enough. She was barely halfway through Hell and the ominous silence from Luce was worrying her. Bidding farewell to Ploutos, she set off for the lower levels of Hell, where she knew Luce had to be hiding.

The mercantile battle behind her may have ceased, but Mel heard more fighting ahead. She wondered if they were fighting over another faulty foot spa or whether there was a far greater prize at stake. Under the clash of metal and shouting voices, she could hear the bass gurgle of water. Standing at the edge of the cavern, her first impression was of the aftermath of the Battle of Arausio. Thousands of men struggling in a river while they sank beneath the weight of their armour, fighting each other all the way down. The Rhone hadn't been so swampy – this underground river looked more like the Styx, though Thessaly was a world away from where she was now.

Mel sniffed carefully, but this didn't smell the same as Level Three's sewage. Not fresh, certainly, but more like artesian water than wastewater. The taint of blood in the air did turn her stomach a little, though.

"Are you looking to place your bet, too?" a voice said. "You're cutting it close. Battle ends in an hour."

"What happens when the battle ends?" Mel asked.

"Same thing that happens at the end of every day. Everyone stops fighting, we count up all the missing bits and announce who lost the least limbs and drowned the fewest times. Wait a few hours, until everything's grown back in the morning, then start over. Are you new?" The tunic-clad demon squinted at her.

Mel smiled. "I wouldn't say that, though I don't believe we've met before."

"Phlegyas. I used to be a king, once, and now I'm just king of the moat. All that rutting fool Apollo's fault. The man thought the sun shone out of his arse, but my daughter knew otherwise. She picked someone better and the idiot got jealous. So now I pole a boat in the dark, in between taking bets on the battle below." He shrugged. "Such is life."

"Phlegyas...Thessaly? I think I was working with Minos then...your reign was cut short before I got a chance to meet you," Mel said.

"Ah, I remember those days. Seems like only

yesterday..." Phlegyas shook his head. "Now they all want minions, weapons of mass destruction and mobile phones. HA! They get a spear, a sword and whatever armour they can find that fits. If they want padding to stop the armour from chafing, they have to source that themselves, or they can go naked." He appraised Mel from top to toe. "I'm not sure we have armour contoured for your shape, but it looks like you're already dressed for the more berserker style of battle. Good luck to you, lady. Probably the safest battle you'll ever be in — no rape and pillaging here. Just hacking off limbs and such. Wait until this one's over and see if you can find yourself a sword small enough. You'll get the hang of things eventually." When he turned to point at the small pile of weapons remaining, Mel saw that his tunic was hiked up at the back over his tail, baring his backside. Sun didn't shine out of his behind, either.

"Oh, I'm not here to fight, Phlegyas. Nor do I wish to place a wager on the outcome of today's battle. I'm seeking Lucifer. I must see him before I leave."

"You sure? I can give you good odds. The favourite is...that big bastard there." Phlegyas pointed at a hulking man who was fighting off three muddy figures in waist-deep mud not far from them. He whirled, sending a wave of muddy water that reached the shore and splattered at Mel's feet, leaving splotches of mud up her thigh.

Mel glanced down and sighed. Between the sewage, mud and cat saliva, she really wanted a bath some time soon. The sooner she found Luce, the sooner she could go home. Maybe he'd agree to share her shower. That was something they hadn't done yet.

"No, I need to get going. I don't have time to watch this battle." Mel nodded at a boat, pulled up on shore. "Will you take me across the river to where the next level is?"

"Not until the battle's over!" Phlegyas said, staring at her. "They'll drag the boat under and add us to the casualty list. I'll take you when it's done, but not before. You could always row over yourself...I won't go near the water until they call a ceasefire."

Mel shrugged. "I guess I'll fly, same as I did on Level Three. Tell me which way to go, please."

Phlegyas' eyes seemed to widen further. "Fly? You some sort of fallen angel or something? You should already know all the lower levels are through Dis, over that side." He pointed into the dark.

Mel laughed, shaking her wings out and letting them lift her higher. "Thank you. No, I haven't fallen yet and I won't if I can help it. That way? So be it."

The cavern ceiling was low, so her wingtips brushed the stone even as her toes skimmed the water. Muddy water splashed over her skin as combatants burst from the water, first fighting one another and then reaching for her. A long wolf-whistle cut through the other sounds, originating from a man with a swastika tattoo on his shoulder. Heads surfaced from the water and more whistles sounded like eerie echoes, pursuing her across the water.

The sounds of battles ceased. "Angel," came the gasped cry from hundreds of throats. "The angel of victory."

"Angel of mud, more like!" Mel called back over her shoulder. The shore approached and it was only a narrow strip of sand, ending in a seemingly solid cavern wall. It didn't look like there was access to the lower levels from here. Mel landed and strode closer to investigate.

"What in Hell? More gates? What does Hell need more gates for? Everyone's stuck in the horrible delusions in their own heads." Mel glared at the barrier, stretching up to meet the cavern roof above her head.

"It's your turn to deal."

"No, yours. I did the last round. You need to learn to shuffle better, Kas."

"I shuffle just fine! You're the one who can't shuffle, Mo — you dealt me that last straight."

The clink hiss of beer bottles being opened, before

the clink of glass.

"To Lady Luck!"

"To her deciding Kas is a poxy whore and smiling at us again!"

"OI!"

Mel laughed softly as she headed toward the voices, her feet almost silent on the cold stone. She saw them before they saw her — three fallen angels, sitting at a square table, drinking beer and talking so loudly they never heard her approach.

"Can one of you open the gate, please?" she called.

"Holy Hell, is that an angel?"

"Fuck, she's naked. No angel would be crazy enough to walk through here without clothes. She'd have Lord Lucifer on her in no time."

"How come he gets all the best girls?"

"He is the Lord of Hell. Must be the title."

"Nah, guys, that's Mel. She'd freeze his balls before she'd sleep with him. Mel! Come have some beer with us," one of the men invited.

"Who's Mel?" she heard a doubtful voice say.

"She's the one who saved me from the crazy harpy in HR. The one who stabbed me with her shoe over some paper. She's no ordinary angel. The rest look through us demons like we aren't really there — but she's different. She acts like she's one of us, only nicer."

"No angel would do that. We're scum to them — as if we'd make them fall if we so much as soiled their eyeballs with a single glance."

Mel heard Merihim's unmistakeable laugh. "You haven't met Mel, then. She went into an adult shop with Lili to get Gerry's mankini for his birthday. They were having a sale on all the Fetish Fantasy range for some bondage book release – everything out on display, including some toys I'd never heard of. Lili said she barely blushed."

A vision of latex tentacles crept into Mel's mind and she banished it quickly. She hadn't needed to know what they were for then and she definitely didn't need to know now. "What sort of beer are you drinking?" she asked, moving closer.

"Duvel, of course! We have plenty. You look like you need a drink," Asmodeus said, flicking the cap off with his claws. He held the bottle out to her.

Mel admitted she was thirsty and took a deep draught. The beer certainly satisfied her thirst – she'd left the stream far behind, many circles before. She'd lost count somewhere along the way, too – but it didn't matter. Luce was on the other side of that gate – that she knew for certain.

"What was the book? Was it that one with the numbers? Fifty lashes or something?" Kasyade asked.

Merihim shook his head. "Nah, a new release. Something about monsters."

"Monsters in the dark?" Mel suggested, taking another sip. "Sex slavery and sadism?"

"That's the one!" Merihim exclaimed. "It sounded really dark, hence the toy sale."

Mel tried not to laugh. "I heard the hero's name was Quincy. It can't be that dark."

All three men stared at her as she took another drink. "You've read it?" Asmodeus asked, looking shocked.

Mel did laugh this time. "No, not my style. Ana from HR had a copy and she and Lili were discussing it. They both really liked it." She shrugged. "I mean, you guys deal with corporal punishment every day here. It must get boring."

"No, we're not on punishment detail," Asmodeus said quietly. "We do guard duty, mostly – here on the inner gate, or relieving some of the inner-circle demons when they're up on the surface. Ana and Lili are into some of the more physical roles here – I guess they like it." He drank so deeply he finished his beer.

He threw the empty across the cave, where the bottle shattered on a stalactite. He reached into the cooler box beside the table, looking at Mel. "You finished that fast. Need another one?" He offered a fresh beer.

Mel licked the foam from her lips. "Thank you. You're right, I did need that. Can you tell me how I open the gate?"

"What for?" Kasyade scoffed. "Nothing in there but the damned and the Lord of Hell himself, and he's in the nastiest mood I've seen yet. Chewed me out for not feeding his bloody dog while he was off with that little princess he left in charge!" He snorted. "Bullshit, too.

The dog wasn't hungry – he'd just finished dinner when I got there, with all sorts of stinking offal. Wouldn't eat it at all."

Mel tried to cover the huge belch threatening to escape. She burped as delicately as she could before admitting, "I fed him. Cerberus looked so sad, I felt sorry for him. I gave him some sausages I'd planned to cook on the weekend. I can always get more once I'm done here."

Asmodeus took a gulp of his beer. "What in Hell are you here for, Mel? I thought you finished up with HELL Corp weeks ago. I figured you'd be back in Heaven with the other angels."

"I'm here to see Luce," she replied cautiously. These were his minions, after all, and not necessarily to be trusted. Luce was the only redeemed demon in Hell.

"What do you want to see that grumpy prick for? Come play cards with us. We'll lend you the money," Merihim offered.

Asmodeus smacked him. "We still owe you for the coffee machine at work. That coffee is heavenly, compared to the instant shit we used to have. We'll pay you back and you can use that money for betting. Can't play poker without some stakes."

"Angels don't gamble," Kasyade sneered. "Not unless they want to fall and stay here permanently. I wouldn't say no to her, but she might have some pasty hypocrite of a cherub waiting for her at home."

"Of course Mel gambles. She won us the office

coffee machine on Melbourne Cup Day. C'mon, Mel. One game and we'll show you how to open the gate. Or give you a lift back up to the surface, if you decide after some beer and a hand of poker that Lord Prick isn't worth wasting your time on."

"Okay, it's a deal – a game for the gate, and you can divide my winnings as interest on the loan, if there are any, for I don't need them and I don't have anywhere to carry cash at the moment. I must see Luce – and I won't go home until I've spoken to him. You don't like him much, do you?"

Asmodeus shrugged. "He's the boss. He gets all the girls and gives us all the shit jobs, like feeding the dog, writing government policy in the office and guarding the gate. We do what he says or he gives us to the Corporal girls – and Lili's real mean to demons."

"Lili's here?" Mel asked in surprise.

Kasyade snorted. "Down on Level Seven. Since the little princess took over the office, she's back full-time with us and she's gotten creative. Hell, the only one angrier than her is Lord Prick himself. You'll see – if Lili lets you past. I bet she'd like to get her claws into a sweet little angel like you..."

Merihim snorted with laughter. "Kas, Mel worked for Lili in the office. They get along just fine. Lili's the last of us Mel needs to worry about." He nodded at Mel. "You look dead on your feet. Grab a seat." Merihim pulled out the fourth chair for her and Mel graciously sat, lifting her wings over the back so they sat comfortably. She shook her hair down over her breasts so she wouldn't distract the demons too much with them. She fully intended to play fair.

"Here," Merihim said, pulling a t-shirt out of a bag Mel hadn't seen until now. "It's my change of clothes for the gym in the morning. It's clean — I haven't worn it yet."

Mel smiled and took it. "Thank you. I'll only borrow it — you'll have it back before you need it for the gym."

"Do you know how to play poker?" Kasyade asked. "Five-card draw, fifty-dollar buy-in and two rounds of betting. No limit to the number of raises."

"It's been a long time," Mel admitted. "Would it be okay if I watched a hand or two, just to refresh my memory?"

"Absolutely," Merihim said warmly. He glanced at her empty beer. "Let me get you another drink while you're watching." He opened and passed her another, taking the empty from her fingers.

"Thank you," Mel said, leaning back into her chair. She hadn't realised quite how tired she was until now. It was one Hell of a relief just to sit and do nothing, no more walking, for a few minutes. The beer seemed like a tiny sip of Heaven, too. Good Belgian beer was a luxury she didn't often spend money on.

She watched Kasyade deal, then Merihim raised and Asmodeus matched him. Kasyade hesitated for a bit before raising, too. The betting ran round the table one more time before the demons traded unwanted cards for new ones and grimaced at the result. Mel found her eyes kept being drawn back to Kasyade, who sat with his arms crossed. She could've sworn he was holding six cards, but she blinked and looked again. No — it was only five, like he was supposed to have.

Merihim folded, but Asmodeus stayed in until the end, when Kasyade's two pair trounced his couple of tens. "Aw, you have all the good luck tonight, Kas," Asmodeus complained. "I swear you've won half my money already and if you keep going like this, I'll be out before the beer's gone!"

"Luck will change with Mel. She's an angel — luck always favours her," Merihim said, smiling at her. "Are you in the next round, Mel?"

"I'd like to watch one more, please," she said. "Then I'll give it a try."

She kept her eyes on Kasyade again and this time it looked like cards were disappearing up his sleeve. His discarded cards never made it to the pile with everyone else's, yet he still drew four new ones. She caught his tiny, relieved smile at the new cards before it vanished, too.

Both Merihim and Asmodeus stayed in until the end, but Kasyade won once more. Asmodeus threw his cards on the table, swearing, as he grabbed another beer, leaving Kasyade to deal again. "It's the cards," Asmodeus grumbled. "The deck likes Kas. Get the other one out, Merih. Maybe these cards will like me instead."

Merihim extracted another, identical pack of cards from his pocket and proceeded to shuffle them. "Are you in?" he asked Mel.

She took a deep breath and set her beer down on the table. "Sure. Why not?"

Despite her protests, both Merihim and Asmodeus set a large pile of cash in front of her. "It's less than the coffee machine's worth," Merihim insisted, so Mel accepted it.

"Buy in," Kasyade grunted. Merihim and Asmodeus tossed in their fifty-dollar notes. Kasyade followed suit and they all stared at Mel.

"Oh, yes," she murmured, looking for a yellow note in her stack. She found one and placed it delicately on top of the other three in the middle of the table.

Kasyade shuffled the cards one more time and started dealing. First Merihim, then herself, before the other two got their cards. Round and round, until each had their five. Mel watched Asmodeus pick up each card he was dealt, one by one, and frown at it. Merihim waited for all five of his before grimacing at his hand.

Mel lifted her cards and fanned them out, pausing to rearrange them a little, before setting the fan back down on the table before her. "Remind me again," she said to no one in particular, "the aim of this game is to get as many of a kind as possible, with as high a number as I can, right?"

Kasyade and Asmodeus exchanged glances. Even Merihim looked startled, but he recovered first. "Pretty much, yeah. Unless you get all five in a sequence or of the same suit, but that doesn't happen often. It's easier to look for two or three or four of a kind, when you're just starting out."

Mel nodded and sipped her beer. "Thank you."

"Right, bets!" Kasyade announced, grinning. "Merih?"

Merihim added five dollars to the pot and Mel followed his lead. Asmodeus shrugged before doing the same. Kasyade frowned and looked thoughtful but, after what seemed like an inordinately long amount of time, chose to place his purple five-dollar bill in the pot with the others.

"Right. How many cards you trading?" Kasyade said with his eyebrows raised.

"I'll go four," Merihim announced, throwing them down.

Kasyade swiped them up neatly and dealt him four fresh cards. Merihim's frown deepened as he looked at the cards, but he didn't say anything.

"Mel?"

"Mm?"

"How many cards are you trading? How many of the ones in your hand do you want to discard and replace with new ones?" Asmodeus asked patiently.

"Oh!" Mel peered at the backs of her cards, still face-down on the table. She looked thoughtful for a moment. "No, thank you. I'd like to keep these, if that's okay."

"All of them?" Asmodeus pressed. "Usually there's one or two, at least, and you could get a much better hand if you trade them in..."

Mel shook her head. "No, it really is okay. I'll keep the ones I have. It's a game of luck, right?" She smiled around the table.

Kasyade stared at her, mesmerised, as if he still didn't believe her. He had the look of a man who had just won a lot of money in a lottery, Mel decided. She shrugged. "Mo's next, right?"

Asmodeus had his two cards up, ready to trade. Kasyade's gaze swung to Asmodeus and he replaced the cards mechanically.

The other demons seemed intent on their own cards, so only Mel watched as Kasyade discarded one of his and dealt himself a new one. His big hands concealed his cards for a few seconds, and Mel wondered what he was trying to hide.

Kasyade seemed to notice her scrutiny and set his cards on the table, clapping his hands. "Right. Next round of betting. Merih?"

Merihim pouted at his cards, then pulled out another five-dollar bill and surrendered it to the pot.

Mel hesitated. "I can match or make a larger bet, can't I?" she asked.

"Or fold," Kasyade added.

"Right." Mel nodded thoughtfully. She glanced at the piles of cash around the table. Kasyade seemed to have about as much as Asmodeus and Merihim put together, which was more than Mel had, too. "If I'm only playing one game, I could bet all of this, couldn't I?"

Three shocked pairs of eyes stared at her. Asmodeus attempted to smile. "You could, but it's usually safer to place smaller bets at first, until you get the hang of the game and the measure of your opponents..."

Mel smiled back. "You mean you all want to play cards with me again some time? When I'm not on such pressing business, of course. That would be lovely."

All three men nodded fervently, their gaze shifting to the money she was carefully transferring to the pot.

"I believe I'm all in?" she said.

"Y-yeah," Asmodeus stammered, throwing his cards down. "I can't match that. Fold."

Merihim dropped his cards, too. "Same."

Kasyade looked at Mel, who kept her serene smile firmly on her face. It was just a game to her, after all, and when it was over, she'd be able to pass through those gates and continue to Luce. The faster the game ended, the better. There definitely wasn't any point in drawing this out.

Kasyade opened his mouth.

Mel said, "Kas, you should probably fold, too. It would be in your best interests." She returned his gaze with concern.

Merihim coughed. "Mel, you shouldn't warn him if you have a good hand. Let him take the risk with his money and his hand – the point of the game is to win. You won't win if you tell people what you have in your hand. You could win some of our money back if you keep your cards a secret."

Mel tilted her head. "I don't understand. If Kas folds, I win. Isn't that the point?"

Merihim started to reply, but Kasyade cut him off. "But the point is, I don't fold, angel. I'll not just match your bet – I'll raise you. I'll go all in, too. And you're out of cash." He grinned. "I'll take payment in other forms. Whatever you're offering."

Asmodeus and Merihim looked from Kasyade to Mel to their remaining funds. In unison, both men pushed their stacks toward Mel. "The rest of the coffee machine money, Mel," Asmodeus said.

Merihim nodded. "Yeah, I'll bet on you over my

own hand any day. Match him."

Once again, Mel hesitated. "Are you sure, Kasyade?" she asked.

"Fold or match my bet, angel. Stop stalling," he replied.

She bowed her head. "I will match it." She counted out the money required and added it to the pot. What remained would barely buy lunch for the three of them on the Terrace.

Kasyade laughed. "Kiss my ass, angel. Four aces, look." He threw the hand down to reveal his cards to them all.

Asmodeus swore, but Merihim's jaw tightened. "What do you have, Mel?"

"I don't have four of a kind," she admitted. "Actually, I don't have more than one of anything."

Kasyade laughed even harder. "You've got balls, angel – I never met one who could bluff like you before. I'll tell you what – I'll buy you a beer out of my winnings." He reached for the pot.

"NO!" The shout came from both Asmodeus and Merihim.

"I believe I have to show you my cards first," Mel stated. Her hands shaking a little, she turned over her fanned cards on the tabletop.

A hush fell.

"A royal flush," Merihim breathed.

"That's not possible!" Kasyade insisted. "I have all four aces. She must have been hiding the cards somewhere!"

Merihim looked from Mel to Kasyade. "Mel only touched those five cards, Kas, and she was naked when she arrived." He addressed Mel. "Where did you get the cards in your hand?"

"Kas dealt them to me," she replied.

"She's lying!" Kasyade declared.

"Angels don't lie," Asmodeus said slowly. "And they don't cheat, either. You've been cheating all night, you son of a harpy!" The table, money and cards went flying as Asmodeus dove for Kasyade. Kasyade got his arms up to shield his head, so all that got hurt was his sleeve, ripped up the seam to his elbow. Two more aces and a king fell out. "Forfeit! Forfeit all your winnings, you lying, cheating..."

Mel heard the smack of flesh on flesh, then bone breaking as Asmodeus and Kasyade hit the floor. She stood, hoping to help, but not sure how.

Merihim spread his arms. "You wanted to open the gate and go through, right? Now's probably a good time." He led her away from the wrestling demons. "How did you know he was cheating?"

Mel shrugged. "He had too many cards sometimes and some of them simply disappeared." She swallowed. "I gave him the opportunity to fold without having to show his hand, so he could make reparation to you both with his dignity intact, but he refused. I had hoped..."

Merihim snorted. "You're too innocent for your

own good, Mel. We're demons. Damned, never to be redeemed."

Mel wished she could tell him that he was wrong, but perhaps Luce was unique among demons. He'd certainly been unusual enough to win her heart. "Call me an optimist, for I'll never lose hope," she murmured.

"Didn't you read the sign over the door? Hope deserts everyone here eventually," Merihim said.

Mel kept her smile soft. "Yet you hoped I'd win against Kas. You even bet money on the outcome."

Merihim coughed. "That's different. I've seen you win every gamble you take — when it's not for personal gain. Where did you learn to play poker?"

"France," Mel answered. When Merihim looked puzzled, she explained, "Poker was played in France before it arrived in New Orleans in America. Most people don't know that Napoleon's Russian retreat was because he lost a game of poker."

"I never heard that!" Merihim protested.

Mel smiled. "He had such an expressive face — he was terrible at bluffing. Given how well I knew him, I could read his hand simply from his expression."

Merihim's face registered his shock and Mel didn't wait for him to recover. "The gate?" she prompted. "I really need to see Luce."

Merihim heaved a huge sigh, shaking his head. "I hope you know what you're doing. Lord Lucifer is...well, he's in one of the darkest moods I've seen him in for centuries. You'd be better off going back to the surface. I'll give you a lift home, if you want."

"I must," Mel insisted. "I won't leave until I've seen him. Please open the gate."

Merihim coughed. "Actually, you have to be born an angel to do it. Just touch it – and it'll swing open. It works for us fallen angels, too, luckily, or we'd all be stuck on one side or the other. Not many angels make it this far without falling." He still looked regretful, Mel thought. "I don't want to see you fall. Even if you make it to Lucifer's lair, he'll do everything in his power to turn you, because he's a sadistic bastard. You don't deserve our fate, Mel. Turn back."

Mel placed both of her palms on the gates and they swung open, as if tonnes of stone were merely paper. She heard moans and screams from the depths below. She turned her head toward Merihim. "I can't turn back. Thank you for your help." She pulled his shirt over her head and handed it to him, before kissing his cheek.

Merihim took the shirt, stunned. "Any time, Mel. Mo and me...we owe you more than ever, now. Kas, too – I'll remind him that you gave him a chance to repent, when he wakes up and his arms grow back." He squinted at Asmodeus in the darkness. "Maybe before his arms grow back. I don't want him taking a swing at me, too." He blushed as he looked at Mel. "Lucifer will probably like what he sees, especially when he can see everything. I hope you reach him. Take care, Mel."

Mel smiled, waved, and stepped through the gates to the lower levels of Hell.

I'm coming for you, Luce, she thought, wishing he could hear her. Walking naked through Hell, just like you said in that café. I never thought it would be me doing it, though.

She stretched her wings and started her descent.

Touching down on the first stone terrace, Mel was greeted by the grumpy receptionist she'd first met at her interview for the HELL Corporation. The girl had lost her clothes and gained a pair of dark, leathery wings, marking her as one of the Dirae, but Mel hadn't forgotten her frowning face.

"What do you want?" the girl asked, evidently appraising Mel's much larger wings.

Mel smiled and let her white wings fade from sight, wishing she had a way to wash some of the mud off the rest of her. "I'm looking for Lucifer. Do you have a switchboard, so you can call and tell him I'm here?"

The girl gave her a look of deep disgust. "No. Why would you...ohhh. You're that angel who wanted a job in the office up on the surface." She managed a nasty smile. "You come to try whoring yourself to Lord Lucifer for another chance? He has all the office whores he needs and the rest are all better looking than you. Maybe he'll find space for you with the harpies on Level Seven. Sometimes they run out of damned souls and they always need practice dummies."

Mel's smile didn't falter, though she wished she could increase the distance between herself and this nasty piece of work. Were all the demons in the lower levels as rude as this? Those in the upper levels had seemed so reasonable.

Mel cleared her throat. "I worked a long contract with the HELL Corporation on the surface. The work was very rewarding – fascinating, in fact. Now I've come to see Luce and I must admit, it's been interesting to see how he runs things in the Pit. What are those?" Mel nodded at several pits placed at regular intervals around the terrace – almost like open graves.

"Those?" The girl's grin became nastier still. "Part of the heating system for Level Seven. Want a closer look?" She gave Mel a shove toward the nearest one.

Sparks showered to the stone from where the girl had touched Mel, leaving scorch marks on her skin and the echo of the initial, painful burn. Mel found herself on her knees, but she rose as soon as the pain started to fade. A fading flash was all it was. Hardly enough to incapacitate an angel. The Dirae girl had disappeared.

Mel looked around. Perhaps the girl had fallen into one of the pits. She glanced into the nearest and saw what appeared to be a human figure, encased in flame as it lay on...was that molten rock? Pipes ran along the sides of the trench, with no markings to say what they contained. That meant they were filled with air or water, Mel knew. With a single thought, she split one of the pipes open. Water cascaded down the walls, rising as steam from the rock below. The pit began filling faster than the heat could evaporate it.

The extinguished but blackened figure disappeared in the cloud of steam, surfacing as the pit started to resemble a hot bath. "Thank you," a hoarse voice said. "They say I committed heresy, but I don't even know what religion they were from." As it rose from the warm water, Mel became aware that the burned heretic was most definitely male. "Oh, wait. They were Romans. I wouldn't give my wife to the slaves during the Saturnalia. Heresy, they called it. Unholy. Ha. My grandsire was a rabbi in Hieroselyma. Now he knew holy. Those crazy Romans..." His voice failed him at this point, to Mel's relief. She'd heard enough to know that this was a very strange level of Hell.

"Please, I was looking for the...girl responsible for this place," Mel said. "One of the Dirae, but I didn't catch her name. I think she might have fallen into one of these pits, but there are so many..."

He cleared his throat, coughed, then repeated the procedure. "Did you ask her name?"

Mel shook her head.

"Did you ever do anything to piss her off?"

"No, I met her on the surface, in an office. She was supposed to be helpful, but she seemed to begrudge even a moment of time to do her job and notify someone I was there to see..."

"Megaera, then. Alecto won't tell you her name and Tisiphone will fool you into thinking she's an angel until you cross her and then she'll rip you apart. Must've been Meg. She deserved a turn, burning in the pits." The man grinned with grim satisfaction. "She'll hurt for a bit, but she'll be fine again by morning. We always are, ready to be tortured all over again."

It was the second time she'd heard about the regeneration powers of Hell. Everything automatically healed by morning. So whatever was causing this silence from Luce should have healed by now, surely. How long had she been here? More than a day? Two? So hard to keep track of time when there was no daylight. She needed to find Luce. Find out why she couldn't even sense his soul.

Still, she could hardly leave the girl to burn. She had to help her first.

Mel ran along the line of pits, calling, "Meg. Megaera. Please, tell me where you are so I can help you out!"

The voice she heard was gravelly. "Bitch." It came from four pits down — she'd flown more than ten metres.

Mel increased her pace, splitting the pipes in all the pits open as she passed.

The dripping Dirae hauled herself out and glared at Mel. "I bet you did that on purpose." She ignored Mel's outstretched hand, clambering to her feet on her own. "Big joke from the bloody angel. I hope Lord Lucifer fucks you with his fork, if you even make it that far. Level Seven will just lap you up, I'm sure. A bit of fresh blood never hurt anybody...oh, except the angel shedding it, of course." Megaera pointed. "On to Level Seven and good riddance."

Mel tried to smile in the face of such malice. "Thank you."

As she left the girl behind, she heard the words, "With the pointy end, bitch."

Well, it was Hell. There had to be horrible people in it. Otherwise, why would the place exist at all? The shadows in the tunnel descending to Level Seven seemed darker than those above, but Mel assured herself she was just imagining it.

36

The smell hit her first. The stench of old blood wafted up the tunnel, like the time Mel's neighbour had applied blood and bone fertiliser to her garden on a hot summer's day. Or the carnage at the Battle of Arausio, all over again. She wondered if the army commanders who led that slaughter were here among the damned. It seemed fitting for such mass murderers to bathe in a boiling river of blood just like the one before her.

She couldn't tell one struggling figure apart from the others — they all seemed to be submerged in the gruesome ooze.

"You're far from home, angel. Want a ride somewhere?"

Mel tore her eyes from the river. She hadn't seen a centaur in years, and this one was leering at her. Combing her memory, she found his name – Nessos, the ferryman who liked to rape his female passengers. "No, thank you. Directions to Lucifer's lair are all that I ask."

"Lord Lucifer?" Nessos scoffed. "He can't fill you like I can. Even humans know that – they say a well-endowed man is hung like a horse, not like Lucifer. If you're looking for some action, demon style, you won't find a rougher rider than me. I can make you scream, angel, so they'll hear you in Heaven."

Mel managed a polite smile. "Tempting, I'm sure, but I need to speak to Lucifer. I take it I'll have to cross the river?"

"And the bank on the other side. You do like it rough, then, if you're headed into the harpies' territory." Nessos stared at her, seemingly impressed. "You're braver than me. I'll just fuck you – those girls will fuck you up."

Struggling not to show her disgust, Mel forced herself to maintain her strained smile as she flapped her wings, trying to rapidly rise above the depraved centaur.

Her shadow darkened the river's sluggish surface, but it seemed to gather density as it lost form. It looked like a dark cloud beneath her, keeping pace with her progress as she trudged deeper into Hell for Luce.

Luce.

Mel reached out for his soul, straining for a sense of him that she couldn't grasp. He seemed so distant she couldn't feel him at all. Had he left Hell while she struggled to make it through to him? That would be the ultimate irony – if he'd left Hell to look for her. Surely Michael and Peter would tell him where she was – even Raphael, for Michael must have told him everything by now. If she reached Luce's lair before he returned, she was claiming his throne while she waited or, better yet, his bed. She couldn't recall ever being so weary on Earth. She longed for rest – but she couldn't stop yet. Luce needed her – that much she knew.

She touched down on the rocky ledge that hung over the river – too high for those poor, drowning souls to grasp, but just high enough for a centaur to poke his spear at anyone who made the attempt.

"I said no! The harpies don't need any more assistants. Only volunteers to be victims and Jez said she doesn't want to see your arse again. Get down!" Chiron the centaur jabbed at a gory figure, who subsided into the red river. "You should fly right back where you came from," Chiron said, leaning on the spear as he squinted at Mel. "There's nothing but pain if you go any further."

Mel smiled wanly. "My feet already hurt and it seems all the foot spas in Hell are broken. I carry my pain with me and the sooner I see Lucifer, the sooner I can head home for a rest."

"No angel should see what the harpies are up to. I'm not even game to go in there. The screams are enough." The centaur shuddered, from his human shoulders right down to his equine tail.

"Is there another way through to Lucifer's lair?"

Chiron shook his head. "Few make it through and they say he won't see anyone. You're wasting your time."

Mel's heart twinged as she wondered if he was right. Perhaps she should just turn around and return home. Luce knew where she lived – if he wanted her, he could find her.

But if he was hurt and needed her help...

"No. My time is never wasted, though there are some things I wish I hadn't seen. I'm sure it won't be as bad as you say – I've worked with some of the harpies up on the surface. This is Lilith's domain, and she and I get along just fine." Mel bowed her head. "Thank you, but I will continue, as I must. If you see Lucifer..." She wasn't sure what to ask for.

Chiron bowed deeply. "In the unlikely event that I see Lord Lucifer, I'll say that you seek him and that he is undoubtedly in your debt. You should have summoned him to the surface and not endured such hardship." A vaguely humanoid figure surged up from the revolting river. "OI! I said no!" Chiron levelled his spear at the offending soul. "Get back in there or I'll..."

His voice faded as Mel entered the next cave and the

chorus of screams drowned out all other sounds. There was so much suffering here.

512

To Mel's surprise, the new cave was a maze of tall partitions, reminiscent of the HELL Corporation offices. The ruddy, flickering light made this scene far more eerie – especially with the screaming. She tucked her wings out of sight, so they wouldn't catch on anything in the narrow passage.

Mel peered around the first partition and wished she hadn't. Light caught the metal barbs on a many-tailed whip as it swished through the air to embed itself in the torn flesh that had once been a damned soul's back.

This soul gave a hoarse groan, as if his voice had fled long since. The whip-wielder yanked her weapon free, pulling flesh and blood with it.

Mel edged away, trying not to gag. She wanted to close her eyes and run right back up to the surface. This was Hell and for her, it was true torture.

She quickened her steps, trying to be silent. She couldn't leave this level soon enough for her liking. As for looking into any of the other cubicles...she wasn't sure she could face it.

A gurgling scream broke her resolve and Mel's eyes darted toward the sound. The sizzle and stench of searing flesh hit her as she realised this demon's weapon of choice was a branding iron. No, a whole collection of the things — she saw the bundle of metal rods protruding from the fire. The soul writhed on the table, pinned there by the demon's weight.

"Oh, yes, baby. Do that again," Jezebeth's voice cooed as she shifted to seize another brand. Glowing metal met flesh and the man bucked beneath her. She rode him with a moan of pleasure.

Surely no one could enjoy others' pain so much that they craved sex while inflicting it.

Jezebeth let out a triumphant shriek. Evidently she did.

Mel hastened away, but not quickly enough to miss Jezebeth's voice saying, "One more orgasm like that, baby, and I'll let you come, too."

Bile rose in Mel's throat and she fell to her knees,

retching. The smells, the sounds and the sheer horror of it all were too much for her. Oh Hell, she had to get out of here. Luce. She had to find Luce.

"One trying to escape? Oh, no, pretty one. I've got a special new steel strap-on I'd like to try out on you. I sharpened it 'specially this morning. Don't worry, your impaled insides will heal again tomorrow. The big question is, which hole do I fuck first?" Like Jezebeth's voice, this one was familiar, but Mel didn't have time to place it.

Claws dug deep into Mel's back, grating on bone, and Mel heard her own screaming. More pain burned and the sharp talons were torn away, taking flesh with them. Mel swallowed carefully before she dared to look at the wound. Her attacker had sheared her shoulder down to the bone, but the blast of their souls touching had cauterised it so the wound wasn't bleeding. There was a chunk of flesh missing from her back and her attacker couldn't be far away.

Mel clambered to her feet, searching the space for her assailant. Ananiel lay sprawled against one wall, like a thrown doll. Her manic grin disturbed Mel deeply and that was before she saw the demon's hands.

Ananiel sniffed her gory fingers with relish. "Mmm, angel meat. Good thing it's not long 'til morning. I'll take burns and a broken back for an hour or so to taste meat this sweet." She poked two fingers into her mouth, noisily sucking the flesh from them.

Revolted, Mel couldn't think of a fitting reply.

She was saved by Ananiel's violent coughing fit. "Fuck, that's too sweet!" Ananiel choked out. "It's like super-concentrated sugar at boiling point!" Her black tongue sent up wisps of smoke as she tried to spit out her mouthful of Mel. "Oh, it burns, it burns!"

"I don't advise you do that again," Mel said.

"Fuck, no," Ananiel spat. "Angel meat's barely fit for dog food. I should've carved you up to serve you to Cerberus."

Mel smiled for the first time since entering this charnel cave. "I've already fed Cerberus. He preferred pork sausages."

"Ana, you're supposed to be bringing the new souls to me, not playing with them in the corridor." Lilith appeared, her breasts bursting out the top of her black leather corset, which was all the clothing she wore. Mel stared at her former boss, reflecting that demons didn't need to wax, as there wasn't a single hair evident from Lilith's breasts down to her black stilettos. Lilith returned Mel's stare until the blushing angel focussed her eyes firmly on the shiny shoes. "What the Hell are you doing here?" Lilith asked.

"I'm here to see Luce."

Lilith snorted. "The big baby's not seeing anyone. Apparently, one of your angels pulled some sort of trick on him and he's sulking in his office." She eyed Mel with a calculated air. "You might be exactly what the devil ordered to cheer him up. Gerry!" she shouted over her shoulder.

Sounding like a large bat, Geryon's leathery wings flapped at the end of the corridor. "I'm not dragging any more souls out of the bloody river for you today, Lili. Jez is due to finish up for the day and she promised we'd spend the evening together. I'm going to wear my...what's Mel doing here?"

"She's here to see Lord Lucifer, apparently. I need you to escort her safely through to his lair. Wouldn't want anything to happen to her on her way to see the boss, would we? He likes his angels as pristine as possible," Lilith purred.

Geryon looked torn. "But Jez..."

"Will be waiting for you when you get back. I'll tell her how eager you are," promised Lilith.

He bowed, gesturing for Mel to go first. "Let's get you to your destination. I'm sure we both have better places to be than the harpies' little club. I don't know about you, but once the blades come out and they start hacking bits off, I always wish armour was still in vogue."

Geryon led the way into a steep, twisting passage. Mel counted three turns before he held his hands up for a halt. "Please," he said. "I want to ask you a favour. I know I have no right to ask and I'm a demon, so you have no reason to trust me. I want you to close your eyes. Your ears. Your whole mind. As you travel through this place, I don't want you to judge me by my job here. This is the worst level of Hell, where even the imps won't come. The souls here are damned for the most heinous crimes and their punishment persists for eternity, in the hope that they might feel some portion of the pain they've caused in their lifetimes. Even Lord Lucifer hates this level – it's where he sends demons for punishment. You're such a sweet angel. I don't want you scarred by what you see here."

Mel was touched. Geryon couldn't know what atrocities she'd seen humans commit – perhaps even some of the very souls entrusted to his...attentions. It was sweet of him to want to protect her. Yet he was a demon and she knew she couldn't trust him.

"I need to reach Luce," she said. "Is there another way to get to him, without walking through this horrible layer of Hell?"

He shook his head. "No. I'll guide you, Mel – every step of the way. Just close your eyes and trust me. Or...or leave. I can guide you all the way to the surface and home. Make an appointment to see him at the office. Mephi will set you up." His eyes looked hurt, she thought.

Looking deep into the demon's eyes, she tried to read his soul. Darkness swirled...and seemed to reach for her. Sighing, Mel retreated. Luce was the only denizen of Hell she trusted, for his was the only soul she could read. "I'm sorry, Gerry, but you won't be able to lead me through without touching me if I'm closing my eyes and ears to everything here. You know you can't do that without getting hurt. If you lead me through as quickly as possible, I'll do my best not to...not to look. This is Hell and you're just doing your job, right?"

Geryon looked hesitant. "I was going to offer to carry you. Fly you over the worst of it and down to the next level. It's how I manage to get through my work day. If you could fly, it wouldn't be a problem..."

His mouth dropped open as Mel unfolded her feathers. Her clawed shoulder ached, but no more so than before. She swung her wings in a powerful beat, rising as only an angel could. "Lead the way."

Leathery wings flapped furiously as Geryon struggled to reach Mel's altitude. "All right. Follow me and don't look down. Even from above, some of the torture bolgies are disturbing. We had to separate them into bolgies or the damned souls complained that other crimes had lesser punishments than theirs. I hate to say it, but I'll take an eternity of screaming over arrogant whining any day."

The demon flew as erratically as a black cockatoo, Mel mused as she glided after him. Strange smells assailed her nostrils – raw sewage, the acrid fumes from boiling pitch, the stench of burning flesh and the underlying notes of spilled blood. She caught a glimpse of flame out of the corner of her eye and directed her gaze at what appeared to be a ditch full of fire, the shadowy forms of damned souls writhing as they burned. Souls burning for eternity – this was the picture she'd had of Hell, repeated incessantly in human media over millennia. Yet it represented one tiny trench amid all the horrors Hell had to offer. A great, dark cloud seemed to obscure all of the sections of this level, as if the flames generated more smoke than Mel thought possible. Yet this cloud looked alive, roiling like a storm and weaving like a snake searching for prey. Hell, it looked like it was staring at her, trying to decide if she'd do for dinner, as it slowly rose for a closer look. Sentient smoke? Oh, how silly. Maybe she really was tired and she should rest.

"Don't look down!" Geryon shouted, and Mel focussed on riding the updraft away from the source of hot air and the curious cloud.

Geryon dived, heading for a black hole in the cavern floor. As they dropped, so did the temperature; goosebumps broke out all over Mel's body. While the air temperature plummeted, their descent remained steady until Geryon touched down on the stony floor of a huge cavern.

Mel's natural glow barely lit any of it, leaving many dark, shadowy corners. She felt surrounded by ominous malice, but she couldn't pinpoint the source. Her feet touched stone so cold that she cried out. It wasn't stone at all, but dirt-encrusted ice. This portion of Hell had frozen over and the air was positively frigid.

"Welcome to Level Nine," Geryon said, gesturing. "The damned souls here are fewer in number, but they're far worse than those in my level. Frozen forever in the lowest layer of Hell, so they won't hurt anyone else, and guarded by Lord Lucifer himself. Most demons never come this deep into Hell unless Lord

Lucifer summons them. As for angels...I don't know any who've ever made it this far." He paused. "Do you think you'll be all right on your own? Jez is about to knock off work and I've got her favourite flogger all ready. If I hurry, I might even have time to slip into my mankini..."

Mel smiled and wished him a pleasant evening – not that she thought any evening involving flogging and the mankini she remembered all too well could be pleasant, but each to their own. Perhaps demons enjoyed inflicting pain on one another while they wore hideous, skimpy clothing. Who was she to judge? They were certainly consenting adults, after all.

She watched Geryon spiral upward, wondering at what seemed to be thickening shadows pouring over the lip of the pit and into the cavern where she stood. Ah, it was only smoke. Mel had more on her mind than the fumes of Hell. She needed to find Luce – he had to be on this level. How could he hide himself from her?

"Have you been torturing the damned in here? You should get someone to clean up – ugh, you should get cleaned up. What possessed you to sleep in a pool of congealing blood? Have you been watching vampire movies again, Luce?"

Darkness, but there'd been Mel. She'd come to comfort him, but she couldn't stay. She'd had a pressing task, someone she'd had to save, and he'd floated in the dark, hoping and waiting for her to return, but she hadn't. It had seemed so real...

Luce lifted his head. There was blood all over the floor and he had a Hell of a headache. He didn't remember torturing anyone...he had agony enough to fell an army, and he...damn. Demons couldn't die after all — and demonic weapons couldn't kill him. Maybe somewhere, that meant Mel was alive, too. He had to hope. Even if he never saw her again, at least he'd know she lived.

"What's up with you and all the extra security? I had to shove through some sort of energy shield to get through here — the static frizzed my hair up something awful. Not as bad as you, though. You look like Hell — no pun intended, because you look worse than this gloomy place. What happened? Did Mel leave you?" Persephone's perky voice grated on his grief. She laughed — deeper and darker than her usual giggle. "You know an angel of her rank wouldn't stay long with someone like you."

Luce lifted his head to glare. He had nothing to say to her.

She perched on the corner of his desk, swinging her leg beneath her long skirt. "I had to attend the Minister's dinner in your stead. He was quite attentive — wanted to give the corporation advance warning of some of the new contracts on the horizon. Privatising the ports under one company...and Lili's very eager about the possibility of winning the Department for Child Protection contract, too. Anything I should know about Lili?" She gave a wicked little smile. "Oh, and I donated all your reserve red wines to a charity auction for the children's hospital, in the company's name, of course. Raised our profile plenty – and now I have that space for my china doll collection. So many pretty porcelain faces, instead of those dusty, dreary bottles..." She prattled on, not seeming to notice that Luce wasn't listening any more.

He'd have shared the wine with Mel happily, but now he didn't care what happened to it. He dropped his forehead to the sticky stone, wishing she'd go away and leave him to his misery.

It took a while for him to realise, but it hit him like a brick when it did: here, he was still the Lord of Hell. He could make her leave.

"Get out," he growled, shoving with all the supernatural forces he could muster to send her back to the surface and out of his domain.

She giggled. "You gave me all your power – everything. You can't order me around in this place – you made me your equal." She lifted her hand eagerly, looking like a naughty child about to steal the moon.

Luce felt the power of her push, but he resisted it. "Not my equal," he grunted. "More like second in charge, when I'm absent. I'm still the lord of this place. Now get out."

"Aww, don't sulk," she simpered. "I came to offer you some solace. You can do anything you like to me, honest. No strings attached." She held up the strings that had tied her dress around her neck, showing him that if she dropped them, the whole outfit would fall to the floor.

The ink on her thighs, glorifying Hell as if it was worth putting permanently on her skin. Ah, Hell – it was like tattooing a blocked toilet on her backside to entice a plumber.

Luce looked. He wondered if he'd ever have been able to summon up some enthusiasm for the young woman who was so willing to bare everything before him. Before he'd met Mel.

He'd never know. After Mel, he felt nothing any more. Not for Persephone; not for anyone.

"I'd rather have Mel's rotting corpse than you. I said get out. Mel's gone. Let me mourn her in peace," he snapped, pointing at the door.

Persephone bristled, tying her dress again with shaking hands. "You're one delusional demon if you believe Mel would ever have any feelings for you."

"She said she loved me," Luce whispered, regretting it the moment he said it.

"And you think that makes you special?" Persephone sneered. "Mel loves everyone. It's just the sort of angel she is."

For a moment, he believed her. The sheer horror that he'd imagined Mel's love...

BULLSHIT.

Mel didn't lie. Not with words, expression or body language. She'd loved him – even as he killed her. She hadn't looked at anyone else the way she had at him.

He rose onto his elbows. "Get out. I won't tell you again. If you think your power matches mine, I'll call in every demon and devil under my command and we'll see who they obey. I'll have them drag you out by your hair – across all the circles of Hell to the gate. And when they dump you outside in the hot desert sands, I'll laugh. I never want to hear another word from you about Mel – and I definitely don't want to see you again."

She lifted her little nose in the air. "You can keep everyone else out, but not me, Luce. Remember that." And with that, she disappeared.

He wanted to follow her and choke the life out of her, but he didn't want to hear any more of her lies. He might not be powerful enough to kill her – he might have conceded too much of his personal power to her in his hope for Mel. Like all hopes in Hell, any chance he'd had with Mel was long gone now – fled far from here.

Stiffly, he rose to his feet and surveyed the mess. The amount of blood looked like he'd slaughtered a pig, or at least butchered several damned souls, instead of attempting suicide. He stared at his wrists, but the holes had closed and healed as if they'd never been. He'd made a Hell of a mess of the floor and his clothes. His fork still had flesh clinging to the barbs – enough to make him feel sick, even though he knew it was only pieces of him.

How did suicide victims' families clean up after a

crime like this? Losing a loved one and having to clean up the mess afterwards? Fury ripped through him. The harpies were hardly punishment enough for them – he was going to make them clean the torture chambers on Level Eight. With tiny toothbrushes and no gloves. Let them deal with blood and severed limbs, the smells and sounds of torture echoing around them every day. It was nothing compared to what they'd put people through in their selfishness, violence and waste as they ended the precious gift of their own lives... Demons couldn't die, but he'd damn well make every suicide sinner wish they could, all over again.

But first, he had to clean up his own mess, or the senior demons would know he hadn't been torturing anyone in here but himself. And the Lord of Hell could never show weakness to a demon, because they knew how to take advantage of that...

Luce summoned a bucket and a scrubbing brush, detergent and hot water. This job required hard work and he couldn't trust anyone but himself to do it. He cleaned up his own messes, damn it, and he wouldn't make the same mistake again.

Right after he'd had a hot shower, he was going to find out what had gone on in Hell in his absence. If the interfering angel who'd made a mockery of the gates and his grief had returned, he'd know about it. He decided to start with the weakest one first.

Mel lost count of the number of times she'd slipped on the gritty ice. At least the limestone dust was white and not black, so she looked like she'd been rolled in flour or sugar, like some sort of scone. How long had it been since she'd eaten something? Hot, fresh scones sounded wonderful, with whatever she could lay her hands on. Butter. Jam and cream. Jarrah honey. A fresh-brewed cup of tea.

As soon as she reached home, she'd do some baking. A trip to the shop for ingredients and an afternoon of domestic bliss, showering her kitchen in flour as she cooked up a storm. Maybe even with Luce, if she could drag him out of this horrible place. Wearily, she reached for his soul, praying that this time she'd sense him again, though she'd been disappointed so many times since she entered Hell that she wasn't sure what to hope for any more.

Misery. Pain. Anger. Frustration that blood was impossible to clean off porous white surfaces. Deep desire for her...

LUCE! Mel stumbled and fell, but she barely felt the pain. She'd found his soul again and he was close. All she had to do was find him.

Rising laboriously to her knees, she closed her eyes and sent her thoughts searching for him once more. A cold gust of wind chilled her to the bone, but she persisted. He was here.

Luce was...somewhere near the source of the freezing breeze, it seemed. She felt him most strongly when she faced into the frigid air current. Opening her eyes, Mel peered into the darkness, seeing only the dark cavern wall. Her eyes moved down and she caught a glimmer of light, through an opening close to the ground. She'd have to crawl through it, but if it led to Luce...it wasn't as if she had any pride to lose. Losing Luce when she was so close would be a far worse fate.

Prostrate, she slid across the ice onto sand. Tears of relief tracked down her cheeks as she pulled her body through the narrow tunnel, wondering if this was what snakes felt like. No, snakes couldn't cry. Nor could they feel the sort of love bursting out of her soul as she sensed the object of it was so close. Oh God, what if she'd given up and left him here to his fate?

The tunnel widened, the walls disappearing into the darkness, and Mel clambered stiffly to her feet, brushing dust off her body. She could see a faint light in the distance, so that's where she directed her weary steps.

"I've had no report from you all week. How are the damned doing on Level Four?" Luce asked.

Ploutos gave a shaky shrug. "Same. They battle pointlessly and the cats play. I took a video of the cats playing and Nybbas uploaded it onto the humans' internet in the office. He called it Cats from Hell and it went viral, he said, which is good. Spreading like some sort of horrible disease among humans. I recorded a few more and he's looking to put in subliminal messages, like 'Greed is good' and 'You need sex now but you don't need to know his name' and 'HELL Corporation is your hero'. All standard propaganda, he said."

Luce stared at him. "Cat videos? Humans can get sick from cat videos?"

"No, Lord Lucifer. Nybbas said it's a sort of sickness of the mind. He said it makes them forget everything else and want more cat videos. They flood the internet with such things. He said it inspires sloth, laziness, procrastination...all things that bring people to us." Ploutos' face moved in a fleeting smile, as if there was more he wanted to say, but wouldn't.

"So there's no change in your domain?" Luce pushed. "No unusual visitors, or anything strange happening?"

Ploutos screwed his face up. "Mmm...mmmy sister came to visit," he managed to say.

"Your sister?"

"My sister...Persephone. She...she comes to visit and asks questions about you, Lord Lucifer. I believe you have a very willing recruit there, if you're looking for junior demons."

"Oh Hell, no! That's the last thing I need – that little nephilim permanently here in Hell. I can't imagine anything worse. I don't want her anywhere near here again, you hear? You go visit her on the surface – every weekend, if you want, but I don't want to see her in Hell." Luce looked down at his list. "Go tell Camael and Samael I need to see them."

"That's all you wanted to know?" Ploutos asked, looking almost happy.

Luce stared at the small man. "Is there anything else I need to know that you should be telling me?"

"Ah...ah...no, Lord Lucifer," Ploutos mumbled. "I'll go get the twins. And then...more cat videos!"

Cat videos. Humans were crazy, Luce decided, and Ploutos wasn't far behind. But if he was related to Persephone, he wasn't surprised.

Camael and Samael, he thought. The experts in animal welfare. He had a job for them.

Mel crossed the cold cavern and found an ordinary door, set in a fairly standard door frame in the rock. The icy blast blew from this open doorway. She didn't need directions or a map. She knew Luce lay through this portal.

She stepped inside, face turned toward the full-bore fan from the air conditioner as it blew a fine mist of dust from her hair. Now she wished she'd brought the tablecloth from Heaven, or, better yet, a coat. But...no. She'd come this far without anything. Her clothes were inside this room and she'd have them back soon enough.

"I don't want to hear any more excuses," she heard Luce's voice state without emotion. "I want to know the dog is fed, twice daily, as he should be. We have a reputation to maintain and that includes animal welfare. I've taken Kas off animal control and I'm making both of you responsible for Cerberus – a hungry dog has questionable loyalty and he's a guard dog, after all. There's always space in the lower levels of Hell for more souls if you feel this is beneath you."

Mel heard sullen voices murmuring their acquiescence. With a degree of pleasure, she noticed it was Camael and Samael, the two former angels who'd coined the animal welfare legislation that had caused so much trouble for herself and Gabrielle in the office. Karma was indeed a bitch – one who liked dogs.

Luce dismissed the fallen angels and Mel stepped back against the concrete wall to let them exit. Both nodded to her in recognition before leaving quickly. Samael shut the door behind him.

She took a deep breath, letting it leave her before she rounded the corner to where she could see Luce. He sat at the desk, his head buried in his hands. He didn't seem to be aware of her presence.

This close, she could tell the darkness he surrounded himself with was guilt. She could feel it rolling off him in waves. The soul within, though despairing, was as light as ever. The dark master of Hell no longer had the heart for the job. She wanted to reach out to him, to comfort him, but she didn't know what to say.

As Mel hesitated, Luce looked up and his eyes met hers. His face was flat, revealing nothing. "A very well-thought out illusion, but not very thorough," he said after some time. She could feel her heart close to breaking at the pain in his, but he showed no outward sign of it at all. He stood and approached her. "You see, you've missed details. The real Mel had a scar on her index finger from a fight with a stapler. She had a half-healed burn on her hand from where she spilled her tea when I surprised her in the kitchen last week. And she had two gaping holes here." Luce pointed at her breasts, making Mel wish they didn't stand out so prominently in the cold air. His eyes were hard as he looked at her. "She'd also be perfectly presentable and clothed, without a hair out of place. You have mud splatters up to your thighs and limestone dust everywhere. Nice try, but you can get out." This time he pointed at the door.

Mel blinked. "I wasn't focussing on blemishes when I assembled this body. They weren't necessary. I've just crossed the nine circles of Hell, looking for you. I felt you were more important than a few streaks of mud or the dust accumulating outside your front door that I had to crawl through to get here, though I'd love a shower if you can point me the way to your bathroom. Mud sure sticks in this place — especially from that swampy River Styx."

Luce laughed. "No angel's ever made it through all

the circles of Hell. They give in to despair, or corruption, or disgust at the array of sins the souls here have committed. You're a demon in disguise, though a good disguise. Did Persephone put you up to this to distract me?"

"I'll certainly be paying Persi a visit when we get out of here, but I haven't spoken to her yet. I wanted to see you first," Mel said, allowing a little of her irritation to colour her tone. Some demons were dense, but today Luce really took the cake. Surely he knew her better than that. "You do know that angels aren't capable of deception, don't you?"

"Which is why you must be a demon, not some decoy sent by those bastards in Heaven," Luce replied bitterly.

"Leave here with me and I'll show you, Luce. I don't want to drag you out of here against your will and I haven't come this far, only to leave alone. I want you to choose to come with me."

"I told you to get out and you will." He waved at the door and Mel felt the full force of his will, pushing her in the direction of the exit. It wafted right past her, though – his power was in no way equal to hers. Even here.

Patiently, she stood her ground and held his gaze.

Luce's eyes widened in surprise. "Persephone? Now you've given yourself away. No one else in Hell has that kind of power. Appearing in Mel's body... This is beyond a joke. You have everything you asked for.

Leave me to my solitude." He walked back to the desk and threw himself into the chair, his eyes staring at the concrete wall.

Mel wasn't sure if she wanted to laugh or cry. How could Luce forget that angels couldn't die? She could feel his grief and guilt, yet he couldn't accept that she was herself.

"Please leave," Luce said again, his voice cracking. Mel could see tears brimming in his eyes as his hand tightened on a bundle of white cloth in his lap. "Please. If there is any sympathy, any kindness left in you at all, I'm asking you to leave. I don't want to see you here again."

Mel reached out. "Luce." If she could touch him, she'd know why he wanted to shut her out. Maybe she'd even know what to say. While she'd been wandering through Hell, what had happened to him? What had Persi done?

He yanked his arms back, as if shielding his heart with them. "Don't touch me. Just get out. Now."

Wordlessly, she turned her back on him and marched toward the door. She didn't want him to see her cry for him. She'd come too late to help. All this had been for nothing and Luce didn't deserve her failure.

Tears blurred her eyes as shadows surrounded her. The darkest shadows she'd only glimpsed as she strode through Hell now seemed to have congregated here, lying in wait. Like the shadows she'd first seen on Luce's soul, which he'd somehow sold to Persephone for her. Or the sort that had hidden him from her as she walked through the deeper levels of Hell. The sentient cloud she thought she'd glimpsed on Level Eight didn't seem so silly now.

Her eyes flew to the open door behind her, which

was darkening already as if beset by black smoke. But there was no fire – this smoke was made from souls. The blackest souls this world had ever known. So dark they couldn't be confined to a single circle of Hell, for its punishments and tortures held no power over them any more. She could feel the malice pouring off them – they had neither name nor identity. They were clouds of hate. And they were headed for Luce's lair, to hurt him more than she already had. To Hell with that.

She shouted, sealing off the entrance even as they deserted the door to attack her. It had been centuries since she'd fought anything stronger than a ladle-jammed drawer – or used a weapon other than words. But today she fought for one she loved. One she'd wronged and owed reparation to, who had begged for her help. Nothing could withstand a righteous angel, and she had a millennia-old wrong to right.

She breathed deep and steady, feeling the malice swirling around her. Closing in. The shadows whispered of failure, of pain, of the day humans stoned her to death for daring to make a difference in Crete so many millennia ago. Angels in Hell would fall because nothing was stronger than they. Not even the Lord of Hell could destroy them, for this was their domain, before it ever was his. Growing in strength through the ages until nothing could match them. They would destroy him.

Mel was painfully reminded of the memory Luce had shared with her before they'd left for Heaven. His fall and the shadows closing in. Not metaphorical shadows, she realised, but these — those that had surrounded his soul and pushed for a way in. A way they hadn't found yet, no matter how hard they'd fought.

The hissing whispers told her what they wished to do. First, they'd destroy the arrogant angel who thought she was better than them, that she could best them with her petty perfection.

"Not your domain. Your prison. I am not perfect and I never will be, but each day I strive to be better and that lies at the heart of an angel." She kept her voice steady.

Weakening in the world, with every step through Hell, the shadows continued. Another angel would fall. Couldn't match their strength. They'd been watching. Still wounded from the harpy. Too weak to fight.

Mel's arms ached from how tightly she held her knees to her chest, crouching on the floor. She'd hold firm and protect herself until they gave up.

Stupid angel to think she could take on Hell. Too weak. Too arrogant. She would fail. Here, they were strongest. She was no match for them. They would never give up, the shadows insisted.

"Nothing can match you in here, but Hell is tiny compared to the world I walk in. The powerful have no need to enter here. You can never leave to see. Never..." She cried for the once-damned souls, driven to madness in this confined space with no chance of redemption, until they became nothing but malicious whispers and intent. The shadows crowded closer to her, as if they would drink her tears. "Take them," she said, flinging her arms wide. "Drink my pity for you."

The hissing continued, No pity for the weak angel. No one would come to help her. She would fall and one day join them. All souls did.

Mel's mouth flew open at the thought of souls that didn't even know of the presence of Heaven, or anything outside this dark cave. And they never would. A dark tendril of shadow, almost like a finger, touched the tear on her cheek. She couldn't see the door to Luce's lair, they shrouded her so thickly, but Mel could see the tendrils forming what looked like a hand. She reached out and grasped it.

That one touch let her read the entire swirling cloud of souls. A miasma...many minds with no recollection of who they once were, but burning with desire...all wanting one thing. To get out and wreak havoc on Earth again, on those who had trapped them here. If they tormented Luce enough, he might send them away far enough to escape...but first, they would imprison this angel's soul like they had everyone else's — starting with the one she'd come to save. Mel watched them remember shrouding Luce the first time he'd fallen into Hell from Heaven — the angel thrown among them — even as he'd tried to shut them out. That's what angels did. They curled in on themselves, tried to protect themselves from darkness as it surrounded them and won. By the time they realised, it was too late — their soul was sealed in with no escape. No angel was brave enough to burn – not after they'd seen the other burning souls in Hell.

Souls fell, but the source of the taint was here. Mel wasn't going to let them surround another soul. Even if she had to surrender her own to destroy them. If they touched her soul, they'd burn with her. Maybe she could light a pyre that even Luce, the hot devil, would notice.

Poor, naked angel. No clothes, no help, no pity. Only tears. Like the day they stoned her to death. She could relive that here. Over and over and over again. Just like the Lord of Hell, remembering the day he killed her. Or his fall from Heaven.

"NO!" She could take her own pain. She knew her failings and her failures. Luce didn't deserve guilt for what she knew was her fault. Hadn't she come this far? To Hell with hiding what she really was – Hell's fires only consumed bodies, but as an angel, she could destroy souls. If the shadows really wanted her, they'd need to be stronger than they thought possible.

Mel shot to her feet. The weight of her wings tugged at her shoulders, but she stood firm. Her soul burned for justice denied and nothing could withstand a righteous angel. It was time for her to show her light. "You will not touch him. You won't touch any angel, demon or the Lord of Hell. Not even the damned, unless they approach you directly. I forbid it." The cave seemed brighter, and the shadows became more insubstantial. She could barely see the tendril fingers she still held in hers. "If you want my soul, take it!"

Her spirit swelled like a supernova, enveloping the cloud and lapping the very walls of the cavern. She could feel them all and they burned. She burned with them, but it was worth the pain. A hundred times worse than the energy surge she'd felt when Merihim had first touched her; ten times worse than the burn that had defended her from Ananiel and the Dirae's attacks, but never more than she could bear. She was stronger than any dark, malicious soul that could only prey on the weak.

"Time weakened you and so it will continue until you are no more! Do not enter my sight again." She pointed at the entrance tunnel to Level Nine and watched as a beam from her fingertip hit the wall with a splash of light. What was left of the shadows seemed like a tiny curl of smoke, rapidly eddying away from her.

The smack of flesh on flesh reverberated through the cave, startling her. Mel heard it again before she whirled around, looking for the source.

Luce leaned against the doorway to his lair, slowly clapping. He still held her clothes in the crook of one arm.

Why hadn't he come to her aid, or even attempted to call off the fiendish souls? Not that she'd needed his help, but it was the principle. Hadn't he cared that she was in danger?

Or had he lured her here, knowing what lurked in

the shadows, hoping their dark malice could corrupt her when he couldn't? Was that why he'd stood back — to watch? Maybe the imps weren't the only voyeurs in this place.

She hadn't journeyed naked through Hell to be anyone's entertainment. She'd come to save him. If he didn't want her help, she was done with him.

"You." Luce's startled eyes met hers. "Give me back my underwear," she commanded, striding forward.

Persephone couldn't...surely she couldn't have done that. She wasn't as strong as he was – and he was no match for those souls. Suddenly, he felt the need to go back to his desk, where he could put a block of solid timber between himself and this angel gone nova. Not daring to take his eyes off her, he backed away. It couldn't be. But if it was...

She passed through the energy barrier as if it didn't exist – the same barrier he'd been trapped behind – and her relentless steps carried her closer to him.

Her wings grazed the doorway, but she didn't stop to fold them back. "I've walked naked through to the very inner circle of Hell and I'll be damned before I leave empty-handed. If you're not coming with me like I thought you would, I can at the very least leave with the clothes you stole from me. You can keep the shirt if you wish, but if you're going to pretend I'm dead or call me by another woman's name, I draw the line at my underwear. I want it back."

He stared at her, keeping a death grip on her balled-up shirt, his retreat halted by bumping into the desk. Persephone. Not Persephone. But who else had the balls to confront the Lord of Hell in his own lair?

He tried not to laugh. It was pretty damn clear this girl didn't have any balls to speak of – but she couldn't have walked through all of Hell naked like this. She'd have to be crazy.

"I've said it before and I'll say it one last time. Get out or I'll summon every demon in Hell to help me evict you. And they'll enjoy making the process as long and drawn-out as possible." He tried to make his voice vicious, but he could feel it shaking a little. He hoped she didn't notice his weakness.

She stood close enough for him to see that her eyes were the same grey he knew and loved – even if the rest of her glowed gold. There was no sign of the red that flashed in Persephone's eyes when she got angry. These eyes looked like clouds threatening rain. "Luce, they're demons. Lazy as all Hell. They'll probably bring popcorn to watch the show and back the winner. Don't get me started on the gambling in this place. Do you really want an audience? I'd prefer not to hurt you or any of the demons at your disposal. Please, just give me back my clothes and I'll leave, if that's what you really want." Her voice had returned to normal and the soft tones were nothing like those of his tattooed former PA.

Luce knew she wasn't Persephone. The nephilim didn't have sufficient self-control for this.

He wasn't sure what he'd just witnessed. The blinding light that had lit up the whole cavern as it burned the dark spirits that had plagued him since the day he'd arrived...it must've come from her. No demon could've done it. That meant she had to be some sort of angel — but angels couldn't lie. And this one had just said she'd walked naked through Hell.

She couldn't be. But if she was, she'd be furious at him even if he wasn't withholding her underwear.

One more step and her radiance would start burning him, just as it had those incorporeal dark souls. He'd had enough pain for several lifetimes and he couldn't take any more now. The sadness in her eyes hurt like Hell already.

He swallowed. "The lace on the bra is ripped," he admitted.

"It doesn't surprise me. Your fork's sharp," Mel said, her eyes straying to the bident in the umbrella stand. "Doesn't matter. It's the principle. You don't want me, you don't get to keep my underwear, Luce." She smiled sorrowfully at him.

Oh Hell – Mel had walked through Hell naked, from the front gate to his lair. For him. And then he'd made a right mess of things. Again.

A tear escaped his control, tracking down his cheek. He swiped a hand across his face, wishing he could hide it. "Mel?" he whispered.

"That's me. Now, are you going to give me my clothes back or not?" Mel's smile was pure summer sunshine as it spread across her face: fierce, but still warm. Yet her light seemed to fade and she wrapped her arms across her chest as if she was cold.

Luce shrugged out of his suit jacket, ripping off his tie, before he started unbuttoning his shirt. He paused to grab the air conditioning remote to turn the fan down. "You must be freezing," he said. "Your shirt's torn. I'm sorry. Take mine." One of his cufflinks tinkled to the floor. He bent to pick it up as Mel moved forward.

He could feel how close she was – her foot landed beside his fingers as he scrabbled at the stone for the cufflink. He wasn't looking at the metal any more. His mind was full of perfect skin, curved over a beautiful body. The smudges of dirt and splashes of mud made no difference – if anything, they only made her more real. This was Mel, the angel he'd loved and thought he'd lost. His own body ached for hers. He dragged his eyes unwillingly to her face, letting her see his damned soul. "What if I do want you?" Luce murmured, leaving her in no doubt that he was telling the truth. He couldn't lie to her if he tried. "I know I've damned myself for eternity by killing you, but I still love you. If I could go back and change what I did, I would."

Mel smiled. "You only damaged the body I'd built. As you said, it had scars, imperfections. It took time to build a replacement. When I returned, you'd left without me. With my clothes. You should have waited – I wanted to show you Heaven." The wicked look in her eyes was far from angelic...and yet, it was.

Luce shook his head. "I'm damned for what I did. I can never leave here."

"You can and you will – I'll escort your soul through the gates myself, without wasting any time. I won't stay here, Luce. Too dark and depressing for me," Mel replied.

He wanted to believe her. Angels didn't lie. But she

didn't know what he'd done while she was gone. And he wasn't willing to tell her. Right now, he just wanted to make the most of the little time he had with her, for once she found out...she'd leave without him.

"Right away? I'd have to make some arrangements here before I could just up and leave. I'm still responsible for this place, Mel – I've signed everything I could over to Persephone, but Hell is still my charge..." Luce stared at her longingly, wanting nothing more than to grab her and leave. To Hell with his responsibilities for this damned place. The demons knew what they were doing – they didn't need him to oversee them all the time.

Mel seemed to understand his longing. "It's all right, Luce. You deal with what you have to. I could probably do with a rest. I'd love a shower, but that'll have to wait 'til I get home, I guess." She looked around the bare cave, searching for something she evidently couldn't see.

Luce smiled. Here was one surprise he could offer her. "Have you never heard of Hell's bathroom?"

Mel started to laugh. "No, Luce. Hell's kitchen, yes, but your realm isn't known for its plumbing – or any water supply at all. None of the rivers here looked particularly clean. Even the air conditioning took me by surprise. What's Hell's bathroom? Some sort of sulphurous spring, a shared latrine for all the demons in the many levels of Hell? I'm sure the description will be enough for me – I don't need to smell it. I smell bad enough as it is."

"Let me show you. I swear you'll have it all to yourself. I don't share my personal apartment with just anyone," Luce said, leading the way to the wall. He rounded a corner and opened a door, set snugly into the stone. Mel laughed as she followed him through.

"I'll never get used to some of the modern things you have here. Doors in a cave?"

He shrugged. "I didn't want the air conditioning in the office to mess with the humidity in here."

Luce stood aside to see Mel's reaction as she entered. This cave was a smaller cousin of the curtain-and-column castle cave above in one of the upper levels, but this was his alone. He'd even arranged lighting so that it looked its best. He flicked the switch, letting the illumination glow into life.

Mel gasped. With her mouth still open, she turned her eyes on him. "How can you keep something this beautiful hidden in the depths of Hell?"

He stared at her, almost hurt by her shock. "What? Just because I've spent millennia running the darkest pit of punishment for the damned, with armies of demons and devils at my command, doesn't mean I don't like beautiful things. You saw the view from my penthouse. I wanted to preserve it, just for me. Not everything in my life has to be all darkness and despair."

She looked uncomfortable. "I'm sorry, Luce. I know you're more than the man in charge of Hell. I just never thought to find such beauty deep beneath so much...horrible..." She shuddered.

Luce tried to smile. "What better place to hide something beautiful? It's yours for as long as you need it. I'll be in the office, trying to get everything sorted so we can leave as soon as possible." He waved his hand and let a pile of towels appear. "Sorry, the colour scheme is a bit limited here." He concentrated hard on the stack and managed to lighten it from black to burgundy. "Will that be okay? Let me know if you need anything else."

"I'll be fine. Thank you, Luce," Mel murmured. She stepped forward to trail her toes through the water. "It's warm!"

"Geothermal," Luce replied. He looked longingly at her as she submerged into the pool, wading toward the trickling cascade. "I wish I could join you."

"I'll wait for you," she promised, closing her eyes as the water streamed over her head. A streak of gold showed through the dusty grey smothering her hair.

He hurried back to the office. He wanted to get the Hell out of here as quickly as possible – but not before he'd enjoyed a long, hot bath with Mel.

Luce buttoned and tucked his shirt in, knotting his tie as quickly as he could. He shrugged back into his jacket and picked up the air conditioning remote. He'd used the air conditioner for so long to remind him to keep his cool, but today he didn't need it. He felt like nothing could break his good mood. Mel was alive and in the next room; and when she left, she wanted to take him with her.

He dropped the remote on the desk just as Asmodeus and Merihim appeared before him. Actually, he'd summoned three demons, not two...where was Kasyade?

He concentrated and Kasyade appeared behind the other two. He immediately tried to put as much distance between him and the two of them as he could.

"What happened to you?" Luce asked Kasyade. He'd rarely seen such injuries on a man who wasn't a professional fighter.

Kasyade tenderly patted both his black eyes and grimaced, revealing the gaps where he'd had teeth the last time Luce looked. "I met with an accident. There was an angel, you see, and..."

"Mel didn't do it!" Merihim burst out. "I blacked his eyes. Mo here broke a couple of his ribs. Should've ripped his arms off again, like he did yesterday, so he couldn't try to cheat us at poker any more. We were trying to help her. We offered her a drink, a rest, a game...tried to get her to turn around and leave. She wouldn't do it – insisted that she had to see you. So she showed us how Kas was cheating and headed through the gates of Dis into the lower levels. We told her how to open the gate. Did she make it through safely?" He looked genuinely concerned.

Luce nodded once. "She did."

"Don't hurt her!" Asmodeus said, sounding as worried as Merihim. "She...she saved me from that harpy in HR. Mel's not like other angels. We don't want her to fall like we did. She's too nice. She should stay the way she is."

"You're both attempting to tell the Lord of Hell what he should do with an angel who managed to penetrate the lowest circle of Hell, wreaking havoc on every level on her way in?" Luce kept his voice very quiet as he looked from Asmodeus to Merihim, before glancing at Kasyade. "What about you? Do you presume to give me orders, too?"

The other two glared as Kasyade and he seemed to visibly shrink, to Luce's amusement. How had he lived without Mel making everything different, by her sheer presence? She could even make a simple disciplinary meeting hilarious – not that he could let on. He was the stern Lord of Hell, after all.

"She gave me a chance to pay for cheating, without telling anyone what I'd done. I didn't listen. I didn't believe she could beat me at poker – she barely knew the rules!"

Luce thought of Mel's angelic smile, which hid more secrets than the whole of Hell. "I think Mel might be the best natural poker player this world has ever seen. I wouldn't play her unless I wanted to lose."

Kasyade grunted. "You got that right. I turned her down, she won the game, and those two beat the shit out of me and took all their money back. It was like she knew...but she wanted to save me. She acted as if I was an angel, like her. I've never met an angel like her before. It'd be sad to lose her." He shuffled his feet on the limestone, looking anywhere but at Luce.

Luce found it even harder not to laugh. How had

Mel managed to charm these three demons? She'd bewitched them to the point where they'd neglected to tell him there was an angel loose in Hell – an angel who'd gotten past the gate all three of them were guarding.

He had to somehow discipline these three to maintain his authority, but for the first time, he was lost. Mel would know what to do, but he'd promised not to disturb her until he was ready to join her. Besides, what would she think of him if it looked like he couldn't control his own realm?

"I'm sending you back up to Persephone. You can be part of the new Children and Family Protection unit Lili's putting together for the latest contract." Luce glared at the three of them. "A month up there should do it."

He dismissed them.

Had he been too lenient? Luce wondered. He could have given them sword practice on Level Eight, but they were used to that. Office work and taking care of feral children would do instead.

"Next!" he called.

Luce dismissed the last of them, wondering just how many demons Mel had met on her journey through Hell...or did she know all of them from the office? There sure seemed to be a Hell of a lot of them – and they all liked her, or owed her a favour, or both. Every senior demon knew her and had something to say.

"Don't turn her..."

"Don't press her too hard..."

"Don't hurt her..."

"Please don't change her in any way..."

"Don't be too hard on her..."

Luce's personal favourite was Ploutos' poignant plea:

"But I NEED her to make more viral cat videos! Cats from Hell wouldn't be an internet sensation if it weren't for Mel and her ping pong balls...it was like *Priscilla: Queen of the Desert* but with cats!"

Some of them even looked like they harboured romantic hopes for her, though they knew an angel would never consider pairing up with a demon.

Well, until Mel had chosen him, but Luce wasn't sure what he was anymore. A demon, an angel, some fallen hybrid between the two... If she'd have him, he didn't particularly care what he was, as long as it was good enough for Mel.

He hung his jacket over his chair, then loosened his tie and took it off. The shirt was next – he shrugged out of it and left it on the desk. She'd liked his wings before and he wanted them out for her. He looked at his pants. On or off? Would he look too eager if he walked in there buck naked, or would she think he wasn't interested if he still wore his pants?

He slowly unbuckled his belt and left it on the desk. He decided to keep the pants on – at least until he got into the bathroom. Then he'd leave all decisions up to Mel. She definitely deserved to call the shots.

He paused at the closed door, knocking lightly. "Mel?" he called. "I've finished with the last meeting for the moment. If you still want me to join you, I can come in now." He waited, but heard no reply. Perhaps she was deep in the pool, or under the waterfall. He opened the door and stepped cautiously inside.

The pool was still, marked only by the slight ripples as the cascade in the corner added to the water. Mel wasn't in the water at all — he could see to the bottom of the clear, deep pool. He scanned the room for her, his heart tightening in his chest. He couldn't lose her again.

The sound of something soft moving across stone caught his attention and it took him a moment to work out what the unusual rock formation was. Mel had wrapped herself in a towel, pillowing her head and body on a few more, and fallen asleep on the floor. The formerly red flannel was now the colour of butter, blending in with the limestone floor, so that he'd barely seen her until she moved in her sleep. She'd been bleaching his towels with her radiance, just like she'd done with his precious red handkerchief.

He'd lost track of time. So many meetings, so many demons...he'd missed out on precious time with Mel. Melody Angel. The amazing angel who'd walked naked through Hell for him, when no one else had ever willingly lifted a finger to help him. He couldn't stop thinking about it. About her.

"Melody. Sweet, sweet Melody." He wanted to take her in his arms and do every pleasurable thing he could think of to do to a woman — Hell, he'd invent a few, just for her. Luce was on his knees, reaching for her, before he realised he should probably wake her first. Not to mention ask what she wanted. The last time he'd touched her was when she'd died in his arms.

"I'm sorry I took so long," he said. "You shouldn't be lying here on the cold stone. I have a bed, you know."

"Mmm," Mel said, sighing. He wasn't sure if she was responding to him or not.

"Did you want me to take you to bed? To rest, of course. You need it."

He waited for some sort of acknowledgement, but he got none. After a few seconds, he decided to do it anyway. He'd prefer her to be angry at him for making her comfortable than to leave her on the floor. Plus, he got to carry her in his arms and lay her on his bed. Plenty of material to fantasise about later...

He lifted her body, letting the covering towel slide off to reveal her flawless skin. No, not flawless, he realised – she had a nasty wound on her shoulder, as if someone had clawed at her recently and it hadn't yet healed. When he found out who'd hurt her, he'd make sure they had time to regret their actions. A bloody long time.

Avoiding the wound, he rose and carried her carefully back to the office. The illusionary wall that hid his bedchamber – and it was a chamber, a cavern within the greater cave – vanished to reveal the bed he rarely slept in. Black silk sheets didn't seem right for Mel, so he tried to focus on lightening the colour as much as he could before she touched them. He managed a brighter red than he had for the towels – more the colour of an open wound than a glass of rich, red wine – but there was no way he could make them as white as hers were at home.

The red seemed to suit her, Luce decided, as he laid her on silk. He stroked her hair, accidentally brushing against her hurt shoulder. She screwed her face up and grumbled under her breath.

"Who hurt you, Mel? Why didn't you just heal it?" he asked, not expecting a reply.

She mumbled something he couldn't understand, so he asked her to repeat it.

"Some harpy," she murmured. "A mistake. Won't do it again."

"Why haven't you healed it?" he asked urgently. He couldn't stand to see her hurting like this.

"Can't. Angels can't heal themselves. Healing is an act of love," she said, still not opening her eyes.

"Mel, the claws went deep. I can see where it tore muscle and..." Luce didn't want to say much more. It'd only sound gruesome. His hand hovered over the wound – he wanted to touch it but didn't dare. "We need to get you to another angel who can heal you."

"You do it," Mel mumbled.

"Mel, I can't heal. I haven't been able to heal since I fell. Only angels can..."

Mel's fingers were warm as her hand covered his to move his palm over her shredded shoulder. "You're an angel, my love. I can't think of anyone else's hands I'd like to heal me more than yours." He found he was staring into her wide open eyes. He couldn't look away. She smiled. "I'll tell you what. I'll even let you keep my underwear, if you like."

Luce laughed. "What if it doesn't work?"

She touched her lips to his fingers. "I believe you can heal me. I'll sleep better without the pain. Hell, I'll give you my underwear simply for trying. Just do it, Luce."

He closed his eyes, summoning a power he'd been without for so long that he'd almost forgotten what it felt like. It flowed like warm water from his fingertips to his palm, heating as it concentrated. He could see the glow through his eyelids, but he kept his eyes firmly shut, concentrating on muscle and tendon, bone and blood vessel. Pain burned in his shoulder – Hell, he'd forgotten about the part where you felt the pain you took away, but for the first time in his life, he welcomed the sensation. Mel's body had to knit perfectly – she'd been damaged while trying to help him.

"You're hurting, my love. Let me take the pain away," Mel murmured. "The least I can do."

Luce felt the healing pain start to fade as her delicate touch caressed his very soul, but he resisted it. "No. You've taken enough pain for me. I deserve this." If she probed any deeper, she'd know what he'd done in his despair...and leave him. Pain was a small price to pay — and perhaps part of his penance, too.

"You don't deserve more pain, but if you wish, so be it."

Luce felt her draw back from him a little and he fought the sensation of loss that followed. She was here and he was healing her, or at least trying to...despite his best efforts, the healing warmth in his hands faded. "Mel, I'm sorry. I can't," he said bitterly, not wanting to see the disappointment in her eyes.

Her hand pushed his down, against her shoulder. The gaping hole was whole now — as if the wound had never been. Smooth and soft, an angel's skin, begging to be kissed, caressed...

Luce opened his eyes to Mel's smile. "I told you," she said. "Thank you." She leaned forward to kiss him. Long and luscious — to Luce, this kiss was as near to Heaven as he'd been in centuries. Standing at the gate didn't come close. But this was the closest he was ever going to get.

Reluctantly, he broke it. "You need to rest. I can wait — we have eternity together, or at least until this world ends." He waited for her to rest her head on the pillow again before he pulled the sheets up to cover her. He stared at the gold silk in his hands. "I'm sure this was..."

Mel laughed softly. "A joint effort, I think. Do you still think you're a demon, Luce?"

"I'm not sure what I am any more," he admitted. "Angel, demon or a bit of both."

"What makes you think there's still a little demon inside you?" she asked.

A little demon. Oh Hell. It was Luce's turn to laugh. "No, Mel. Not a little demon at all. The biggest, scariest, darkest demon you can imagine. I've heard men on Earth described as being beset by demons, but they have nothing on me, for I've been beset by, surrounded by and possessed by demons since the day I arrived here. And nothing will banish the worst one of all — because the big boss demon, the one in charge, is me. I'll always have a demon inside and that demon is me."

"Show me," Mel commanded, her voice deceptively soft.

"I don't want you to see it. It's the very worst of me — the horns, the hooves...all the darkness and horror of Hell that helps me keep order here. What an angel like you hates."

"An angel doesn't hate." Mel's eyes seemed to burn into his. "Whatever body you wear, I still see the soul inside. Show me."

Perhaps if he managed to distract her with his

demonic body, she'd neglect to look too deeply into his soul. Reluctantly, Luce unzipped his fly and started pulling his pants down.

"You keep your demon in your pants?" Mel laughed.

Luce felt his cheeks redden. "No," he mumbled. "Just that this form isn't so good for clothes. You know how I said I walk around Hell naked to remind the other demons who's in charge?"

"Well, it's a relief to know I'm not the only one to walk through this place without my clothes," Mel replied. She crossed her arms over the gold sheet that hid her breasts, as if reminding him what lay beneath. "Please, continue." Her avid eyes watched him finish stripping.

"You asked for it," he said, grinning as he closed his eyes to keep that image of her face in mind. He didn't want to see her expression change to horror as his body showed her the monster that lived inside the man.

Muscles bloated and bulged as his skin hardened. The weight of his wings settled into place – leather was lighter than feathers, though most wouldn't think it. A slight air current chilled his bare head as his horns pushed their way through the stretching skin. His feet tightened, forming hard hooves. He flexed his fingers, feeling the claws extend as his teeth did the same. His mouth felt full of rocks, as it always did when he shifted to this form. He hoped he wouldn't bite his tongue in front of Mel. The skin of his back stung as his tail poked its way through, point first. He drew a breath into his expanded lungs, feeling the power in this body. He was the Lord of Hell – and he was afraid to open his eyes to see what Mel thought of him.

He heard the light slap of her feet on stone as she approached. Would she keep going, running past him and all the way back up to the surface, to Heaven where she belonged? Or would she have the courtesy to say farewell first? Luce clenched his fists, squeezing his eyes shut tighter still.

Gentle fingers trailed up his spine, stroking the soft membrane between his wing digits as she somehow soothed away his fears. "This body has harder skin than the form you usually wear. I miss the plumage, but your wings feel so delicate when they're bare like this. It's hard to believe something so fragile can carry your weight, let alone anything else." Her lips touched his back, between his shoulder blades. "You're so much hotter in this form, too." She sounded amused.

Impulse drove him to whirl around and whisk her

into the air, wings beating as he shot upwards with her. He'd never thought of his demon body as big before, but she seemed so small in his arms as they soared high above the Styx and the walls of Dis.

Mel placed her hand over his heart and the beat quickened for her.

"So much suffering in one place," she murmured sadly, surveying the scene spread below her. Her hair felt tantalisingly soft against his skin as she laid her head on his chest. Luce breathed deeply, savouring her scent. "I don't know how you can stand it."

"I belong here. This is Hell and I am the lord of this place. Torture, torment and all the despair I can't stomach. I can never be an angel again for you, Mel. Behold, the demon!" He threw his arms wide, releasing her.

He expected her to cling to him in fear, or fall into the Styx below, so he'd have to catch her. How many times had he underestimated Mel?

"Not all angels fall, Luce." Her wings shone far too bright for this dark space, seeming to give off their own light as they fluttered gently to buoy her. Her hand remained on his chest. Her touch was so light it might have been the feathers in her wings instead of her fingers. Mel lifted her head to look into his eyes. "You're not a demon and you belong with me," she said, smiling.

Luce wanted to believe her, but the evidence wasn't looking good. "Angels don't have horns or tails or wings without feathers...and they don't have claws, either."

Mel's white wings lifted her higher than Luce. Her lips touched the top of his head, right between his horns, as she treated him to a lovely, close-up view of her breasts. *Angels probably don't get this horny, either,* Luce thought, enjoying what was offered so freely.

Her eyes met his again as she sank a little lower. Luce froze as he felt her reach around behind him, her fingers drifting down his lower back, one vertebra at a time, until they closed around him completely. He stared at her as her hand slowly stroked the length of his tail, stopping only at the tip, which she brought to her lips.

If there was someone he could have sold his soul to so that she'd continue, he'd have done it on the spot.

"The Lord of Hell does, for he has a reputation to maintain with the demons he rules. The body you wear is not a representation of the soul inside – merely what is appropriate for the time and the circumstance. I know you, Luce." Her words echoed in his head as she took his tail-tip in her mouth, sucking it like a spoon of that chocolate raspberry mousse she'd loved.

Oh God. Did she know how many nerve endings she'd just electrified with one stroke of her tongue, arcing up his spine to his euphoric brain?

Luce felt like he was going to burst out of his pants. If he'd been wearing pants...well, she'd be under no illusions that his body enjoyed the attention. He clenched his eyes shut so she wouldn't read the desire consuming his soul. She'd already read deeper than anyone else. "How can you possibly think you know my soul? I killed you once. The darkness you didn't see could rise and do it again." Sweet torment as her tongue tantalised his tail. She would have made as good a demon as she did an angel. With an effort, he wrenched his tail from her grasp, trailing the damp tip down her cheek, her throat, caressing her skin as he moved the point slowly down.

"Because my soul is bonded with yours," she whispered.

Horrified, he jerked away from her. "No, Mel. I never asked for your soul. Never wanted to damn you with me to this place..."

She sniffled and smiled as she lifted her head, wiping her tears away with careless fingers. "Of course you didn't. You came to me and asked for my help. I shared it with you freely. I breathed my spirit into you, expecting your demon spirit to fight me and carry you home to Hell to escape from being burned by the brightness of mine. But there was no darkness shielding you from me — instead, your soul welcomed me in with...with love." She swallowed as an untended tear trickled down her cheek. "How could I respond with anything else? I felt the bond form — surely you did, too! — and when we parted, the connection between us remained. It helped me find you, but it doesn't hold me here. My soul is still my own — just linked with yours."

Luce swallowed painfully. "If...if that's true, I didn't know about any bond. If I'd known you were in Hell, searching for me, instead of dead or in Heaven...I wouldn't have...I wouldn't have..." He'd thought he'd heard her voice, encouraging him to hold on when he'd wanted to die, but that was easily dismissed as wishful thinking.

"Show me," she said softly.

Fateful words.

"You don't want to see," he whispered, as the horrors came unbidden. The despair that drove him to his own weapon, ripping flesh, bleeding on the floor...and waking to Persephone, as he lay puddled in his own blood. Saying Mel couldn't...didn't...would never love him.

Falling. He plummeted into darkness again. This time, strong hands caught him. No one had ever...no one...yet he was rising. Mel. How could she bear his weight as well as her own? Her fragile wings were smaller than his, but together they ascended.

"Hold on, Luce. I'm so sorry. I should've come sooner. Left clearer signs. Like the one at the entrance. Didn't you see?" she entreated through her tears.

Red glitter. Not Michael. Mel. He closed his eyes. "I thought it was someone else, trying to torment me by reminding me of you. I never thought you'd come here for me. That you'd want to..." He stared at her, not even sure how to finish his sentence.

"I've never...I never wanted to bond with anyone

before. You...I've read so many souls, but I've never tried to share what lies in mine. Please...tell me if this reaches you." Mel closed her eyes tightly and frowned as she attempted whatever it was she meant to do.

He watched her but felt nothing. "It's all right. I'm probably not perceptive enough to pick up on..."

"Oh, to Hell with it," she exclaimed and kissed him. Leathery lips, mouth full of fangs, forked tongue and all.

Her love burst upon him like a depth charge, leaving him breathless. How could her body hold all that feeling in? All for him. "Mel," he choked out, desperate not to hurt her even as her tongue caressed his. His mouth was a bloody booby-trap for him – he was terrified he'd bite her. God knew he'd bitten his own tongue often enough.

"A demon would feel unbearable pain from my first touch and I didn't hurt you," Mel said, licking her lips. Her tongue looked miraculously unhurt, too. "You're no demon, my love."

"No," he agreed. He became uncomfortably aware of where they were. "How about we take this back to my office, instead of in front of an audience that includes half of Hell?"

Mel surveyed the hundreds – perhaps thousands – of demons and damned souls who were looking up in what might have been the first time in millennia. Self-consciously, she folded her wings. "Yes. Please, take me down, Luce."

Holding as tight to her as he had during their ascent, he mirrored her smile. He had her all to himself, now without an audience, and she loved him. His hooves had barely touched the stone floor of the cavern before he kissed her deeply.

"I don't deserve you," he said.

"You didn't deserve centuries in Hell. I hope you might consider what I have to offer some small consolation for what you've suffered."

"Hardly small, Mel," he murmured.

"There's something else that isn't small..." She glanced down, blushing. "I can certainly see why you intimidate the demons so much in this form."

He'd never been glad of his red skin before, but he was now. She didn't see how his blush burned darker than hers. "I'm not normally this big," he insisted. "It must be because I'm so close to you. You could help me relieve the pressure a bit..." He pressed hopefully against her.

"Luce, you're huge," she protested before he cut her off with another kiss.

He concentrated on bringing his body back to be the man she'd known on Earth. Perhaps he had overdone the size of his demon body a bit...but it had all been proportionate. When his claws retracted, Mel didn't seem so small any more. Secure in his arms, she felt...perfect.

"When I leave here, I want you to come with me," Mel said, bringing him back.

He found himself, lost in her eyes. "That sounds wonderful." It took him a few moments before he added, "Hop on and I'll take you anywhere you want to go." He sat on the bed and patted his lap.

Mel laughed, shook her head, and sat beside him instead. "Heaven. I want to take you home to Heaven with me, Luce."

Luce wanted to drop everything on the spot and go with her. Even to Heaven, if that's what she wanted. He opened his mouth to offer.

Someone started beating down his door. "Lord Lucifer! I need to speak with you!"

Mel shrugged. "You're still the Lord of Hell. I bet you have a fair few demons who are wondering what exactly you were doing with the strange angel."

He pulled on his pants and stood up. "I'll let you rest. If you need anything, I'll be in the office next door, working as hard as I can to get the Hell out of here as soon as possible. With you."

She smiled, nodded, then sighed and settled deeper into the pillows. A thin silk sheet covered all he wanted in this world and he hoped he'd never have to give her up again.

Luce concentrated on concealing the chamber where she rested with an illusory concrete wall once more. She didn't deserve to have demons staring at her as she slept.

When she was hidden from sight, he waved the office door open to allow the knocking nuisance entrance.

He leaned on the desk, doing his best to sound stern even as his thoughts were still flying with Mel. The doorway stood empty. "Well? What's so urgent? Have you decided you don't need to speak to me after all?"

The old ferryman, Charon, stepped hesitantly inside. His approach was painstakingly slow and he seemed to consider each step before he took it. Almost halfway to the desk, he stopped, lowered his hood and said, "Lord Lucifer, I came to ask about...the lady."

The lady. Mel was all that and more. "What about the lady?"

Charon twisted a fold of his robes in his hands. "The lady...I wanted to ask if she was safe and well."

Luce stared at the man. "I don't see what it has to do with you. My business with the lady is hers and mine alone. Now, did you have something to tell me or not?"

"Lord Lucifer, I do need to tell you something," Charon admitted. "You can't keep Lady Muriel here. She belongs on Earth, not in Hell."

So the old ferryman knew her, though he'd never met her in the office. Had Mel managed to charm him here? Luce tried not to laugh. "Aren't you going to tell me not to try to turn her? That's the first thing everyone else said."

Charon choked out a laugh. "You've got to be arrogant or stupid to think you can best her – and your arrogance always was legendary. Lord Lucifer, not even you can turn Lady Muriel. She's one who'll never fall. She's too sure of her path. And you'll have every angel in Heaven and on Earth come looking for her if you keep her here much longer. You can't hold the Domination of Heaven and Earth and Hell."

For a moment, Luce was reminded of Michael. "What does my fall have to do with Mel? Michael said that, too — but he wasn't talking about Mel. He was talking about..."

Charon howled with laughter, almost doubling over in mirth. "You're a fool, Lord Lucifer. You mean you didn't know..."

"Well met, ferryman," Mel said softly. She stood before the illusion of a wall, draped only in a gold sheet. Luce's fingers itched to tear the sheet away from her body so he could see her in all her glory. "You never gave Luce my message that I was looking for him. You could have saved me a lot of time and a fair bit of trouble if you had."

Charon's chin jutted out, showing his Adam's apple as he swallowed nervously. "I still hoped you'd turn back, Lady Muriel. This is no place for you, and I worried that he'd keep you as he tried to turn you. The world needs you above, not hidden away here, until he gave up."

Mel strode to Luce's side. "Luce knows he can't keep me here and I won't stay long. He will come with me."

Luce stared into Mel's eyes. She was right. Of course he would. How could he not?

Charon started to laugh. "I didn't think it was possible for an angel to fall twice. Michael will have a fit when he finds out."

"He already did," Mel admitted. "But he knows he's powerless to do anything about it."

"You two are talking in riddles," Luce grumbled. "This is my office and I'm supposed to be in charge of this place."

"Is he?" Charon asked Mel. She smiled and nodded. He turned to Luce. "Do you know who leads the choir of Hashmallim?"

"Sure," Luce responded. "That's...Raphael, the archangel who's Mel's boss at the agency. He led them into battle against me when..."

"No," Mel interrupted. "It's me, Luce. Raphael acts as my second in charge. He insisted that we needed to be present at the battle and he begged to be the one to lead them. Boys and their battles – I wouldn't stand and watch that idiocy. He took those who agreed with him. He left me a lot of work to do and no angels to do it. No wonder I summoned both you and Michael to Earth to speak to me when I found I couldn't leave." She looked almost angry. "If you'd bothered to accept my invitation, I could have saved you a lot of pain."

Luce shook his head. "I didn't get any message from you, Mel. Never. I swear..." His memory gave him a kick. "Wait. One of the Grigori brought me a crazy message he said was from Michael. It made me laugh. Something about how I should go down to Earth before offering battle and beg some girl to help me..." He stared at her in horror. "Mel, I'm sorry. If I'd known..."

"You've paid your penance, Luce. How many centuries have you served here? All you had to do was ask for my help and you finally did, on the floor of my little house. And Michael said you'd never find me, the Domination of Heaven and Earth, in such plain surroundings."

Charon coughed. "I'll be going. Don't linger too long, Lady Muriel. The world needs you above, and soon."

Mel smiled. "Oh, I know."

Luce repeated the old ferryman's words and saw in Mel's expression that she knew his thoughts, too. Hell, she knew his soul. How could she not know what he was thinking?

"I was sent here so that I'd never have the Domination of Heaven and Earth. Set upon by that bloody sword, forced to fall against my will to land, shattered, HERE. I wanted to prove that arrogant angel wrong. I could have control of Earth in legal contracts, because humans are stupid and they'd do anything for money. All along...the Domination of Earth wasn't a vague concept. It was YOU?" Luce kept his voice level for most of it, but the line of reasoning seemed too preposterous to be true.

"Yes. The Domination of Earth is me and...Michael believed he was protecting me. If you sought my help...he foresaw that I would enter Hell." Mel's words were quiet and careful.

"So he hid you. For centuries, he's hidden you. How could you go along with it? He sent me here – forced me to fall. Every other angel had a choice, yet I had none. And what was my crime? That he feared I'd take you from him?"

Mel bowed her head. "They told me that you wanted me to guide you, and you alone. That you were evil and would use me for your own ends, which would not match mine. Michael, Raphael – those who witnessed your fall – they said you would confine me in Hell; that Michael had seen that in my future. If you found me, asked for my help...I would come here and you would never let me go. So I did what I had to – and hid from you. I can see the currents of future events – all bar those that involve me. I could only trust the foresight of others. I'm sorry."

Luce's voice died and what came out was a hoarse whisper. "I didn't know you. I didn't know who you were or how important you could be. I never hunted for you, never wanted to hold you against your will. I never knew your name until you told me, Mel. I swear I never would have wanted you to share my fate — confined to a Hell you didn't deserve." He stared into her eyes, willing her to read his soul, if she hadn't already. "Please, believe me. I had no idea of any of what Michael accused me of wanting."

"I didn't understand what he'd done until outside the gates of Heaven, Luce. They wouldn't even use my true name. Lying in your arms, I saw it all...but the only place I could make amends was in Heaven. I let my damaged body disintegrate and headed home to straighten out the tangled mess Michael had made. And when I returned to tell you...you'd gone. How could I not follow you into Hell? An innocent man has no place here." Mel looked determined. "I want you to come with me, to walk triumphantly into Heaven. To show them they were wrong. About you. About me. But only if you're willing."

Luce snorted. "Mel, I've committed most of the sins the damned are in here for. Suicide. Murder. Betrayal. Lust. Bad counsel...and that's just this week. No one in their right mind will let me into Heaven. I should apply to Minos for my level assignment here..."

"Angels aren't perfect, Luce," Mel began.

"DON'T!" he snapped, breathing hard. "She...she said that. Angels aren't perfect, they're just better than everyone else..."

Mel's eyes turned hard. "Persi. I'm going to have some serious words with that girl when I see her next. She should never have come here..." Her gaze softened.

"She was misquoting me, Luce. I told someone once that angels aren't perfect, but we try to be. That's what sets us apart. The soul I see inside you belongs in Heaven. Perhaps not in the highest ranks of angels yet, but we all have to aspire to something. They won't keep you out with me at your side."

Luce managed a grin. "And you'd stay at my side this time? What if we run into more crazy, weapon-wielding mothers?"

Mel's smile spoke of untold power. "Ah, but I have nothing and no one to hide from any more. They'll face Lady Muriel of the Hashmallim and not just Melody Angel. What I did to those dark souls here is nothing compared to what I can do."

"And the gatekeepers – Michael with that damn sword and the dude in the dress?" Luce persisted.

"They wouldn't dare challenge me if they have to acknowledge my rank, and they will." Mel held out her hands to him. "Come to Heaven with me, Luce. You offered to show me Heaven once, on Earth. While that was wonderful, I can show you a time far more sublime in Heaven." Her wicked grin returned.

"How can any man refuse an offer like that?" Luce replied. "When do we leave?"

Mel looked down. "After I've had another bath. It looks like I missed a bit of mud before...and I'm not taking any part of Hell home with me."

Before he left, Luce had one final matter to attend to: finding the harpy who'd attacked Mel so he could make the bitch pay.

Lili gave him a searching look as she led two other harpies into his office. "I take it you're feeling better?" she asked, glancing around.

"I have no idea what you're talking about," Luce replied.

She smiled. "So you've broken the new toy I sent you already? Impressive."

Mel. She thought he'd harmed Mel and she seemed happy about it. Was Lili the one who'd attacked his angel? Surely not. Lili wouldn't have sent the girl to him if she'd already damaged the goods. But she'd seen Mel, so she must know something.

"Time for an update on Level Seven. Do you have any issues to report?"

Lilith, Jezebeth and Ananiel exchanged glances but didn't seem to want to respond.

"I heard Level Eight's looking for more personnel again. I'll volunteer all three of you until someone else more appropriate chooses to take your place," Luce offered lazily, watching all three and wondering which of them would break first. One of them had to know who'd hurt Mel.

"The heating system's not operating as well," Jezebeth volunteered. "Meg on Six must've turned one of the graves into a hot tub again. I wouldn't mind if she invited us, but she only invites men, and when she's done with them, she boils them alive. I don't see why she has a hot tub and we don't."

Luce nodded, scribbling down notes. "I'll send one of the engineering demons to take a look. The pipes might just need replacing again. Anything else?"

Lilith cleared her throat. "We need replacements for some of the barbed whips. They seem to wear out far faster than the smaller floggers. I'm not sure if it's overuse or poor workmanship."

"More whips, too." Luce scrawled another line.

"Anything unusual?"

"There are rumours that the illusions on Level Two have failed and the place has turned into a mass orgy," Jezebeth said, glancing at Ananiel. "Right, Ana?"

Ananiel glared at her. "I wouldn't know anything about orgies or Level Two. I've been working hard in Level Seven the whole time."

Jezebeth burst out laughing. "The Hell you have! For the last two days, you've been practising double stuffing on Two with any men that'd have you. I heard you even had the new fallen angel twins – at the same time! I'm surprised you can walk after all that sex, let alone work. No wonder you just mess with the women on Seven, and the little ones, at that, like the one you carved up today – you're too spineless to dominate a man."

It was Ananiel, Luce realised. She'd attacked Mel.

"I do my fair share of torturing damned souls!" Ananiel shrieked. "You take the floggers home to use on your horse of a husband. I've seen you! Just because I don't have a permanent partner, you're making me look like some sort of slut!"

Lilith sighed. "Ana, I counted twenty-five men yesterday and thirty the day before that. You don't need any help from the rest of us to make you look promiscuous. All you have to do is open your skinny legs. Lord Lucifer doesn't need to know about your insecurities. I'm sure I can reassign you to work in the office on the surface if you wish. You can go back to running your little illegal brothel in the disabled toilets at the food court, in between hiring more office whores for the CEO to bend over his desk."

Luce wondered when they'd be finished with their silly spat. Hell, he could hardly believe he'd accepted Ananiel's services or that of any of her stable of office girls. After Mel, he couldn't contemplate even touching one of them again, least of all the crazy Ananiel. His thoughts strayed to Mel, behind that door, who'd be lovingly soaping that sweet skin of hers, like a perfect, living statue in his private pool. And she was waiting for him to finish so he could join her. He couldn't wait.

Silence fell and Luce dragged his eyes back to the bitching harpies. "I'll be shifting the suicides to Level Eight for clean-up duty. They're not much use to you on Seven, are they? That'll give you more space for usurers – we seem to be getting a Hell of a lot of them the last few centuries. Does that work for you, Lili?" He stared at the harpies – now reduced from three to two. "Where's Lili?"

"She left," Jezebeth replied. "Can we go, too? I have another six souls to torture today and Ana's behind again."

Luce considered this before saying, "I'll speak to the imps about the issues on Two. Ana, you're confined to Seven and if I hear a single tale about you turning the tables on the damned souls so that you're the one being tortured, I'll send you down to Eight permanently. This is Hell. Damned souls aren't supposed to enjoy themselves. Now get back to work." He waved them away and both harpies hurried out.

Alone, Luce had an important decision to make: to join Mel now or be responsible and sort out Level Two and the imps first? Luce knew what he wanted, and it most definitely involved Mel. Duty or one Hell of a lot of pleasure? Such a tough choice.

Mel lingered to enjoy the cool cascade over her shoulders for just a little longer. She would simply have to find similar bathing places on Earth, if she could. Small streams created such cascades the world over, surely – she'd never paid them much attention before. She thought about seeking some out in Korea – though she'd settle for hot springs in their cold climate – and wondered if she should take Luce with her. Perhaps it was too soon for such things.

She thought she saw movement out of the corner of

her eye and called out, "Show yourself. If you were after a glimpse of my body, you've had time to grab an eyeful as I travelled through Hell. I have nothing to hide."

A shadow stepped from behind a column. "You've certainly been showing off, angel. You have the male half of Hell talking about you, and a fair few of the women, too. No one can believe an angel would cross Hell just to see its lord."

Mel strained her eyes to recognise the face that matched the familiar voice. "Lili?"

The red-skinned female demon who stepped into the light resembled Lilith, though any sign of humanity was gone, as was evident in her clearly visible horns. "Did you think you were the only woman he's had here? There's something about him in the water that's made so many female angels fall that I lost count a long time ago."

"I don't need to count," Mel replied with a smile. "It's all in the Book of Judgement, outside Heaven's gates. Over a hundred and fifty thousand, I believe, though perhaps he didn't bring all of them here." She shrugged. "As long as I don't have to bathe with them all, I don't mind."

"He's not yours. He'll never be yours, because he's always loved me," Lilith snarled.

"Who?" Mel asked, confused.

"Lord Lucifer. He's mine — has been for millennia. I've stood by his side through the centuries, his right hand and his partner in all his grand plans. He'll discard you when he's done using you, yet another fallen angel...just like all the others. So fresh-faced they hardly recognise who he is before he's turned them into his personal playthings. That's when he throws them away – to be harpies in Hell, or errand girls in his office." Lilith stepped to the edge of the pool, dipping her hoof into the water. "He's mine," she repeated.

"No," Mel said softly. "He's...his. Luce is his own man, neither yours nor mine. Demons can't love, Lili. He can't have loved you. I'm sure he's grateful for all your help and your companionship through so many dark years, but he couldn't love you. And you can't love him."

"You know nothing, you little angel bitch!" Lilith screeched, launching herself at Mel. The demon was so fast, she blurred as she hurtled through the air.

Sighing, Luce decided to deal with work before he joined Mel. Hopefully, he'd have longer to spend with her, without interruptions. What demon would dare invade his personal bathroom?

He summoned the imps' leader, then sat back to wait. Despite their appearance, he never mistook them for demons – they were his allies. How in Hell was he going to keep them amused now that he only wanted Mel? Even the thought of those voyeurs watching him with the woman he loved put him off. Especially as they communicated in a form of soul-to-soul telepathy. The thought of them in his head was worse than them watching him and Mel.

"Greetings, Lord. Where sexy Lady?" Sptlk's amusement coloured his soul-voice.

Luce's mind immediately brought up the delightful picture of Mel's naked body submerging in the pool. He quickly shut it down, not wanting Sptlk to see her naked or to know his weakness for the angel.

"Lady safe. Wish to offer respect. Will wait."

The imps had never offered him respect, Luce reflected, but quelled that thought quickly, hoping Sptlk wouldn't catch it. "I don't want to discuss Mel. I want to ask about the illusions on Level Two. There are reports that the damned souls are without illusion on that level. Can you confirm?"

Sptlk's amusement increased. "Illusions gone. Orgy entertaining. Many hours, many souls. Many demons, too. Many thanks to Lady for spectacle. Debt now owed."

Luce tried to wrap his head around this. "Are you saying Mel dispelled your illusions? Before Mel instigated an orgy?"

"Lady order. We obey. Much amusement. Lord learn from Lady for eternal loyalty."

The graphic pictures Sptlk conveyed showed an intimate knowledge of Mel's body as well as some of his own fantasies, Luce realised with horror. The imps had watched him and Mel when they'd...oh, she'd kill him if she knew. Gaining the imps' eternal loyalty wasn't worth losing Mel if she found out he'd let them watch the couple make love.

"Lady already knows. Imps cannot hide from Lady. Lady sees through all illusion. Gracious permission from sexy, seductive Lady. Honour for us. Great honour for you. Redemption, too."

They knew. The imps had helped him disguise his soul for centuries – hiding it behind an illusive shroud so thick that none could penetrate it – so that no one else could know that his was the only soul in Hell that wasn't completely tainted by malicious shadows.

"I need the illusions restored on Level Two and the shroud around my soul must remain, for no demon can know I'm not one of them. Can you do it?" Luce crossed his fingers. He knew he didn't need to ask for their price – Sptlk would show him.

The imp flashed his pointed teeth in a wicked grin. "Can, yes. Will, if Lady does not order otherwise. Lord must pay reparation to Lady for disrespect." Pictures flowed through the Sptlk's mind, each more detailed than the last, showing Mel's impassioned face as Luce pleasured her body in every way he knew how.

"She won't let me do that," Luce said hoarsely, unable to get the erotic images out of his head. If Mel let him do any of those things, he'd be in Heaven.

"Kneel and beg." Sptlk laughed and disappeared.

Aching for the angel, Luce strode across the office toward the private pool where Mel and Heaven awaited.

Mel languidly lifted a dripping hand and Lilith splashed into the pool. Mel sighed and waded through the water to the edge, stepping onto the limestone beside her bath. The demon charged through the water at the angel's unprotected back, her claws out and ready to rake.

"No," Mel murmured, turning and holding up her hand again.

Lilith stopped in her tracks, one hoof raised to take a step that she couldn't complete. "What have you done to me, bitch? This is some trick. A new angel like you doesn't have the power to stop me like this. Even if he'd turned you, you couldn't!"

Mel shook her shoulders, the rippling movement flowing into her wings as they faded into sight.

"What in Hell? Those aren't real!" Lilith hissed.

Mel turned sad eyes on the angry, immobilised demon. "Lili, I did everything you ever asked of me in the office. You, of all people, can hardly doubt my angelic patience. Even an archangel would have snapped at least once. But I never did. You owe me more favours than the rest of your corporation combined – and, one day, I will collect. I always do. As for the power to stop you...I can, and I will. Even here, I hold greater power than your lord. I am Muriel, leader of the Hashmallim, and I have come for him."

"Bullshit," Lilith spat. "The leader of the Dominations is Raphael. Everyone knows that. I've never heard of a female Domination."

"Do you remember Luce as an angel, Lili? When his wings were white?" Mel asked gently.

"His wings were never white. They were blacker than the night sky when he came to me. He sought solace in my body and I gave him everything. My life and my heart. He loves me, angel. You lie."

"You were human," Mel breathed. A tear slipped down her cheek. "Then you can never understand. Angels don't lie. And demons don't love. If he met you after he fell, he was no longer capable of love, Lili. He's deceived you for centuries, if he told you he did." She sniffled and struggled to smile. "He had the biggest, whitest wings of any angel I'd ever seen. I only saw him once, when I was in Heaven on business. He breezed past me, deep in conversation with two other Seraphim. I don't think he even saw me. I thought he was an arrogant prick then, too."

Lilith struggled, but after a few seconds, she burst out laughing. "Yeah, he's an arrogant prick, all right." She seemed to calm a little as realisation crossed her face. "If he can't love me, you know he can't love you, either."

Mel smiled sadly. "But he does, Lili. It almost destroyed him as half his soul fought the other part of itself. I had no idea. He gave up everything to find me, because he thought I could help." She hesitated. "I did what I could. I had to help. Angels always do." She bowed her head. "I'm sorry."

Lilith's expression hardened again. "Not as sorry as that bastard will be."

The door swung open and Luce stood in the doorway, beaming. "Mel, my love, I'm finished. May I join you?"

Lilith let out a scream of rage and Mel released her in shock. The enraged demon launched herself at Luce.

Mel looked miserable, Luce thought. Were those tears on her cheeks, or just water from the pool?

Weight and pain hit him all at once. Something sharp seared his shoulders as he fell back against the floor, cracking his head on the stone. The blow blinded him, so he couldn't even see his assailant.

"Mel?" he gasped out. He tried to fight off the crazy, clawed beast, but its frenzy lent it more strength than he felt he had.

He got his hands around the creature's neck and

squeezed, trying to crush the air out of it so it would stop.

"NO!" Mel shouted.

Luce felt the weight lift off him. Blinking through his pain, he saw the red, clawed creature suspended above him. He stared at it and it stared back.

"Lili?" he asked, mystified. Why would his most loyal lieutenant attack him?

"You're a fucking lying bastard, Luce, and I should never have trusted you. I'd give anything, never to have met you!" she screeched.

"Lili, I..." Luce struggled to sit up, but the pain in his head made him wince. What he saw of his chest was a mess of blood and ripped flesh. Lilith's claws had dug so deep she'd shredded skin and muscle. It made Mel's shoulder wound look like a slight scratch. He could see his own ribs and some of the organs beneath. Wait, was that his...

Mel's feet made no sound on the stone. She was simply there, kneeling beside him. "Shh, let me." She laid her hands on his chest, stroking the stinging wounds, and the burning started to subside. Mel lifted her fingertips to his temples, and his blurred vision cleared. "You have blood everywhere, Luce. I need to get you to the pool to wash it off." Luce felt his body leave the ground, floating on nothing.

"What the Hell?" He started to struggle, trying to find what, if anything, was supporting him.

"Luce. Just hold still," Mel murmured. He felt air on

his skin as his clothes vanished, before it was replaced by cool water. Wavelets lapped the pool as Mel's gentle hands sluiced water over his chest. "It's in your hair, too. Immerse yourself completely – duck your head under for just a moment."

"What did you do to him? Why is his blood red? Did you turn him human, angel?" Lilith demanded, her voice shaking. Her red face had paled to pink in what Luce thought might be fear.

"He's taken his true form – that of an angel, as he originally was. Not as powerful as he was, or I am, but an angel, like me. One who is capable of love," Mel said. "It was his choice."

"And what about me, Lord Lucifer? Do all these years of service mean nothing?" Lilith spat at Luce.

Love and Lilith – now there were two concepts that didn't go together. He'd repaid all her services with his trust, as he let a former human rise in the ranks so that she was on the same footing as the senior fallen angels. What more could she possibly want from him than the power she so ardently craved? He didn't know how to answer her, so he continued to stare.

"I'm done, Luce. You should probably get dressed," Mel said.

He dragged himself out of the pool and began to put on the clothes that Mel had left on the floor. He gave the shirt up as a loss, but his pants were intact. "What about you, Lili? You just tried to claw my heart out of my chest." He coughed and it bloody hurt. Perhaps she'd punctured a lung before Mel had patched him up. "I'm sure we have a circle in Hell reserved for souls who betray their sworn liege lord. I think it's a particularly nasty one, too."

"So demons can't love and angels can't lie? What can you do now?" Lilith asked bitterly.

"Demons don't love. They fuck and form alliances — that's all. You chose to become one. I never forced you." Luce shrugged.

Lilith flexed her claws and reached for Luce. "Are you just going to leave me hanging here, angel?" she demanded. "Let me down!"

"Are you going to try to hurt him again?" Mel asked.

"He seduced me with promises he couldn't keep, lied to me for centuries! I deserve retribution!"

"I understand your anger, but you deserve no such thing. You chose your fate and he's served his penance. Heaven accepts his contrition, Lili — you should, too."

"Go to Hell, angel. I don't want your pity or preaching. You've turned the Lord of Hell into a lapdog. Take him to Heaven and castrate him — see how long you can keep him then! Leave and let me down."

Mel nodded. "You've made your point clear, Lili. If I ever see you again, it will be to collect what I am owed. Nothing else." She turned a smile on Luce, who finished buttoning his pants. "Let's go, Luce." She held out her hand and he took it.

Soft cloud formed beneath his feet as a gentle breeze caressed his freshly healed skin. He should be wearing a shirt, he decided, concentrating. No, a whole suit. This was definitely a formal occasion. Maybe even a tie...no. A shirt unbuttoned at the throat looked far sexier. Such a pity all he could manage was black.

"What do you think?" he asked Mel.

She smiled as her eyes wandered across his body. How did she do that? The longer she looked, the more turned on he became. Oh God, he was going to walk into Heaven with a hard-on. Hell was one thing, but here...

"You need your wings, Luce. This is one of those times when appearances count. You're making an entrance that no one dreamed was possible. Make them remember who you are — the angel Lucifer, Lord of Hell." Mel's voice was mellifluous, her warmth melting the icy fingers that clutched at his heart.

He hesitated. "Wings and shirts don't go so well together. I always end up ripping things. Ripped clothes won't work if I'm trying to look impressive."

"Like everything in this place — your body, your clothes, all of it — your wings and your clothes are simply an illusion. It's all about appearances." She reached for his chest and tapped a shirt button, which glowed gold. Mel smiled. "Even the blood my body shed the last time we were here was an illusion."

It had seemed so real — Hell, her blood had even tasted real. He couldn't lose her again. He wouldn't lose her again. He seized her hand and spread his wings. He breathed deeply and prayed that this time, for the first time ever, he'd be allowed happiness.

The breeze ruffled his feathers as Mel's musical laughter rang out. "As if I needed more feathers," she said, so quietly it was barely audible. "I'd forgotten how heavy they are."

Luce looked and looked again, just in case he'd been mistaken. He didn't remember her wings being quite so wide — surely they were bigger than his! She flapped them twice, her feet leaving the cloud beneath them as the powerful lift carried her body with it. She was still laughing as she drifted down, folding her wings neatly behind her. Her pearlescent skin glowed from within as Mel turned her dazzling smile on Luce.

"If it's all right with you, I'd prefer not to give fuel to the rumours that I walked naked through Hell for you," Mel said.

Luce's heart dropped faster than she had done, just moments before. "You're ashamed of what you did for me? Even I can't believe you did it. I want to see the faces of some of those righteous angels when they realise what you've done..."

Now Mel's smile was serene. "I don't regret my actions for a moment, but it might be easier for the angels and souls waiting for judgement if I have some clothes on, is all. I'm sure they'll all hear the truth and it will only add colour to the legend. Most of them won't notice the angel beside you, but if they do, it might be best if my arse is covered. Like this, we look like something off the cover of one of Lili's dark erotica books – the CEO in a suit, with a scantily clad young woman at his side."

Luce grinned back. "Well, if you put it like that...if you're going to wear sexy lingerie, I think I'll be walking behind you to take in the view, instead of beside you."

"Then I'd best be a little more modest," Mel said softly, closing her eyes. A shimmer began over her breasts, cascading over curves to dim her steady glow, so that her skin was merely glittering instead.

Luce blinked and managed to miss the final step that set her transparent dress opaque, but it was the colour that arrested his attention. She wore the gold silk dress he'd seen in her wardrobe, clinging to every curve as if it loved her as much as he did. His knees went weak. He was going to kneel and beg, the moment he got her all to himself in Heaven. "I thought you wore white," he said.

"I did, and sometimes I still will," Mel responded, glancing down. "I like the simplicity of being Melody Angel, but your escort must be Lady Muriel. My time for hiding is done. Today it's time for a show of power, and an angel of my rank must be clothed in gold." She lifted impish eyes to his face. "I need to look good enough to be seen with you, Luce. I believe the human term is arm candy."

Luce leaned in close so that his lips brushed her ear. "You know that'll make me think of how sweet you taste, every step of the way."

"As long as you look impressive, your thoughts can wander wherever you like," Mel replied, turning her head to claim a kiss. "Are you ready, Luce?"

He released her reluctantly, so that their only contact was their joined hands. "As I'll ever be."

Together, they strode forward.

A billow of cloud blew aside with a flutter of Mel's wings. Now he could see the crowd that awaited them — the benches bridging the gap between them and the Book of Judgement were full of angels and some saintly souls, too. Far more than on the day they let Mel die.

Mel wouldn't die today, Luce swore. At the slightest hint of trouble, they'd both fly and to Hell with the consequences.

His eyes kept straying to their audience. There were very few wings in sight, and none as magnificent as

Mel's. Even his stood out, both for their colour and size. Perhaps he should have thought to wear something lighter – a grey shirt and suit, instead of his customary black. He wasn't sure he could do anything about the colour of his wings.

Luce glanced at his sleeve, which looked a little lighter. He focussed harder on the fabric, willing it to change.

"Relax, Luce," Mel murmured. "I won't let anyone hurt you."

He laughed. "I was thinking that I should've worn a lighter shirt."

"Let me help you with that." Her voice was barely a whisper, but he heard it clearly. Her hand landed on his thigh and stroked up his side to his shoulder before caressing his arm.

Under her lingering fingers, his sleeve shifted a few shades lighter still. He glanced at the seated souls and their escorts to see if they had noticed the change. He couldn't catch anyone's eye, he realised, watching each of them look down as he passed, as if they were afraid to lock gazes with him. Just like that innocent little escort last time – the one who'd been terrified of him. Now Luce dropped his own gaze to his feet. His pants were dark grey, he noticed, but the lightening colour wasn't enough to lighten his heart. He didn't belong here.

Mel stopped, and, touching his cheek, she looked into his eyes so that he could see the love that filled her soul. "Don't forget that you're the angel I love, claiming your rightful place at my side in Heaven. Every angel here aspires to what you have. Do you want them to remember you as the arrogant angel who strode into Heaven, the miracle of redemption no one believed possible, or the broken demon who was beaten by a girl and dragged back here?"

Luce couldn't help it – he burst out laughing. "Which would you prefer me to be?"

"If I wanted to drag in a broken demon, would I have given you a choice?" Mel whispered. "Though I think we could make quite an impression if you go for the red, bulging muscles and I fly in, with you hanging from my hand by one huge leg..." She glanced down, smiling wickedly. "I think you might intimidate angels as much as demons that way – but it's not particularly dignified. Best if you keep your pants on, I think."

"I love you, Mel. Lucifer the arrogant angel, at your service." He straightened his shoulders and lifted his chin, sensing her merriment but not daring to catch her eye or they'd both laugh. She knew him better than he knew himself. He'd had centuries of practice being an arrogant demon – an arrogant angel couldn't be much harder, surely.

They continued past the line of benches and he tried not to look at the watchers any more. All that mattered was Mel and their destination.

Luce fixed his eyes firmly on the gates as they grew larger with every step he took. Glowing pearl and not steel; the base of the bars shrouded in misty cloud. Today his misgivings were gone – today they would swing open more smoothly than the stone gates of Dis. Somehow, Mel had infused him with her certainty. He prayed for her to be right.

Mel drew him to a halt beside the gate guard, who still wore a white dress. The angel bowed deeply. "Welcome home, Lady Muriel. I think I speak for every angel in Heaven and Earth when I say we're relieved to see you return, safe and sound."

"Did you really think I wouldn't, Peter?" Mel asked gently.

He straightened so he could face her. "Many of us were worried for you. When you ventured where no angel has returned from...and you, an angel we could scarce do without...we feared the worst. To see you return, with the one you said you'd save...I am in awe, Lady Muriel." He bowed again, this time from the waist. "May I be the first to congratulate you on your conquest of Hell?"

Luce laughed so hard he almost choked. Mel and whose army? She'd have had to bring all the forces of Heaven to Hell and she couldn't conquer the whole place without defeating every single senior demon in addition to himself. Lilith would never give up without a fight – nor would any of the others, if only out of pride.

"You make it sound like some sort of violent battle. I merely travelled through Hell to help Luce and bring him here," Mel said softly, her now-watery smile melting Luce's heart. Mel wasn't the conquering type.

Movement caught Luce's eye on the edges of his vision. Those on the benches were standing and bowing, too – all in Mel's direction. Even he felt compelled to pay her the same homage. They hadn't been avoiding his eyes at all, he realised – they'd all been showing their respect to Mel.

Mel's fingers tightened around his and Luce lifted his head to look at her. She'd turned pale and the smile that lifted her lips was nervous and uncertain. She'd stayed on Earth, avoiding this kind of attention for centuries. Yet when she'd had a message to convey in front of a pack of human reporters in the office, she'd frozen and fallen to her knees in tears. The indestructible angel who'd fearlessly taken on all the forces of Hell and won...suffered from stage fright.

Luce slipped an arm around her waist and pulled her close. His now-white sleeve disturbed her feathers, marring their perfection, but she didn't make a sound of protest. "You don't know how happy I am that you did. How about we get the gate, Mel, and leave this bloke to deal with the backlog of work he has queuing up?"

Mel nodded jerkily and allowed him to lead her to the shimmering portal to Heaven.

"So, how do we do this?" Luce asked, looking at the bars preventing his passage.

Mel smiled wanly. "At least we don't have to play a game of poker to find out. The same as your gates to

Dis – the touch of an angel."

"Well, do the honours then, Melody Angel," he replied with a flourish of his hands.

"No, together. We do this together," she insisted, her voice still small but gaining a little volume as it stopped shaking. She held tight to his hand, stretching her left hand toward one gate as he extended his right toward the other. "Now."

Her delicate hand and his larger one touched the bars at the same instant, sending the gates swinging wide open to permit them both passage into Heaven. With their hands still joined, they stepped forward together.

He could feel her shaking, but she continued to take one step after another and he kept pace with her until she stopped. Mist swirled around her bare feet, making his light grey trousers look even lighter beside her creamy legs. "If I asked you to turn my wings white as well as my clothes, would you do it?"

"No," Mel replied. "Only you can change those and the colour is a part of who you are. You're still the Lord of Hell, as well as an angel, Luce. That makes your wings...quite striking, as well as unique." Her smile seemed genuine again. "Besides, you know how I feel about dark wings. Think of the swans." She stretched out her fingers, caressing his feathers. He didn't want her to stop, but he didn't want to embarrass her in front of the audience.

Luce glanced back to see if the crowd at the gates

were still watching them, but they, the gates and everything outside of Heaven were no longer visible. He sighed his relief, understanding why Mel had relaxed.

"Congratulations, Luce. You're the first fallen angel and the first redeemed demon ever to enter Heaven. I'm honoured that you let me be the one to escort you this far." Mel's expression glowed with joy.

Centuries...millennia...they'd kept him out. No more – all thanks to Mel. "Thank you," he managed to say before he grabbed her, crushing her wings in his fierce hug. He kissed her next, repeating his thanks when she broke for air.

He could have gone on kissing her forever, but she disengaged from him gently. As if to offer some compensation for the end of kisses, she clasped his hand between hers.

"So, what do you have in mind for your return to Heaven, Luce? What would you like to do first?" Mel asked with a smile.

Luce eyed her hungrily. "I want to do you first. All this about how it'll be better in Heaven...I want to see for myself. And I really, really want to use these." He produced the handcuffs from his pocket. The very special new ones that featured in his favourite fantasy about Mel.

Mel cleared her throat, her eyebrows lifting almost to her hairline. "You're finally redeemed, allowed to enter Heaven for the first time in centuries, and the first thing you want to do is handcuff me to a bed and..." Her hands seemed to convey quite eloquently what she failed to find the words to express.

Luce chuckled. "No. These are for me. Lady Muriel, illustrious leader of the Dominations, I was hoping you might..."

"I hardly need handcuffs to hold you anywhere I want you, my love." Mel's smile turned decidedly wicked. "Maybe later, if you like. First, I think I should show you how angels do it in Heaven."

Luce woke from his blissful slumber and untwined himself from Mel. She may not have conquered Hell, but she'd conquered him so completely he never wanted to be apart from her again.

Something kept nagging at his mind. The old ferryman, asking if he was still the Lord of Hell, but he'd been looking at Mel.

And she'd nodded...

She'd have had to defeat all the senior demons in Hell in order to conquer the place. But Mel didn't work that way. Her style was more subtle – persuading them all to mutiny in her favour, perhaps.

By all that was holy...she had. Geryon, Merihim, Kasyade, Ploutos...even Lilith.

He cuddled up to Lady Muriel, conqueror of Hell. It's not like she'd needed to go to so much effort, he mused. He'd give her anything and he'd go to Hell and back to get it for her. All she had to do was ask.

"Lady Muriel. Lady Muriel. Please forgive the intrusion, but Michael sent me. Raphael said it was urgent..."

Surely she'd earned a longer rest than this. Evidently not. Reluctantly, Mel unwound herself from Luce's embrace. "What is it, Jehannette?"

"It's Persephone. She's disappeared."

Mel felt Luce's interest arouse. "She has? That's wonderful news!"

"No, it isn't," Mel said gently. "I know you don't like her, but I need to see her. Raphael was supposed to bring her to me for a meeting regarding her recent conduct in Hell. If she's disappeared, then who's running the HELL Corporation?"

"That's her problem, not mine any more. I gave all that up, remember?" Luce cuddled closer to Mel.

"You signed it over to the agency, not her personally. If she's not taking care of the company, it falls to Raphael," Mel replied. She turned to Jehannette. "How long has she been gone? Does he have a suitable caretaker?"

"I don't know, Lady Muriel. Both archangels told me I needed to find you, tell you the news and beg for your help." Jehannette's barely-contained panic said more than her words.

Mel relaxed as she said, "Go tell them that I'll return to my little house on Earth as soon as I can. I'll find her and make sure the corporation is well cared for."

Jehannette hurried off, her relief as visible as the cloud beneath her.

"I still don't see how it's your problem," Luce grumbled. "Don't go. Think of all the trouble I'll cause, up here alone without you."

Mel drew away from him completely, feeling bereft already at the slight parting. "That's why you're coming with me, Luce. We'll return to HELL together. Just think — you'll get to wear pants again."

Melody Angel's Guide to Heaven and Hell

DEMELZA CARLTON

Introduction

Not everyone has personal experience in both Heaven and Hell. Nor have many people met most of the immortals who inhabit one or both of these places – at least not those on Earth, the realm in between.

There are countless more immortals than I have introduced you to here, but I hope this will serve as an introduction to my realms and those who live here with me.

Melody Angel

Heaven

Heaven is the domain of angels, enlightened and non-damned souls.

Three Triads

There are nine choirs of angels, divided into three triads or spheres that each contain three choirs.

The Lowest Triad

The first and lowest triad consists of Angels, Archangels, and Principalities. These three choirs deal with the minutiae of the universe – including humans. Guardian angels are some of the lowest level of angels in this triad.

The Middle Triad

The middle triad is responsible for maintaining large-scale order in the universe, throughout both space and time. They delegate lesser tasks to the angels on the lowest triad. The choirs in this triad are the Powers, Virtues and Dominations.

The Highest Triad

The highest triad are the furthest from Earth, spending all their time in Heaven or on higher planes of existence. These are the ones who have a reputation for singing, as they are tasked with contemplating and conveying the glory of this universe and communicating with other universes. Thrones, Cherubim, and Seraphim are the three choirs that make up this triad.

Seraphim

The Seraphim are six-winged angels who stand highest in Heaven. Each pair of wings has its own purpose:

- One pair for covering their faces
- One pair to cover their feet
- One pair for flying

In Hebrew, Seraphim means flaming, which is how these angels are meant to appear, as they are aflame with love for the higher beings they stand so close to, while they are adept at kindling love in those around them. Lucifer was once a Seraphim and this is probably where he gets his affinity for fire and his legendary capacity for seduction.

Cherubim

Cherubim are next down from Seraphim and they are said to be very wise, with many eyes and four wings. They are supposed to have the greatest knowledge of this universe and also the greatest capacity to convey this knowledge.

Thrones

Thrones (also called Ophanim and Galgallin) are the conduit between lower angels and higher beings, dispensing justice. They're symbols of the universe's highest authority and justice.

The form of these angels is quite odd – they are described as wheels within wheels, with many eyes set around their rims. Admittedly, they sound a lot like modern reports of flying saucers.

Dominations

Dominions (also known as Dominations, Lordships or Hashmallim) are described as glowing or amber ones, as they are clearly recognisable as angels who wield light. They preside over all the other angels and nations on Earth, but they rarely make themselves known to humans.

Their appearance is the closest to human – though they are meant to have a pair of feathered wings. They are freer than the higher triad of angels, so their service is voluntary. They help ruling bodies on Earth to govern with prudence and wisdom. Dominations are so named because of their control over their senses. They teach how to subdue dissolute desires and passions, through enslaving the flesh to the spirit, and how to rule one's will and be above temptation.

Various sources name different angels as the leader of this choir of angels – some name Raphael; others Zadkiel, Hasmael, Muriel or Zacharael.

Virtues

Called Virtues, Strongholds or Dynameis (which means forces in Greek), these angels work miracles, or convey the power to work miracles on those who deserve them. They also assist those who are overburdened by those they owe fealty to, apparently, and grant patience to those who ask for it. They also control the elements, nature, seasons and celestial bodies. Stars, planets and satellites, of course. What were you thinking?

Powers

The Powers (also known as Potentates, Authorities and Exousiai) get their name from the power they hold over the devil and demons. They can prevent demons from harming people, restrain their power, and assist those who wrestle with demons. They have the power to cast out evil and conquer the devil and his demons, too.

Led by Freyja, angels considered candidates for this choir are subject to extensive training before being selected for duty.

Principalities

Principalities (also called Archai) are a lesser form of Dominions – they, too, are responsible for maintaining order in the universe, but they convey orders from Dominions to angels and archangels, as well as carrying these out themselves. They are assigned to groups of people to help them choose good leaders and to individual leaders, in order to assist them in good government.

Archangels

Archangels are heralds and they are allowed to reveal knowledge, prophecies and a deeper understanding of the higher authorities' will. These angels frequently appear in religious texts, as they interact with humans and enlighten a select few. Gabriel, Michael, Uriel and Raphael are described as archangels.

Angels

While all those in the nine choirs of angels are angels, those in this lowest choir are just angels – angels of no higher rank than that of an angel (sometimes called Malakhim). These angels have the most frequent contact with individual humans and are always with them. They are guardian angels, angels who escort souls to judgement and Grigori or watchers, who observe humans – just to mention a few roles these angels play.

Hell

Hell is also known as the Pit, the Inferno, a place where damned souls go after they die and they don't come out. It's run by demons, devils and Lucifer. It has nine circles, plus a vestibule and a pool, specially designed for Satan himself.

Before humans were allowed into Heaven when they died, their souls were sent to the Underworld, consisting of Tartarus and the Elysian Fields. The Underworld eventually became far too crowded and a new solution was needed, which included Heaven and Hell.

The Gates of Hell

Hell's gate appears to be simply a cave entrance, with the following description over the arched portal:

Through me you pass into the city of woe
Through me you pass into eternal pain

Through me you pass among the lost.
Justice moved the founder of my fabric,
Divine power raised me
With the highest wisdom and primeval love
Before me, nothing but eternal things
Were created, and eternal I endure.
All hope abandons ye who enter here.

Hell's Vestibule

The vestibule of Hell – the bit just inside the portentous gate – is full of people who did nothing in their lives to warrant an afterlife in a specific place. They're not truly in Hell, nor anywhere else, either. Their punishment is to be plagued by stinging wasps and hornets, while their blood and tears are drunk by maggots and other insects. Plenty of suffering for a place that's not even Hell yet.

The Vestibule is separated from Hell proper by the Acheron River.

Acheron River

This river gets its own special mention, as the souls of the damned need to cross it in Charon's ferry to reach Hell proper. In Greco-Roman myth, Acheron was originally a god who got himself turned into a river by offering the wrong gods refreshment during battle.

First Circle of Hell

This circle is described as a lesser version of Heaven for unbelievers who have lived good lives – similar to the Greco-Roman Elysian Fields. It has a castle with gardens.

Second Circle of Hell

This one's reserved for those who've committed the sins of lust or adultery and their punishment is to live in a realm of constant storms. Strong winds, hail, heavy rain…blowing them around the way their passions did in life. Because of the constant storms, they know neither peace nor rest.

Third Circle of Hell

The third circle of Hell is for gluttons – those with addictive habits, be it food, drink or drugs. Their realm is one with continuous, icy rain, turning the ground into a constant, muddy slush. This is where Cerberus, the legendary three-headed dog lives.

Fourth Circle of Hell

This is where greedy people get sent. The guardian of this realm is Ploutus, the god of wealth. Souls sent to the fourth circle of Hell spend their time fighting each other with great weights, pushing either the weights or each other with their chests, much like a pack of aggressive elephant seals.

Fifth Circle of Hell

Angry and sullen souls end up in the fifth circle of Hell, which is in the swampy River Styx. The angry ones fight each other on the surface, while the sullen ones gurgle on the riverbed.

The River Styx guards the walls of the underworld city of Dis, which contains the deeper, darker circles of Hell.

City of Dis

Dis is a walled underworld city, surrounded by the River Styx. Guarded by fallen angels, the city gates can only be opened by an angel.

Sixth Circle of Hell

The sixth circle of Hell is for heretics, whose fate is to buried in flaming tombs, burning for eternity.

Seventh Circle of Hell

This one's for violent criminals, divided into three circles, each of which has differing levels of punishment. Those in the outer circle are submerged in a river of boiling blood and fire. The depth they're submerged is dependent on their crime – and there are centaur archers patrolling the outside of the circle, ready to fire arrows at anyone who tries to get out of the river. Those in the middle circle are at the mercy of the harpies and whatever punishment the harpies conjure up. The inner circle is subject to burning rain falling from the sky in a desert of burning sand – and this includes usurers or anyone who lends money for interest.

Eighth Circle of Hell

A demon named Geryon presides over the eighth circle of Hell, which is divided into ten "bolgies" – each bolgia separated from the others by stony ditches with bridges between them. Punishments and crimes vary between each of the bolgies, but they include being forced to march while being whipped by demons; burial head-first in a rock; having their heads twisted around so they walk backwards; sitting in a lake of boiling pitch if you're a corrupt politician; being bitten by snakes and lizards if you're a thief; concealment in individual flames; repeated dismemberment by demons; and affliction with various diseases if you're an alchemist.

Ninth Circle of Hell

This circle is reserved for treachery. All the residents of the ninth circle are frozen in an icy lake. The depth they're frozen in depends on the extent of their crimes. This part of Hell really is frozen over.

Centre of Hell

The centre of Hell is where Lucifer lives in his own icy prison. If you make it there, he might give you a guided tour.

The Immortals
Who Inhabit
Heaven and Hell

Alecto

Alecto is one of the three Dirae. Alecto's name means endless or unceasing in anger.

Ananiel

Ananiel's name means rain of God and she's a fallen angel.

As one of the harpies in Level Seven in Hell, Ananiel's job is to mete out punishment to damned souls at the end of a whip, burning brand or other torture implement. Far from being a natural dominatrix like Lilith or Jezebeth, Ananiel prefers to be on the receiving end of such treatment, so she's frequently in trouble for turning the tables and allowing damned souls to enjoy themselves as they punish her instead.

In the HELL Corporation, Ana works in Human Resources, recruiting administrative staff for Lucifer to corrupt before using them as prostitutes in her illegal brothel in the HELL Corporation building's food court toilets. She has a deep, abiding hatred for Mel.

Acheron

Acheron is both a river in Hell and a man. It's also a river in the Epirus region of Greece, but this entry is only about the man and the infernal river Acheron.

Acheron was the son of Helios by Demeter, though some say his mother was Gaia. As he shares a mother with Persephone, this makes him Persephone's half-brother. When Zeus was fighting the Titans, Acheron offered the Titans a drink, which refreshed them and prolonged the fight. The angry, victorious Zeus cursed him, turning him into the river.

Now, Acheron crouches in the river in Hell that bears his name, lonely and forgotten, as no one can see through Hell's illusions to the man in the water.

Asmodeus

Rumour has it that Asmodeus is the son of the angel of prostitution, Naamah, and Adam, the first human man, so it may come as no surprise that he's the demon of lust. He's also responsible for inciting gambling and most of the gambling in Hell is overseen by him.

He once fell in love with a woman named Sara, murdering her husbands until the archangel Raphael chased him away from her and back to Hell. His favourite pastime is tormenting newlyweds with all sorts of problems – both in the bedroom and in the rest of their lives.

In Hell, he guards the gates to the underworld city of Dis, along with Kasyade and Merihim. They generally play cards to pass the time. He once had a brief love affair with Lilith, before she grew bored.

In the HELL Corporation, he's known as Mo, the policy officer in the Brothel Regulation Unit who seems to always have to fill the printer with paper – a dangerous task in stationery shortages.

Baraqiel

A fallen angel and former Grigori whose name means lightning of God. He is reputed to have taught humans astrology in the time of Jared or Yered. He's possibly also the father of Hazael.

In the modern day, he was the first Chief Financial Officer at the HELL Corporation, because of his (self-reported) talent at financial predictions. When his talent proved to be losing money on bad investments, Lucifer sent him back to Hell in disgrace and didn't replace him. The HELL Corporation's financial standing improved immediately.

Beelzebub

A prince of demons known as Lord of the Flies, Beelzebub was originally a Philistine deity and oracle. There are rumours that he once successfully led a revolt of the forces of Hell against Lucifer, but this seems unlikely, as Beelzebub is one of the demons Lucifer often leaves in charge of Hell in his absence.

Not only is Beelzebub one of Lucifer's most senior demons, he's married to another, equally important demon — Mephistopheles, who calls him Bob. Occasionally, he acts as CEO to the HELL Corporation when Lucifer is called away on urgent business. He lacks Lucifer's long-term views on business strategy and makes some very short-sighted decisions as a result.

Belial

Once an angel, Belial is now one of Lucifer's most senior demons. With a name meaning without worth, Belial brings about both wickedness and guilt. In the HELL Corporation, he's known as Lial and he's the director of the state-run art school.

Camael

Samael and Camael are twin fallen angels whose names mean the blind God and one who sees God, respectively. People often confuse the two, because the brothers are identical. They were the angels of death before Lilith seduced the two brothers and they both fell together.

Cerberus

Cerberus is the giant, three-headed dog who guards the gates of Hell. Some accounts say he has more or less than three heads and others give him other roles, too. One particularly lovely description says he has three heads, a dragon's tail, a mane of snakes and the claws of a lion.

Apparently, he fawns over those entering Hell, but he'll attack anyone who tries to leave. The exception to this is Persephone, who he adores.

He seems to pop up in various places. Some say the mouth of the Acheron River; others the gates of Hell and Dante places him as the overlord of the third level of Hell, where the gluttonous and greedy writhe in their own filth. When Mel encounters him on Level Three, all three heads are hungry because the lazy demons who feed him have been slack. She takes pity on the poor, mutated puppy and gives him a snack fresh from the butcher.

Charon

Charon is the cloaked ferryman in Hades who ferries newly dead souls over the River Acheron and possibly the River Styx to the underworld. He requires payment, in the form of a coin that was placed in the dead body's mouth after death.

He's described in various sources as being an old man with a long beard and poor hygiene.

In Dante's *Divine Comedy*, he's said to beat slow-moving souls with his oar to get them into his boat.

When he sees Mel, he refuses to carry her across the river – and he's even more emphatic in his refusal when he recognises her.

Chiron

Chiron is a centaur – half-man and half-horse – but he's unlike the others of his kind. This might be because he was the son of the nymph Philyra and Kronos, who transformed himself into a horse so his wife wouldn't recognise him while he was busy with Philyra. Other centaurs are the children of King Ixion and the cloud nymph Nephele.

Considered very wise and just, Chiron was a teacher and mentor to many mythical heroes, including Jason, Hercules, Peleus, Asclepius, Patroclus and Achilles.

He died after being accidentally struck by one of Hercules' hydra-poisoned arrows.

Chiron is the leader of the centaurs in Hell, where they patrol the banks of the River Phlegethon in Level Seven, firing arrows at any of the violent souls who attempt to leave the river of fire and blood.

Cresil

Cresil is known as Sil in the HELL Corporation, where she works in the Human Resources department, conducting orientation and training for new staff. Cresil is a demon of impurity and laziness.

Demeter

Demeter is known in Greco-Roman mythology as the goddess of agriculture, fertility and the harvest. She had several children by different fathers, including Ploutos, Acheron and Persephone. While it's believed that Persephone's father was Zeus, Demeter will only say that Persephone's father was built like a Greek god, but about as useless in bed as one of his statues. She's Mel's cousin.

One of the Dynameis, Demeter is responsible for agriculture and the conditions required to ensure its sustainability – though this is not always what humans would prefer, as droughts, floods and other weather variabilities still occur under her care.

Dirae

The Dirae are also known as the Furies or the Erinyes. They're the three daughters of Uranus and Gaia – Megaera, Alecto and Tisiphone. The furies are the bat-winged spirits of vengeance and they guard the gates of Dis, the city of the underworld. As well as administering punishment to those in Level Six in Hell, they take new souls down to the lower levels when they're delivered to the gates of Dis.

These three are so implacable in their fury that most called them the Eumenides (soothed ones) or Semnai Theai (honourable goddesses) so as not to incur their wrath.

Freyja

Freyja is a goddess in Norse mythology. She chooses which souls may be suitable to be trained as Powers or Exousiai – so called for their power to banish demons. After they are trained, she selects which warrior souls are worthy of fighting demons on Earth in the present day and at the apocalypse.

Gabrielle

Gabriel (or Gabrielle, also called Jibra'il) can be either male or female. This angel's name means both man of God and God is mighty. She chooses to be female at the time of Mel Goes to Hell.

As an archangel, Gabriel is responsible for delivering messages from Heaven to individual humans. Some of the more notable people who received these messages were Daniel in the Book of Daniel; the Prophet Mohammad in the Qur'an; Mary, Jesus' mother, and Zacharias, John the Baptist's father. Because of Gabriel's important role as a messenger, he's considered to be the patron saint of communications workers.

Gabriel is the archangel who first appeared to the Prophet Mohammad and revealed the scriptures of the Qur'an to him.

At the beginning of the Mel Goes to Hell series, Gabi is working with the archangel Uriel, her partner, in Russia. As the situation in the HELL Corporation heats up, Raphael summons her to Perth to help Mel out in the office – and to positively identify Lucifer. Being the patron saint of communications workers, she's ideal for the position of temporary receptionist and switchboard operator.

Gabrielle is a very traditional angel, who believes that demons are damned and should be shunned at all costs. You can't trust them not to taint anything – including the office coffee machine.

A fan of sweet, iced, frothy coffee, Gabi makes it her mission to keep Mel out of Lucifer's clutches, enlisting the help of some well-built Grigori angels in the Agency – though Mel has already made her own plans.

George

Saint George was born in the third century AD in Cappadocia, which is modern-day Turkey. Following the death of his father, he became a soldier in the army of the Roman Emperor Diocletian. He rose to the rank of Tribune, but he objected to the Emperor's campaign of persecution of Christians.

In punishment, he was imprisoned, tortured and dragged through the streets of Diospolis (present-day Lodd) or Nicomedia (present-day Izmit) before he was beheaded. Understandably, he's a bit hazy on the details of which city it was.

He's most famous for his defeat of a dragon. This dragon lived in a lake outside the city of Silene in Libya, where it terrorised the city and the surrounding countryside. The people of Silene appeased it by sacrificing sheep and then its own people. The human sacrifices were chosen by lot and one day the lot chose the king's unmarried daughter.

George approached the gates of the city and noticed the princess, who exhorted him to leave before the dragon attacked him. Instead, he battled the dragon and had the princess lead the dragon into the city, where he killed it.

The story of Saint George and the dragon first appeared in the 13th century in England, suggesting that this may have occurred as a miracle after his death and not during his life.

As an angel, Saint George is one of leaders among the Exousiai, warrior angels whose sole purpose is to battle and banish demons.

Geryon

Geryon was the grandson of Medusa, but he quietly kept red cattle on the island of Erytheia with the help of Cerberus' two-headed dog brother, Orthrus. That is, until Hercules came to fulfil his tenth labour, by stealing Geryon's cattle. Hercules clubbed Orthrus, the watchdog, then Eurytion, Geryon's herdsman, so Geryon donned his armour and attacked Hercules. Hercules was the victor – Geryon died with a poison-tipped arrow in his forehead.

Geryon is the guardian of the eighth level of Hell, where some of the worst sinners are sent. His demonic form has a human face, lion's paws and a wyvern's body, complete with leathery wings, and a tail with a venomous tip. He lives in the caves in the cliffs between Level Seven and Level Eight in Hell with his wife, the harpy Jezebeth.

In the HELL Corporation, he's known as Gerry and he reports to Merihim in the Health Unit. He's particularly partial to a bit of bondage and discipline with his wife, Jezebeth, when he dons his mankini and she pulls out the flogger.

Grigori

Grigori are in the lowest choir of angels. With no wings and no higher rank than that of an angel, they are still very important. These angels are Watchers, watching humans and occasionally stepping in to assist them.

Some of the first Grigori fell when they went native, taking human wives and siring children with them. These half-angel children are known as Nephilim.

Working as a Grigori does have its risks because they work so closely with humans and forming close, personal relationships is very easy to do.

Hades

Known as the Greek god of the Underworld, Hades was Lord of the Underworld when Lucifer was still an angel. Neither an angel or a demon, he feels he's been hard done by in ruling over the dead and not the living. His main interest is in increasing his subjects. His weapon is a bident, much like Lucifer's.

When Persephone was very young, Hades abducted her from her mother, Demeter, ostensibly so that the girl could become his wife. Demeter went to great lengths to rescue her daughter from Hades, enlisting the favours of several other immortals before the girl was freed.

Harpies

Level Seven in Hell is where harpies are allowed to punish the damned as they see fit. Having spent some time up in the HELL Corporation offices, indulging their tastes for dark erotica, Lilith, Jezebeth and Ananiel have remodelled their level to look more like a modern-day BDSM dungeon. Taking inspiration from this genre of books, these ladies are dark, dirty and definitely in control.

Homusubi

Homusubi, whose name is made up of the kanji symbols for to shine and force or power, is known in Japanese culture as the god of fire.

He's one of the Dynameis, the choir of angels who take care of the elements, and he's responsible for the volcanoes on the western side of the Pacific Ring of Fire.

Imps

Imps are a race of small, demon-like beings who were resident in Hell before Lucifer got there. Led by an imp named Sptlk, they specialise in creating illusions so realistic, they can even fool angels and demons.

Lucifer has an arrangement with them for their assistance in running some of the lesser punishment levels of Hell, as their illusions reduce the number of staff and the power required to exact punishment on the souls confined to the first four circles of Hell. The imps' voyeuristic tastes are reflected in the payment they receive from Lucifer for their services – he allows them to watch his conquests.

Jehanette

Known to most modern readers as Saint Joan of Arc, the patron saint of soldiers and France, the girl's name in her own time was Jehanette.

Born in 1412, Jehanette grew up in the village of Domremy in Champagne, France. From an early age, she was visited by Saint Michael, Saint Catherine and Saint Margaret, but it wasn't until 1428 that they instructed her to go to the aid of King Charles VII of France (then known as the Dauphin, as he hadn't yet been crowned) and assist him to take back his kingdom from King Charles of England.

She earned the name of the Maid of Orleans after she led a small army to lift the siege at Orleans in 1429. Following several more victories, she stood at Charles VII's side at his coronation in Reims.

Taken prisoner by the English during a battle at Compiègne, she was imprisoned in Rouen. Following several months of imprisonment, Jehanette was tried for heresy and condemned to death in 1431. The next day, she was burned at the stake.

In the present day, she is a messenger angel (Malakhim) who assists Saint Michael the Archangel.

Jezebeth

Jezebeth is a demon of falsehood and lies, which is why she naturally excels at public relations and graphic design in the HELL Corporation. Except for the unfortunate James Pond campaign, which brought Mel to Lucifer's attention.

She's particularly skilled at possession and she prefers to take over humans when they're at the peak of fury. Naturally, that makes her perfect for her role as a harpy who tortures damned souls in Level Seven.

As the wife of Geryon, she takes her dominatrix role seriously – both at work and at home.

Kasyade

Kasyade is one of the fallen angels guarding the gates of Dis and he often passes the time by playing poker with Merihim and Asmodeus, the other fallen angels on guard duty.

Kasyade means both observer of the hands and covered or concealed hand or power. So while he's the dealer and generally the one who watches his fellow poker players for untoward behaviour, he's definitely demonic in cheating whenever no one else is looking.

Koyane

Ame No Koyane No Mikoto, known in the present day as Koyane, is one of the kami or deities of the Shinto religion in Japan. He's one of the four kamis of the Kasuga shrine in Nara, and he may have human descendants.

One of the Hashmallim, he's the angel who advises the Emperor of Japan and other leaders in eastern Asia.

Lilith

Lilith is the leader of the harpies in the seventh level of Hell and the demon of waste. When on Earth among humans, she amuses herself by searching for children to kidnap or kill.

In many religious sources, Eve (or Khavah in Hebrew) is supposedly the wife of Adam, who is described in Islamic, Christian and Jewish creation myths as the first man. Yet in early versions of the Jewish Talmud, Eve is Adam's second wife. The story runs that Adam was created from clay alongside Lilith – his first wife.

Like a far more modern woman, when Adam decided he was superior to his wife, Lilith told him to get stuffed. She wasn't the submissive sort. Then she left him for Lucifer. Though both she and Lucifer corrupt many lovers as the desire takes them, she still considers the Lord of Hell her personal property.

Lilith is Lucifer's mistress and one of the senior demons in Hell, which naturally entitles her to be one of the senior managers in the HELL Corporation. She's also Mel's boss, inventing odd tasks to make Mel's work day Hell and deriving considerable enjoyment from it.

What neither of them counted on was that Mel and Lili, as she's known in the office, look similar — making Mel very much Lucifer's type. As he's had Lili for millennia, his eye is most certainly caught by the fresh-faced angel.

Lucifer

The mythical figure commonly known as the devil and the prince or lord of Hell has many names. The most common ones are Lucifer, Iblis and Satan (also spelled Shaitan or Shaytan).

Lucifer's name means lots of things:

- light of the morning
- morning star
- son of the morning
- daystar
- shining one
- son of the dawn
- light-bringing

None of these meanings match the concept of a dark, demonic figure and that's because, according to various religious sources, Lucifer was a Seraphim – one of the highest choirs of angels. He was reputedly as close to perfect as an angel could be:

"…the seal of perfection, full of wisdom and perfect in beauty." – Ezekiel, 28:13

He is believed to have fallen from his exalted position through pride. Christian Biblical sources indicate he wished to be worshipped as a god and Heaven objected to this. He was thrown out of Heaven by the archangel Michael, which was a calculated insult, as archangels are a much lower choir of angels than the Seraphim. According to Saint Jerome, the name Lucifer is what the devil laments losing in his fall from Heaven.

Jewish sources suggest he was cast out of Heaven because he was envious of Adam, the first human man. Adam had been granted dominion over Earth and Lucifer refused to bow in homage to the man.

In Islam, the Qur'an indicates that Iblis, as he is known, was banished from Heaven because he wouldn't bow before Adam. Iblis isn't confined to Hell in Islam – instead, he spends his time tempting human beings away from the true path of their religion, thereby condemning the erring humans to Hell.

Aside from his supposed perfection and six wings that marked him as a Seraphim, Lucifer is described as being able to change his form and appearance. He's reputed to be able to appear as a snake, a dragon, a cormorant, an angel with dark wings and a demon in various shapes.

He's portrayed in all of these forms in art throughout the ages – though few chose to show him in his initial perfection, preferring to give him one of his more bestial forms to match the dark soul within.

Christian sources suggest that he actively tries to subvert humans and win their souls through trickery so that they can worship him in Hell, as he's reputed to have tempted Jesus during his time on Earth. Some Christian works, like Dante's *Divine Comedy*, suggest that Lucifer is confined to Hell for eternity.

Conversely, Islamic sources indicate he only tempts humans to reveal their true nature, as he has no power over those who are true to their religion.

In the present day, Luce Iblis is the overbearing, alpha-male CEO of the HELL Corporation. A superb body, an apt mind and a penchant for power make him hard to resist, but he is a fallen angel and synonymous with evil in many religions. As a villain, he comes equipped with a fiery underground lair and myriad minions with a capacity for violence and pain.

Whether he's a villain or a possible hero who can win the angel he's set his sights on, though…only one thing is for certain: he's a sexy devil to watch out for.

Megaera

Megaera is one of the three Dirae. Megaera's name means grudging or jealous rage. In Hell, she's one of the guardians to the gates of Dis and she's responsible for torturing the inhabitants of Level Six.

Megaera not only works in Hell, but occasionally mans the reception desk for the HELL Corporation. She was the receptionist on the day of Mel's interview and grudged the angel everything from information to common politeness to a smile.

Meness

Meness, also called Menuo in Lithuanian, is known as a moon god in the Baltic region. His preferred mode of transport is a chariot pulled by grey horses. After a lengthy courtship, he married Saule, the Baltic sun goddess, but he was unfaithful to her with the morning star and punished accordingly.

Both Meness and Saule are Dynameis, angels responsible for the moon and sun, respectively.

Mephistopheles

Mephistopheles means doesn't love the light. This isn't entirely accurate, as Mephi's greatest desire for centuries has been a tropical beach holiday with her husband, Beelzebub. There's no love lost between her and Lucifer – she feels her husband has as much right to be Lord of Hell as Lucifer does, though she invariably rules the roost where her husband is concerned.

She's the demon who tempted Doctor Faustus and made a deal for his soul. It's made her a formidable personal assistant to Lucifer in the HELL Corporation, as she's the expert on legal contracts with humans. From occupational health and safety to sexual harassment in the workplace, Mephi knows what Lucifer can and can't get away with. But, Lucifer being the Lord of Lies, he manages to get away with it anyway.

Merihim

Merihim is the dark prince of pestilence, but in the HELL Corporation he's known as Merih, the manager of the Public Health Unit. He has a bit of a crush on Mel.

He's one of the fallen angels guarding the gates of Dis and he often passes the time by playing poker with Kasyade and Asmodeus, the other fallen angels on guard duty.

Michael

Saint Michael the Archangel is one of three archangels mentioned in the Christian Bible, together with Raphael and Gabriel. In the Qur'an, only two angels get mentioned – Michael and Gabriel.

Healer, protector and leader against the armies of Satan, Michael's name means he who is like God. He's described in Christian, Jewish and Islamic religious texts and he's believed to be the angel responsible for Satan's defeat and banishment from Heaven.

He's suggested to be the leader of the Seraphim, but also just the Archangel in charge of the lowest level of angels, those who have no other choir.

Michael is described in several sources as the rescuer of faithful souls. He's reputed to have stood guard over Moses' body and over Eve's body, too. He fought Samael (described in some sources as a fallen angel, who grabbed Michael's wings and tried to pull him down with him when he fell) for Moses' body.

In the Catholic faith, Michael has the interesting task of giving souls near death the chance to redeem themselves in their last hour. Seeing as he's usually in the right place at the right time, he also brings newly-dead souls to judgement at the gates of Heaven. This is consistent with his depiction as the leader of the lowest choir of angels, who fulfil similar roles in guiding souls to their final judgement.

Michael has a reputation as a heavenly physician. He's believed to have appeared to the Emperor Constantine at Sosthenion, south of Constantinople.

Egyptian Christians placed the Nile under his protection, as this river was so important in their lives.

Michael is frequently portrayed in religious art in armour and armed with a sword – sometimes with or without flames.

In Lucifer's war against Heaven, Michael was the leader of the armies who opposed him, as well as the one who personally dispatched Lucifer to Hell.

In the present day, Michael is an archangel – one of the guardians at Heaven's gate who stands in judgement over souls who wish to enter. Clad in armour and bearing a flaming sword, he makes quite an impressive guard. Since he banished Lucifer, he stands guard to make sure the fallen angel doesn't return to Heaven.

However, there is another side to Michael. He's Melody Angel's younger brother – and he's very protective of his sister. He and Raphael met as brothers in arms during the Heavenly War against Lucifer and it's hard to say who's more important to him – Raphael or Mel. Both he and Raphael are united in their mission to protect Mel at all costs.

Minos

As Saint Peter is believed to judge souls at the gates of Heaven, so Minos is the man who hands out accommodation assignments in Hell.

Minos was a legendary king who appears in many stories involving other, equally mythical characters. There are so many of them that there may have been more than one man with that name, so archaeologists are uncertain whether Minos was really a name or the title of the king – but the Minoan civilisation was named after Minos by an early 20th century archaeologist, Sir Arthur Evans.

Around 4000 years ago, the decentralised cultures on Crete formed a new political system, headed by a single person – their king. Large palaces were constructed, which were for administrative and storage purposes as well as living spaces. Roads were built between their cultural centres, which exhibited set class structures…and the beginnings of an established bureaucracy.

This king – the legendary Minos – brought about peace, prosperity and the political system that supported it. His navy was the first of its kind in the ancient world – or at least the first documented navy. To put this into perspective, this was before the Trojan War.

Minos' kingdom was modern-day Crete and there are still ruins from his reign dotted around the island. The earliest known buildings from the Minoan civilisation are around 4000 years old. For around 500 years, the Minoan civilisation was one of the most advanced of its time, as evident by its art, written language, functional indoor plumbing and structures that have withstood centuries.

Minoan cities were open to the sea and their pottery has been found throughout the Mediterranean, indicating that they traded far and wide, presumably by sea. Minos lived in Knossos, the largest Minoan city, where he was reputed to hear leadership advice from Zeus. This he translated into legislation and a complete constitution for Crete.

To reward him for his good judgement throughout his life, Minos was made the judge of the dead in the Underworld, possibly with his two brothers. According to Virgil, he decided who went to Elysium or Tartarus.

In Dante's epic Christian poem, *The Divine Comedy*, Minos judges souls in Hell. He has a very long, serpentine tail which he uses to indicate the level number the damned soul belongs to. He'd wrap his tail around himself the same number of times as the level number.

Minos in Hell is every bit the retired, wise ruler, whose wisdom was derived from divine advice. Seeing as divine advice to rulers is definitely Mel's speciality, who better to have been his advisor? So when he sees Mel again after thousands of years, he doesn't recognise the young, modern woman…but he's never forgotten the angel who taught him how to rule.

Like many of Hell's denizens who date back to the time when all human souls were confined to the Underworld, Minos is neither demon nor damned – his immortal soul has taken on the job of judgement. Though he's kept very busy, he does find time to leave Hell on occasion. When he does, he meets up with Saint Peter and Saint Michael the Archangel, both colleagues in their roles as final judges of human souls, and the three find a quiet spot to enjoy a barley beer or six.

Some of the Greek legends surrounding Minos are far from the benevolent ruler who united the communities on the island of Crete, which suggests that there was more than one Minos…or the man was both brilliant and a complete nutter. Ancient historians like Plutarch support the theory that the benevolent Minos was the ruler who started a navy and wrote the laws; but that the original Minos' grandson gave rise to some of the more colourful legends of the time. The following legends pertain to Minos' grandson, who is presently one of the denizens in Hell.

Minos was the stepfather of the Minotaur. The sea god, Poseidon, was angry that Minos hadn't sacrificed a bull to him, so he made Minos' wife, Pasiphae (the daughter of the sun god, Helios), fall in love with the bull. With some help from Daedalus, she managed to somehow seduce the bull and conceive a child – the half-man, half bull known as the Minotaur – the Bull of Minos.

Minos didn't like the Minotaur much, so he ordered Daedalus to build a palace to hide the creature. The result was the Labyrinth. A less than grateful ruler, Minos then imprisoned both Daedalus and his son, Icarus, so they couldn't tell anyone else how to get through the Labyrinth.

One of Minos' sons, Androgeos, attended the athletic games held by King Aegeas of Athens. He was so successful at the events that the local competitors conspired to murder him. When word of his death reached Minos, King Minos declared war on Athens.

On the way to Athens, Minos besieged the coastal city of Megara. Megara's king, Nisus, had an unusual gift: as long as he retained a lock of red hair, which he hid under the rest of his white hair, his city would be safe.

Minos seduced his daughter, Scylla, who cut off her father's lock of red hair so she could offer it to Minos. Her father died, Megara fell…and charming Minos drowned the treacherous Scylla.

Minos did reach Athens and he conquered it, too. He required that Athens send him seven of their best young men and women every 7-9 years (sources are a little hazy on precisely how many years), which he then sacrificed to the Minotaur.

On the third such sacrifice, Theseus volunteered to go. With the assistance of one of Minos' daughters, Ariadne, and a ball of string, Theseus found the Minotaur and killed it, thus ending the slaughter of Athenian children.

Daedalus and his son escaped from their prison by creating wings from feathers and wax. Icarus flew too close to the sun, so his wings melted and he drowned, but Daedalus made it to the mainland and into hiding. Minos set off to search for him and found him in Sicily. With the help of King Cocalus of Sicily and his daughters, Daedalus managed to kill Minos…by scalding him to death with boiling water while he was in the bath.

Muriel

Her name means perfume of God and the myrrh tree was named for her. Unusually, Muriel is an angel who appears female, while most others are male or androgynous in form.

Very little is known about this angel, except that she is one of the Hashmallim. Some accounts place her as the leader of that choir.

Nessos

Nessos is a centaur who used to ferry people across the Euenos River on his back. One day, his passenger was Hercules' wife, Deianeira. During their short ride, Nessos decided he wanted a ride of a different sort and attempted to rape Deianeira while Hercules was still on the opposite bank of the river.

Hercules shot Nessos in the heart with a hydra-poisoned arrow. As the centaur lay dying, he told Deianeira that his blood was a powerful love charm that would ensure that Hercules remained faithful to her. She took some of his blood and later stained one of Hercules' shirts with it. When Hercules wore the poisoned shirt, it burned him to death.

Nessos is now the ferryman for the River Phlegethon in the seventh level of Hell and he hasn't lost his taste for personal payment from his female passengers.

Nybbas

Nybbas is a demon whose speciality is visions and dreams, but he's a charlatan and a fool. He's said to be able to create anything he can dream about.

This may be why he's in charge of IT at the HELL Corporation – and he's the main liaison to the imps, a race of winged, demon-like beings who create illusions so realistic they even fool angels and demons. He's reputed to have been instrumental in the start of the Thai adult film industry (though he hasn't said how) and his public speaking skills are comical at best.

He has something of a crush on Mel.

Patrick

Man or myth? Did Saint Patrick really banish snakes from Ireland?

Saint Patrick most certainly did exist. Some of the documents he wrote (or copies of the originals) have survived more than 1500 years to the present day.

While Patrick spent most of his life in Ireland, Patrick wasn't born there. He was born around the year 385 in Kilpatrick in Scotland. He wasn't Scottish, either – his parents, Calpurnius and Conchessa, were Romans tasked with taking care of the Roman colony of Britannia. His father, Calpurnius, was a deacon and his grandfather was Potitus, the priest of Banna Venta Berniae (a town believed to have been near modern-day Carlisle).

When he was a teenager, an Irish raiding party captured him and took him home with them. In Ireland, he was a slave shepherd until he was twenty.

He escaped and took ship for home in Scotland, but he was persuaded to return to Ireland – to convert its people to Christianity.

He didn't go right away – he studied to be a priest instead. It wasn't until 433, when he was ordained as a bishop, that Patrick returned to Ireland. He spent more than thirty years of his life in Ireland, where he died on 17 March 461.

There are several tales about how Saint Patrick rid Ireland of snakes. Some say that snakes attacked him while he was fasting and praying, while others state that his beloved wife was bitten by a snake. Either way, he took a distinct dislike to the creatures, so legend says he drove them into the sea.

Actually, no human intervention was required to rid Ireland of snakes – as a combination of ice and sea water is responsible for that. In the last Ice Age, which ended around 10,000 years ago, Ireland was too cold for snakes to survive there and by the time it was warm enough to be hospitable, the sea level had risen, isolating the island from anywhere snakes might migrate from.

Ireland isn't the only island that doesn't have snakes – New Zealand, Antarctica, Iceland and Greenland don't have any snakes, either. This might account for Patrick's preference for Ireland – he has a healthy fear of snakes.

In the present day, the saint has become one of the Hashmallim – the first human-born soul to do so. His area of responsibility is the leaders of the UK and Europe, which is mostly where he spends his time. He's an old friend of Mel's and has worked closely with her many times over the centuries when she gets involved in European politics.

Persephone

Demeter's daughter, known as Persephone, Proserpine, Kore or Kora, prefers that her close friends call her Persi.

Abducted by Hades when she was very young, to be forced into a marriage she didn't want, Persi's had a tumultuous life which has left her less than angelic.

She's fond of ink and has a particularly detailed tattoo inspired by a Luca Signorelli painting in Orvieto Cathedral in Italy.

As Demeter's daughter, she's also Mel's cousin and Persephone looks up to Mel as friend, confidante and authority figure. Persi aspires to be angelic, but her penchant for bad boys and other Earthly delights get her into trouble more often than most.

Peter

Saint Peter, also known as Simon Peter and Cephas, was both a fisherman and one of the twelve apostles of Jesus Christ, the leaders of the early Christian church. Along with Saint Paul, he's believed to be one of the founders of the See of Rome of the Catholic Church.

He died in Rome during the reign of the Emperor Nero, crucified upside down on a cross on the Vatican Hill, where he was later buried. St Peter's Basilica was built on top of his grave, or where his grave was believed to be.

Since his death, the saint's soul stands in judgement at the gates of Heaven. With the Book of Judgement, he weighs whether souls may enter Heaven or not. Up until recently, he's only stood in judgement over human souls and when demons attempt to enter Heaven, he defers to a higher authority like Saint Michael the Archangel.

Philatanus

Philatanus, known as Phil in the HELL Corporation, is the demon who assists Belial in sodomy. As the two men are lovers, they tend to focus on each other more than tormenting unwilling humans.

When he's working, Philatanus is the director of the HELL Corporation's Research Division.

Phlegyas

Originally the King of the Lapiths, Phlegyas was the son of Ares and Chryse. His daughter, Coronis, was one of Apollo's lovers. When she was pregnant with Apollo's son, Asclepius, she fell in love with someone else – Elatus' son, Ischys. Apollo was so angry at Coronis that he sent his sister, Artemis, to kill the girl – but the baby survived, to be brought up by the centaur Chiron.

Phlegyas responded by torching the Temple of Apollo at Delphi, so Apollo killed him, too.

Phlegyas is in charge of the fifth level of Hell, where those who committed the sin of wroth endlessly battle it out with each other in the swampy River Styx. He has a boat and occasionally ferries souls across the river, but at their peril.

His particular enemy in Hell is Megaera, one of the three Dirae, who imprisoned him in a rock where he could see an eternal feast, but never eat any of it.

Ploutos

Ploutos was the Greek god of wealth – not to be confused with Pluto, otherwise known as Hades, the Lord of the Underworld. Ploutos was Demeter's son by Iasion, conceived when the couple were attending a wedding. He's tasked with distributing wealth, which is why he's often pictured with a cornucopia, but some accounts state that he's blind, because he distributes wealth so blindly.

Ploutos is responsible for maintaining order in Level Four of Hell, where the greedy are punished. He continues to distribute wealth by managing the gambling in Hell – betting on which of the greedy souls will win their bout of fighting.

He's Persephone's half-brother and particularly fond of cats.

Raphael

He healed a blind man, saved a woman from the devil, buried a demon in the desert…Raphael heals and likes hot places.

Recognised in the Bible, Torah and Qur'an (where he's known as Israfel) as an archangel, very little is known about Raphael.

Some sources say that he's on the same level as Michael, Gabriel and four other archangels in the angelic hierarchy, where archangel can be either one of the lower tiers of angels or simply a title for the leaders of each of the tiers.

Raphael has been described as the leader of the Hashmallim, the choir of angels who have domination over Earth and the rest of the universe. If that's true, he's a bloke with huge responsibilities.

The Book of Tobit in the Bible describes how Raphael disguised himself as a human and escorted a young man named Tobias from his father's house in Nineveh to Media and home again.

During his journey to Media, Raphael and Tobias stopped at the Tigris River to wash. Like something worthy of *Crocodile Dundee* or *Jaws*, a large fish attacked Tobias from the river. Tobias cried out for help, but Raphael told him to catch the fish instead. The two ate part of the fish for dinner and retained the rest for its demon-banishing and healing qualities.

After catching the fish, Raphael and Tobias arrived at the settlement of a man named Raguel. Raguel's daughter, Sara, had quite a serious problem – she'd been betrothed to seven men, yet each man was killed by demons on their wedding night. Raphael persuaded Tobias to ask to marry the girl and gave him advice on how to survive the wedding night. Tobias had to pray for the first three days of his marriage; burn the fish's liver to keep the demon away; spend a night with the girl under the observation of some holy patriarchs; wait for a blessing…and think of nothing but children during the consummation of his marriage, on the fourth day. Evidently she wasn't the dinner, chocolate and flowers sort.

When Tobias burned the fish liver, it drove away a demon called Asmodeus. Raphael pursued the demon into the deserts of Upper Egypt. According to the Book of Enoch, Raphael bound the demon hand and foot and cast him into the darkness, beneath rough and jagged rocks, where the demon wouldn't see light until the end of the world – when the light would be a fire to devour him.

On their return to Nineveh and Tobias' blind father, Raphael told Tobias to rub the fish gall on his father's eyes to allow the man to see again. This treatment worked.

Some texts state that Raphael revealed his identity before he left the family, while others say he kept it secret.

Raphael is the Director of the Helpful Angels Agency, the temp agency Mel works for. His relationship with Mel is quite complex – they're not simply a boss and employee. He pops in to her house unannounced for dinner, worries about her (especially when Lucifer starts paying an increasing amount of attention to her) and he definitely owes her a favour for helping him out in the HELL Corporation.

He has good taste in clothes, food, wine and beer, but as a Domination, he doesn't let his passions and pleasures rule him. He spends some of his time on Earth, but takes regular trips back up to Heaven.

Samael

Samael and Camael are twin fallen angels whose names mean the blind God and one who sees God, respectively. People often confuse the two, because the brothers are identical. They were the angels of death before Lilith seduced the two brothers and they both fell together.

Sarkis

Saint Sarkis was a military commander who lived in the fourth century AD. Born in Cappadocia, Sarkis was an Armenian who was appointed as Roman Emperor Constantine's general in charge of the Roman troops of Cappadocia.

When Constantine was succeeded by his nephew Julian, Sarkis objected to the new emperor's persecution of Christians and left Cappadocia to command the armies of the Sassanid Empire instead. When Sarkis destroyed a Zoroastrian temple, Shapur, the Sassanid Emperor, retaliated by killing Sarkis' son, Mardiros. Sarkis was then imprisoned and executed.

Saint Sarkis is the patron saint of Armenia and young people.

In the present day, the saint was recruited to the Exousiai to fight demons alongside Saint George and other warrior angels.

Saule

Saule is the Baltic sun goddess and her duties include the wellbeing and regeneration of all life on Earth, through taking care of the sun – quite a responsibility, but as one of the angels in the choir of Dynameis, she can certainly handle it.

Her preferred mode of transport is a chariot with copper wheels and at the end of each day, she retires to a castle to watch the setting sun as she lets her horses play in the sea.

She married Meness, the Dynameis responsible for the moon, but he betrayed her with the morning star.

Saule likes to attend midsummer festivals or those at the summer solstice, where she dances in silver shoes. She's particularly fond of green snakes.

Tisiphone

Tisphone is one of the three Dirae. Tisiphone's name means punishment, vengeful destruction or avenger of murder.

Turiel

Turiel is a fallen angel whose name means rock of God or mountain of God. His name is on a counterfeit magic manuscript, the Secret Grimoire of Turiel, which is plagiarised from other historical magic books in the middle of the twentieth century.

In the HELL Corporation, he's the demon responsible for intellectual property and copyright, given his experience in plagiarism.

Uriel

Uriel is an archangel who is bonded to Gabrielle.

Author's Note

Readers of my Mel Goes to Hell series have often asked for a guide to the angels and demons contained within the pages. There are so many of them and each have their own story, often outside the pages of Mel's books. *Melody Angel's Guide to Heaven and Hell* is that guide.

Another question I hear frequently from my readers is, "When is your next book out?"

The good news is the next book in this series is out now.

So if you'd like a taste…read on for THREE bonus chapters from *To Hell and Back*, the fourth book in the Mel Goes to Hell series.

"You're coming with me, Luce. We'll return to HELL together."

Luce watched the chainmail-clad girl clink off. Armour on a guy just looks old-fashioned, but on a woman…it made him feel a bit nostalgic. If Mel had fought in the Heavenly Battle all those centuries ago dressed in mail like that one…Hell, he'd have fallen to his knees and begged to surrender to her. Maybe if he hinted to Mel, she'd consider…

"Just think – you'll get to wear pants again."

Pants. Damn. That meant no fooling around. At least, not yet.

"Any chance you'll let me lose the pants later?" he asked eagerly.

"Luce."

"It looks just like we left it," Luce said, looking around as he headed for the bedroom. He stumbled over a shoe and kicked it away, swearing. "Who left all these here, where I could trip over them?"

"They're yours, Luce. You were wearing them when you kicked the juvenile swan and earned yourself a nasty nip, back at the office Christmas party," Mel replied, stepping daintily over the obstacles as she made her way to the kitchen. "Would you like some tea? I find it always helps ground me when I've been without a body for a while."

"Sure," Luce said, grinning. "Boil the kettle. I've been thinking about your body all week and I have some ideas I'd like to try out." He pulled out a dining chair and sat down, patting his lap. "We could get started while the water heats up. Maybe heat things up a little more."

Mel laughed, crossing the kitchen to fill the kettle. She clicked it on, returned to Luce, and lowered herself onto his lap, crossing her wrists behind his neck. "I have some ideas, too," she murmured, drawing him in closer for a kiss.

His hands caressed her back through the silk of her dress and his arms tightened around her as she slipped her tongue between his lips. Mel could feel the love spilling out of his soul and hoped he could feel the same from hers. So many centuries of soul-reading without revealing her presence…but she was learning to let Luce sense her.

Her body betrayed her thoughts, making Luce break the kiss to whisper, "You're too tense, Mel. Don't think about it. Only share what you want to. Your body is expressive enough for me to read plenty from you, without you needing to share your whole soul. Humans manage love like this just fine." He chuckled. "Focus on my body for once and not my soul. I made sure it was perfect for you, Mel. I promise you'll enjoy it." He pressed his lips to the side of her neck, trailing kisses down to the neckline of her dress.

Mel tipped her head back, closing her eyes as he kissed her breasts – or what little he could reach without her taking her clothes off. "Luce, I'd like to…"

"So would I," he said, returning to her lips. He deepened the kiss, tightening his hold on her as if he'd never, ever let her go.

A new and distinctly annoyed voice rang out, killing the moment. "Kissing demons is disgusting, Mel. I didn't believe you'd ever…"

"If the lady will let me, I'll show you just how wrong you are," Luce offered instantly.

"No, Luce, that's not…" Mel pulled away from him. "Raphael, you should really knock first. You could have saved yourself from seeing things you don't like. You'd best remember to be polite to my guest, too – Luce is an angel, the same as you. Definitely not a demon any more."

"Fine. Former demon, then. You look like you're about to…sleep with him! Ex-demon or not, I wouldn't have thought you'd stoop so low as to…"

"Low is condemning an innocent man to Hell, Raphael," Mel said coldly. "What Luce and I do is really none of your business, nor your concern. Why are you here? If you've only come to lecture me on going to Hell and bringing Luce home with me, you may leave." Gracefully, she rose from Luce's lap and headed for the kitchen, smoothing her dress down along the way.

"I came here to tell you about Persi and the mess she's left us in. It has nothing to do with him." Raphael glared at Luce. "He's the one you should ask to leave."

Mel spooned tea into her teapot. "Luce is my guest and he's free to leave whenever he wishes, but he's here at my invitation now. My love, I think you should stay to hear what Raphael has to say."

"Why?" Raphael spat.

Mel poured a steady stream of hot water over the mixture of leaves and flowers. "Because I need Luce to help me clean up Persi's mess. He's going to return to his old job as CEO of the HELL Corporation."

"WHAT?" the two men shouted together.

Luce recovered first from his shock. "Only if you're working there, too. I'm not going back to HELL without a small slice of Heaven. You can have the office across from mine and I'll make you coffee every morning."

Mel's smile lit up her whole face. "That sounds lovely. Of course I will, Luce."

Mel carried her cup of tea to the armchair by the window and settled into the well-padded cushions. Luce clunked his cup on the coffee table and sprawled across the sofa, leaving Raphael the other armchair. He watched in fascination as the archangel dragged one of the dining chairs over and parked his backside on that instead. He sat stiff and silent, making Luce wonder if he was going to say anything at all or if he was just wasting their time.

"Raphael, didn't you come here to tell me about

Persi?" Mel asked. "I mean, do you know who the last person was to see her before she disappeared?"

"Me," he said hoarsely, then cleared his throat. "Me. I was the last one to see her. We were discussing the dismantling of the demon corporation and their banishment back to Hell. Persephone worried about sending anyone back, because that would only strengthen this guy's army." He shot Luce a cold glare. "He was pining for you, she said, but he'd soon realise you wouldn't have feelings for the likes of him and take up arms against Heaven again. I told Persephone that she'd have some time, as the devil had managed to lure you into Hell and under some sort of spell that made you forget who and what he is." Raphael's eyes glittered. "She said —"

"Hang on," Luce interrupted. "You fed her a line of bullshit about how I've worked some sort of hocus pocus on Mel? I thought angels couldn't lie."

Raphael glared at him again. "I don't know how you did it, but there's no way Mel would give you the time of day without some sort of magic. Persephone said she'd find you and make it right. But instead, she disappeared." He dropped his gaze to the floor. "She was supposed to visit her mother in Heaven after our meeting, but she never arrived. Demeter said Persephone would never have forgotten — she's very close to her mother."

The same mother who'd tried to take a sword to me, Luce fumed.

"If he wasn't with you at the time, Mel, I'd have suspected him," Raphael continued. "After what he did to Persi last time –"

Luce jumped to his feet. "I didn't touch the little bitch! She's feeding lies to the lot of you. Say it to my face, angel. If you want to accuse me of crimes I didn't commit, we can take this all the way to Heaven's gates. Go on!" He advanced on the wide-eyed angel – or at least he tried to, but he couldn't seem to move.

Raphael rose. "Not so tough now, are you?" he taunted, yet when he tried to step forward, it looked like he'd run into an invisible wall.

"Enough," Mel said softly, her eyes darting from Raphael to Luce and back again. The edge of steel in her tone made it an order neither of them could disobey. And neither of them could move…

She was doing it. Luce realised a split second before Raphael did.

"Whatever you believe about Luce, you're mistaken," she said to Raphael. "Do you know anything else about Persi?"

"No," he said sullenly. "So I should go." He attempted to, but Mel's invisible grip still held him fast.

Luce grinned. "Now who's tough?"

Mel placed her hand on his chest. "Luce, please. The more polite you both are, the more smoothly this will go and the sooner it'll be over. Now, I want both of you to sit down, please."

Luce finally capitulated and, a moment later,

Raphael followed.

"Better," Mel said. "So, I gather that the problem is that Persi's missing and no one's in charge of Hell. Yes?"

"No," Luce replied. "I think Lili and the other senior demons are in charge. The HELL Corporation could be run by a concussed monkey right now, for all I know. I only signed over the company to the nephilim girl."

Mel inclined her head. "Okay. So no one's in charge of the HELL Corporation and the best qualified person to replace her is the retired CEO – you, Luce. As we've already agreed, I'll assist. Raphael, if you find Persi, or if someone else does, you already said she's looking for me, so I want to know if you hear anything about her."

Raphael nodded, but the calculating look in his eyes showed that his mind was working overtime. "I'll give you regular updates about anything we hear to do with Persi."

"I also want a team of angels to assist me in the office, with some Exousiai, if George can spare any."

"Oh no, not bloody Powers!" Luce groaned. "Last time I ran into one of them, he pulled out a damn sword and tried to butcher me in the middle of the street. The last thing I need in HELL is a bunch of archaic warrior angels who think I have a target painted on my arse."

"Wearing pants might help fix that problem, Luce." Mel's eyes danced with laughter before she resumed in a more serious tone, "Exousiai are experts at dealing with demons, so I need some. I'm sorry. But Raphael can explain the terms — no drawing without provocation and they must stay away from you. I'll give you a list of who I want, Raphael."

Raphael nodded again. "Is that all?"

"No," Mel said slowly. "There's also the matter of the underwear you owe me. And a new shirt."

Luce smirked at Raphael, only to find the angel wore a similar expression. So who owed her underwear, then?

"Raphael, I was helping out the Agency when my clothing was damaged. I require replacements," Mel explained.

Luce sniggered.

"I'm not...not shopping for women's clothes!" Raphael spluttered, flushing.

Mel shrugged. "Fine." She held out her hand. "Then give me your Agency credit card, please."

Raphael pulled out his wallet and handed over the card, glowering. "He better not be helping you."

A wicked smile spread across her face. "That's none of your business, Raphael. Now, if there's nothing else...keep me updated. I'll see you out."

When the door closed behind Raphael, Luce said, "I can help you. I know this shop that sells the sexiest —"

"Luce. Though I don't do it often, I'm familiar with clothes shopping. I'm sure I'll be fine. Besides, I have to do something on my lunch break and there are plenty of suitable stores in the city near the office." Mel's eyes met his. "Now, what were we planning on doing before we were interrupted?"

Luce grinned. "Let me refresh your memory."

The tale continues in

To Hell and Back

ABOUT THE AUTHOR

Demelza Carlton has always loved the ocean, but on her first snorkelling trip she found she was afraid of fish.

She has since swum with sea lions, sharks and sea cucumbers and stood on spray drenched cliffs over a seething sea as a seven-metre cyclonic swell surged in, shattering a shipwreck below.

Demelza now lives in Perth, Western Australia, the shark attack capital of the world.

The *Ocean's Gift* series was her first foray into fiction, followed by her suspense thriller *Nightmares* trilogy. She swears the *Mel Goes to Hell* series ambushed her on a crowded train and wouldn't leave her alone.

Want to know more? You can follow Demelza on

Facebook, Twitter, YouTube or her website, Demelza Carlton's Place at:

www.demelzacarlton.com

Books by Demelza Carlton

Ocean's Gift

Ocean's Gift (#1)

Ocean's Infiltrator (#2)

Ocean's Depths (#3)

Water and Fire

Turbulence and Triumph

Ocean's Justice (#1)

Ocean's Trial (#2)

Ocean's Triumph (#3)

Ocean's Ride (#4)

Ocean's Cage (#5)

Ocean's Birth (#6)

How to Catch Crabs

Nightmares Trilogy

Nightmares of Caitlin Lockyer (#1)

Necessary Evil of Nathan Miller (#2)

Afterlife of Alanna Miller (#3)

Mel Goes to Hell

Welcome to Hell (#1)

See You in Hell (#2)

Mel Goes to Hell (#3)
To Hell and Back (#4)
The Holiday From Hell (#5)
All Hell Breaks Loose (#6)

Romance Island Resort

Maid for the Rock Star (#1)
The Rock Star's Email Order Bride (#2)
The Rock Star's Virginity (#3)
The Rock Star and the Billionaire (#4)
The Rock Star Wants A Wife (#5)